BEYOND SUPERHERO SCHOOL

Also by Gracie Dix

Journey to Superhero School
An Oliver and Jessica Prequel to
THE VORK CHRONICLES™

Welcome to Superhero School
Book One of
THE VORK CHRONICLES™

BEYOND SUPERHERO SCHOOL
Let The Games Begin!

Book Two of
THE VORK CHRONICLES™

GRACIE DIX

TOAST INDUSTRIES
2025

TOAST INDUSTRIES. 14643 Dallas Parkway, Suite 1050, Dallas, TX 75254.

This book is not sponsored by nor affiliated with Marvel Comics or DC Comics.

Cover by Biserka Design

Library of Congress Cataloging-in-Publication Data has been applied for.

ISBN 9798280000520

www.GracieDix.com

I dedicate this book to my real-life Super Dad for everything he has ever done to support me and my career. He is definitely the best Dad in the world, although I might be a little biased. His pure soul and loving heart make him a perfect candidate to be a character in my book.

Main Characters and Their Superpowers

STUDENTS

Avery (Kendal). Freshman. Dragon Abilities, Fire, Foresight.

Darla (Madison). Eighth-grader. Finger Laser, Fire, Invisibility, Sneak Magic, Super Heat.

Jake (Stanford). Freshman. No Superpowers.

Jason (Mackenzie). Freshman. Fire, Super Intelligence, Water.

Jessica "Jess" (Fletcher). Eighth-grader. Force Field, Mind Reading, Scar Reading, Super Sensing, Super Speed, Wind.

Josh (Stanford). Freshman. No Superpowers.

Mason (Mackenzie). Freshman. Earth, Wind.

Michael (Atrius). Freshman. Aura Decoding, Electricity, Energy, Flight.

Nick (Gator). Sophomore. Dark Magic, Energizer, Energy Transference Power, Friendly Killing, Healing, Power Steal, Sensing, Super Intelligence, Super Strength, Vocal Manipulation.

Oliver (Fletcher). Freshman. Analytical and Processing Intelligence, Flight, Super Intelligence, Super Sensing, Wind.

Ondrea (Kendal). Sophomore. Healing, Levitation/Molecular Kinesis, Telekinesis, Mind Reading, Super Speed, Super Strength.

Rachel (Fletcher). Eighth-grader, when human. Morphing.

Spencer (Knight). Sophomore. Dark Magic, Super Sense, Visions.

Sydney (Atrius). Not in School. Dark Magic, Morphing.

Teddy (Baird). Freshman. Earth Magic, Teleportation, Super Speed.

Will (Brookes). Sophomore. Heat Vision, Ice Powers, Invisibility, Super Strength, Super Stretch, Water.

ADULTS

Damian (Fletcher). Dark Magic, Fire Power, Hypnosis, Shadow Power.

John (Atrius). Black Magic.

Steven (Stanford). No Superpowers.

Super Dad (Dadicus). Elemental Powers, Flight, Speed, Strength.

Vixsten (Knight). Dark Magic, Hypnotic Powers.

ONE

In Which They Musn't Stand Out

Hey! Spencer! How was summer vacation with your dad?" Nick yelled on the first day of school. Nick had just spotted his friend walking down the hall at Lily Flower High School, talking to a girl Nick had never seen before.

"Shut up! Stop being loud!" a hall monitor hissed, shushing Nick aggressively.

Nick just rolled his eyes and said, "Sorry."

"Nick! Dude, summer vacation was great!" Spencer exclaimed. "My dad and I actually bonded really well. Hey, man, it's so great to see you. I wasn't actually sure if we would all be able to get into the same school".

"I haven't seen the others yet," Nick said, suddenly upset.

"Hey, don't worry. I'm sure they'll be here for their classes. Classes don't start for an hour. We got to school a bit early," Spencer assured him.

"I've already been to all my classrooms and visited my teachers," Nick said.

"So did we," Ondrea whispered from behind Nick.

He jumped in surprise. "Dang! I should have Sensed that," Nick yelled, laughing. He turned around and noticed Avery was holding onto Ondrea's shoulders. "Hey, guys! Good to see you. How did you sneak up on me like that?" he wondered. "I swear I should have Sensed you."

Ondrea leaned in and gestured to the boys to lean in as well. "I used my Super Speed Powers!" she whispered excitedly.

Nick jumped back. "Are you stupid? Did anyone see you? If you were caught… that would be horrible!" Nick whispered frantically.

"We're totally screwed now! Ondrea, when you run at light speed, you leave behind this gust of wind as a result of going so fast! You could have done any number of things: knocked someone over, rustled papers, closed lockers, or even closed doors!" Spencer hissed rapidly.

"I told her not to," Avery said. "But she's my stubborn older sister. I figured if she's going to do it, I might as well get a ride."

"Relax, you three! No one saw me, and no one will! Have you gotten a little rusty over the summer? Have you forgotten that when I run at the speed of light, no one can see me?" Ondrea asked. "Have you come across any of the others yet?"

"No, we haven't seen them yet. Jason's probably glued to his TV screen. He wouldn't stop texting us about this stupid game show he found on TV over the summer," Nick said, sighing and rolling his eyes. "I hope Mason will be able to pull him out of it so they won't be late."

"Yeah," Avery mumbled.

There was awkward silence.

"Hey, everyone!" Oliver called from farther down the hall. Behind him trailed Jessica and Rachel.

"Ollie!" Nick called happily. "I texted and called you like 500 times!"

By now, Oliver, Jessica, and Rachel were standing in front of Nick and the others.

"Well, we had a little… stress issue," Jessica explained.

Rachel grinned with embarrassment. "Sorry. I don't know why I'm so anxious right now," she said.

"It's alright, Rachel. Really, it is," Oliver assured quickly.

"It's the first day of school. It's okay to be nervous!" Avery exclaimed, smiling sincerely. Avery had gotten down from Ondrea's shoulders and now put her hand on Rachel's. "Plus, you, Jessica, Darla and the other eighth-graders are younger than the rest of us since they brought the eighth grade into the high school this year. We're really glad you're here, but I get why you're anxious."

"Besides, you have the right to be nervous," Spencer said. He lowered his voice. "After all, we do have something to hide."

"Yeah, we sure do," a breathy voice whispered.

"Did anyone else hear that?" Rachel questioned, her voice rising.

"Hello!" Darla shouted, suddenly appearing right next to them. Everyone jumped in surprise. Darla burst out in laughter.

"Darla! No! Don't do that!" Ondrea hissed.

"Don't laugh?" she wondered, frowning.

"No! Don't use your Powers!" Ondrea exclaimed.

"Fine!" she grumbled, crossing her arms.

Oliver grinned. "Gosh, I missed you guys so much!" he said, laughing. "I even missed Darla's snappy attitude."

At that, Darla smiled.

Suddenly, the hall monitor tapped Spencer on the shoulder. Spencer turned around and said patiently, "Yes?"

"You've been loitering here for too long," she said pointedly.

"It's a school hallway!" Nick countered angrily. "What's your name anyway?"

"My name is Jackie Peterson, and don't you forget it!" Jackie demanded. "Move along."

"We won't forget," Avery stated plainly.

Rachel growled at Jackie. Just as everyone began walking down the hall to go 'loiter' somewhere else, they heard a familiar voice.

"You don't know who you're messing with, tough guy!" the voice said. Ondrea realized It was Will.

The gang ran around the corner and saw Will pinned against a set of lockers by a big guy.

"Tough guy. Yeah, I like the sound of that. Thanks for the nickname. I'll call you 'skin and bones,'" the stranger said menacingly. "Get it? Because you're wimpy!"

"So what? I'll… I'll beat you before you can beat me!" Will yelled. By now, other kids had gathered around in a scattered form to watch the scene. Ondrea and the gang stayed just out of sight so they wouldn't stand out.

"Where is the hall monitor when you need her?" Darla mumbled.

"That sounds like a fun game, S&B. Let's play!" the big guy growled. He drove his massive fist into Will's ribs and hit home with so much force that Will doubled over against the lockers.

"Oh no," Jessica whispered. "We have to do something!"

A barely visible icy mist began to curl from Will's fingers. Oliver, Jessica, Nick, and Spencer began to sense a minuscule drop of temperature.

"Crud!" Rachel exclaimed. "His Ice Powers!"

"I'm about to go and super punch the guts out of that guy!" Ondrea muttered intensely.

"No. Ondrea, don't!" Nick said quickly.

"Why can't she, Nick? Is it just because she's a girl?" Avery pestered.

Nick felt defensive and said, "Okay. First of all, why would you jump to that conclusion? Second of all, yes. It is. Will is the type of guy who will never live it down if he's saved by a girl on the first day at a new school. Third, because I'm about to…"

The air around them suddenly began to feel hot. Everyone noticed, including the bully. The gang peered back around the corner and then stepped into the hall out of pure shock.

Two familiar and identical figures stood in the hall. Everyone was watching them.

"Alright, everyone! By order of the principal herself, I am here to announce that the air conditioning system just broke. This corridor is about to feel really hot. Some might even say too hot. So, you'd best go to some other area for now. Go!" Mason shouted confidently.

As students evacuated the hall, Jason kept using his Fire Power to discreetly push heat from his palms into the air. Only the eleven other Superheroes could see the waves of heat being emitted from his hands. Once everyone had gone, the twelve Supers remained.

"Jason, you can stop now," Mason said, nudging him with his elbow.

Oliver raced over to Will who was slumped over against the lockers. Nick and the others followed.

"Hey, bud," Oliver whispered. "It's good to see you. I see you haven't changed a bit."

"Gee thanks. It's really good to see you too," Will said, attempting to right himself. He grimaced.

"I've got you," Nick said, suspending his hands above Will's ribcage to use his Healing Powers. But before he did anything, he stopped and looked around nervously.

"Something's happening," Jessica mumbled. "There's an aura in the air."

Suddenly Teddy Teleported behind everyone. "Geez. I've been looking for your Power signatures for too long! What happened?" he wondered, bewildered.

"Will got beat up," Rachel exclaimed, blinking with surprise.

"Shut up, Rachel," Will muttered defensively.

"All of you, shut up!" Darla shouted. "Hello, Teddy. Good to see you. Get back to your Healing thing, Nick."

Once more, Nick set his hands to hover over Will. Red and white mist surrounded Will.

"His ribs are broken. That guy can surely pack a punch," Nick said. He had to stand still for a full minute, as Healing was a tedious process. By the time he had finished, the bell for first period had rung. "How do you feel, Will?"

"Good I guess," he mumbled. Will began to get up slowly, but Mason came and helped him up the rest of the way.

"The bell rang. This hall is about to fill with people, so we have to get to class ASAP," Jason exclaimed, shifting his backpack on his back. "I don't want to be late!" Jason began running to his first period class.

"Jason!" Mason yelled as the hallway filled with students. "Jason, you're going the wrong way!"

Jason didn't stop, but people were now staring at Mason.

"Crap," he muttered. He began to look around for his friends, but he realized he was the only one of the group still there. All his friends had gone to class.

"Jason didn't go the right way!" Mason thought. "With that bully running around, he could be in trouble—or worse! Oh, man. I didn't think being in a school of normal people would be so stressful!"

Mason went off to find Jason. "Why am I even worried about him? I know he can take care of himself, but he's my…"

"Lost?" the annoyance known as Jackie snipped.

"What?" Mason asked. He looked up and saw someone standing directly in front of him.

"I'm the hall monitor!" she said. "You should be in class!"

Mason suddenly felt overwhelmed. "Geez. Um… okay. Look, I'm trying to find my brother. He looks exactly like me and…"

"Yes. That Jason kid. He told me his name. He also told me he had a twin. You're going to the same class as him," the hall monitor stated.

"Which is…?" Mason urged.

"Chemistry with Mr. Parker. Room 122. Just down that hall there. Now get to class!" she exclaimed, shoving Mason toward the hallway.

Mason shot a look of disdain at the back of her head and walked slowly down the hall. Once he had made it to the door, he silently opened it and walked in. The classroom was very big and bright due to the massive windows on one side of the room. In front, there was a chalkboard and a plain brown desk. Chairs were connected to the student desks, and all but three were filled with random students he did not know. He was able to recognize Oliver, Ondrea, and Jason, but that was it.

Mason had tried to come in quietly, but his plans were foiled when Mr. Parker announced, "I see our last student has finally arrived. Obviously new."

Heads turned in Mason's direction and Mason went red with embarrassment.

"Why am I so embarrassed by this?" Mason wondered to himself.

"Nothing to say? I see. Go sit by your brother then. Detention after school today, and don't be late this time!" Mr. Parker demanded.

"Y-yes sir," Mason choked, nervously.

TWO

In Which Will Steps Up

After first period, Jason walked briskly over to Mason and put an arm around him. "Hey, you didn't deserve that whole public humiliation," he said to his brother.

"Yeah, but I still got it," Mason mumbled.

"Just six more classes to go," Ondrea said.

"Don't remind me!" Mason snapped.

"Alright. There's no reason to lose your temper. We're all in the same boat," Oliver said, running to catch up with the others. He had been a bit slow to pack up his things.

Nick turned the corner, and Jason, Mason, Ondrea, and Oliver spotted him.

"Hey guys!" Nick called.

"Hi, Nick," Oliver said, "Who do you have first period?"

"I have Mrs. Pain first period. She's the art teacher. She is actually a lot nicer than her name gives her credit for," he yelled, still speeding toward them. Although it was hard to tell, Oliver Sensed there was something bothering Nick. He thought it would be best not to ask yet.

Mason sighed irritably. "You're lucky. Mr. Parker is a bit of a crabby little…"

"Point is, he's not that cheery," Jason interrupted quickly.

"Aw. Sucks, dude," Nick exclaimed. "I've got to go." Nick kept walking past the group.

"We should get to our next class too," Ondrea said, looking at the clock on the wall.

"I hate school," Mason said with a sigh.

2.1

"Rachel! You survived one class period!" Jessica exclaimed loudly.

"I couldn't have done it without you," she whispered, her eyes glancing in every direction.

"Relax! Have fun! You love art! You have art next, right?" Jessica wondered.

"Yeah, I do," Rachel said.

"And Mr. Jackson wasn't that scary, was he?" she questioned, trying to make Rachel feel better.

"I guess not," she admitted. "And I'm much better at art than I am at math."

Rachel filed into her art class as she and Jessica went their separate ways. The art room was a quaint place with four tables lined up in a row. Each table had three chairs, and there was a colorful desk at the front. On the side of the room, there was a long counter covered with brand new art supplies. On the board—also at the front of the room—the teacher had written "Mrs. Pain." Rachel prepared herself for the worst.

Once she had found a seat at the back table, she took her backpack off and waited anxiously for the teacher and other classmates to arrive. Kids began filing in. She only recognized two: Will and Avery. When Avery saw Rachel, she grabbed Will's arm and pulled him toward Rachel's table. Soon, all the seats were filled and the teacher had finally walked in. She had been organizing blank papers when the second-period bell rang. The teacher opened her mouth to speak. Rachel held her breath.

"Good morning, everyone! How are you guys adjusting?" she asked, smiling sweetly. No one spoke. "Oh, well. That's alright! My name is Mrs. Pain, but you can call me Angelica if you'd like." No one spoke. "Okay! So, we have a few new students in class today! Please come to the front when I call your name. Avery, Hannah, Rachel, and Will."

Avery hopped up quickly, excited to be recognized in art class. She gave Will a nudge—surprising him because he had been asleep—and he popped up. Rachel slowly got up and walked behind Avery and Will to the front. Hannah already appeared to be at the front of the room. She had shiny orange hair and a glowing smile. She looked very beautiful, especially to Will. As soon as Will, Rachel, and Avery had lined up in the front, Will was able to see everyone in the class better.

"Oh crap," Will muttered as he saw the same big kid who had confronted him earlier.

"Will, would you like to introduce yourself first?" Mrs. Pain asked.

"Um. Okay. My name is Will Brookes. I… uh… like to play… video games," he said awkwardly. He looked at the bully in the middle of the class and saw him grinning maliciously.

Avery put a supporting arm on Will's shoulder and spoke. "Hi everybody. I'm Avery Walker, and I love art."

"Um… Hi. I'm Rachel and I like wolves and… other animals. I like the dik-dik," Rachel said, nervously. The kids in the class burst out in laughter. "No, no!" Rachel stammered. "It's like a deer! A baby deer!"

"It's okay," someone muttered to Rachel. "Hi guys! I'm Hannah Moler and I like animals too! I also like to build and talk to people," she said happily.

"Thank you so much, children!" Mrs. Pain exclaimed. "Now, before I let you sit back down, I am going to assign what I like to call Art Associates! Please sit down with your double-A as I call them out. There will be three per group." Once she had called out a majority of the names she finished with, "Will, Peter, and Hannah will be a group. Lastly, Avery, Rachel, and Caleb!"

"Which one is Peter?" Will mumbled to Hannah.

"The big guy over there," she said, pointing to the guy who had bullied Will in the hall. "We should stick together. I don't like being much of a gossip, but I hear that he's so mean, he kicked some new kid's butt this morning!"

"Yeah. You… you shouldn't believe everything you hear," he mumbled nervously.

Will and Hannah walked over to Peter, and Will let Hannah take the seat next to Peter.

"What's going on, loser?" Peter taunted, "Why do you look so nervous, loser? Afraid to take another beating?"

Will said nothing. Hannah looked back and forth between them, confused. Then she gasped. "Oh! You're the one…. OMG! Peter! You jerk!" Hannah yelled.

"Is there a problem?" Mrs. Pain asked, sounding genuinely concerned.

"No, Mrs. Pain. Of course not," Peter cut in, sounding as innocent as possible.

"Well, alright then. Everyone! Get to know your Art Associates! Ask questions to get to know each other better," Mrs. Pain announced. She walked over to her desk and sat down.

"You know what I'd like to get to know more of?" Peter asked. He waited a second. He suddenly stood up, his bulk creating a shadow over Hannah and Will. "I'd like to know how much of my fist fits into Will's face."

Will shrunk back into the corner of the art room. Avery and Rachel noticed his distress and looked at him in concern.

"What's going on, Peter?" Mrs. Pain growled, suddenly losing her kind demeanor.

"Uh… Will is refusing to get to know me!" Peter yelled, faking sadness.

"No, no, no," Will mumbled fearfully. He crouched farther back into the corner. If he were still at Superhero School, he would have gladly used his Superpowers to defend himself. But tragically, that school was gone. He was in new territory and didn't want to stand out. Bottom line, he didn't know how to handle this situation. Will's adrenaline was flowing through him at this point, and using his Power of Invisibility, he disappeared for a second, his conscience urging him to hide.

Avery and Rachel saw his Powers flash and shared a panicked look. They both got up from their chairs and grabbed Will's arms.

"We need to be excused for a second," Avery said loudly and firmly. Without waiting for a reply, they raced out of the room and into the empty, quiet hall.

"Will, are you okay?" Rachel asked, concerned for her friend.

"Yeah. I just… I don't know!" he exclaimed, pacing down the hall. "It's just… Peter. He's so awful! I want to beat the crap out of him, but…"

"Will, I know he's a jerk, and I know you feel… defensive, but you can't pick a fight with everybody. Also, stop hiding! Stand up for yourself without fighting him!" Avery demanded, putting a supportive hand on his shoulder.

"Remember, we've got your back," Rachel stated, a strong look in her eyes.

Will, Rachel, and Avery walked back into the art room. "Well, I hope that was necessary. I hope everything is solved," Mrs. Pain said happily.

Everyone went back to their groups and got along for the rest of class. For Peter, that was just a facade. When the class ended, everyone left smiling and laughing. Will, Avery, Rachel, and Peter were the slowest, therefore the last, people in the class. The teacher had left the room to grab a print from the printer. Will had just begun walking out the classroom when he heard, "Dork" and was suddenly tripped.

"Geez. Ow!" Will mumbled, rubbing his elbow. Rachel and Avery stood in the door, silently urging him to stand his ground. Will slowly got up from the ground and turned to face Peter.

"Back off!" Will yelled firmly.

"I'm sorry, what? Loser!" Peter taunted.

"I said leave me alone! You're horrible, mean, disgusting, annoying, and the biggest pain in the… You're a villain!" he screamed. Promptly, Will stomped out of the room along with Avery and Rachel, leaving Peter standing speechless.

"Nice," Avery laughed, high-fiving Will.

THREE

In Which The Teacher Is Mean

As Teddy exited second-period science class, he sighed sadly. "How could I not have any of my Superhero friends in either of my first two classes?" he asked himself.

"You must be lonely if you're talking to yourself," Darla said, jabbing him from behind.

"Darla. Hey! Are you in my next class?" Teddy asked hopefully. "Do you know if Ondrea is in my next class? I miss her. Do you think she misses me?"

"I don't know the answer to any of those questions, weirdo," Darla remarked. She peered at Teddy's face and wondered what he was thinking. Darla noticed he looked anxious, and she suddenly felt bad. She realized she could be a little less sassy. "Alright, I'm sure Ondrea misses you. She's your girlfriend, Teddy. Cheer up, okay?"

"Yeah. You're probably right. Thanks, Darla," Teddy mumbled.

"I have English with Mrs. Cross next. You?" Darla questioned.

"Yeah! You are in my next class. Finally!" Teddy cheered.

Darla, who normally would have rolled her eyes at his excited outburst, found herself smiling a little at his enthusiasm. She realized Teddy was holding out his hand for a high five. At that, Darla slightly rolled her eyes—but only after high-fiving Teddy.

"Birdbrain," she muttered under her breath.

Teddy and Darla entered Mrs. Cross's class and sat down next to each other. As the bell rang, Teddy said, "Man, that reminds me of the same bell at… our old school. Sounds the same, I mean."

Darla nodded her head in acknowledgment. "Yeah," she whispered sadly.

"Good morning, everyone. I wish you the most pleasant of first days," Mrs. Cross said in a monotone. Darla looked at Teddy and raised an eyebrow. Teddy looked back and just shrugged.

"For our first assignment, we will be writing haikus," Mrs. Cross said and sat down at her desk. She opened a drawer and passed around notebook paper. Once everyone had paper, she said, "Begin!"

While the other students grabbed some kind of writing utensil from their bags and began to write furiously, Darla and Teddy just sat there, clueless as to what had been assigned. Teddy cautiously raised his hand.

"Excuse me, but what is a haiku?" he asked reluctantly.

Mrs. Cross looked directly at him, as if in shock that he would ask such a question. "Well, I never! I suppose you don't know what a haiku is either, Darla?" she accused, with fire in her eyes.

"Obviously I don't, or I would have started doing your dumb assignment. What are you going to accuse me of next? Murder?" Darla exclaimed with the biggest attitude she could muster. "I don't understand what the big deal is about not knowing something."

Mrs. Cross darkened her expression and said aggressively, "A haiku is a poem consisting of a syllabic pattern of five—seven—five! Now you will complete your assignment!"

"She's not really the best, is she?" Teddy mumbled to Darla. She silently nodded in agreement. Teddy then said, "I've got an idea."

"What are you thinking?" Darla asked quietly.

"Just follow my lead," he responded. Teddy immediately sat straight up in his chair as if he were a model student and said, "Mrs. Cross, I forgot a pencil."

She looked up at him. "Not my problem. You should have come prepared! Borrow one from your friend," Mrs. Cross ordered. There was a slight pause, then Darla caught on. Teddy was trying to test Mrs. Cross to see what kind of a teacher she really was.

"I also forgot my pencil," Darla called out, even though she had a tiger-print pencil case in her bag that was so full, it was nearly bursting.

Mrs. Cross muttered something inaudible and began digging around in her purse. Two minutes later, she pulled out a pink pencil and a blue pen.

"Here! Come to the front and take these!" she barked, already looking as if she wanted to go home. Teddy and Darla walked slowly up to the front while Mrs. Cross held the writing utensils out impatiently. After Darla and Teddy had taken the pen and the pencil and walked back to their desks, they both stared at their blank notebook papers.

"So, what is the theme we're supposed to be writing about?" Teddy questioned loudly, only to annoy Mrs. Cross. She didn't respond. "Mrs. Cross?" Teddy yelled.

She nearly jumped out of her chair. "What?" she hissed. "Yes, the theme… There isn't one! Write about whatever! But just remember—five, seven, five!"

"Well, that isn't much to go on," Darla said in a girly, innocent voice. "See, I'm not good at writing poetry, and I think I need some kind of theme. Unfortunately, both Teddy and I seem to be having trouble picking something."

Mrs. Cross sighed intensely. "Do something about nature then," she mumbled just loudly enough.

Teddy and Darla stared at their papers again and realized they actually were having trouble coming up with something to write.

This was no longer just testing the teacher. They realized they needed to finish the assignment. Teddy began, "We can't think of anything about…"

"Fine! Fine! Um… you're new students! Write something about your previous school then. And if you ask me another question, you will be writing a million haikus! In detention!" she said hastily.

"We're just asking questions," Darla peeped, realizing they might have pushed Mrs. Cross a bit too far. Mrs. Cross just sighed. That was her signal that she was done talking to them. Teddy gave Darla a sympathetic look.

"Let's just try to write about something from… Superhero School," he whispered, leaning in closer when he named the school.

After some thought, Teddy and Darla began writing until the bell rang. In the hall, they shared their haikus with each other.

Darla said, "Mine says: 'School was fun, I guess. Although, I hope that's over. It was action-packed.'"

"Hey that's pretty good!" Teddy exclaimed. "My turn! Mine says: 'I'd never forget—It. But if I told you why—I'd have to kill you.'"

Darla laughed. "Hey! I like that!" she giggled. "I hope Mrs. Cross doesn't take off points for the last line though."

"Man, I hope not!" Teddy exclaimed.

The two friends came to a hallway intersection and stopped. "I guess this is where I say 'goodbye for now,' Teddy," Darla said, staring down the hallway as if it were made of lava.

"Bye, Darla, and good luck with fourth period!" Teddy called, walking down the hall.

"Right back at you!" Darla yelled, walking down the opposite hallway and earning a "shush" from Jackie, the hall monitor. If you looked hard enough, you could see Darla smile just a little bit.

FOUR

In Which Nick Struggles With His Past

Jessica sat attentively in Mr. Casey's fifth-period history class. She had rushed from her previous class to get there on time, but it turned out she was earlier than anyone else. Mr. Casey smiled at her, clearly appreciating the fact that she had been early. A group of kids began to file into the classroom. Nick was tangled in the middle of them. Once he was spit out of the group, he walked over to a seat next to Jessica and put his head down on his desk.

"Tired already?" Jessica wondered, putting a supportive hand on Nick's back.

"Nah, I've just got a lot going through my head right now," Nick said, sitting up. "How are you holding up?"

"I'm doing pretty well," she said, raising an eyebrow in suspicion. "How are you?"

"I… I just told you," he stammered.

"You were trying to change the topic," she stated, hiding a small grin.

He just stared at her blankly, and then it dawned on him. "You used your… your Super Sense!" he whispered, appalled. "You know we're not supposed to use our Superpowers here. We're In a normal school now!"

"Why are you so surprised? It's not noticeable," she responded innocently.

"What's not noticeable?" Spencer asked said he walked into the room just as the bell rang.

"Nothing," Nick muttered, putting his head back down.

The teacher looked around the classroom as everyone was getting settled. Spencer chose this time to speak again. "You okay?" he whispered to Nick.

Nick gave him a hard stare. "Sure," he said. Although he was being sarcastic, Spencer noticed he kept a firm tone and a steady expression.

"Hello, everyone! Welcome to the first day of school. I'm sure you're tired of hearing that," Mr. Casey laughed. "As you should know, this is history. Not U.S. history, but world history. Although, if you have any questions about space, I'd be happy to answer!"

Nick smiled, finding the teacher's happy mood funny. He kept his head on the desk. "I love this guy," he muttered.

"My goal this year is to not stress you out, but to make sure you have the best time while also appreciating history and its key players!" he said, always keeping a smile on his face.

"Geez. It's as if he's brainwashed," Spencer mumbled.

"Excuse me?" Jessica called to the teacher, "What will we be learning about today?"

"Ah, yes! I'm glad you asked. Don't mind me and my rambling!" he said in a light-hearted joking tone. "Today, we will be talking about World War II. Actually, we'll be watching a video about it."

Nick's head snapped up, and he felt his insides jump. "Why?" he asked suddenly and loudly.

The teacher paused and looked at him strangely. "Well, because this is history class, and World War II is a part of history," he explained, still smiling.

"But why a video?" Nick asked frantically.

Nick's mother had sent him away to the military even before he could finish high school—because she couldn't handle a child with Superpowers. That's where Nick met Spencer, who had been sent to the military by his evil father.

In the military, Nick had seen so many things he wished he could forget. The bloody deaths, the torturous nights, and the horrifying last screams of companions dying in battle. He could remember all the friends he hadn't reached in time to help with his Healing Powers. There were so many.

Nick glanced at Spencer, sighed, and then took a few deep breaths. Nick thought about the fact that Spencer almost died too! When Nick looked at Spencer more closely, he noticed Spencer had a grim and nervous expression on his face too.

"I can tell you're upset, but this is just an educational video," the teacher said. "It's already happened. You don't need to worry. Thankfully, no one In this room has had to deal with any of this war stuff personally, so it's going to be okay. Let's start the video now."

The video began to play on a TV screen located in the front of the room. A deep voice narrated as the actors reenacted WWII. Nick put his head down to avoid looking at the screen. Even though he knew it was a just a reenactment, the fake blood looked too real.

"I can't," Nick just barely whispered. He flinched when he felt a gentle hand on his shoulder. He looked up and saw Jessica staring at him with great concern.

"You don't look too good," she whispered.

"It's a war thing," Spencer stated quietly. His voice wavered, "PTSD."

"Oh, no," Jessica gasped.

Nick glanced at the screen. The narrator was no longer speaking. Instead, the video showed men in green military outfits eating the military MREs—Meals Ready-to-Eat—in the tent.

"I'm going to ask to go to the bathroom to get away from this. I just… I can't watch it," Spencer choked. "Do you want to get away too?"

Nick hesitated and then said, "No. I'll be fine. You go."

"I understand you're mad at me, but if this is too much for you, you should just… go," Spencer murmured, gesturing to the video. Nick didn't say anything. He just stubbornly put his head back on the desk.

"Okay, fine," Spencer hissed.

"Mr. Casey! May I go to the bathroom, please?" Spencer called out.

"Of course! Who am I to stop nature's call?" Mr. Casey answered. With that, Spencer quickly got up and left. A minute later, Mr. Casey spoke again. "Nicholas, do you think you could put your head up and pay attention to the video please?"

"Yeah. Sure," Nick called back. He sighed and stared at the screen before him. Now it depicted people out in battle and, since the narrator was no longer talking, Nick could hear every fake scream and every fake gunshot. It all sounded surprisingly real. It almost sounded as if he were there.

A gunshot went off really close to the camera taking the video, but to Nick, it sounded as if it was right next to him. He shook his head violently, trying to convince his brain that it wasn't real. He closed his eyes, but discovered that was a mistake; a ghostly image of Spencer's "dead" body floated into his vision.

"No! Not again!" Nick yelled out, shaking his head again.

"Nicholas! Are you alright?" Mr. Casey asked, sounding genuinely concerned. But Nick couldn't hear him. All he could hear were the gunshots and the screams. He heard the sound of what he had thought was Spencer's last laugh. His last breath. Then, he saw them. All of them. Through his closed eyes, he saw all the people he hadn't been able to save. He saw his friends murdered before him, the blood on his hands.

"I can't be here!" Nick screamed, pain coursing through his heart at the sight of it all. He was sweating. Spencer—the real Spencer, who had now come back into the class—slapped Nick in the face. The images stopped. The sounds faded. Nick realized it was all in his head as the teacher had paused the video after his first outburst.

"It's all over. It's all over. Everything is over," Spencer cooed gently to Nick.

Nick could barely hear it, but it was there. That soothing tone of his friend who was still alive and no longer bleeding on the ground. He began to hear the murmurs of his classmates and the warm, loving voice of Jessica. He became aware that he was sweating, crying, and breathing. Nick became conscious of the space around him and the life he was living in the present.

"It's not real anymore," he whispered to himself half-heartedly.

"It was real. But it's over now," Spencer said, his voice coming in more clearly this time.

"Alright. Stop babying me," Nick muttered, not really knowing what to say or do. He decided to stand up abruptly. But that was not really the best idea. The crowd around him shifted as quickly as they could after he stood up. Spencer stood in front of him with a pitiful smile on his face. Nick breathed deeply and coughed, realizing that he had been hyperventilating. He looked at his arms, slick with his nervous sweat. He looked around and remembered that not only was he in a building, but he was in a classroom. Nick spotted the door and took a step toward it, as the room seemed too crowded. "So many bodies in one space," he thought.

But instead of taking a successful step forward, Nick stumbled and almost fell. Someone caught his arm. It was Mr. Casey.

"You should go to the nurse," Mr. Casey said very firmly.

"More like the hospital," another student said sincerely.

"No! The insane asylum!" a different kid exclaimed, laughing.

"We'll take him to the nurse, sir. He may need two people to help him," Jessica suggested, grabbing Spencer's arm.

"Alright then. Go on," Mr. Casey hurried them, eager to get Nick to the nurse.

Once they were in the hall, they traveled to a nearby water fountain and bench to sit down. Spencer sat on one side of Nick and draped his arm around Nick's shoulders. Jessica sat a few inches away on the other side of Nick so as to not interrupt their war talk.

"Geez, man. I told you to come to the bathroom with me," Spencer teased softly. "I'm sorry I didn't stay with you. Though I wouldn't have been much help."

"I hate… you," Nick said through gritted teeth.

"I'm sorry that I have to leave. I told you during first period that I had to go take care of some VORK stuff with my dad. To be fair, you're the first one I told. Honestly, now is not the time to be having this discussion. Do you want to talk to me about anything else?" Spencer asked.

"No. I'm fine," Nick whispered. He suddenly felt as if he had the weight of the upon him. His eyes and head felt as heavy as lead. His stomach churned and felt hot like lava. "No," he muttered again. Nick jumped up, fighting back the dizziness and pain. He rushed to the bathroom and threw up.

Nick spent ten minutes throwing up. When he came out of the stall, he saw Spencer waiting by the sinks.

"You don't have to follow me everywhere," Nick said, his voice shaking.

Spencer rushed to Nicks' side and wrapped his arm around his back to support him. It was obvious why Spencer did this. First, Nick was trembling horribly from throwing up. Second, Nick had been through so much in the last twenty-five minutes. And third, Nick's face had gone so pale; Spencer was afraid he'd disappear.

"We should get you to the nurse. Now," Spencer said, not letting Nick talk him out of it. After a few minutes of Jessica and

Spencer dragging Nick to the nurse, they finally arrived. In the nurse's office, there was a small, blue, bed-like object obviously meant for lying on.

"Oh, my heavens!" one of the nurses exclaimed when she caught a look at Nick. "Oh dear! I shouldn't have said that! That was insensitive. Are you religious? Oh, never mind! He looks horrible! Oh, sorry! I just meant he looks like he's feeling horrible. What happened?" she shouted. "Quickly, quickly! Lay him down!"

Spencer and Jessica helped Nick onto the bed-like object, but instead of lying down, he curled up with his head on his knees.

"Nick, lie down," Jessica said, pulling his arm a bit.

"Nick!" Spencer exclaimed worriedly. When Nick didn't respond, Spencer lifted Nick's head up and saw closed eyes. "Well, that's just great," Spencer sighed, throwing his hands in the air. "He's unconscious."

The second nurse came by and laid him out on the temporary bed. Once she had done that, she felt his forehead.

"He does feel warm," she said. Then she measured his temperature. "Oh my! Did he come to school with this fever?" she questioned. "If not, can you tell me what caused this so suddenly?"

"It was… um PTSD. Post Traumatic Stress Disorder. That and a lot of hyperventilating and sweating. He also threw up," Spencer explained reluctantly.

"All the stress made him really tired too," Jessica cut in, trying to be as helpful as Spencer.

"PTSD from what?" one of the nurses asked. "Because, since everyone has the same schedule, different teachers, I can figure that you kids just came from history."

"The war!" Jessica blurted out. She immediately slapped her hand over her mouth.

The nurses both raised their eyebrows. "Really?," they both said, skeptically.

"Yeah. Yeah. See, his dad was in the military, and he was… critically injured. He turned out to be okay, but Nick still has major trauma from that," Spencer lied quickly.

"He should go home then. There's something strange about this fever," the nurse mentioned. "I'll call home."

"No! Um…. No!" Jessica shouted, making everyone flinch. "It would be better if he heard it from us, Nick's friends. He'd worry less if the call came from us."

"Alright. We'll just hand you our phone," the other nurse agreed, searching a very cluttered cabinet for a phone that was most likely out of place.

"It's fine! We have our own phones," Spencer said.

Behind Spencer, Nick stirred slightly. "Ondrea…" Nick gasped.

The nurses were suddenly at attention.

"Oh, he's just rambling. Isn't that right, Nick?" Jessica questioned as a cover-up. Nick was unconscious again.

"It's lunch now, right?" Spencer wondered, pulling out his phone.

"Yes," one of the nurses replied simply.

With that, Spencer walked out of the Nurse's office and into the mostly empty corridor. He made a phone call.

FIVE

In Which Spencer Disappears

Guys!" Spencer called, running up to the lunch table.

"What's going on?" Teddy asked.

"Why do you look so pale?" Avery wondered.

"Whoa. Bro! You okay?" Will questioned, laughing.

"What happened?" Rachel asked with a nervous look on her face.

Mason began to add to the commotion too. "What's…"

"Maybe if you all would shut up, he'd be able to explain!" Darla yelled, accidentally drawing attention to their table. She looked around at the people staring. "Oops. Sorry."

"Okay, it's pretty bad. Jess and I are thinking that the reason Nick passed out was because his Powers were somehow silently triggered by his PTSD and, yes, he had the regular symptoms of PTSD, but he also just fainted!" Spencer rambled quickly. "The nurse says he has a bad fever. She's saying we have to call his dad, Damian, and send Nick home now! Jess is with him in the Nurse's office, and we didn't know what to do, but I guess Nick did. He muttered something about Ondrea. I assume it's because she has Healing Powers, but I can't be too sure and…"

"Hey! Slow down, man!" Teddy exclaimed.

"Yeah! We have some questions! What do you mean Nick passed out?" Oliver wondered.

"Well, he obviously developed PTSD from…" Spencer lowered his voice, "the war. And in history class, we were forced to watch a reenactment of WWII. I went to the bathroom because I couldn't take it, but Nick stayed. I didn't exactly see what happened, but when I came back in the room, Nick was sweating, crying, shaking—and I don't even think he was aware of it. I slapped him out of it."

"You mean snapped him out of it," Jason stated.

"No. No, I totally slapped him out of it. In the face. It worked!" he argued when he saw his friends faces. "It did!"

"I know we're not really supposed to use our Powers here, but Nick looks a bit fried so…Ondrea needs to use her Healing Powers to help him. Now! Go, go, go!" Jason urged, dragging Ondrea out of her chair.

"Are you sure? Because you know that if anyone sees us using our Powers, the government will find out! And if they find out, we have no idea what they'd do, and . . ."

"Whoa! Whoa! We know how dangerous it is!" Spencer said. "But Nick is more important than that. Please, Ondrea! Go on!"

"Okay, okay! Geez. I'm going!" she mumbled, running to the Nurse's office. At that moment, the bell rang. The rest of the gang stood up abruptly and followed Ondrea while the other students quickly cleared the lunchroom and headed to their classes. Avery and Spencer lagged behind.

"Why do you look so pale?" Avery asked, putting an arm around Spencer as they followed everyone.

"Well, obviously the video had me a little shaken up, but that's not all. I saw the way Nick looked at me after I slapped him," Spencer confessed.

"He was probably mad," she stated.

"No. That's the thing. He looked at me as if I were a ghost. Dead! After a few seconds, his expression returned to normal, but I think this whole day has really messed him up. And you're only the second person I'm telling this to, but… I'm leaving. And I feel terrible because I think Nick still needs me around," Spencer continued.

"What do you mean you're leaving?" Avery asked, suddenly shocked. "You can't! After all everyone has been through?"

"That's just it. I'm leaving to help my dad with some VORK stuff. I can't stay here. You heard what happened to Nick! It's just too much pressure!"

"I get it. But what are you going to tell everyone else then?" she asked, stopping Spencer in his tracks.

"I… I can't. I mean, they're my best friends. I can't tell them I'm leaving them! I don't want them to think I'm abandoning them!" Spencer cried.

"You know what, I'll tell them," Avery decided. "Just don't stress yourself out anymore. You don't deserve any of that. But just know this: if you tell them yourself, they might take it better." Avery walked into the Nurse's office and left Spencer standing in the middle of the lunch room.

"I don't know what to do. I…don't know what to do. Why don't I know what to do?! This is so frustrating!" he yelled aggressively. He closed his eyes in an attempt to calm down. His emotions began to overwhelm him; he didn't notice the black tendrils of smoke curling out of his fingers, filling up the lunch room.

"I mean, I'm leaving my best friends! The only friends I've ever known! How could I possibly tell them I'm leaving? I don't know how long I'll be gone either! I could die, and they'd never know. What could I do without them? My dad can't always look after me. What if my friends still need me? What am I going to do?" Spencer thought anxiously.

By this time, nearly the whole space had filled with black smoke. Spencer felt as if the world were closing in on him. When he finally opened his eyes, he saw only black smoke. He felt more alone than he ever had in his life. He felt like a disappointment and a traitor. Spencer started running away from the black smoke as if attempting to outrun his pain.

Will, Darla, and Jason raced out from the Nurse's office. "On no!" Jason shouted as he saw the smoke. "This has got to be Spencer's doing."

"Why would he do this?" Will questioned in a distracted tone. Darla glared.

"He would never do this on purpose! And stop swiping at the smoke, would you?" Darla scolded.

Will looked ashamed and stopped. "Sorry," he mumbled.

"Good news—the smoke isn't toxic. Bad news—the air is littered with smoke. More bad news—we still have enemies out there. And even more bad news—they can sense this!" Jason said.

"Uh. More bad news," Oliver said, appearing out of the smoke. "I can't Sense Spencer's presence anymore."

"Does that mean what I think it means?" Darla asked, grimacing.

"That Spencer's gone," Will whispered. "He left."

"Well, that's just great!" Darla yelled.

"How's Nick?" Jason wondered.

"I feel as good as new," Nick announced, coming up behind Will and making him jump. "But something tells me there are bad things happening."

"I'm glad you're good now, but something's come up," Darla said nonchalantly.

"Oh really!" Will exclaimed, his voice filled with sarcasm.

"Yeah, I can tell," Nick stated.

"Look, we are hidden by the smoke for now, but it needs to be dealt with!" Oliver cut in.

"What are we going to do about it? This is smoke produced by Dark Magic!" Darla hissed.

Oliver felt his mind buzz as if he could suddenly think more clearly.

"I know what to do," he muttered. He began to close his eyes and concentrate to let his Super Analytical Processing kick in. "Hmmm... This isn't smoke. It can't be," he thought aloud. Everyone looked at him strangely. Oliver opened his eyes and looked at the blackness around him carefully, processing every molecule. He began to see black splotches pulsating in the air around him. "That's what I thought!" Oliver exclaimed loudly. "Guys! This isn't smoke at all. It's all Dark Magic! Do you know what this means?"

"Uh, no," Will said, shrugging.

"This means we can trace Spencer's location!" Jason said excitingly, catching on to what Oliver was to so amped up about. "He has left a trail of tracer magic!"

Ondrea, Jessica, Rachel, Teddy, Mason, and Avery ran out of the nurse's office just then.

"Sorry!" Jessica called, "The nurse made us... whoa!"

"What happened here?" Mason gasped.

"Oh, no," Avery murmured. "Spencer had an emotional burst of Dark Magic, didn't he?"

"That would explain this," Nick agreed. "Do any of you guys know where he is?"

"Oh," Jason said, "We haven't told you yet that he disappeared."

"Wait... you don't know where he is?!" Nick yelled frantically.

"Why do you think we were trying to find him, buddy?" Oliver added cautiously.

"Do you have any ideas on where he could be?" Teddy asked, now also in a frantic state.

"We need to find him fast! I mean really fast! This is bad!" Avery shouted, grabbing Oliver by the shoulders.

"Alright, why is this happening? Why did this happen? I thought I would like this school! I just want to go home now!" Rachel cried.

Jessica hugged her sister tightly. "Everything will be fine," she reassured her.

"Avery, why are you freaking out so much about this? You're usually pretty calm in these situations," Oliver said, using his Wind Element to encircle the Dark Magic in the air in an attempt to move it.

"He hasn't told anyone else, but he has to leave with his dad to go take care of some VORK stuff, and I'm guessing he felt a bit overwhelmed," Avery sighed, gesturing frantically to the obvious Dark Magic in the air.

Everyone just stared at her for a second. "What?" Will yelled.

"Oh, come on, Spence!" Teddy mumbled to himself.

"We need to find him!" Rachel yelled. "Oh, no! He must be so scared."

Will rolled his eyes. "Oliver seemed to be on the verge of something great before you guys came out."

"Uh. Right. The trace location," Oliver started. He was clearly getting ready to explain more when Jessica asked, "What's a trace location?"

Ondrea answered instead. "A trace location is the invisible Magic left behind after it's been triggered by an emotional outburst."

"That's cool. What does it do? Come out of his butt?" Will asked with a goofy look on his face.

Everyone sighed and Will looked as if he were about to argue when Jason cut him off. "A tracer location is provoked when a Superhero lets off a large amount of what we like to call 'Emotion Magic'. It's like stress and hormones for regular kids, but in the form of a trail."

"Wait, do we have hormones?" Darla wondered.

"Of course we do!" Avery exclaimed, still worried about Spencer.

"Anyway…" Jason continued pointedly, "the Magic produces a… sort of… magnetic pull to the person who unleashed it. But it's such a slight pull, that the Magic is nearly invisible. That's what we need to follow."

Mason's expression suddenly turned dark. He said, "Well, then we'd better find him as fast as we can because…"

"Because VORK will find him!" Nick finished, nearly yelling.

"Oh no! You're right!" Jessica cried.

"Before we do anything, we need to clear this up, right?" Will asked, gesturing to the giant, black cloud.

"Duh," Darla said. Will glared at her.

"We'll take care of it," Mason volunteered. He was talking about himself and Jason. Teddy suddenly Teleported out of the area. To feel useful, Rachel Morphed into a fly. A minute later, Teddy Teleported back, and Rachel Morphed back into a human.

"The perimeter is clear!" they both exclaimed at the same time. Will cringed.

"Alright," Mason said. "Shoot fire at the thingy I'm about to do something with," he told Jason.

Jason rolled his eyes. "Real specific," he muttered to himself.

Everyone moved out of the black mass in order to let Mason and Jason do their cool twin thing.

"Okay, so I learned I could do this awesome thing…" Mason explained, moving his pointer finger in a counter-clockwise motion. "Where I… I manipulate the air circulation around me and…"

Everyone could feel the air suddenly shifting, but not strong enough to pull them off their feet.

"I can turn it into this tornado-like thing," Mason said.

A Dark Magic funnel began to form with Mason standing right inside it. Jason suddenly worried that Mason didn't know what he was doing.

"And then, then I can squish it into a tiny ball of Dark Magic," Mason said. He began to bend the finger that he'd been moving counterclockwise. He curled it into his thumb, which looked as if it were a struggle for him. The funnel began to shrink, and it became more rounded in a matter of seconds. Everything went dead silent, and the ball of Dark Magic was trembling—when really, it was the exertion of the Wind Power trick making Mason tremble.

Finally, Mason finished off with, "Jason, Fire it up, baby!"

Jason smiled and used his Fire Power to shoot light-green flames out his palm. Before the fire had vanished, it flashed a rainbow of color and then dissipated. The ball of Dark Magic was gone.

Everyone stared in amazement—first at Jason, then at Mason.

"What?" Jason asked, smirking. "Mason's performance was so epic, I thought I could spice up my Fire a bit."

Everyone began to laugh as the tension suddenly dissipated, just like Jason's Fire Power.

Nick suddenly stopped. "Guys! That was really cool and all, but we have to go! We need to find Spencer!" he yelled. "Oliver, any ideas?"

"Because of our weird twin-thing and our Super Sensing, Jess and I can follow the trace location," Oliver said. His expression was now serious. "Follow us! I hope he hasn't left the school."

Oliver and Jessica linked their hands together and began running to follow the path of tracer Magic.

SIX

In Which Spencer is Found

W e've got to find him!" Nick said for the thirteenth time as they walked around the school.

"Where is everybody?" Mason asked, not seeing anyone around them in the building.

"Well, they probably thought there was some kind of fire going on," Jason answered. "Because of the Dark Magic in the air—which any passerby would interpret as fire smoke."

"Do you think they'll take roll or something?" Darla wondered. "In all our commotion, I hadn't actually noticed the fire alarm going off."

"Yeah, they really should make them louder," Will agreed.

"Guys, are we still looking for Spencer or what?" Nick asked, pushing between Will and Darla.

"Yeah!" Avery yelled.

"Alright guys! Calm down!" Oliver shouted. He suddenly lowered his voice. "We have to be kind of quiet since there might be firemen coming into the building."

Ondrea shouted in surprise and stopped in the middle of the hallway. She held her hands against her ears and crouched down.

"Whoa!" she gasped.

Even though Teddy was only a few feet away, he immediately Teleported to Ondrea. "Yo, babe! What's going on?" he yelled, feeling flustered.

"Geez, Teddy. Nothing is wrong. I just… I hear someone's thoughts!" she stammered, using her Mind-Reading Powers. "I think they're Spencer's!" Ondrea stood up, ran over to the supply closet at the end of the hall, and threw open the door. "He's here!"

Everyone sprinted over to the closet, Nick running faster than the rest. Nick squeezed past Ondrea and crouched down where Spencer was sitting. He grinned ever so slightly. "Nice and dark in here, Spence. I should have known."

Spencer's head popped up and he gasped. "You're okay!" he said weakly. "I… I didn't know what to do. I'm sorry."

Avery walked in and crouched on the other side of Spencer.

"We're here too," she stated compassionately.

"I smell people coming down the hall," Rachel said, using her animal instincts.

"Right, let's get in the closet and shut the door so people don't realize we're still inside," Jessica suggested. The Superheroes smooshed into the small space and closed the door.

"Hey, Nick?" Spencer muttered, "Now it's really dark in here." He flashed a small grin. No one saw it, but Nick just knew.

"Why didn't you tell us you were leaving?" Will blurted out.

"Bad, Will!" Mason exclaimed. "Dude!"

"No, no. It's okay. I… wait. Avery? Did you tell them?" Spencer wondered.

"Yeah. I'm sorry. I guess we panicked when you were gone, and I thought you would get in trouble," she replied.

"Well, I'm okay," Spencer sighed. "I'm leaving next week. I just thought I should say that now that the cat is out of the bag."

"I've never heard that expression before," Rachel cut in, the curiosity obvious in her voice.

"That's because old people use it," Darla replied.

"Uh. Okay. "We're getting off topic," Oliver stated awkwardly.

"Right. There really isn't anything else to say other than the reason I'm leaving," Spencer said.

"Avery told us that too," Jason stated, twiddling his thumbs.

"Go figure. Hey, I'm sorry about that Dark Magic explosion in the dining hall," Spencer apologized sheepishly.

"I'm honestly curious. I can't hold it back anymore!" Will giggled, "Which…. body… part did the 'smoke bomb' come from?"

"Will!" Jessica sighed, exasperated.

Spencer began to chuckle. "That was pretty good," he affirmed.

The whole gang shuffled out the closet just in time for their sixth-period classes.

6.1

For the rest of the week, everyone acted as if everything were normal. And everything was—until Friday.

"Alright, Will. What's the big news?" Oliver asked.

"Yeah, why'd you call us all here?" Mason wondered, feeling overly excited about the prospect of going home for the weekend.

Jason was standing next to his twin, peering at his watch. "Will, hurry up! I want to get home in time to watch my game show!"

"You will not believe what he has to tell you!" Rachel exclaimed.

"We're Superheroes. Try us," Ondrea said, putting her hands on her hips.

"Okay, okay! I have a girlfriend!" Will screeched.

Everyone just stared at him with grins plastered to their faces.

Avery stepped in. "It's true, guys. It's… weird, but true."

"Who is it?" Darla asked as if she were interrogating him.

"It's Hannah! And wow, is she hot!" Will yelled, laughing.

"Geez, man," Mason whined. "That's a bit TMI. Besides, don't let everyone know you think that. They might judge you."

Will just stared at him. "When has that ever bothered me?" he asked defensively.

"Always," Rachel answered plainly. She just looked at Will and blinked. There was a moment of silence.

"Alright, we're going home then," Jessica said, grabbing Oliver and Rachel.

"Yep, bye everyone!" Spencer yelled. Everyone left school for their homes. All but Spencer. He left for something else.

SEVEN

In Which Nick Has a Heart-to-Heart

Teddy was sitting at home with his younger sister Tilly, watching cartoons when the doorbell rang. Teddy hopped off the brown leather couch and walked toward the door. "I'll be back, Tilly!" he called out.

He walked past the kitchen where his mom and dad were whipping up a large meal, even though the only people in the house were Teddy, Mom, Dad, and Tilly. His parents always cooked when they were stressed, and that was usually around the time school started for Teddy.

Their stress had been even worse since his old school, Superhero High School, had burned down the previous year, and Teddy had gone back to a normal public school. At the sight of his parents in a crazed cooking frenzy, Teddy sighed and rolled his eyes as he continued to the door. The doorbell rang again, and Teddy walked faster past the stairs that led to the kids' bedrooms. By the time he got to the door, it had rung four times.

"Alright! I get it. I'm here!" he shouted at the door. Teddy opened the door with an angry expression. But that instantly vanished when he saw Nick standing there with a look of pure terror on his face. Nick rushed inside.

"Whoa. Hey what's going on?" Teddy wondered, turning around.

"Bro! Spencer's gone! Man, he's gone!" Nick yelled, grabbing Teddy by the shoulders.

"What do you mean he's gone?" Teddy asked as he was now becoming worried.

"He left! He left! He went to his dad's. He never said anything! He just… went!" Nick shouted.

Teddy glanced around and saw his parents doing that thing where they pretended to not be listening. Around the corner, he spotted Tilly looking at the chaos.

"Nick. You need to calm down. My little sister is watching!" Teddy whispered in Nick's ear.

Nick took some deep breaths. "Sorry," he mumbled. Nick slumped against the wall of the stairs and slid down to the floor. He put his knees up and hid his head down on them.

Teddy slid down beside Nick. "Look, man. I'm sure the only reason he left early without saying anything is because it would be too hard for him—and for us – to say goodbye," he said. Teddy hoped he was being comforting; he had never been very good at comforting anyone but Ondrea.

"So, you're just okay with him leaving like that?" Nick cried, appalled.

"Whoa! No way. That's not what I was saying at all! I was… I was just saying that… No! Of course, I am not happy with him leaving early, but I'm sure it's for a good reason. I am upset that he didn't say goodbye. Don't accuse me of not being upset! After everything we've been through, I would be upset if anything happened to any of us!" Teddy exclaimed.

"R…right. I'm sorry, Teddy," Nick sighed, clearly exhausted.

"It's okay. We're a team. We've been through so much already, so I know we'll get through this. Do the others know?" Teddy wondered.

"Yeah. I've already had this lecture six times. Will's wasn't that good, but he's not much of a people person," Nick laughed.

"Good! Then you know that you're going to be okay. Don't tell me I need to give you a seventh lecture," Teddy joked.

"No. One lecture from you is all I need. Yours did the trick," he said seriously. "But Teddy, I have a favor to ask you." Nick hesitated and took a deep breath. "See, my dad needs to keep his job in New York. So, unfortunately, he can't move here. And I really appreciate your letting me use your Teleportation to go back and forth between school and my dad's place. But…I don't want to keep doing that. And…"

"You can stay with us," Teddy interrupted.

"Oh. Uh, thanks. How'd you know I was going to ask?" Nick questioned, staring at the floor.

"Just a hunch," he responded, getting up. He offered a hand to Nick.

"I got it," Nick peeped awkwardly. He got up himself and met eyes with Teddy for a second then looked away.

"Everything's going to be alright," Teddy assured him. He believed it too.

"Yeah," Nick muttered. There was a silence.

"Do you want some dinner?" Teddy wondered. "My parents seemed to have cooked for about 5,000."

Nick smiled ever so slightly and said, "Nah. I'm good."

"Alright. Go to your dad real fast and grab some of your stuff, then you can come back," Teddy advised.

Nick nodded, but before he left, he asked, "Hey, can I borrow your Teleportation Power for a bit?"

"Of course," Teddy responded.

7.1

Nick Teleported to his dad's apartment in New York. As soon as Nick arrived, he saw a man in a blue police uniform.

"Hey, Dad," Nick muttered.

Damian put on a wide smile and gathered Nick in a hug. "Hey, bud! How did you do that?" he wondered.

"Teddy let me take his Power," Nick answered quickly.

"Well, that was nice of him," Damian said.

"Dad! Stop acting like a parent!" Nick demanded. "It's… weird."

Damian's smile lessened a bit as he said, "I am a parent. I'm yours. Remember? Is everything okay?"

"You know how I called you last week and said Spencer was leaving? Well, he left early. Without saying a single word to anyone," Nick said, plopping down on one of the green chairs in the living room.

"Oh, wow! That's huge. That's upsetting," Damian noted. "I talked with Vixsten, Spencer's father, recently, but he said they were leaving the week after this one. How peculiar…"

"Spencer hasn't really been having the greatest time fitting into this new school and stuff, so I guess that makes sense why he left early," Nick shared.

"I could call The Boss for you and talk about it," Damian offered.

"No. I wouldn't bother Vixsten over it. He's probably busy working to get more information about the criminals of VORK," Nick said with a sigh. There was silence. Finally, Nick asked, "So, how are things going for you here in The Big Apple?"

"It's going alright. There's been a recent increase in drug dealers around the area. All the dealers I've caught and brought in had strange weaponry on them," Damian reported.

"That's not good," Nick said, putting his head in his hands.

"Hey, don't stress about it," Damian exclaimed.

"Damian! This is dangerous!" Nick yelled. "Where exactly have the 'drug dealers' been with the strange weapons?"

"They've been… around. Mostly around this apartment complex or in the nearby area," Damian admitted.

"VORK! It has to be VORK!" Nick shouted. "I mean, Spencer left school to help his dad because VORK criminal activity has been going up around the entire world, Dad!"

"W… what? The world?" Damian whispered.

"Yes! If you continue this, you'll be found out and they'll kill you!" Nick cried. "You can't keep doing this! I don't want you to die, Dad. No one wants you to die! No one except for ALL the VORK members and the ALL the VORK leaders!"

"Son, we've already been over this. I'm a police officer. This is what we do," Damian said. "I'm in danger every single day, Nick. But there are still many safety protocols and lots of training we go through to assure our safety. And even though it sounds like we're in danger, we're usually not. Most police officers never pull their weapons out even once in their entire careers. It's not like you see on TV," Damian explained, slightly surprised by his son's outburst.

"I know, but this is different! It's VORK, Dad, VORK! You know, that evil organization that wants to exterminate us! They want to wipe us out, kill us, murder every one of us with Superpowers as if we're nothing important! Nothing at all!" Nick yelled, tearing up.

Damian knelt down next to Nick and took his son's hands. "How's school going, bud?" he whispered cautiously.

Nick stayed quiet for a moment then said, "I had an episode of PTSD I might not have told you about."

Damian gasped and sat down on the same chair next to Nick.

"Over what? Why didn't you call?" he wondered, pulling Nick in for a hug.

Nick didn't really want to talk about it, as he knew it was a sore subject for him and his dad. He remembered that his mother was the one who had sent him to military school—and not his dad, Damian, as Nick had previously thought.

"It was an incident in history class. That's all. It's over now. No need to dwell on it," Nick stated quickly.

Damian raised an eyebrow and looked at Nick. He stared hard for a second, as he always did when he was concentrating. Realization dawned on his face. "The… war. Was it, uh, World War II?" he whispered.

Nick pulled away from his dad. "Uh. Yeah. Let's not talk about it. I just came here to get my stuff anyway. I'm going to be staying with Teddy for a bit. It's just easier," Nick said cautiously. "To be honest, I'm just tired of having to borrow Teddy's Teleportation Power to get back and forth between your place and school."

He stood up and ran into his room to get his stuff.

"Was it something I said?" Damian muttered to himself.

EIGHT

In Which the Twins Receive Great News

It was a Sunday afternoon in the Mackenzie household and Jason was intensely focused on the TV screen, shouting in excitement. He was halfway through that month's first episode of his favorite game show, *Unleash Your Wild Side*.

"Get over it!" he yelled. "It's just a frog!"

"Well maybe some people are afraid of frogs, Jason," Mason suggested.

At this point in the show, participants were shown their worst fear through high-tech holograms. The holograms could talk, walk, and act—and they were so realistic, participants could even touch them, and they would feel real.

The game-show host hooked the participant up to a few wires and projected them into a dark room where their worst fears were waiting for them. From there, they had to face their fears, no matter what.

That afternoon, the participant was standing in front of a giant frog and cowering in the corner.

"Oh my gosh! Just touch it!" Mason yelled at the TV, getting annoyed as well.

"Look who's being impatient now!" Jason exclaimed, jokingly punching Mason on the shoulder.

On the TV, the frog must have been getting impatient too.

"Touch me. Face me," it croaked in a terribly scratchy and deep voice.

"Creepy," Mrs. Mackenzie mumbled, coming up behind the boys.

"No! This is awesome!" Jason shouted, pumping his fist in the air. "I mean, look at those projections! It must have taken years of scientific research to make something like that. This technology must be years ahead of its time!"

Mrs. Mackenzie rolled her eyes and smiled. "Well, I'm glad you love it so much—because I have something for you boys related to this show."

Mason now noticed that his mom had been hiding her hands behind her back the whole time. He started to ask about it. "What do you…"

"Quiet! Quiet!" Jason shouted, pointing to the screen where the frightened participant was slowly reaching his hand to the face of the frog.

"He's finally going to touch it!" Mason said happily.

As soon as the participant touched the frog's face, the hologram projectors turned off, and the game show stage suddenly appeared again. The other participants just looked away, appearing bored. Mason and Jason cheered.

"Now we can finally get to the best part of the show— the Environmental Dome! Now that's some advanced technology!" Jason explained, jumping off the couch. "They project an entire environment and atmosphere into a dome, and you can do everything you'd be able to do in a regular nature setting. You can even eat the food that's projected!"

As soon as Jason had finished speaking, the TV game-show host said, "Now it's time, boys and girls, for the Environmental

Dome! Participants will spend two weeks in this dome and attempt to survive whatever environment they are put in!"

"Man, this part is boring," Mason whined. "They don't need to survive if there's no danger!"

"Maybe it's like false advertising or something," Jason suggested. "Maybe there are dangerous animals. They might just not show them on TV."

"I'm pretty sure that is false advertising," Mason said.

"Hold on, I think that's illegal," Jason said, now confused.

"Yeah, that has to be illegal," Mason agreed, with certainty.

"Boys! Announcement!" Mrs. Mackenzie reminded them.

"Right!" they both said at the same time.

"Wait!" Jason exclaimed, "Can we finish this episode first?"

"Boys! This is a chance you may never get again. It's related to your game show, Jason. I believe this is a rare and lucky opportunity! Do you really want to wait?" she questioned.

"Well, not when you hype it up like that!" Mason shouted, happy to pull his attention away from the Environmental Dome.

"Alright. What is it?" Jason asked with a suspicious look on his face.

Mrs. Mackenzie pulled out a blue envelope and opened it ceremoniously.

"Hello, Mackenzie twins!" she read. "We see you have been tuning into our show ever since it started. Quite amazing, isn't it? That is why we officially invite you two—plus nine people of your choice to accompany you—as our next participants on our game show, *Unleash Your Wild Side*. We will be providing three additional team members once you accept our invitation. We can't wait to see you! Signed, your favorite game-show host, Steven Stanford."

The twins just stared into space for a minute and then screamed with excitement.

"We're obviously taking all of our friends! This is awesome!" Mason yelled happily.

"Yes, this is great! It's what I've always wanted!" Jason shouted, jumping on the couch.

"When do we go?" Mason questioned.

"And where do we go?" Jason asked, staring at his mom like a puppy begging.

"Wait, wait, wait!" Mason screamed dramatically. Everyone stopped. "Listen to the TV!"

"That's all for today folks. Now here's when I announce the next participants for the show! ... Ah! Psych! It's going to be a surprise! Next participants," the game-show host began, addressing the audience, "You know who you are! And we know *where* you are. So, we'll be coming to your home to pick you up in our game van in exactly two days! Don't worry about clothes or packing. Everything you need will be supplied. See you next time, folks!"

"Whoa," Mason sighed.

"Yeah," Jason whispered.

"Let's call our friends!" they both screamed at once, causing Mrs. Mackenzie to jump in alarm. "This will be so much better than school!"

NINE

In Which There Are New Twins
And a Gargantuan Beast

This is totally awesome!" Jason shrieked as he saw the game van driving down the street toward his house. Mason, Jason, and the others were standing outside the Mackenzie house, waiting for the game bus.

It had been a process, but with the help of their parents, all the students had gotten an approved break from school for this "educational experience." When they returned to school, they would have to catch up on their classes and make a report on what they learned while they were gone, but everyone agreed it would be worth it to be a part of *Unleash Your Wild Side*.

The game bus stopped in front of their house, and a man with brown curly hair and a bright blue formal jacket stepped out.

"Oh my gosh! Steven Stanford!" Jason screamed happily.

"Ah yes, that's me!" Steven said. "Are you kids ready to go?"

"Um, yeah," Oliver said.

"Alright! Hop on in!" Steven exclaimed, with a smile plastered on his face.

"You take care of my boys now, Mr. Stanford," Mrs. Mackenzie said.

"You know I will," he answered enthusiastically, and then turned back to talk to the boys. "There are two more participants waiting in the bus for you to meet. And, just like our prize winners, these participants are twins as well."

The gang smiled, happy to meet newcomers and possibly make more friends.

"Why are you so… smiley?" Darla asked Steven.

"Rude, Darla," Ondrea muttered, quietly enough that only Darla could hear.

"It's quite alright. I understand her type," Steven stated simply.

Ondrea looked shocked. "How could he say that?" she thought to herself.

Will got defensive. "What do you mean 'her type?'" he growled, stepping forward.

Steven looked flustered. "Ah. I meant nothing by that," Steven exclaimed, brushing it off.

"Maybe we should go," Mason said, walking toward the entrance of the bus. When Mason entered, he found two boys, who looked exactly alike, arguing.

"Josh, stop being so introverted!" one of them said.

"I'm not being introverted. I'm being Josh!" the other one countered, with a smug smile on his face. "What do you have to say to that, Jake?"

"Well… well, I'm being Jake!" he said with a mocking expression.

"Uh, hi," Mason interjected.

"Oh, hi! I'm Jake Sta… Um… So sorry you had to witness that! Josh can be a bit of a pain sometimes," Jake exclaimed, getting up from one of the seats. Jake had dark brown hair with a slight curl to it and somewhat of a long, thin face. He was wearing orange shirt and gray basketball shorts. The boy next to him had the same face shape, and looked exactly the same as Jake, but his hair was even curlier. He wore blue basketball shorts and a white shirt with a back hoodie.

Mason awkwardly stuck out his hand, assuming Jake would shake hands with him. Jake just stood there, smiling. Mason withdrew his hand and decided to break up the awkward tension.

"Your twin's name?" Mason asked, gesturing to the boy he assumed to be named Josh.

"Don't worry about it. That's just Josh," Jake said, rolling his eyes. "Josh!" he teased, "Stop being shy!"

Josh smiled sheepishly and slowly got up. He walked to his brother and stood beside him. "Uh. Hi. I'm Josh" he said.

Mason decided to introduce himself. "Well, hi. I'm Mason and..."

"Fun time! Here we come!" Will yelled, practically jumping into the bus.

"Oh, my gosh! Shut. Up. Will," Darla growled, tromping onto the bus after him.

"Be nice, Darla!" Ondrea warned. "He's just excited."

"Yo, wait up, girl!" Teddy called to Ondrea. He grabbed her hand and tried to pull her close, but she stopped him.

"Guys, we have to all be in this together during this weird process, so remember to stick together and take a buddy with you," Oliver called looking into the bus and at the remaining people outside.

"That means no PDA on the bus, Teddy and Ondrea!" Jessica added, shoving past Oliver.

"They can do whatever they want!" Avery shouted defensively, while pulling Rachel into the bus behind her.

"No, please!" Rachel begged, "No weird things on the bus, guys. Not now."

"Did Mason already get on this thing, or did he ditch?" Jason wondered, hauling himself into the bus. Mason face-palmed at all of his friends' outbursts, which is how Jason spotted him.

"Ah, there you are, Mason." Then Jason saw the other set of twins and stopped. "Oh… hi," he said. Mason rolled his eyes and pulled Jason next to him. Everyone in the bus went quiet to watch how this exchange would go.

"Hi, I'm Jake! This is Josh. It's nice to meet another set of twins," Jake exclaimed.

"I'm Jason," the Mackenzie twin stated, still in a bit of shock.

"Soooo… What brings you fellas here?" Will asked suspiciously. "Are you just lucky winners like us?"

"No, we just got a letter in the mail, and then we got picked up," Jake answered while staring intently out the window.

"That makes us lucky winners, dummy," Josh said, smiling.

"Oh yeah. Right," Jake said as he turned around to face Josh.

"Hello everyone!" Steven yelled, jumping onto the bus and closing the doors. "After talking to the lovely Mackenzie parents, I have procured all of your permission forms, and we are all good to go. I assume you have all gotten acquainted with my sons?"

"Whoa, what?" Mason yelped. "Why didn't you tell me? Holy crap! That's awesome. I can't believe you are the sons of the Steven Stanford!"

"Hmmm…I wonder why," Josh muttered sarcastically.

"Well, time to get this bus moving! I'll be driving, obviously, and our trip will take about five hours. We will stop to refuel at some point, so that would be a good time for a bathroom break," Steven continued.

"What are we going to do when we get there?" Oliver wondered, taking the initiative.

"Well, we're going to jump right into the first leg of the show!" Steven announced. "Now, everyone sit down!"

"Dad, that was a bit aggressive," Jake said, performing a mock flinch.

"Ah. My mistake. Never mind, then. Now we're off!"

Everyone went silent for a while. The gang was traveling into new territory and had no clue what they were going to face. They knew the first portion of the game show—the part before the Environmental Dome—was about their fears, but some of them had no clue what their own deepest and darkest fears were. A few were afraid because they did know their own fears; they knew the others would see not only their fears but also how they faced them.

Oliver was the most terrified.

"Steven?" Oliver called to the front. "Has anyone ever had a really dark fear that they tried to overcome?"

"Nope! The people on our show are boringly normal. Although it is possible to have a dark fear," Steven answered, still looking at the road in front of him. "Why do you ask?"

"I was just curious, that's all… no, wait. Let's say theoretically, what if one of our fears is dangerous? Would our fear be able to attack us?" Oliver questioned.

"Well… I'm not sure. But, if that began to happen, we should be able to shut the system off before anything bad happened. I mean, we certainly would if it were anything someone could sue us about," Steven responded, now staring straight at the road again. With that, the entire bus got silent. Quite some time passed with everyone mostly silent.

"About three more hours until we reach our final destination," Steven shouted out. "How's everyone doing?"

"I'm good," Oliver said in a tone indicating that he was not, in fact, good.

"I'm…hanging in there," Rachel peeped from the back of the bus.

"I've been better," Nick called, staring down at his phone in his lap from the seat behind Oliver.

"I'm doing so great!" Jessica cheered a bit too enthusiastically. She was clearly nervous as well. Oliver, who was sitting next to his sister, gently grabbed her hand and gave it a reassuring squeeze.

"We're fine!" Jason and Mason said together as if speaking at the same time were a normal thing. They were sitting behind Jake and Josh.

Will and Darla were both asleep in front of Oliver and Jessica. Darla was snoring softly. Ondrea and Avery were sitting in the row in front of Jake and Josh. They both had headphones on and were listening to music. Jake tapped Ondrea's shoulder.

"How are you doing? Dad wants to know," he said, gesturing toward Steven.

"We're doing alright," Avery answered, sharing a confirming glance with Ondrea.

"I'm pretty good too!" Teddy called from the row next to Ondrea. "I miss you, baby."

"I'm right here if you need me, my Teddy Bear," Ondrea assured him, reaching across Avery and giving his shoulder a loving squeeze.

"Gross!" Will yelled, waking up suddenly.

"Yeah, shut up, love birds. We're trying to sleep!" Darla hissed.

Josh's eyes went wide as he said, "Geez, what's their deal?"

Darla, who had heard this comment, growled in his direction.

"Alright, sorry!" he apologized, sitting back further into his seat.

"Anyway… how are you guys doing?" Ondrea asked Jake and Josh.

"I'm fine," Josh answered. "For some reason, Jake seems nervous, and I honestly don't understand why."

"Shut up, Josh," Jake mumbled. He turned from the window to face Ondrea. "Besides, I'm probably just worrying over nothing."

"From what we've experienced, nothing can certainly be something," Jason intervened, having been listening to the conversation.

"Facts," Will muttered, seeming to be suddenly interested in the conversation too.

"What's going on?" Oliver asked, walking over to where Jake and Josh were sitting.

"Speak now or forever hold your peace," Mason added, laughing to himself. Jason rolled his eyes.

"Okay, okay!" Jake exclaimed. He turned to face the Mackenzie twins. "There's been this weird bird following the bus since we left your house."

"Yo, what?" Teddy asked, surprised. "I expected it to be something bigger. You're worrying about a bird?"

"It *is* pretty big," Rachel said, now moving a little closer to the conversation. "Maybe it's a morph…um… some kind of coincidence," she corrected herself.

"A what?" Jake asked. "A morph-what?"

"Forget it," Rachel responded softly.

"Where is it?" Darla wondered, climbing across a drowsy Will to get to the aisle.

"Right there! See it! It's like the only bird in the sky!" Jake shouted, seeming anxious.

"Come on, kids. Stop creating a ruckus back there," Steven called from the front.

"Sorry, Dad!" Jake said, his voice cracking.

Ondrea glanced out the window of the bus and spotted the bird Jake had been talking about. It was completely black with a bright red beak. The bird was huge, and its wingspan appeared to be half the length of the bus.

"OMG!" Ondrea gasped. "How in the whole wide world did we not see that thing? It's like the size of a teenage dragon!"

"Uh… how do you know how big a teenage dragon is?" Josh asked, flashing an amused smile.

"From books, right, sis?" Avery insisted, nudging Ondrea in the side.

"Right. Yep," she said quickly. Ondrea and Avery knew exactly how big a teenage dragon was, and Ondrea felt ashamed that she had almost given them away. She reminded herself again that they had all to hide their Superhero status. But maybe she was thinking too far into it. How much could their new friends really put together from what she had just said?

Everyone else had migrated to the window at this point and gasped at the large bird gliding high above the bus.

"That's legit!" Will stated, still in awe.

"You said it," Darla agreed, smiling like a child during Christmas.

Jessica saw everyone grinning and shouted, "Guys this is not a good thing!"

Oliver saw her stress and put his arm around her, trying to comfort his sister.

"Guys, she's right. We need to take care of this strategically and attempt to get the bird to go away," he stated.

Mason opened the window and did possibly the worst thing he could have done.

"Hey, bird!" he screamed, leaning the top of his body out the window, "Go bother someone else!"

Jason immediately face-palmed.

"Mason!" Oliver whined.

"Come on, dude!" Teddy sighed.

The giant bird suddenly turned its head and focused its beady eyes directly on Mason. The bird made a screeching sound and rocketed toward Mason at a nearly impossible speed.

TEN

In Which Mason and Jason Have a Spat

Mason!" Jason screamed. Jason grasped Masons' arm in an iron grip and yanked him back into the bus. Mason screamed and slammed the window shut.

Steven slammed on the brakes and turned around. "Kids, what's going…"

Everyone in the bus screamed and jumped back just as the giant bird's head smashed into the closed window. The bird miraculously recovered, screeched at Mason through the window, and flew out of sight. They all tried to breathe normally again. This silence continued for a moment.

"Holy crap," Will muttered at last.

"What just happened?" Steven questioned, having stopped the bus. He unbuckled and walked to the back with the rest of the gang.

"Did you not just see that beast bird attack us?" Darla yelled furiously.

"Whoa. Down girl!" Ondrea stated, putting her hand on Darla's arm.

"Is everyone okay?" Oliver wondered, his voice slightly shaking. He realized he still had his arm around Jessica and subtly put his arms down.

"R-Rachel?" Jessica asked, turning her head in Rachel's direction. "Rachel, are you okay?"

Rachel was sitting on the seat curled up in a little ball. Tears were streaming down her face. "Mason could have been killed!" she cried. "We all could have been killed."

"Now, now. Calm down everyone. I'm sure Mason would have been fine," Steven said.

"Ha. Killed by a giant bird. Who would have guessed?" Mason laughed.

"How could you laugh at that?" Jason yelled, suddenly infuriated. "What is it with you? Do you not care about your own life? I can't even begin to count all the times these passed years that you have nearly killed yourself doing stupid, nonsensical things!"

"Um, can you use smaller words?" Mason joked. No one laughed.

"That's just the way it is with you, isn't it?" Jason continued. "You can't take anything seriously! Not even your own life. You're so stupid sometimes, Mason!" Jason's voice began to shake. "You can't even think about how other people feel about you for one second! I love you! You're my twin! Apparently, that doesn't matter! Apparently, you have to always take life by the horns and take unnecessary risks! This isn't a joke! Nothing we've been through has ever been a joke!"

Tears were now dripping off Jason's chin. Jason shuddered as he finished his rant. "I couldn't live without you," he whispered. Jason quietly got up and went to sit down on the other side of the bus.

An awkward silence commenced. After a few moments, Steven turned back to the front of the bus and said, "We'll be at the gas station in thirty minutes." He walked back to the steering wheel, sat down, and began driving. Then he added, "And try not to kill each other."

Mason tucked himself against the wall and hid his head in between his knees. His whole body shook. The kids went back to their seats and silently continued their activities. Oliver and Jessica shared a glance with each other and nodded their heads, both sure of what they needed to do.

10.1

Mason didn't know how to respond to his brother's anger. He didn't know how to respond to the bird attack. He knew he wasn't the best when it came to understanding his emotions. All he could react to right now was the painful silence he could hear all around him. He hid his head in between his knees, hoping maybe the darkness could shelter him from his guilt and pain. But it didn't. The darkness just forced him to think about his brother's words. All he could think about was how much they hurt—and how true they were.

"Hey," someone peeped up from beside him.

Mason looked up. It was Oliver.

"H-hey," Mason stuttered quietly. As he looked at Oliver, a sulking Jason came into his peripheral vision. "Oh, hell. Why did I do it, Ollie?"

"Hey, it's going to work out. It doesn't matter what you did— only that you'll recover from it. And so will Jason," Oliver said, placing a hand on Mason's shoulder.

Mason buried his head in his hands. "Geez. I-I'm such a wreck. More like a wrecking ball. I just screw up everything," Mason cried. "No wonder my own brother hates me! All I do is ruin our relationship with my stupid, nonsensical actions, whatever that means. He was right."

"He may have been right about a few things, but you're not a screwup, Mason! You are yourself, and you're amazing!" Oliver stated.

"No, I'm not. Don't even try to convince me otherwise. I'm just horrible. I'm just m-me," Mason sobbed.

"Yes. You are you. You may not know who you are, but I do and so does everyone else. You are funny, charming, cool, and insecure. You need your friends. And your relationship between you and your brother means the world to you. You make mistakes. You get beat down, then you get back up. Then… you make things right again. You're relentless, you're stubborn, and you're not super mature yet. You're fun to be around no matter what you do, and Jason loves you or else he would have abandoned you years ago," Oliver said.

"Well, thanks Oliver. But…" Mason sighed, "you don't understand."

"Tell me then," Oliver said, inviting Mason to say more.

"I guess I kind of like being me, but… I really want to be like Jason. He's so calm and cool in every situation. I can't possibly imagine how he feels right now. All I know is he has never before made me feel like I do now. I really want to be him," Mason explained.

"Then be more like him," Oliver stated plainly. "If that's what you truly want, you can be more like him."

"I-I just can't! My whole life, I felt like being his opposite is how people could tell the difference between us. I'm the fun one. He's the smart one. That's how it's always been. I feel like I'd be lost if I tried to be like him. I want to be me, but I hate myself, Oliver," Mason cried.

"Wow. Okay. Then don't be him," Oliver muttered, becoming confused.

"Oliver! Didn't you come over here to help me or something?" Mason whined.

"Uh, yeah," Oliver countered in a tone that implied he obviously came over to help Mason. "Listen to me, Mason. You don't hate yourself. You love yourself. I know this! You always have so much fun when you're being yourself. You're always confident in everything you do. I know you want to be yourself. Admit that to me, at least."

Mason looked up at him wearily. "Yeah. Fine. I like being myself, but… but it's so hard! There's this fun part of me—and then the part that just makes messes," Mason complained.

"I get it. If you want to stay yourself, but slowly start to get rid of that destructive side, try this: Be yourself, but be more careful," Oliver instructed. "It's going to be difficult, but you need to use your better judgment."

"Man! You're so right, Ollie. Why didn't I think of that? I still feel bad about what I did to Jason though," Mason said, sitting up straight now.

Oliver sighed. "Look, that will work itself out. I just know," he stated, beginning to feel impatient. Oliver started walking back to his seat, but before he left, he said, "By the way, Jason really loves you."

Oliver went back to his seat, and Jessica was still with Jason. Oliver smirked as he noticed her arm around Jason's shoulders.

"Ten more minutes until the gas station, kids!" Steven yelled to the back.

10.2

Jason felt the tears running down his cheeks as he moved to the other side of the bus. Once he sat down, he looked outside, hoping the view of nature would help him clear his head, but all he saw was his own reflection staring back at him.

"Stop crying," he mumbled to himself. Jason turned back around to look at his brother. He saw him shaking with his head buried in between his knees. Mason was shaking. Jason knew he shouldn't feel upset since his argument was justified, but he did. Mason was so… irresponsible. Jason felt like it wasn't fair to accuse Mason of not caring, though. Jason just didn't know how to feel or what to do. He leaned his head against the window attempting to calm down.

"Jason?" a female voice said. He turned to look and saw Jessica.

"Hey, Jess," he whispered. "What are you doing here? You don't want to get involved in this."

"Well… too late. I already am, and I'm going to help you two! You guys are brothers. You guys are twins! This is the last way you should be acting," Jessica proclaimed.

"What, so you and Oliver have never gotten into a fight?" Jason asked.

"Yeah. We have. Not recently though… which is great!" she exclaimed.

"Good for you, Jess," Jason retaliated.

"Why are you so upset?" she asked cautiously.

"Mason almost got stabbed in the face by a giant dragon-bird! He doesn't even seem to care. Why do you think I'm upset?" Jason hissed.

"Okay, I got it. I got it. The major issue here is that you were a bit too harsh," Jessica said plaintively.

"Yeah, I know that. I feel bad, okay!" Jason stated. "I know this is my fault. I mean, Mason was just being Mason. He's always been like this. I don't know why I snapped the way I did."

"You reacted like that because you love him," Jessica told him, hanging a supportive arm around his shoulders. Jason flinched but didn't push away.

"I've always loved him. Still do, so why wouldn't I have reacted earlier?" Jason wondered.

"Could it be because of the competition coming up?" Jessica asked, raising her eyebrow as If she knew the answer to her question.

"Possibly. Maybe I'm just worried about him. Jess, what if he starts acting like this during the competition and gets hurt or… killed? I-I couldn't handle it. I've seen him almost die like 500 times. How do I know he won't handle this the same way he always does?" Jason questioned, leaning his head into Jessica's shoulder.

"You can talk to him about this. Tell him how much this really means to you—calmly. Being civil makes a pretty big difference." She laughed, then smiled a pretty, genuine smile and looked down at Jason.

Jason never realized how pretty she was when she smiled. This cheered him up a bit more. "You're right. I can only just hope he'll listen to me," Jason told her.

"He really loves you. I'm sure he'll listen to you. But don't forget to remind him," Jessica added.

"Remind him of what?" Jason asked eagerly.

"Try to remind him that you love him as much as you can. It will do him good," Jessica explained.

"Ah. Thanks," Jason said, truly grateful for the pep talk.

"You should apologize," Jessica reminded him.

"I'll do that once we get to the gas station," Jason mumbled, feeling tired. He didn't want to admit that the reason he didn't want to get up right that minute was because he was so comfortable.

"Please don't leave," he said to Jessica.

"I won't," she said supportively.

With Jason's head against Jessica's shoulder and her arm around him, he began to doze off. Back where Oliver had sat down, he was looking at them and grinning. "I think Jason likes my sister," Oliver laughed quietly.

Steven Stanford made an announcement, "Five more minutes until the gas station, kids."

ELEVEN

In Which There Is a Laser Gun

Once the bus arrived at the gas station, and Steven began to refuel, the kids hopped off and ran inside the store. Ondrea was wandering down the chip aisle when she spotted Nick.

"Hey," she said softly, concerned by the sad look on his face. "Are you still upset about…you know, Spencer?"

"I don't know! I just don't want to talk about this right now," Nick exclaimed, pushing past Ondrea.

Meanwhile, Jake and Josh were roaming the drink aisle together. "Whoa. Look at all this! Five liter bottles of soda!" Josh yelled.

"No way. Josh, you don't need any more sugar," Jake said sternly. "Besides, having sugar isn't going to magically make you sweeter."

"Aww. But aren't I just so sweet?" Josh asked, batting his eyelashes.

"Ew. Get away from me, weirdo," Jake stated, pushing Josh away.

"Maybe you need some sugar," Josh said in a huff.

"It wouldn't make me any sweeter either," Jake reminded him with a humorous smile on his face.

Mason suddenly turned down the candy aisle looking sad and lonely.

"Hi," Josh said, bringing attention to the fact that Mason wasn't the only one in that aisle.

Mason looked up and jumped, still very shaken up, grasping onto the shelf so he didn't fall over. "Hey guys," he sighed.

"Don't let your brother get to you, okay?" Jake said, attempting to reassure Mason.

"Yeah, yeah. I'm not worried about that anymore. He'll come around. I'm more worried about the contest. Like are we going to be pitted against each other? Or are we going to have to work together?" Mason asked. He shoved his hands in his pocket and bit his lip nervously.

"What else are you worried about?" Jake wondered, stepping closer to Mason.

"Nothing!" he said quickly. "It's… it's just nothing!" Mason turned around and walked out of the store, heading back to the bus.

"Look what you did, Jake," Josh said.

"Not right now, Josh," Jake countered, looking at his shoes.

"Actually, I'm sure you didn't do anything wrong. He's just got some issues he needs to sort out," Josh whispered, squeezing Jake's hand.

"Yeah," Jake responded.

Suddenly, someone screamed.

"Everyone on the ground!" A man's voice yelled from the door of the store.

Jake and Josh immediately obeyed. For some reason, they noticed that the others hesitated.

"I said: 'On the ground!'" The man screamed again.

Jake tapped Josh's arm to get his attention and then slowly began to crawl forward to get a better view of the situation. Josh followed. At this point, the others obeyed and got to the ground. Jake froze in horror. He didn't know what to do! He had never been in a situation like this before. What Jake saw was a man dressed in all black holding a… laser gun.

11.1

Jason, Darla, and Will had been milling around the store and looking for Mason when the armed man burst into the store. When the man yelled for them to get on the ground, the three could see their friends hesitate. They were probably all thinking the same thing: "We're Superheroes! We can take them!"

Jason saw that Jake and Josh had already gotten to the ground. Oliver and the others had seen them do this and, after the man yelled at them again, Jason made eye contact with Oliver. With his eyes, he gestured to where Jake and Josh were crouched down. Oliver got the message and began to lower himself to the floor. The rest of the gang followed his example.

As Teddy and Ondrea crouched on the floor, their hands met in a firm grasp. At this moment, Teddy's first thought was, "Couple's goals—hold hands during an armed robbery." Teddy looked over and saw Ondrea terrified. He squeezed her hand as if to say, "We've been through worse. It will be okay." She gave him a nervous smile. In truth, Teddy was also very nervous and didn't know how this situation was going to resolve itself.

The man locked the doors to the store so no one could get in or out, and he stepped forward.

"Phones!" he yelled. "I'm going to collect them, and then you'll listen to me!"

The cashier flinched. The man first went to Nick, who muttered a complaint under his breath and handed his phone over.

"You have something to say, kid?" the man demanded. Nick shook his head begrudgingly. "That's what I thought!" As he passed to go to the next person, he kicked Nick in the ribs and laughed. Nick bit his tongue and stayed silent.

Next the man went to Jake and Josh.

"Phone," he commanded. When nothing happened for a second, the man became impatient. "I said: 'Phone!'" He screamed and grabbed Jake by his shirt collar.

"Here!" Josh yelped quickly, not wanting Jake to get hurt. Josh whipped his phone out of his pocket and gave it to the man.

The man laughed as if Josh's fear was incredibly amusing to him.

"Ha ha! Good little boy!" he cackled. He let go of Jake's collar and said, "Now give me your phone, or I'll take your brother!"

Jake didn't want to hesitate and get Josh in trouble, but he really didn't want to give up his phone.

"I don't have a phone!" Jake said, his voice shaking.

The rest of the gang knew he was lying, and Jake heard some of them sigh.

"Yeah right, idiot!" the thief screamed. "GIVE. ME. YOUR. PHONE!"

"I-I don't have it!" Jake screamed back.

"Okay. Since you clearly don't care enough about your brother to sacrifice your phone for him, what about yourself?" The man asked, now holding his laser gun against Jake's head. "Do you care enough about your own life?"

"He really doesn't have it!" Rachel piped up weakly from the frozen food aisle.

"Right! He doesn't!" Jessica shouted.

Everyone else began to shout proclamations about the fact that Jake didn't have his phone, when the man blasted a laser beam at the ceiling to get their attention.

"Alright! I get it!" he yelled. "You guys are the most annoying set of kids I've ever held up in an armed robbery with a laser gun. EVERYONE, SHUT UP!" He screeched.

His shout—combined with the noise of plaster falling from the ceiling—managed to shut everyone up. The psychotic man went around collecting everyone else's phones without problems.

Once he was done collecting phones, he walked up to the cashier and pointed the laser gun at him.

"What do you want?" the cashier whispered, cowering in fear.

"All the money from your register… NOW!" He yelled. "NOW! NOW! NOW!"

"Okay, okay! Please stop!" the cashier cried, opening the register.

The crazed man laughed again.

"I'm getting bored!" he screamed. His head swiveled in Jason's direction, and Jason flinched. "You! Come to me!"

"What? M-me?" Jason stuttered.

"Yes! You! Don't try any funny business now," he growled. But Jason was barely able to move because he was frozen in fear. The man shot Jason in the arm with the laser gun. Jason yelped as it burned his arm, pain searing through his body, causing him to shudder. He felt dizzy, but he was pulled out of the dizziness when the man grabbed his other arm and yanked him upwards. Jason let a whimper escape his lips. Looking toward the window, he thought he saw Mason in the bus.

"One casualty wouldn't hurt me," the man said as he laughed.

11.2

Mason had been waiting for fifteen minutes, but it felt like hours. He was too upset to even think about talking to Jason.

But then he had a sudden feeling that something was very wrong. Something worse than his argument with his brother.

"When will those kids be done in there?" Steven asked from behind the steering wheel.

"I'm not sure. Do you… do you want me to go and see when they'll be done?" Mason asked. Now that he was more focused on his friends, he could clearly sense they were in trouble. More importantly, he could sense Jason was in trouble.

"That'd be great!" Steven agreed, opening the doors to the bus.

Mason stepped off the bus and started running to the store, but stopped short and hid behind a concrete column. He couldn't believe what he was seeing.

"Holy crap. There's some kind of robber in there," he whispered to himself. Once he felt his composure returning, he glanced at the store window again. He nearly froze when he saw that the man had Jason in his grasp and that Jason looked like he was in pain. Mason looked closer and saw a burn on Jason's arm. He had to do something! Should he go get Steven? No, Steven didn't seem very capable, and he wasn't any help at all when the bird hit the window. What about calling the police? That wouldn't work either; he left his phone on the bus.

"Oh no, no, no!" Mason cried. "No! Get composure, get it together, save everyone. Okay, just another day. I have to think. I can't just rush in there…" Mason thought for a second and then an idea sparked. "I got it!"

Mason tapped into his Wind Power and, at first, tried a small gust of wind against the doors. The man with the weapon put it against Jason's head.

"No! Not now," Mason thought. When the doors didn't open, he tried again, but he pushed bit harder. He heard the doors shake, but they didn't open. "Come on!" Mason urged himself. The man with the blaster looked straight toward the door, but Mason didn't care.

Mason used his Wind Power to push with everything he had. Wind rushed past his head and filled his ears as if he were sky diving. The doors flew open, and he could hear everyone shouting. Mason full out sprinted toward the doors. The man, who was obviously very surprised, turned and fired laser beams in rapid succession. Mason barely managed to dodge the onslaught. The last one singed the ends of his hair.

Mason focused his attention back on the man and noticed the man was smirking. That was not the reaction Mason expected, so he slowed down. The man with the blaster began to laugh as he figured out that the boy he had hostage and the boy who was charging at him were twins. He pointed the blaster back at Jason's head and laughed even harder as if he would enjoy killing Jason.

"No!" Mason shouted. He pushed his Wind Power as hard as he could so the wind would give him a speed boost. Mason made a leap for the man and hit him with such force that the man screamed in pain and anger. Everyone else took this as a sign to spring into action. There was so much commotion that Teddy was able to Teleport to this villain without being noticed. Teddy snatched the laser from his hand and threw it on the other side of the room. With Teddy and Mason now on top of him, the man didn't notice Nick coming up to side kick him in the ribs until it happened.

"Pay back!" Nick shouted angrily.

Oliver looked at Jessica and said, "Quickly! You grab Jason and Nick. We have to get them out of here! I'll think of an explanation for Steven of why everything just happened, but you need to take them to the bus. I'll grab Ondrea, Jake, and Josh."

"Why Ondrea?" she asked quickly.

"Healing," Oliver stated, gently shoving Jessica toward where Jason was standing in the back, away from the fight.

"Okay, I'm going," she said, rushing toward Jason. She ran up to him and saw his face contorted in pain. His hand was squeezing his arm over the burn.

"Is it that bad?" Jessica asked while grabbing Jason's other arm and pulling him toward the door.

"Yeah. It hurts pretty bad," he confirmed. "Hey, where is Mason? Is he okay?"

"He's somewhere in that dog pile the boys have created on top of the idiot who did that to you!" Jessica exclaimed. At this point, everyone left in the gas station tackled the man, holding him there. In the commotion, the cashier had called the police.

"Gosh, I hope Mason's okay," Jason said anxiously.

"I'm sure he's okay. He's a strong kid," Jessica reassured him. Once they had reached the door, Jessica said, "Wait here for a sec!" She ran to the dog pile near the register and pulled Nick out of it.

As she pulled on him, he came up and yelped. That man had done some damage to Nick's ribs. But when he saw Jessica's concern, he had to say something so she wouldn't worry. "Hey, they're just bruised," he mumbled with a small grin.

"Yeah, whatever," she said, rolling her eyes.

"It's true!" he insisted.

Jessica pulled Nick to the door where Jason was. "Stay!" she commanded sternly.

"Geez. Yes ma'am!" Nick exclaimed, sitting down.

When Jessica went off to get Ondrea, Nick slid to the floor next to Jason. "Hey, you okay?" Jason asked, putting his hand on Nick's shoulder.

"Yeah, I'm doing alright…" Nick answered. He looked at Jason's arm and gently touched it. Jason clenched his teeth.

"Sorry, man! This is bad!" Nick said.

"Yeah. Hurts too," Jason gasped.

"I can use my Healing Powers on this for you," Nick stated, looking around. Suddenly, Oliver ran past them with frightened-looking Jake and Josh in tow. Nick watched them run out of the store and onto the bus. Jason and Nick looked at each other, and then shrugged.

Nick began to push Healing Energy from himself when he felt a jolt of pain. "Ouch! Nope. Can't do it," Nick whispered, gingerly touching his ribcage.

"It's fine. Ondrea can do it. Besides, you need to conserve your energy," Jason said, forming a pained smile.

"Dude, you know I'm a replenishable energy battery," Nick countered, laughing to himself.

Jessica came back with Ondrea and Rachel following her. She gestured for Jason and Nick to get up, and all of them ran to the bus. She led them onto the bus with Oliver, and then went back into the store.

"Guys, we've got to go before the cops get here!" Jessica yelled, grabbing the attention of all her friends. "We can't explain how a bunch of kids beat up a psycho with a laser gun."

"But… but the bad guy!" Will whined, still wanting to show him who was boss.

"I'm sure you've cut off his air supply long enough. We've got to get going, guys!" she insisted.

"I'll keep him here until the cops show up!" Darla shouted, jumping up and down.

"No way! We're not leaving you here!" Jessica yelled as if Darla had lost her mind.

"I didn't say anything about leaving me here," she exclaimed, smirking. By this time, the rest of the dog pile was with Jessica by the entrance. The bad guy thought he could make an escape. But boy, was he wrong. Darla brought back her arm and punched him in the side of the head, causing the man to groan in pain and pass out. Darla, being Darla, stood up and bowed. Everyone clapped humorously, but Will clapped the hardest.

Everyone turned and went back to the bus. Teddy picked up the man's laser and brought it with him. Before he left, he pulled three 100-dollar bills of his emergency money from his pocket and gave it to the cashier.

"Keep this on the down-low," Teddy said to the cashier. "Don't say anything about anyone else being here. Just tell the cops you threw some kind of heavy object at his head. I hope we didn't ruin too much of your day. Okay? Thanks! Byyyeee!" Teddy called, sprinting after his friends.

TWELVE

In Which a Subtle Calm Descends
After the Storm

After everyone was back on the bus—and Oliver had made up some crazy but convincing story for Steven, who was oblivious—they all began to talk at once. No one could hear what anyone else was saying. After five minutes, Steven yelled, "Quiet! I'm trying to drive!"

Everyone immediately silenced themselves. For thirty minutes, the gang went about doing their own things with the event at the gas station still in mind.

Will noticed Darla had been staring out the window for the past thirty minutes without saying anything. He pushed her shoulder gently.

"Hey, you okay?" he whispered.

"Yeah, I'm good," she responded, not turning around.

"Um. Are you sure?" he wondered. Will tried to lean forward to get a better look at her face, but she turned away from him.

"I'm just great, Will!" Darla yelled. Still looking out the window, she crossed her arms and bowed her head.

Will was taken by surprise. He nearly jumped out of his seat when she yelled at him. He'd thought their friendship was in a good place. Will rose out of his seat and began to walk toward the back. Nick tugged on Will's shirt sleeve as he passed.

"Hey, you can sit with me if you want," Nick said.

"Uh. Okay," Will mumbled. He sat in the aisle seat on Nick's row.

"You should talk to her," Nick stated quietly.

"Nah. She doesn't want to talk to me," Will muttered as he fidgeted with his hands in his lap.

"She may not want to talk to you, but trust me when I say that she wants *you* to talk to *her*," Nick said. He gave Will a hearty pat on the shoulder.

"What kind of logic is that?" Will asked, his voice raising an octave.

Nick sighed wearily and took a deep breath. "She likes you, Will. A lot."

"Wait, you mean she… um … likes me—likes me a lot?" Will wondered nervously.

"Yeah. Is it not obvious to you?" Nick asked.

"Well, clearly not," Will grumbled.

"You should talk to her. Not about the whole 'liking' thing, but ask her what's got her so upset," Nick suggested, gesturing to how she was slouched over in her seat.

"Alright," Will said. He began to walk nervously toward Darla.

Once Will sat down, Darla said, "I don't bite, you know."

"Right, I know. Sorry. I… I uh. I wanted to ask you again. I… Are you okay?" he stammered.

"Let me guess. You're just asking because you're my friend, and you feel it's your 'duty' to see if I'm okay?" Darla mumbled, finally turning her head away from the window to face Will.

"Well, I wouldn't call it a burden," Will said. "It's certainly not my duty. I could have just ignored you, but I didn't so… what's up?"

Darla sighed heavily. "I don't know. Doesn't it just seem like we're in a constant state of peril all the time?" she asked, slumping back into her seat.

"Yeah. It kind of comes with the Superhero job description, Darla," Will answered, awkwardly scooting closer to her.

"I know," she sighed. Darla stayed quiet for a couple minutes longer while Will just sat there.

Finally, she said, "Why are you here? You don't seem to be very comfortable."

The question surprised him. "I just wanted to make sure you're okay. Do you want to… I don't know… talk more about this 'constant state of peril' thing?" Will asked.

"There's no point. We're teenagers, Will. We're not supposed to be living this kind of life. Complaining and talking about it won't change that, so what's the point?" Darla mumbled.

"Well, yeah. But… maybe talking about it might help just a little," Will suggested.

"Well, we talked about it enough already," Darla exclaimed.

"Darla, are you mad at me?" Will questioned, scooting away from Darla now.

"No! I'm just… I'm just lonely. I feel like I'm living in a world by myself a lot of the time," Darla confessed. "It's just… It's hard."

This time, Will scooted closer once more. He put his arm gingerly around Darla's shoulders.

"We'll do this together. You're not alone. You have us," Will said, smiling. "You have…me."

Darla glanced up at Will and grinned sadly. She leaned her head into his shoulder and closed her eyes. As shocked as Will was at this display of emotion, he found it comforting. He didn't get up to leave.

For the rest of the bus ride, he stayed right there with her head on his shoulder.

12.1

"That was insane," Jake whispered to Josh. The two had decided to sit by each other.

"Yeah. That was pretty crazy. Are you okay?" Josh questioned, fidgeting with the latch on the window.

"I'm alright. What about you?" he replied. When Josh didn't answer, Jake nudged his brother on the shoulder.

"I'm a bit shaken up. That's all," Josh answered, turning to face him.

"Hey, what was that guy carrying, anyway?" Jake wondered aloud.

"I don't know. It looked like some kind of laser gun, like you'd see in a video game," Josh responded.

"Yeah, that was weird," Jake stated, staring straight forward.

"Hey guys, you okay?" Nick asked from the row in front of them.

"Yeah, we're fine. Are you okay? That guy nearly kicked your butt!" Jake said.

Nick noticed that Jake didn't say this with a humored smile on his face, but a look of concern. If they had been through everything that Nick and the rest of the gang had, they would probably be having very different reactions.

"I guess I'm okay. It doesn't hurt too much anymore," Nick lied. The truth was that it didn't hurt at all anymore. Ondrea used her Healing Powers on him as soon as Nick had arrived in the bus. Same with Jason. Nick had to lie to them. Jason even had a bandage wrapped around the area where the burn used to be just to provide the illusion that it was still healing.

All of that just so the Stanford twins—Jake and Josh— wouldn't be suspicious. "My ribs are just a little bruised," Nick assured them.

"You should probably get that checked out by a doctor, still," Jake suggested.

"Trust me," Jessica said, barging into the conversation, "he's fine!"

Oliver looked over at Jessica. She and Oliver were sitting in the row across from Jake and Josh. Nick also glanced over at Jessica. "After that harsh tone, I think I might need to go to the hospital!" Nick exclaimed. He stared at Jessica with an eyebrow raised.

"Ugh. Sorry," Jessica sighed. "I guess I'm just a bit tense from the whole armed robbery thing."

"Speaking of the armed robbery," Jake began, "I'd just like to mention that, for an armed robbery, you guys handled that situation pretty well."

"Actually, yeah. How did you know how to handle that so well?" Josh asked, now facing the others.

Teddy turned around in his seat. "Yo, we were born to handle oddly precarious situations," Teddy called.

"I second that notion!" Avery exclaimed from the middle section of the bus.

"Me too!" Rachel insisted. Rachel and Avery were sitting next to each other in the same row.

"Okay," Oliver mumbled, clearly not wanting to discuss their Powers in front of those without Superpowers. "Now that we've determined we're all psychotic maniacs with all the basic characteristics of over-powered adrenaline junkies, let's talk about why Jake insisted he didn't have his phone on him in the store."

"Wait a minute, yeah!" Teddy called, "You could have easily gotten all of us killed!"

"You're the ones who backed him up on that!" Josh muttered.

"Hey, why are you saying that?" Nick asked. "You're the one who almost had to pay with your life for that!"

"But I didn't!" Josh yelled. "Then he moved on to nearly murdering my brother with his 'laser'."

"Besides, I kept my phone so I could potentially call the cops!" Jake whined.

"Well, aren't you just a little hero?" Teddy said sarcastically.

"Guys! Calm down!" Jessica yelled.

"Please!" Rachel insisted.

"But you didn't call the cops!" Teddy exclaimed, pointing accusingly.

"Teddy Bear, please," Ondrea sighed. "I'm not sure he meant to cause any harm by keeping his phone." She put a gentle, but firm hand on Teddy's shoulder.

Teddy turned back around to face forward and plopped into his seat once more.

"Whatever," he said with a huff, crossing his arms.

"Well, I feel attacked," Jake whispered.

"I'm sorry," Oliver mumbled. "I wasn't trying to start that."

"It's fine. I'm sure people are just a bit wound up," Jake responded.

Josh glanced over at Jake's face and gave him a lopsided smile. "I understand, Jake. I understand why you kept your phone," Josh said supportively.

"Thanks," Jake muttered. "I hope we're close to the game-show place."

Everyone went back to their seats.

12.2

"One more hour, kids!" Steven exclaimed from the front of the bus.

"Well, that was chaotic," Mason whispered to Jason. Jason hadn't said a word to Mason since he had gotten on the bus. "Bro! Please just talk to me!" Jason still didn't say a word. "Jace!" Mason begged, "You nearly died back there! Please talk to me!" Mason's voice cracked. His eyes began to water as he saw the clear vivid image of Jason in the gas station. "Please," he whispered.

"I guess we're even," Jason stated, his arms crossed. Jason was still looking out the window and hadn't turned to see Mason's face yet.

"W…What?" Mason stammered.

"You almost died. I got mad at you for it. I almost died. We're even," Jason repeated.

"But I'm not mad at you! It wasn't your fault you nearly died," Mason insisted. "I'm sorry for sticking my head out that window! I'm sorry that GIANT BIRD almost ate my freaking head! I don't know what else you want me to say!"

"Okay," Jason said.

"Fine. Whatever," Mason mumbled. He turned to face the aisle. He suddenly felt so alone. Mason and Jason had always been as close as any pair of twins could be. Now, he felt as alone as he ever had. They'd never fought like this before.

Jason continued to stare out the window contemplating Mason and his relationship.

"I love my brother," he thought to himself. "That's why he needs to learn to be more careful. Maybe by ignoring him, I can teach him to value what he has." His thoughts were interrupted when he heard someone call his name.

Jason turned around to see Jessica and Ondrea standing in the aisle. "Hey, can we talk to you?" Ondrea asked sincerely.

"Uh. Of course. What is it?" he wondered.

"In… private," Jessica said awkwardly.

"Of course," Jason mumbled as he squeezed passed Mason. Jason had a feeling he knew what Ondrea and Jessica were going to talk to him about. If the only two Mind Readers in the group came up to you when you're having a bad time and ask if they can talk to you in private, you can be sure that they know what's going on.

Ondrea and Jessica led Jason to the very front and sat down on the opposite side of the bus across from Will and Darla, who were both asleep. Darla had her head on Will's shoulder, Will's arm was around her shoulders, and his head was against the back of the seat, snoring gently.

"So, what's going on with you and your brother?" Ondrea questioned.

"Subtle, Ondrea. Real subtle," Jessica muttered underneath her breath.

"It's alright, Jess," Jason sighed. "I know you guys have Mind Reading Powers. Get on with the lecture, please."

"Don't think of it as a lecture," Ondrea said with a small grin.

"Yeah, think of it as friendly advice," Jessica agreed. Jason didn't say anything. Jessica continued. "Jason. Even we aren't perfect. It may seem like we're all perfect with all our Superpowers and everything, but you know what a mess we are. Even by normal human standards, we aren't perfect. We can relate to any human on an emotional level. Even you—the one who thinks he's perfect and tries to be perfect—aren't perfect. You know what I'm saying?"

"Yes," Jason whispered, feeling ashamed.

"I hope it doesn't feel like I'm attacking you." Jessica said, putting a supportive hand on his shoulder.

"That felt a bit like an attack, but you're not wrong. I get it," Jason exclaimed sadly.

"That's why we're here to tell you that ignoring your brother is wrong on every single level," Ondrea explained. "He's clearly already 'learned his lesson,' whatever that means. Also, he is a Superhero teenager with a huge risk meter. Putting himself in danger comes with the job description."

"Plus, he's done it so many times before. Why are you so upset with him just now?" Jessica added.

"I guess I'm just tired of it all," Jason stated. "It's been happening our whole lives. As you can imagine, since we're twins, we discovered our Powers at the exact same time—when we were both five and a half. Since then, it's only been trouble. I thought I had learned to live with it by now, but… I don't know."

"What don't you know?" Jessica asked.

Jason hesitated. "I… I don't know! I'm not sure! It's just every day, he's putting himself at more and more risk. I'm so scared. I'm terrified that, one of these days, it'll be over for him. I'm afraid I'll be brother-less," Jason exclaimed.

He began to look incredibly flustered. His eyes were watering. Jason glanced back at Mason who was now at the window seat, facing the window. When Jason turned back to the girls, they saw tears dripping down his face.

"I don't know what I'd do without him," Jason whispered, his voice cracking. He looked down at his hands and saw they were shaking. "I love him," he croaked. Finally, the tears cascaded down his face and his whole body began to shake. Jason looked up and, through blurry vision, he saw Mason staring at him, giving him a confused look. Jason turned away in shame.

"If that's how you feel," Ondrea began. "Then that's what you should tell him."

"No need." Jason looked up in surprise and saw Mason standing in front of him. "I heard everything." He bent down so he was eye-level with his twin.

"I promise, Jason, that I will be more careful in the future," Mason said as he looked Jason directly in the eyes. "I had no clue this is how you felt. I'm really sorry, bud. I love you, too." Jason didn't say anything, still. Mason sighed. "Just please don't shut me out of your life because of this one incident," Mason whispered.

Jason threw his arms around Mason and began to sob. Steven looked at them from the front, but Jessica gestured that they had it all under control. Mason didn't appear to be shocked by Jason's hug. Instead, Mason wrapped his arms around his brother and let him cry.

THIRTEEN

In Which There Is an Important Discovery

Alright, boys and girls! We're here!" Steven announced happily from the driver's seat. Will's head was the first to go up. He carefully took his arm back from Darla's shoulders and wiped the sleep from his eyes. He gently shook Darla.

"We're here, Darla," Will said. Darla's eyes fluttered open and she began to stretch. She stuck her arms and legs out, accidentally hitting Will in the face.

"Sorry!"

"It's cool," Will assured her.

Jake and Josh had already gotten off the bus with their dad and were waiting outside. Jason, who had cried himself to sleep in Mason's arms, sat straight up. Mason startled.

"We're here, bro. You okay?" he asked, helping Jason out of his seat.

"Yes. Bad dream. That's all," Jason muttered. Mason knew whenever Jason spoke in chopped up sentences, there was something else on his mind. Mason, Jason, Will, and Darla ventured off the bus. Oliver and Jessica followed behind them.

Rachel was having a panic attack, and Avery was attempting to help her calm down. Teddy and Ondrea walked past the two of them.

"Is there anything we can do to help?" Ondrea questioned as she saw Rachel's state.

"No. I've got it," Avery said. "See you out there, sis." Ondrea and Teddy walked out of the bus and told the others that Rachel and Avery would be a minute.

"Rachel, I promise you're going to be okay. If you need to step out, you can. I know this is a new experience and it's frightening, but we're here for you. And again, if you need to step out, you definitely can," Avery explained calmly.

"Thanks," Rachel whispered. "Can we go now?"

"Sure. Let's go!" Avery said. She put her arm around Rachel's shoulders and walked like that all the way inside the studio.

13.1

The second Jason walked into the studio, he perked up. The Mackenzie twins, along with everyone else, looked around the room in awe. Not only was the ceiling incredibly high, but it was completely colored with LED lights. A glow of blue and purple filled the room and made everyone's skin and clothes glow the same colors. A polished wooden stage ran the length of the entire front part of the room. On that stage, a small circle was marked with tape.

"That's where Steven stands during airtime," Jake said, as he noticed everyone staring at it. His new friends just nodded their heads, still admiring the room.

An all-black box sat in the middle of the room. Above it—so the cameras could project what was inside the box—were black screens. The outside of the screens were outlined in red LED lights, adding a cool extra glow to the room. There were twenty podiums spaced out on the stage, each outlined in a different color LED.

Steven grinned as he saw the looks on the kids' faces. "I see you like the studio?" he asked, even though he knew the answer.

"Yeah!" The gang all said at once.

"This place is awesome!" Mason yelled.

"You can definitely say that again!" Darla exclaimed. She too had perked up.

"This is pretty cool," Rachel agreed, standing up a little bit straighter.

"Yeah, this is pretty cool." Oliver repeated. "Although the lights are giving me a huge headache."

"Me too," Jason seconded.

"My apologies. I can fix that," Steven stated. He walked over to the wall right next to the door they had just entered. He flipped a black switch that blended in with the rest of the black wall. As soon as he flipped it, the LEDs turned off and normal lights appeared.

Oliver and Jason's headaches instantly went away. Oliver walked over to Jason while the others explored the building.

"That was weird," Oliver whispered.

"Yes, that was very strange," Jason agreed quietly. "Perhaps that had something to do with our Super Intelligence or what you call your 'Analytical Processing.'"

"Yeah. It didn't seem to be anything sinister. Maybe the LEDs were just messing with our heads, since our Super Intelligence enhances our senses," Oliver suggested.

"Until we investigate this further, which I don't think we'll need to, let's… let's just keep it to ourselves," Jason said.

"Good plan," Oliver stated distractedly. "Whoa. This place is so cool."

"I know! It's everything I've ever dreamed it would be!" Jason said excitedly. Oliver smirked and walked off to check out the rest of the building. Suddenly, Mason, Will, Teddy, and Darla walked up to Jason.

"Hey, brother!" Jason exclaimed.

"Hey, Jace. Guess what?" Mason asked.

Before Jason had a chance to answer, Darla said, "Steven said we could go backstage!"

"Seriously!?" Jason questioned.

"Yeah, man!" Teddy confirmed.

"Let's go!" Mason shouted. He grabbed Jason's hand and began dragging his twin toward the backstage area. Once they all made it backstage, they spread out.

"Guys, look at this!" Will called. He'd spotted all the ropes and strings.

"This is probably where the backstage crew controls the lights up front," Jason said, coming up behind Will.

"I think I found some crew rooms!" Teddy yelled from somewhere further back.

"Stay out of those, Teddy! They're not yours to go into!" Darla shouted loudly.

Mason ventured further onto the stage. He saw the chair the participants were strapped into in order to enter the Virtual Reality room.

"Jason! Take a look at this!" Mason called. Jason ran to his twin and studied the chair excitedly.

"Wow, this is so cool!" Jason whispered, clearly awe-struck.

"Aren't all these wires a little unnerving?" Will asked, coming up from behind.

"They would be if they weren't so fascinating," Jason replied.

"Jason!" Darla yelled. Jason cringed and turned around.

"That was very loud, Darla," Jason said, rubbing his head. He could feel a bit of his headache returning. "What do you need?"

Darla peaked her head out from behind the backstage curtain.

"Teddy went into one of the crew rooms. I need your help to drag him out," she explained. Darla finished her statement with a dramatic sigh: "Boys."

"Why can't you just use your pushy personality and your genuinely terrifying presence to goad him out?" Mason asked sincerely.

"I tried that already. It didn't work!" she hissed.

"Alright, here I come," Jason sighed.

"He's in there," Darla whispered. She pointed to the room in the middle of his vision.

"Why are you whispering?" Jason asked, also whispering just in case something was afoot.

"It's weird in there. It's eerie. I just feel like whispering," Darla answered.

"Eerie?" Jason wondered. He stepped inside the room and shivered. "She's right."

"Yeah, it's real creepy in here," Teddy said as he fidgeted with something in the corner. "I think there's something in here."

"Just ignore it, Teddy. We've got to get out of here. Something's not right with this room," Jason warned.

"Wait! I almost got it, man," Teddy insisted. Jason heard a startling thumping sound from whatever Teddy was doing.

Jason scoffed impatiently and walked over to Teddy. Right before he reached Teddy, Teddy gasped. It wasn't a good gasp; it was definitely a bad gasp.

"What is it, Teddy?" Jason questioned cautiously.

"Look," Teddy whispered, his voice shaking. Jason peered over his shoulder and saw a drawer. Teddy must have been messing with the lock to get it open.

When Jason saw what was inside the drawer, he gave a startled shout. "That's the laser gun the guy had at the store!" Jason gasped.

"N…No. I took THAT laser gun and disposed of it," Teddy said. "But this looks just like it. That's for sure," Teddy said.

"What's going on? Is everything okay?" Darla wondered, coming through the door.

"Darla, look!" Jason hissed. "It's the laser gun."

Darla peered over Jason's shoulder and jumped back.

"Okay!" she began. "Let's not jump to any conclusions. Maybe it's… a prop! It has to be a prop. Teddy, don't touch it!"

Teddy's arm was midway into the drawer, and he was about to pick up the laser gun.

"Yes ma'am!" he stated, making a show of pulling his hand away from it.

"We need to tell the others about this as soon as possible," Jason suggested. "For now, we've got to get out of here and back to the group."

Teddy stepped back, closed the drawer, and relocked it.

"Wait," he said. Teddy saw a second light switch on the wall. He flipped it. Suddenly, the mirror's LED light came on.

Jason's headache immediately returned, although it seemed more intense. He glanced toward the laser gun, and he saw a few black sparkly particles floating in the air. "Wow. Ow. Please, Teddy. Turn those off. Now!" Jason gasped, gripping his head.

Teddy turned them off as fast as he could. Jason's headache immediately subsided. A look of horror was all that remained on Jason's face.

"Jason!" Darla said, placing her hand on his shoulder. "What's wrong?"

"You're not going to believe this!" Jason said.

"Just tell us anyway," Teddy insisted with a deep look of concern plastered on his face.

"There are Dark Magic particles floating in the air. This room contains Dark Magic," Jason croaked.

"Oh boy," Darla sighed. "You know what that means."

"Yep," Teddy mumbled. "VORK."

"VORK," Jason hissed venomously.

13.2

"Hey, where are the others?" Jessica questioned.

"I think they may be exploring the back," Avery answered. Rachel, Nick, Jake, Josh, Jessica, Ondrea, and Oliver had decided to go the opposite way.

"All the fun stuff is where we are," Jake exclaimed. "All the wires and ropes."

"Yeah," Josh agreed quietly.

"This place must be really expensive!" Nick stated, still in awe.

"Yeah. It's pretty expensive," Jake confirmed.

Josh went to open a peculiar purple door over to Oliver's left, but when he pulled the handle, the door remained closed. It was locked. Josh stopped for a second. Jake glanced at Josh and shook his head ever so slightly.

"Right, I forgot that we weren't supposed to go in here," Josh said.

Jake slapped his forehead and sighed. "You know you weren't supposed to even say anything, Josh," he mumbled. "We're not even supposed to want to go into that room," Jake rolled his eyes.

"Why not?" Ondrea wondered.

"We have no clue, but Dad seemed really freaked out when he told us to–and I quote–*never* go in there!" Jake answered.

"When he told us, he looked like he was terrified. It's hard to explain," Josh added.

"Try us," Oliver challenged.

"Okay. Well, Dad seemed like he was afraid—afraid for his safety," Josh said.

"Or maybe afraid for our safety," Jake added, shrugging his shoulders.

"Have you seen anything suspicious lately?" Rachel asked suddenly.

"Uh, no," Jake replied with a confused expression on his face.

"We shouldn't even be talking about this!" Josh snapped. "Dad told us not to."

"You're not even supposed to TALK about it?" Oliver asked.

"That's right," Josh answered.

"Speaking of Steven, where is he?" Avery wondered.

"I saw him go back to the bus," Jake said. "I think he's just grabbing your bags and putting them in the rooms."

"We get our own rooms!?" Jessica shrieked happily.

"Yeah. Your rooms are in a building off to the side of this one. Steven, Jake, and I live in this building, one floor above the studio," Josh explained.

"Yep. Your rooms are sort of like hotel rooms," Jake explained. "Luckily, there are five rooms. Each one has two twin beds and a couch that folds out as a sleeping mattress. Since there are eleven of you total, that will work," Jake finished.

"That's great!" Nick cheered. "I'm just glad we start tomorrow, so we get to rest up before the game show."

"We're excited too! This is the first time Dad has ever let us participate. We don't know why he's letting us join in this time, but it's really thrilling," Jake said, grinning.

"There seems to be a lot you don't know," Rachel whispered just loud enough. "Isn't that a little strange?"

"No. Not really," Josh said. He shoved his hands in his pockets. "We just do our thing, and Dad does his."

This time, the gang didn't try to stop Rachel from asking too many suspicious questions. In fact, they continued the topic.

"Wait, so you're never curious to know what exactly is going on around here—around you?" Ondrea pushed.

"Nah," Jake stated. "We trust Dad."

"We're not trying to tell you to NOT trust him. We also trust Steven," Jessica began, "but… you never thought to ask why he does what he does? And why you aren't even supposed to TALK ABOUT that locked purple door?"

"I'm going to be honest here," Jake answered. "Ever since Dad got an anonymous investor to help him fund the show and keep this place open, he's been a bit more hesitant to share. But, it's fine. We don't push. We're just glad he still has the business."

"Um, okay," Nick muttered. Then he took a deep breath. "Anyway, what's for food?"

"Oh, right!" Josh said, relieved to have a different topic of conversation. "You guys are eating dinner with us and then going to your rooms."

"Does Steven cook?" Avery questioned.

"Believe it or not, he does," Jake replied. He gave a small laugh. "I think he's serving chicken tonight!"

"Awesome!" everyone cheered.

Suddenly, Steven came into the studio and yelled, "DINNER TIME!"

Jake and Josh rushed forward. As soon as they were out of sight, all the Superheroes eyed each other. Whether the Stanford twins knew it or not, the Supers knew there was something strange going on here. They knew it even before dinner—before Jason shared his unsettling news.

13.3

All fourteen of them sat around a large table on the second floor of the studio building. That included the three sets of twins—Jason and Mason, Jessica and Oliver, and Jake and Josh—plus Darla, Will, Teddy, Ondrea, Avery, Rachel, Nick, and Steven. Plates of half-eaten chicken sat in front of each of them. The kids were halfway through their meal, and that's when Jason decided to uncharacteristically cut the idle chit-chat.

"So, what's with the crew rooms in the backstage area?" Jason asked.

Steven put down his fork and stared at Jason. Jake and Josh also looked at him curiously.

"They're just crew rooms," Steven answered. "You didn't go in them, did you? They're private to my crew. Between *Unleash Your Wild Side*—the game show—and the Environmental Dome, we employ a sizable crew. They expect their privacy."

"It's true," Jake added in a slightly annoyed tone. "My dad takes pride in keeping those rooms completely private. Jason, I already told you that."

Jake and Josh glanced at each other. "Why are you guys so curious about those rooms?" Josh questioned.

"We're just curious people," Will said, shrugging.

Oliver face palmed. "Hey this is really great chicken!" he cheered, deliberately changing the topic.

"Why, thank you, Oliver! I made it myself!" Steven replied, clearly pleased that someone had complimented the chicken.

"Oh, yeah!" Jessica added. "Jake and Josh told us you like to cook."

"Very true! Cooking is hobby of mine," Steven exclaimed with a grin.

The rest of dinner was actually rather nice except for the few other times Oliver and Jessica had to cover for their friends' curious behavior. After dinner, everyone graciously thanked Steven, said goodnight to Jake and Josh, then followed the instructions leading them to their individual rooms in the building next to the studio.

Jason and Oliver decided to room together, and Mason took the couch in their room. The rest of the friends paired up to room like this: Avery and Ondrea, Darla and Jessica, Teddy and Will, Nick and Rachel.

Back in the trio's room, Oliver was fuming.

"Why was everyone acting so rude at dinner?" he exclaimed, his fists clenched. "I mean, Steven invited all of us to do this fun game show. Everything is supposed to be normal and fun, but they're acting like there's something to be afraid of!"

"Not afraid," Jason began, "Just cautious."

"Yeah, but… I kind of agree with Oliver," Mason said timidly. "I haven't really seen anything suspicious yet."

Jason sighed as he remembered he still hadn't told the others what he, Darla, and Teddy saw. He sat on the bed, suddenly feeling weary.

"Oliver," he mumbled, "our lives will never be normal." Jason stuck his arms out to the side and flopped back on the bed, closing his eyes. He inhaled deeply as he took in the gravity of their existences.

"Wow, there was a lot going on in that sigh, brother," Mason stated, coming over to sit on the same bed as Jason. "Want to tell us what's going on in your mind right now?"

He sat up suddenly and put his head in his hands. "We just have to accept that our lives will never be normal," Jason repeated.

"I know!" Oliver hissed, "But it would be nice if, for once, SOMETHING NORMAL could happen to us!"

"Normal's boring, dude," Mason said. And as if to prove his point, Mason did a cartwheel in the middle of the room. "See?" he asked. "What normal person would do a cartwheel in the middle of a… whatever this room is?"

"That's just you being you, Mason," Oliver grumbled.

"Alright, settle down, Oliver," Jason warned.

"Nah. It's fine. I take that as a compliment any day. I am me, and that's just great," Mason explained, hyperactively skipping around the room. "I don't care how many flaws I have—as long as I have you guys and myself."

"Are you on drugs or something?" Oliver asked with an eyebrow raised.

"No!" Mason said happily, "But I am high on life!"

"Oh my gosh," Oliver muttered. He plopped down on the couch and mirrored Jason's body language, putting his head in his hands.

"Hey, Mason?" Jason said. He lifted his head and stared pointedly at his twin. "Do you think you could tone it down for us a little?"

"Uh… yeah. Sorry," Mason sighed. The room was quiet for a minute and then Mason said, "Okay! What can we do to get you two in some kind of better mood?"

"I have something incredibly important I need to get out of my head," Jason explained. "But the whole group—excluding Jake and Josh—needs to hear this."

"I guess I can get them over here," Oliver suggested.

"That'd be great," Jason agreed. He sighed heavily as he mentally prepared himself to give the bad news.

Oliver immediately texted the group chat and told them Jason had urgent news he needed to share. Surprisingly, despite the lateness of the hour, no one complained, which reminded Oliver of his "leadership position" once more. Oliver then texted them the directions to their room. Twenty minutes later, everyone had arrived.

"Sorry we took so long," Rachel said as she and Nick hurried into the room.

"We got a little lost, man," Teddy said.

"Yeah, us too," Ondrea added. "This housing situation feels more like a stressful college campus tour."

"College is not so far away," Nick sighed.

"Let's not think about that," Will intervened. "Instead let's think about the probably horrible news Jason needs to share with us."

"Exactly!" Darla agreed, happy to change the subject. She'd hate to admit it out loud, but even though some of her friends were only in ninth grade, she already knew she'd miss them when they were gone to college.

"Guys!" Jason announced, standing up. He began to pace nervously. His gaze flickered to the eyes of Darla and Teddy. Teddy came up to Jason and put a supportive hand on his shoulder. Jason smiled at him. Darla came over too, but she just stood beside Jason, which forced him to stop pacing.

"Earlier this evening, Darla and I were attempting to get Teddy out of one of the crew rooms when… when I…. spotted…" Jason didn't want to say it. Even the aspect of putting the news out there made him worried. The moment the others heard the news, everything would change.

Unfortunately, or fortunately, Darla didn't think that. In fact, she finished his sentence for him: "Dark Magic particles. Jason spotted Dark Magic particles."

Before people could start mumbling, Teddy added, "But he could only see them when the LEDs were on."

"Wait!" Jessica called over the stirring commotion. "Are you sure that's what you saw?"

"Yes, that's… that's what I saw," Jason stammered. "But… but there's more."

Suddenly, everyone went silent again. They all waited for Jason to speak. Despite Jason's intelligent charm, he had never been much of a public speaker. Even among friends, he felt nervous. Maybe this was the case now because of what he had to say. He didn't know. This time, Teddy spoke up.

"We saw the same laser gun that was used on us at the gas station in one of the drawers of a crew room," Teddy announced. "The drawer was locked, but I picked it. I don't know why I did. I just felt I had to."

"Hold up!" Will exclaimed, "The exact same laser gun?"

"No. Sorry, I meant a replica of the laser gun, the same kind of laser gun," Teddy corrected quickly.

"A replica?" Oliver questioned. "Did it work? It could have been a prop."

"Well…" Teddy began with agitation in his voice. "I would have touched it but…"

"But I didn't let him," Darla finished. "I'm surprised you didn't notice why, Jason."

"Wh… what do you mean?" he asked, taken by surprise.

"The light on the mirror wasn't necessarily LED," Darla said. "I don't know what kind of light it was, but I saw a couple of bright yellow fingerprints on the side of the mirror when the lights were on, and on the lock Teddy was fidgeting with. Whoever that crew room belongs to is either a neat freak or really paranoid."

The room was silent for a couple seconds until Teddy spoke up once more. "Jason determined that a VORK member could be living in the crew room."

Mason stepped forward. "A couple months ago, I saw online that our game show, *Unleash Your Wild Side*, had been having funding issues. I read…"

"You read?!" Will interrupted, legitimately shocked.

Mason sighed and continued, "I read that a couple of days before the article came out, *Unleash Your Wild Side* had gotten a new investor who was living on site with Steven, Jake, and Josh. Being interested in the show, I tried to look up more about it, but nothing came up. It was as if their investor was keeping a really low profile and a really clean record, whoever it is. That interested me even more, so I scrolled all the social media sites I could find. I searched for anyone who had the tag '*Unleash Your Wild Side*' 'face your fears game show,' 'environmental dome' and even 'virtual game show' in their posts, but I couldn't find ANYTHING about a new investor."

"Wow, that's pretty thorough!" Avery exclaimed, impressed.

"Thank you!" Mason said. "But I'm not done. After I looked through social media and found nothing, I figured the article I'd first read might have been fake. I did the obvious thing and looked all over the Internet for more articles discussing a new investor. I found twelve more and read them all several times over. They didn't say anything specific about the investor, just that it's a dude.

I began looking to see if there was any news footage about this, and I found two reliable sources. I watched both videos several times, but, once again, nothing useful. I went back to the articles and scanned through them a few more times, but still nothing.

"Finally, I called a couple of the publishers and asked them for any and all information on this investor. They said they would only talk to reporters and that I seemed to be a little young for a reporter. I told them I was a reporter, just a really young one, an aspiring journalist. They asked for a name, so I gave them a fake one of course—Joshua Green. They believed me. Back to the point: I asked them for all the information they had, but they only told me what they wrote in the article. For one of the publishers, I didn't believe them when they said that was all they had, so I asked mom to drive me to their building."

"Wait, when did you do that?" Jason asked, also impressed.

"Remember when I told you I was going to the park?" Mason said, clearing his throat.

"Yes. Wait, that was when you went?" Jason questioned, mentally hitting himself for not figuring out Mason was up to something.

"Yeah," Mason responded. "Anyway, they were located near enough to where we live that mom could take me. I went to their building and asked the security guard if I could speak to Grace Springfield, which is the name of the publisher I thought was holding back the most. The security guard looked at me curiously and asked if I was a reporter. I said yes that I was a student reporter and told him my reporter name. He said I couldn't go through without a reporter's pass, so I told him I left it at home. Mom then took me home and I made a fake reporter's pass—which really isn't that hard. I took a note pad with me and asked mom to drive me back. God bless that woman."

"Anyway, Mom took me back, and the security guard let me through. I went up to Grace's office and told her I was the reporter who called on the phone. She told me I sounded taller over the phone, but I expected as much. She kept insisting she had told me everything, but I saw through her lies. I grilled her hard. Finally, she gave in and told me that during her interview with the investor, not only did he remain behind a curtain, but he also used a voice changer. She did confirm with me that even though he used a voice changer, the investor is definitely a dude."

"Are you going to keep telling this for much longer?" Darla asked.

"Don't worry, I'm almost done. Don't ruin my mojo," Mason replied. "Anyway, I asked her to keep me in the loop. But she said that was a strange request, especially for a kid. So…I told her I'd give her money."

"WHAT?" Jason shouted. "Mason! You're in too deep!"

"It's fine!" Mason argued. "She must have been desperate or something because she said yes. And even I know that reporters do not usually pay for information. She gave me her number for business purposes and told me she'd contact me if she had any more info. I told her that for every useful piece of information she'd give me, I'd give her 200 dollars.

"I then asked her if she could get on the case right away, and she was hesitant about it. I gave her 100 dollars up front since I conveniently had that much in my pocket. Don't ask why. She then said she'll dedicate her weekdays to the case, but not her weekends. I said that's fine. Obviously, I thanked her, then left."

"Wait. That's it?" Darla asked. "What about . . . "

"Let me finish, please," Mason said. "So, I've been scrolling through social media on my phone since that day, trying to see what I could find on my own—but nothing. Still nothing. So, now, here we are. That's the end of the story. As you can see, I'm pretty dedicated to this. I really want to see this through, and I'm willing to go any length to do it."

"You could actually be a reporter when you're older, Mason," Jessica exclaimed. "You'd be really good at it."

"Thanks," Mason responded.

"You realize I could have assisted you if you'd just asked for assistance," Jason mentioned, slightly irritated.

"You actually assist me pretty often," Mason said. "Remember how I asked if you could do my homework for me a lot of times and, for some reason, you said yes?"

"Oh," Jason mumbled. "I see."

"Hey, don't be mad. You really did help me a lot. Thank you, Jason," Mason cheered.

Jason sighed. "Alright, alright. Thank you, Mason," he chuckled.

"Back to the point at hand…" Oliver prompted.

"Oh! Speaking of the point at hand," Avery called. "Remember that purple door?"

"What purple door?" Darla asked.

"You guys were doing your own thing then. Basically, Josh tried to open the purple door, then remembered no one is supposed to go in there. Jake seemed really nervous when we questioned him about it," Avery explained.

"I think I see where you're going with this," Nick said, smiling. "So, the door combined with Mason's life story equals a very suspicious situation."

"Exactly!" Avery confirmed. "Because Mason said the investor is living in the studio and that door was the only purple door in the studio."

"Not a very manly color," Will muttered. "But it certainly is an EVIL color!"

"Yeah, I guess," Ondrea agreed. "If you want to think about it like that, Will. But remember how Jake and Josh were telling us how scared Steven had been when he was telling the boys not to go in there?"

"Yeah, how could we forget?" Rachel said. "There were really bad vibes coming from that door, I'm telling you."

"Rachel, what did it smell like?" Jason questioned, genuinely curious.

"Evil," she whispered and shivered. "It smelled like evil."

"Okay, guys," Oliver began, "I think we're being a bit dramatic here. I now believe 100 percent that there is something evil going on at the studio, but there's no need for extra theatrics, Rachel."

"You were there, Ollie." Jessica reminded him. "I could sense it in you. You felt uneasy."

"We all did," Ondrea mumbled.

FOURTEEN

In Which Jake Disappears

Good morning, kids!" Steven announced as the gang of Superheroes groggily sulked into the studio the next morning. "Hey guys!" Jake greeted. "How'd y'all sleep?"

"Sleep, what's sleep?" Will said, rubbing his eyes.

Everyone had trouble sleeping since their discussion lasted long into the night and gave them a lot to think about. Josh looked around at everyone and saw the sleepy and solemn expressions on their faces.

"Did you guys just not sleep at all?" he asked, slightly concerned.

"We had a lot on our minds," Oliver said, yawning.

"Well, IT'S TIME TO WAKE UP!" Steven shouted playfully. "Besides, someone with high authority decided that it's time to add our final participant to the mix."

All of the kids perked up immediately.

"Wait, a new person?" Darla wondered.

"I know, I know, quite a shock," Steven said with a small chuckle.

"Is that even allowed?" Teddy questioned.

"Wait, hold on!" Jake interrupted. "We weren't informed about this, Dad."

"Yeah! Why didn't you tell us about this?" Josh exclaimed, annoyed.

"Do I need to run every decision I make by you boys?" Steven scolded. "Besides, you two are participants just like everyone else."

"But we're your sons!" Jake stated.

"Yes, and I love you both, but this is my business, not yours," Steven responded, attempting to stay calm.

Josh began to speak. "But…"

"NO BUTS!" Steven yelled, his patience now gone. "Now, go and gather with the others!"

Jake and Josh silently and stiffly walked toward Oliver and the others. Their expressions reflected the fact that their father had never yelled at them like that before. Never. Oliver put his hand on Jake's shoulder and gave him a sympathetic look. Neither Jake nor Josh said anything.

Nick inched next to the twins and said, "Hey, it's okay. My mom used to yell at me all the time. Besides, we're all in this together."

"Thanks," Jake mumbled sincerely. Josh just nodded in Nick's direction. Nick gave him a small smile.

"Bring on the newbie!" Will shouted, purposely attempting to break the tension.

Steven shook out his shoulders and cleared his throat.

"Well, may I introduce you to Michael Atrius!" Steven shouted as a brown-haired boy stepped out from around the corner. He wore a black jacket and blue jeans with black tennis shoes. He was tall and skinny, and his arms were held awkwardly down at his side. He looked around nervously at everyone.

"Um… hi guys. I'm pretty sure I've met some of you before," he said.

Jason recognized him immediately, but it took the others a second.

"I remember you! You're the one who saved my brother's life!" Jason exclaimed only to realize what he had just said after Oliver's sharp gasp. Jason had been referring to Michael's Superpowers, which he suddenly remembered he wasn't supposed to talk about in front of non-Supers. "I mean… you saved his life… last year when he had to study for that test, and I was busy," he corrected.

Michael snuck a smile in Jason's direction.

"Anyway, we'll begin with the show this afternoon," Steven announced. "For now, I'll let all of you get acquainted."

Once Steven left the studio, Jake said, "So, you guys have met before?"

"Yeah, Michael Atrius used to go to school with us," Will confirmed.

"Well, Michael, we don't know you all that well," Ondrea said.

"My lady makes a fair point," Teddy agreed.

Jessica added, "Yeah, we've only ever seen you when you saved Mason's life… by helping him study for that test… when Jason was busy."

"Exactly, man," Mason said, selling the lie a bit too much. "I forgot to thank you for the study help. You really came in clutch… like really, though."

"Okay, weirdo clan," Darla cut in. "Despite the importance of the test, I think we've talked about this for long enough, so cut it out."

"You want to talk about something else?" Josh asked rhetorically. "Then why don't we talk about your old school?"

"Exactly what I was thinking, Josh," Jake added, crossing his arms. "What exactly was this school's name?"

Jason looked toward anyone else and quickly said, "Nick, why don't you take this one?"

Nick shook his head furiously in protest. "Are you kidding? I didn't join until... like... the middle of the year."

"You'd still know the name of the school though," Jason insisted. "So why don't you just say it?"

"Um... Rachel! How about you take this one?" Nick exclaimed.

"What? But I didn't join until the middle of the year too!" she snapped. "Don't ask me! Teddy, you can handle this question, I think."

"I... can't remember!" Teddy proclaimed. He threw his hands up in the air as if enhancing his statement. "I'm sure my wonderful girlfriend remembers the name of our previous school."

Ondrea sighed heavily and said nervously, "I may be smart, Teddy Bear, but I don't... I don't know everything."

"Oh my God. You've got to be kidding me!" Avery said, as she face-palmed in an exasperated fashion. "Since everyone seems to have caught a temporary case of amnesia, I'll be happy to answer your question for you! We went to Leader Garden Academy."

Jake and Josh now looked both baffled and incredibly confused.

"What? I've never heard of it," Jake said, glancing at Josh.

"Uh... you wouldn't have heard of it!" Oliver exclaimed. "It's very remote."

"And elite!" Will added with a huge grin on his face. "It's a school for special people!"

Oliver swiveled his head in Will's direction and raised his eyebrow. "Oh, yes... very special," he said, teeth clinched.

The gang all stared at Will. When he didn't say anything else, Nick said, "Hey, buddy. Why don't you tell our good friends why the school was such a great fit for us SPECIAL people?"

Will was no longer grinning proudly. "Uhm... it was... You see... Uh. Oh God. Well... We're all REALLY smart. Yeah, that's it," he stammered.

It was silent for a moment before Josh finally said, "Well, okay then."

"Okay, I can't take this anymore!" Jake yelled. "What is going on with you guys? This is ridiculous! Are you trying to tell us that you're EXTRA smart, but no one could remember the name of your school?"

"Jake, calm down," Josh said, abruptly turning to face him.

"But we've only known them for two days and I'm already sick of their games!" Jake whined. "They're hiding something!"

Josh turned to face the gang. "I think what he means to say is that you guys have been acting kind of strange, and we just want the truth," he stated calmly.

Nobody spoke.

Michael cut in after a minute. "Um… I don't know what's going on, but…"

"Why can't you guys just be honest with us?" Jake asked angrily. "We all need to be honest with each other! You do realize that later on, after the game show part, we're going to be in the Environmental Dome, right? That's survival! We'll have to work as a team. We can't afford any secrets here!"

Oliver stepped forward hesitantly. "Look, we can't tell you anything… right now. Just know that you can trust us. We mean you no harm."

"What does that even mean? Alright, alright, I get it! No harm. Whatever!" Jake shouted. He waved his hand in the air as if to aggressively dismiss Oliver's assurance.

"Oh, come on, Jake," Josh sighed. "You're usually a lot calmer than this."

"Well… I just feel… I just feel left out," Jake stammered loudly. "It's just that there's so much weird stuff going on recently! It's all happened because of them. First the bird, then the robbery…"

"Okay! The robbery wasn't even our fault!" Will argued.

"Will, settle down," Jessica stated calmly. "Jake, I'm sorry. Strange things just tend to follow us. Are you okay?"

"I… think I just need some air," Jake muttered. He walked outside as quickly as he could.

"Wait, we're sorry!" Nick called out desperately. He began to go after Jake, but Ondrea and Josh stopped him.

"What are you doing?" Nick asked. "He could get hurt out there!"

"Nick!" Mason hissed.

"Nick, just let Jake cool off," Ondrea suggested.

"What do you mean 'he could get hurt'?" Josh questioned, tightly grasping Nick's upper arm nervously. "If he could get hurt… then… I need to know what's going on!" Josh shouted.

"Guys, he's scared," Rachel stated sympathetically.

"Please!" Josh begged.

All the Supers turned their heads toward their leader. Oliver shared a grim smile with them and then spoke. "Fine. It's only fair that we explain EVERYTHING. First, someone go and get Jake from outside. We need to tell him too."

Jason ran outside to grab Jake. About a minute later, he burst back into the studio doors nearly breathless. "I… can't… find him," he gasped, in between breaths. "He's gone."

14.1

Jake walked out into the desert area in front of the studio. Whenever he felt upset in his life, he would do something he liked to call "walk and talk." It was sort of like his own kind of ritual. So, that's what he did. But he continued to walk well past where he meant to go, not realizing how far he had gone until it was too late.

"I knew this would be a bad idea," he said to himself. "Coming onto this game show. I knew everything bad was going to happen! Then, I got into it and thought 'Hey, this might not be so bad.' Well, it was bad! It IS bad! I thought these new guys would be cool, but they don't even trust me! Granted, they've only known me for like two days, but I thought we were bonding."

He kicked at the dust coating the ground and continued. "Why does Josh seem so cool about this?" he asked. Then he shook his head and continued to speak out loud. "Who am I kidding? Josh is always cool about everything. It's so annoying. There's no way Josh is better than me, right? He's not worse than me either, but still! Is he just more trustworthy or something? Now that I've left, those guys are probably blabbing secrets left and right."

Jake sighed and then remembered Steven. "Oh, and Dad! He's never yelled at us before! How could Josh be so cool about that! He totally embarrassed us. Why is it so hard to be friendly and perky?"

Jake could feel anxiety coursing through his body and he had no clue what to do. "I need Josh," he said. "I need… I need to escape."

Jake began to sprint as fast as he could, not caring where he was going. He ran and ran and ran. As Jake's head began to clear, he slowed and then stopped, bent over, and put his hands on his knees.

"Oh, my God," he said. "I have no clue where I am."

FIFTEEN

In Which There is Darkness

Jake stood up and looked around at the vast expanse of empty land. "What am I going to do?" he wondered. "Just… what would Josh do?"

He sat crisscross on the dirty ground to think. But his thoughts were abruptly interrupted by the screaming of a bird. Jake looked up to see a large bird circling him. Was it the same bird from the bus? He realized he would never forget that bird's face. Jake knew vultures circled dead animals in the desert, and he became alarmed.

"I'm not dead, yet!" he called to the bird.

As if it understood him, the bird tilted its head and dive-bombed toward Jake. Jake curled into a fetal position in an attempt to protect his head, but it wasn't his head that the bird was going for. Jake screamed as he felt the bird's talons rake violently down his leg. Next, he felt the bird attempt to dig its talons into his shoulder.

Jake braced himself for the worst.

15.1

"This isn't good," Josh stated. "I'm sure Jake will be okay, though."

"We should still look for him!" Nick exclaimed, gesturing wildly toward the door.

"He's right. We should," Oliver confirmed. "We should split up into groups. Jess, you can take care of the grouping. I need to talk to Josh for a minute."

"Okay, Ollie," Jessica said. She began to sort the groups. "Teddy, Will, and Rachel. Darla, Oliver, and Ondrea. Jason, Mason, and Josh. Lastly, Nick, Avery, and me." Jessica glanced toward where Oliver and Josh were talking then lowered her voice. "Teddy's group. You guys go south. You guys can Teleport the distance. Darla's group, wait for Oliver. Then, go west. Oliver can help you with his Flight Power or his Wind Power."

Will suddenly burst out laughing. "Oliver's Wind Power!" he shouted. "We can surf his wind!"

Jessica rolled her eyes and waited until Will was finished being immature. She continued, "Nick, Avery, and I will go north. Jason's group, you go east. You guys might just have to do things normally since Josh is…"

"Roughly informed," Oliver interrupted while walking toward Darla's group.'

"You guys have Superpowers!" Josh stated, clearly impressed. "Cool. Let's go help my brother."

Suddenly, Nick's phone began to ring. He pulled his phone out of his pocket with the intention to silence it. But when he saw who was calling, he picked it up.

"Spencer!" Nick yelled happily. Nick's expression changed as he listened to Spencer and then said, "Alright." Nick held the phone out in front of him and put it on speaker.

"Guys!" Spencer called. "Look, I miss you guys and I'm really sorry I left so suddenly! But that's not what this call is about."

"So, what is it about?" Darla asked.

"I had a Vision. These Super Visions are somehow always connected to you guys, so I thought I should tell you about this,"

Spencer explained. "I was in this desert-like area, and there was literally nothing around. There was a boy, though. He was lying on the ground and was being attacked by a huge bird. That's all I can really…"

"Did the boy have an orange shirt? Brown hair? Screaming like a girl?" Josh asked frantically.

"Uh, yeah. All that," Spencer replied. "Who are you?"

"That's not important. Are there any more specific details you can give us? About the location?" Ondrea questioned.

"No. I'm so sorry," Spencer said solemnly.

"We'd better get going then," Jessica commanded quickly.

"Good luck, guys. Bye," Spencer stated. Nick's phone clicked indicating that the call was over. Nick shut his phone.

15.2

"What would Josh do?" Jake asked himself as the giant man-eating bird attempted to rip away the flesh of his shoulder. "Well, actually, Josh probably wouldn't do anything. He's kind of wimpy."

Jake felt a sharp pull on his shoulder and yelped in surprise. "Josh would run! I would run!" he exclaimed.

Jake began to get up and noticed the hot blood trickling from a gash in his leg. "That's going to be a problem," he mumbled. He started to limp away from the bird as quickly as he could. Even though waves of pain shot up his leg, he tried to ease into a steady run. The bird followed close by. It peered at the back of Jake's head as he ran as if to say, "I know I can outfly your run. Time to play with my food."

Jake, now at a run, headed in the direction he had come from. He could tell that was his original path because he was able to see where his shoes had stirred the dirt.

After an hour of running, he believed the bird had stopped chasing him.

"Oh, God. That… thing is… insane," he sighed, short of breath. Jake fell onto the ground, feeling exhausted. His leg felt sort of heavy, and although it was almost numb, he could still feel a sharp burning sensation. He hugged his legs to his chest and rested his head on his knees. Jake realized that, in his entire life, he had never felt more lost and alone than he did at that exact moment.

15.3

"Dad," Spencer began. "I have to go help my friends." Spencer and his father were holed up in an underground lab. The lab had been built by Spencer's father, Vixsten, when he had been known as 'The Boss'. In the lab, Vixsten and Spencer had been attempting to unlock the secrets of the evil VORK and, more importantly, to find out what VORK was planning to do next.

"I'm sure they're fine, son," Vixsten Knight assured him. "Besides, we've been doing plenty here to help your friends whether they realize it or not."

"But I had a Vision! I told you!" Spencer argued.

"Yes, but it appears the child you described doesn't match the description of anyone in your group of friends," he counter argued.

"Look, I know what I saw!" Spencer exclaimed. "Besides, I called Nick and they sounded pretty frantic over this kid. He must be important to them and if he's important to them, he's important to me!"

Vixsten sighed wearily. "Yes," he began, "I know you're worried about your friends, but we're on the verge of something important here, Spence!"

"Dad! You know how guilty I felt about leaving them. What if they need me now, and I don't show up!" Spencer stated, putting his head in his hands.

"Spencer, I understand you're feeling guilty, but you cannot be there for them all the time. This is more important right now," Vixsten explained.

Spencer looked at his father as if he had just stabbed his son in the back. "More important than my friends?" he whispered venomously. "What happened to you? When did you stop caring?" With that, Spencer turned around and sprinted into the next cavern.

15.4

Mason was in his element—two elements, actually: Earth Power and Wind Power. He could feel the dry Wind passing through his hair and he could smell the dry Earth surrounding him. Despite the barren landscape and the drastic situation, he felt strengthened by the land.

"Oh wow, I feel awesome, baby!" Mason yelled at the top of his lungs.

Jason and Josh trailed behind him. "Hey, you think you could say that a little louder?" Josh asked, sarcastically.

"Yeah, I don't think VORK quite heard you," Jason sighed. Mason had practically been frolicking the last half mile while Josh and Jason were trudging in the heat and dirt.

"Oh, come on, guys," Mason cheered. "We don't even know if VORK is out here."

"Well, you could still be conscious of the fact that we, unlike you, are not in our elements," Jason mentioned, jogging lightly to catch up with his twin.

"I don't remember the last time I walked this much," Josh added, obviously struggling to keep up.

"I'll slow down a bit. Fine," Mason said, pretending to pout.

Jason let a small chuckle escape his lips. "Don't take it too hard, brother," he stated.

"Hey, still back here!" Josh called.

"Yeah, how could we forget? The deadest dead weight of them all," Mason said in a joking manner.

"Well that wasn't very nice. Especially considering the circumstances," Josh said, finally catching up.

Mason gave him a friendly punch on the shoulder. "Yeah, you're right. Sorry about that one," he apologized. "Hey, let's pick up the pace a bit, huh?"

Jason and Josh groaned wearily as Mason sped to a jog.

"Mason, wait!" Jason yelled as he slowed to a stop.

"I'm not slowing down for slowpokes!" Mason jokingly yelled over his shoulder.

Jason felt the strangest pressure in his head. It reminded him of the headache the Dark Magic particles had given him. He bent down and sat on his knees in the dirt. It was as if every fiber of his being were telling him to go no farther. Josh slowed down and came to a stop behind Jason. Jason rested his pounding head in his hands and took a couple of deep breaths. He heard Josh call out to Mason.

"Mason, stop!," he yelled. "Seriously. I think your brother is hurt."

When Mason heard "I think your brother is hurt," he immediately came to a standstill.

"God, what am I doing?" he asked himself. He shook his head clear and used his Wind element to jet himself over to his twin. Mason knelt down in front of Jason and put his hands on Jason's shoulders.

"Hey. Hey, Jason. You alright?" Mason questioned softly. "What's going on?"

"My head… it's pounding," he muttered. "Mason?"

"I'm here," Mason reassured him. "What is it, Jace?"

Jason lifted his head, looked at his brother right in the eyes, and said, "It's not Nick's Dark Magic. It's someone else's. But… Dark Magic particles. They're here."

15.5

"You see anything up there, guys?" Jessica wondered. She, Nick, and Avery had been searching for Jake for at least an hour now.

"Nope," Avery said, using her Dragon Abilities to fly back to the ground. She folded her dragon wings away, and they magically disappeared—to be used when she needed them again.

Nick lowered himself off his Dark Magic cloud and back onto the ground. His cloud immediately dissipated into the air.

"I don't see anything. Although, I do Sense some strange Magic in the air," Nick stated.

"It's most likely nothing. As far as we know, the only people in this wasteland are Supers," Jessica said. "There's always going to be Magic in the air."

"Have you seen any clues on the ground, Jess?" Avery wondered. Jessica had taken ground patrol while Nick and Avery volunteered for sky patrol.

Jessica sighed. "No. Haven't seen a thing," she said sadly.

"Cheer up, Jess," Nick exclaimed. "We'll find Jake." Nick put an arm around his cousin's shoulders and playfully messed up her hair.

She gave him a small, amused grin. "You know I hate it when people do that," she reminded him, although not bothering to try to fix it.

"Well, I'm not just 'people.' I'm your cousin," Nick mentioned. "Plus, you know I hate it when you get all pouty."

"Then we're even, I guess," she said.

Nick sighed and let Jessica walk a bit ahead of him.

"She'll be okay," Avery assured him.

"I know," Nick said. "I just hate seeing her so down. Hey, Avery? I've been meaning to ask you something."

"Ask away," she said.

"You're part dragon, but Ondrea, your sister, isn't," Nick began. "How does that work?"

"Our mom is a Morpher and our dad was just your average guy. A couple of Powers, but that's it," Avery explained. "Our mom's favorite animal was a black dragon, and she changed into it a lot. I guess her genetics changed into the genetics of a dragon when she was pregnant with me, but not when she was pregnant with Ondrea. Ondrea got more of my dad's side."

"Cool," Nick said. "Do you ever wish you were more like her?"

Avery raised an eyebrow. "Excuse me?" she asked.

"No, I just mean Power-wise, with her Healing and Mind Reading and all. Do you ever wish you were more like her Power-wise?" Nick corrected quickly.

"Not really," Avery said. "My Powers are pretty rad, especially my Dragon Abilities."

Nick smiled. "Yeah, I guess they are," he agreed.

"Guys!" Jessica called frantically. "Something's wrong!"

Nick and Avery shared a worried glance as they ran to catch up with her. "What's going on?" Avery asked.

"It's Ollie!" she gasped. "I think…"

"Is he hurt?" Nick demanded, his friend now being the only thing on his mind.

"I'm not sure," she responded. "It's more like a headache of some kind. It's just not normal. I think he'll be okay, but something is going on!"

15.6

Darla was blasting her Super Heat and using it like jet-pack propulsion. "Despite the seriousness of this terrible situation, this is pretty fun!" she shouted.

"I'm glad you're having fun, Darla, but we need to focus," Oliver scolded her. "Besides, I thought I told you to patrol the ground with Ondrea."

"Fine, 'Dad,'" Darla sighed, rolling her eyes. She reduced her Super Heat and slowly lowered herself to the ground, which now mainly consisted of black dirt.

"If I have to ask you again, I'm taking away your TV privileges for a week, young lady!" Oliver joked.

"Whatever," Darla stated. She jogged toward Ondrea just in time to hear Ondrea snicker. Darla shot her a stone-cold glance.

"What?" Ondrea asked innocently. "You have to admit that was pretty funny."

"Yeah, yeah, yeah," Darla said, grinning. Ondrea was silent for a moment, and Darla knew what Ondrea wanted to do. "You want to ask me something a bit personal," she stated.

"Okay, so… how about you and Will?" Ondrea asked with a smile.

Darla was caught completely off guard. "What… there's… Hold on. What do you mean?" Darla stammered.

"You know what I mean," Ondrea goaded. "I saw all that action on the bus."

"What do you mean 'action?'" Darla questioned loudly. "All we did was take a nap!"

"Uh huh," Ondrea replied. She then jogged forward to catch up to where Oliver was Flying over.

Darla scoffed. "I really don't understand women," she sighed. "I didn't even think I had to worry about understanding women, but I guess that's what friends do to you." She too ran forward, not wanting to be left out. She was a bit afraid that Ondrea would start gossiping to Oliver about her.

"Ondrea! Darla!" Oliver called from the sky. "I don't feel too… my head hurts." He suddenly began falling from his position in the sky.

"Ondrea!" Darla yelled. "Do your floaty thing!"

Ondrea pointed her fingers toward Oliver and used her Molecular Kinesis to catch him before he hit the ground. She gently lowered him to where Darla was waiting.

"What happened?" Ondrea wondered.

"I dunno. You're the smart one, right?" Darla said.

"Well, thanks for helping the situation, Darla," Ondrea exclaimed sarcastically.

"Okay. I'm sorry," she admitted. "Try using your Mind Reading to see if you can get anything since, he's…. you know… unconscious."

"Good idea," Ondrea agreed. "Here goes nothing." She focused on clearing her own thoughts so that she could listen to his. After a minute of searching, her brain was able to make a connection with Oliver's brain waves. She listened.

"Oh my God!" Ondrea gasped.

"What? What is it?" Darla said, beginning to lose her cool.

Ondrea spoke slowly. "There's Dark Magic in the air, and it isn't Nick's. It's someone else's."

15.7

"How's it looking over there, Teddy?" Will called.

Teddy Teleported to Will's side. "Nada! Nothing! Zero! I can't see anything out of the ordinary!" he yelled angrily.

"Teddy, I'm all up for a good yell, but I don't think now is the best time to do it," Will reasoned. "See, as your friend, it's not necessarily in my job description to be your therapist, but if you have any feelings you want to…"

"Can it, Will!" Teddy exclaimed. "Now is not the time for jokes."

A large bird landed beside the two boys.

"How did it go?" Will asked. "Did you see anything?"

The bird began to Morph into a human girl. "Uh… yeah. I went a little bit out of the range that I was supposed to, but I did see something," Rachel stated.

"What?" Teddy wondered. "What was it?"

Rachel hesitated for a second before answering. "I saw… blood," she whispered. "It was fresh. I could tell."

"You think it's… Jake's?" Will questioned.

"It very well could be," she replied. "The blood looks like it's been there for at least two hours. Maybe three."

Teddy felt like she was holding something back. "Did you see any evidence that it could be Jake's?" he asked.

"Yes. In fact, I'm sure that it's his!" Rachel exclaimed in a worried voice. She pulled out a small piece of orange fabric. "Orange. Just like Jake's shirt."

"We have to get the others!" Will shouted. "I mean, this is huge!"

"Not yet, Will," Teddy warned. "We don't know what happened to him."

"I do," Rachel stated. "It was a person. A Super maybe. Like you and me…but it wasn't me!"

"Obviously it wasn't you," Will mumbled.

"How do you know?" Teddy questioned. "I don't really want to call this in with just a theory."

"Well, his shirt ripped, that's for sure. Plus, I found some fabric from his pants there. There wasn't anything around there for him to trip over or on unless he just straight up fell. That's not too likely though."

Will waited for her to say more. When she didn't, he said, "Wait, that's all you were going to say?"

"Yes. Is there a problem?" Rachel asked impatiently.

"Guys!" Teddy yelled.

They both turned their heads to look at him. "What?" They said at the same time.

"Shut up!" Teddy said. "We need to add to Rachel's theory. Anyone got an add-in?"

"No add-ins, but we should probably call Jess and tell her that we all need to regroup," Will said.

"Fine! I'll call her, but we still need at least one add-in!" Teddy exclaimed as he walked a couple feet away to call Jessica.

It was silent for a second before Rachel asked, "So you really have no theories or add-ins?"

"What if it wasn't a person?" Will suggested. "What if it was that bird? The one that tried to attack Mason."

Rachel and Will didn't speak for at least five seconds. Then, Rachel came to a conclusion and voiced it.

"Then Jake is most likely already dead."

SIXTEEN

In Which Evil Secrets Are Discovered

Spencer was lying on a mattress in his makeshift bedroom when Vixsten entered. "Son, I'm sorry," he stated. "You were right."

Spencer sat up and sighed. "What do you mean?" he asked as he brushed his fingers through his hair.

"You were right," Vixsten repeated. "Your friends need you." He walked over to his son, sat on the mattress beside him, and put his arm around Spencer's shoulders. "Go."

Spencer's head snapped up. "What?" he asked, fixing his father with a surprised stare.

"Go," Vixsten said once more. "Go help your friends."

"Wait, but… why?" Spencer questioned. "What made you change your mind?"

"You did, actually," Vixsten admitted. "You're my son, not my business partner. You've been doing so well here, you know, helping me out and all."

Spencer smiled. "Thanks, Dad," he said.

"Hold on, I'm not done," Vixsten warned. "I've been… a questionable father all these years and still, here you are. Not only are you still here, but you're HERE. You traveled halfway around the world on your own just to meet me here and help me with this. You're my son and I want you to be happy and have control in your own life. I'm going to let you help your friends because I trust you'll be safe. Okay?"

Spencer nodded his head slowly.

"Okay. Yes, you've been questionable. But that's history now. You've changed. You're a good dad now. Don't be so hard on yourself. You've always had my best interests at heart," he said. "Besides, I… I love you."

"Thank you," Vixsten said. That was all he could say before his eyes began to water.

"Are you okay?" Spencer wondered. He turned to look his father in the eyes.

"Yes," he answered. "I'm better than okay. I have you. Just… go. Be safe and please come back."

"Sure thing, Dad," Spencer exclaimed. "I love you."

16.1

Jake opened his eyes and slowly lifted his head. "How… how long have I been asleep?" he asked himself aloud. His voice sounded scratchy and dry. The first thing Jake registered was that he felt incredibly dehydrated and the back of his neck was horrendously sunburned. He took a shaky breath and looked at his leg. A trickle of blood was still dripping down his leg, to his foot, and into a small puddle of blood. "Oh, no."

Jake tried to stand but fell back into the dirt. When he tried to stand again, he realized his leg was numb.

"Help!" he tried to scream. His throat hurt too much to make a loud sound. Jake knew he needed help, but he had no clue how to get it. That's when he realized he just needed to suck it up. He rose from the ground and began limping forward. Although all his muscles screamed in pain, he knew he had to just keep going. No matter what.

16.2

After Teddy called Jessica, she made some calls to the others, and Teddy took the liberty of Teleporting everyone to the same spot so they could begin discussing the situation. After a while, Oliver pulled out his phone and looked at the time.

"It's 2:30," he said. "Soon, Steven is going to expect us all back at the studio to start the game show—including Jake."

"Based on everything we've been told, I have to assume that Jake walked away," Jason said.

"But how could he walk away from a killer bird?" Will asked. "Usually, Darla and I are the downers, but Rachel said that he could seriously be dead."

Josh's eyes went wide as he sat on the ground with a thump. Ondrea looked at him and quickly said, "Well, he could also be alive. I mean, how much blood did you really see?"

"I didn't see a whole human's worth of blood, so Ondrea could be right," Rachel said.

"We could scan the desert for a specific temperature. Like a heat signature," Oliver suggested.

"And just how do you plan on doing that, Oliver?" Darla questioned. "Do you have some kind of handy-dandy machine on you that can scan for heat signatures?"

"Uh… no, but we've got to do something," Oliver replied.

"I could use my Dragon Abilities to fly up and shoot out my Fire breath like a homing beacon," Avery suggested.

"No way," Teddy stated immediately. "Even if Jake recognized the signal and knew what it meant, what if he couldn't walk?"

"I'm not really the smart one, but what if Darla used her Fire and Super Heat Powers to seek a certain temperature for a certain distance," Mason chimed in. "Kind of like if she emitted a heat wave that would bounce back to her and give her some idea of where Jake could be. Kind of like echolocation."

"I couldn't possibly do that!" Darla yelled.

"That's a perfect idea, Mason," Jessica said. "And yes, Darla, you could."

"Before you ask, my brother can't," Mason stated, "even though Fire is one of his elements."

"I'm sorry," Jason apologized. "I'm still a little weak from that Dark Magic surge."

"Are we just not going to talk about that?" Will wondered, raising his eyebrow. "Because that seems pretty important. Just saying."

Oliver sighed wearily. "Yes, Will. It's important, but we have a bigger issue at hand. Back to the current problem. Darla, you have to."

"Fine! But, how would I make a 'heat wave' that wouldn't melt all of you into putty?" she asked.

Jason decided to help talk her through it. "It wouldn't be a wave of heat. It would be a wave that detects heat. I know I would be ideal for this, but, as I mentioned before, I'm too weak right now," he said. "But the reason I would be ideal is because I have both Water and Fire elements. My Water can counteract my Heat and stop it from getting out of control."

"I get it!" Avery shouted triumphantly. "Darla, you need a Water element to be your support."

"The only ready Water element here is Will," Nick said. "Or me, of course. I can borrow Powers from anyone else."

"I… I think I can do it," Will muttered nervously. "I don't want to accidentally hurt Darla, and I really don't know how to do this, but…"

Oliver took Will's shoulder and led him a few feet away from everyone so that Will could really focus on what Oliver was about to tell him.

"Do you remember your first and only year at Superhero School?" he asked. When Will nodded, Oliver continued, "I assume you remember how you blasted my sister down in the gym, right?" Will grinned and nodded again. Oliver continued. "I need you to remember how you honed your Powers into that one specific area, and then I need you to do it again now. Instead of jetting water, you're going to fine tune it to a trickle. Like a steady stream.

"What you need to do for this to work is to hold Darla's shoulders and let your Energy flow into her like water flowing down a peaceful stream. Not a river. A stream. You'll need to take it slow and steady. Since you are her opposite element, too much of your Power could hurt her. Slow and steady wins the race, bud."

"What… what if I do hurt her?" Will asked, his voice trembling.

Oliver put on a supportive smile. "Will, buddy, you can do this. You won't hurt her. You're over-thinking it. Remember that you can only do as well as you think you can do. Besides, I know you have the hots for her, so…"

Will's eyes widened, and he lightly punched Oliver on the arm. "Dude, come on!" he hissed.

Oliver laughed. "Yeah, dude!" he joked. "Come on! Let's do this!" Oliver walked back toward the group. "He's ready."

Will took a deep breath and walked up behind Darla. He gently placed his hands on her shoulders and closed his eyes. Will then pictured his Power going through her like a ghost. He felt Darla tense up. The only thought in Darla's mind was Jake. She had to find Jake.

The others observed the outline of a faint orange ring pass through the two of them and to out into the vast expanse of desert. After a minute or two went by, Darla finally spoke. "He's just thirty minutes west of us!" she yelled happily. "Also, I'm really tired all of a sudden." Will felt sort of dizzy and, without thinking, reached out a hand to steady himself. But since he was in the middle of the desert, there was nothing around to lean on—except his friends.

Thankfully, he had friends. Nick caught Will's forearm and began to push his unlimited supply of Energy into Will.

"Thanks," Will mumbled. He shook his head as if to wake himself up, and he stood up straight. Nick then did the same for Darla.

"Half of us need to go back to the studio to ward off any suspicions Steven may have. After all, we've been gone most of the morning and quite a bit of the afternoon," Oliver commanded. No one argued. "Okay," he continued, "these are the people who will be going back to the studio: Jason, Darla, Will, Ondrea… Wait a minute. Oh God. Has Michael been at the studio alone this whole time?"

Everyone went wide eyed and didn't say a word until Avery said, "Um. Yeah, I'm sure he's… probably fine."

"Okay," Oliver sighed. "Jason, Darla, Will, Ondrea, Avery, and I will stay at the studio while the rest of you go rescue Jake. Yes, I am allowing Josh to continue the search for his brother, but I need him protected since he can't protect himself. No offense, Josh." Once more, no one argued.

"The group going to rescue Jake should go on and head out," Ondrea suggested. "I'll lead," Jessica said.

"So, thirty minutes west we go," Mason exclaimed, thrilled that the 'anxious waiting' part was over. He began lightly skipping west.

"Sorry," Jason said. "He does this. It's like his thing."

"Ugh. Why does Mason always do this?" Jessica asked the air.

"You may be the leader right now, but Mason likes to lead usually," Teddy mentioned, laughing as he ran after them.

"Okay, everyone else, follow me," Jessica commanded as she too ran after the others.

16.3

Michael knew the others had gone on some mission to save Jake without him, but he didn't mind too much; he was used to being excluded—whether it was accidentally or purposefully. Michael figured this time was accidental.

Michael used the time to explore the studio by himself. While he was behind the stage flipping the lights on and off—which one wouldn't usually do—he noticed some bulbs were out. He also noticed that he blew out about five of them while flipping the switches.

"Typical," he said to himself as he used his Electricity Power to harness electricity from the air around him to try to revive the bulbs.

Michael had felt like a social outcast his whole life. He guessed some people didn't see him that way, but he definitely did. When he spoke, people tended to listen, because he didn't speak very often. But he thought of himself as just a regular angsty, depressed, social-outcast teen.

Michael was lying on the stage, sprawled comfortably on his back daydreaming about what it would feel like to be socially acceptable, when someone entered the studio. He wouldn't have looked up if he hadn't felt a strong magical presence. But he did, so he looked up.

Michael saw a man trying to sneak past the main room. The man was wearing a black suit jacket and black pants—and he had a giant vulture-like bird resting on his arm. This didn't catch Michael by surprise, though. Not much ever caught Michael by surprise.

Luckily for Michael, the man did not see the boy lying on the stage, and he swept right past him in a hurried fashion. When the man had left the main room, Michael stood up and blinked.

"That… was a normal occurrence…" he stated, trying to convince himself.

Michael quietly followed the man. How did he know where the man had gone? Michael could see his trail. He was able to see every Supernatural trail—whether it was left by a ghost or by another Superhero.

He followed the man's tracer until it ended at a purple door. Michael attempted to open the door, but he found it was locked.

"Curious," he whispered to himself, studying the door handle. He formulated a plan in his mind that seemed simple enough, so he zapped the handle with a small bolt of his Electricity Power, and the door opened. When he looked inside the room, Michael was definitely surprised. He hadn't expected to find a different-colored door hidden in Steven's studio, and he absolutely didn't expect to find an evil lair hidden behind that door.

Michael stood in the doorway, stiff as a board and quiet as a mouse. Most people probably would have explored the room to find its hidden secrets, but not Michael. At least, not this time. An evil lair was an evil lair. That was that. Michael knew one should never trifle with evil—especially when one was alone. He shut the door and left.

The man with the bird on his arm lurked in the shadows of that room. He realized he'd have to be more careful from then on.

When Michael got back to the main room of the studio, he saw Steven sitting in a chair by the door.

"Why, hello Michael!" Steven cheered. "Are you enjoying this facility and all that it has to offer?"

"Um… yes," Michael responded.

Steven didn't say anything for what seemed like ages and then said, "Well, that's great! Hey, have you seen the other kids?"

Michael knew he had to think fast, so he told a partial truth.

"They went out," he answered quickly.

Steven sighed. "Yes, but where? And when will they be back?" he questioned.

"I'm not sure, but they should be back soon," Michael said.

As if on cue, Oliver burst through the door, followed by several others.

"Hi!" Oliver gasped. "Sorry we were out for so long!"

"Yeah, we got a little lost," Will said as he held the door ajar for the others. When Will saw the concerned expression on Steven's face, he added, "But we're okay now!"

Steven did a head count and noticed that half of their group was still out. "What happened to the others?" he asked, his concern growing.

"They got just as lost as we did," Darla said, rolling her eyes. "They'll be back soon."

"Alright," Steven sighed. He was about to head off when he turned back around to face the kids. "My sons, Jake and Josh, are they alright?"

The kids were hesitant to answer. It was all too obvious that Steven was worried about his sons. You could see the anxiety all over his face. No one had the heart to answer Steven, but someone had to do it, so Jason chimed in.

"Yes, I'm sure they're fine. I promise they'll be back soon. Don't worry," he assured him. Steven knew that Jason was a very trustworthy individual, so he gratefully took Jason's word for his sons' safety and headed off once more. When Steven had left the area, Jason sighed and said, "God, I hate lying to him. Especially about his kids. You could see the worry plastered all over his face."

Avery punched Jason's shoulder gently. "You're a good person, Jason. Never change that," she told him.

He smiled at her. "Thanks, A.," Jason mumbled.

"Besides, we know they'll be okay," Will added. "Nick is with them. He's the best Healer around!"

"I'm a Healer too, Will," Ondrea said pointedly.

"Right. Sorry, but Nick is a Master Healer," Will said, shrugging his shoulders.

Oliver noticed Michael standing off to the side.

"Michael!" Oliver said as he walked toward him. "I'm so sorry that we left you behind!"

"It's fine," Michael stated. "I'm used to it, so… it's fine."

"Don't say that," Ondrea mumbled, now feeling extra sorry for leaving him behind. "We don't want to be those people, Michael. We want to be the people who DON'T leave you behind."

"Exactly!" Will agreed. He walked to Michael and put a hand on his shoulder. "From now on we will take you everywhere all the time every single day for the rest of your natural-born life!"

Michael's eyes went wide. "So, this is what it's like to have friends," he thought.

Darla smirked when she saw Michael's expression.

"He was joking, doofus," she said to Michael with a laugh. "You should have seen your face! Priceless!"

"Darla," Avery said sternly. Darla looked at Avery's expression, and that face said it all.

"Alright, alright. I'm sorry, Michael. I shouldn't have said that. I'm working hard to be a better person and yada, yada, yada," Darla said with a sigh, waving her arms around as if to emphasize her point.

Will snickered. "That's a good start," he muttered. Darla glared at him.

Michael actually smiled and said, "I like it when people are real around me. A lot of people in the past think I'm so weird that they don't know how to act around me."

"We understand how you feel, bud," Oliver exclaimed with a huge grin.

"Yeah," Will seconded. "We've been dealing with that our whole lives!"

"He's right, you know," Darla stated.

"There's no need to be anyone but yourself around here, Michael," Ondrea explained. "We're just glad to have you along for the ride."

Avery was the next to speak. "I will admit, you seem like an interesting person. I can't wait to get to know you better throughout the course of this… game show and Environmental Dome thing."

Michael smiled again. He found that he'd been doing that a lot lately.

16.4

"Yo, I thought Darla said only thirty minutes!" Teddy exclaimed.

"Teddy!" Jessica scolded. "Stop complaining! It's annoying, and it does nothing but lower morale."

"Man, I miss my girl!" he continued. Jessica just sighed and kept walking.

"Guys. I think I smell Jake!" Rachel exclaimed. She stopped to smell the air once more. "I do! I do!"

Nick, Rachel, Jessica, Teddy, Mason, and Josh suddenly added a little bounce to their step. "What do you mean you smell him?" Josh asked.

"Well, I smell human blood, a lot of sweat… or maybe those are tears," Rachel stated. She continued on, oblivious to Josh's expression of horror. "Also, it smells like he hasn't bathed in at least three months, but that may just be because my sense of smell is 100 percent better than yours…"

Nick put his hand on Rachel's shoulder. "Hey, could you stop talking?" he asked. "You're freaking Josh out."

Rachel looked at Josh and shrugged. "Sorry, I was just telling you what I meant," she stated, walking ahead with her nose held high, sniffing the air.

When Josh stopped walking, Mason went forward and put an arm around Josh's shoulders. Mason kept walking, urging Josh to take steady steps. Josh was now so focused on the thought of his brother being potentially dead, that he forgot to feel uncomfortable at the physical interaction.

"Hey," Mason said, slightly knocking Josh out of his stupor. "No matter what has happened to Jake, we've got a great Healer in our group. Nick is great. I know you're scared. I remember all the times I was scared that my brother would be hurt or dead. It turned out alright. I mean, we're here aren't we?"

Josh looked up from his shoes and shared a small grin with Mason. "I know," Josh said.

"Good," Mason continued. "You know, not only is he your brother, but he's also your twin. Twins can be hard to come by, but we like twins in our group!"

Mason laughed. Josh smiled a bit more and said, "Thanks."

Suddenly, everyone began running. "I think I see him!" Jessica called to Mason and Josh. Their eyes briefly widened. Josh and Mason sprinted after the others.

16.5

Jake felt like he'd been walking for days even though it had only been a few hours. He still had no clue whether or not he was going in the right direction, but he had to have faith. Jake longed for the witty banter of Josh and the welcoming arms of his new friends.

"I made a mistake by walking away like that," he said to himself. "Even if they were lying to me, or not telling me the whole truth, it was probably for a good reason."

As Jake walked, he realized just how exhausted he felt. In fact, he could no longer feel either of his legs. Then, he made the mistake of looking down. Jake's legs suddenly collapsed, and he fell gracelessly to his knees.

"No," he whispered. Jake tried to get back on his feet, but all his muscles shrieked in protest. Then he heard voices. Distant at first, then closer.

"Now I'm going crazy," he thought. Jake pictured his brother making some joke about his predicament and an empty smile formed on his face.

Jake flinched as he felt someone grab his shoulders and shake them violently.

Josh sprinted ahead of everyone else. He had to get to his brother!

The sight of Jake falling to his knees put a lot more stress on Josh. His brother was facing away from him, so Jake couldn't see Josh running, practically tripping, to get to his twin. Josh, now panting hard and just a couple of feet away, skid in the dirt and grabbed Jake's shoulders. He gave his brother a violent shake.

"Jake!" he yelled loudly. When Jake didn't stir from his trance, Josh slapped him in the face.

"Geez!" Mason exclaimed, coming up on them. "Give your brother a break. He's been through enough."

"He's bleeding," Rachel observed.

Josh looked down to where Rachel was pointing and noticed that Jake's leg looked as if it had been cut open. He gasped.

All of Josh's focus returned to his brother's face as he saw his eyes blink. "Jake?" he said again.

"J... Josh?" Jake stammered. Then his eyes closed, and he fainted.

Teddy Teleported the rest of the way and caught Jake's head before it hit the hard earth.

"Nick, you need to help him!" Jessica demanded.

Nick stepped forward. "Right, I've got this," he whispered. Nick knelt down by Jake's leg and hovered his hands above the gaping wound. Nick thought it was probably infected. White and red mist enveloped Jake's leg as Nick poured his Energy into Healing. A minute or two of tension and anxiety passed. Once Nick was finished, he took his hands away and admired his work.

"Wh... what?" Josh mumbled. "His leg is completely healed!"

"I know! It's awesome, isn't it?" Mason exclaimed. "Although, he still isn't waking up."

"His body has obviously taken a huge hit," Rachel stated. "He's incredibly dehydrated, probably really hungry, exhausted, and smells like absolute dog poo. That last one really doesn't matter, but the point is that he's wiped."

"Nick," Teddy said. "Maybe you can do a quick Heal on his whole body."

"You know, I could," Nick agreed. "It wouldn't last though. The body can't survive on Magic Energy only."

"Meaning?" Josh questioned, clutching Jake's forearm.

"Meaning the second we get back to the studio, he needs food, water, and most importantly, sleep," Nick explained.

"Do it," Josh said. "Please."

Nick stood over Jake's unconscious body and let the white and red mist flow all around it. Thirty seconds later, Nick finished and was surprised to find that he felt tired, which is strange because his Power was supposed to be limitless. His posture slumped and Jessica, from behind him, put her hands on his shoulders to steady him.

"Are you okay?" she asked. "It's not like you to get tired like that."

"It's just the heat, and it's been a long, hard day for all of us," Nick sighed. He hoped that was the truth.

16.7

Jake felt strange as energy flowed into him. He didn't know how or why, but it felt right. He began to regain his senses and noticed that not only could he feel his legs, but neither of them was in pain. He also noticed that he did not feel sore or thirsty or hungry. He did, however, feel someone gripping his hand. He wiggled his toes and felt a few grains of what he believed to be sand in his shoes. Sand? Sand! Everything that had happened to him came flooding back.

Jake opened his eyes and shot up into a sitting position, causing his rescuers to jump. He looked around. He noticed a bunch of hard dirt around him. That's what he was sitting on. He also noticed that his brother, Josh, was holding his hand. Jake coughed and tested his voice.

"Josh?" he said.

Josh grinned like an idiot and responded as if nothing had happened.

"Yes, Jake?" he asked.

Jake released a string of questions. "How am I alive? How are you here? Wasn't there a giant gaping hole in my leg? Also, why am I not tired, hungry, or thirsty? Where…"

"Slow down. Slow down a bit, Jake," Mason suggested.

Jake turned his head, and for the first time, noticed Mason, Rachel, Nick, Jessica, and Teddy.

"Whoa!" he exclaimed. "Did all of you guys save me?"

Josh stood and held out a hand for Jake. He took the hand, stood up, and tested his legs. It felt as if nothing had happened.

"We should get back to the studio," Josh said.

"Yeah," Jake muttered absentmindedly. "Did I dream the whole thing?"

The gang smiled knowingly. As they began to walk back in the direction they knew was the studio, Jessica said, "It's time we tell you everything. We'll talk on the way back to the studio."

SEVENTEEN

In Which There Is an Emotional Conversation

Back at the studio, Oliver and the others were just hanging out when Steven came in once more.

"Are the others back yet?" he questioned, now looking worried. "We need to start in two hours!"

Jason stood and spoke. "No, not yet, but they should walk through that door any second now," he assured him. "For some reason, our team has really impeccable timing."

"Did someone say, 'Impeccable timing!'" Teddy announced as he opened the studio door and walked inside. Following him were Jessica, Nick, Jake, Josh, Rachel, and Mason.

"We found him!" Mason called as he marched through the door. He closed the door behind him and then turned around to see Steven looking at him questionably.

"What do you mean you found him?" Steven asked, his eyebrow arched.

Jessica quickly covered for him. "We were playing hide and seek!" she said.

Steven remained skeptical and spoke again. "In the middle of the empty barren desert?" he asked.

"Yep!" she responded with a smile.

The room was silent for a moment, then Steven said, "Well, at least you kids are playing outside."

Steven was about to walk off, but he took another glance at everyone in the room. "By the way, the game show begins in two hours. Just meet back here. Also, please clean up beforehand. You all look as if you have been rolling in dust."

The kids just nodded and smiled as Steven left. Once he was gone, everyone let out a sigh. Jake stumbled and Josh used an arm to steady him.

"Acting normal is hard," Jake sighed. "I don't understand why we have to keep any of this information from my dad."

"The less the adults know, the better!" Nick snapped. "Trust me."

"Okay," Jake whispered, surprised by the outburst. "Sorry."

"It could happen to anyone, Nick," Jessica said sadly. She knew Nick was referring to the tragic death of their beloved teacher, Mrs. Thomas, just a year or so earlier and how Oliver and Nick had almost shared the same fate.

Oliver's eyes widened as he remembered. He blinked away tears. Jessica walked to her brother and put her arm around his shoulders. Ondrea and Avery moved toward Nick's side, and his stiff posture relaxed a bit when he felt Avery grab his hand supportively. All of this reminiscing brought to Jason the painful memories of Mason's brush with death, and he stumbled as if the memories caused him physical pain. Mason sensed his twin's pain and sadness. Mason wrapped his arm around his brother's waist both for physical and mental support.

Darla, remembering Mrs. Thomas, looked as if she were about to be sick. Silent tears trailed down her face as Will reached out his shaking hand and lightly grasped hers. Rachel nervously pushed a bit of her brown hair behind her ears and slinked back so she could lean on the wall.

Michael, remembering he was a factor in Mason's revival, but also very uncomfortable with emotion, just fidgeted with his fingernails as he rocked slightly back and forth on his heels. Clearly, everyone in the group realized that they had shoved their past traumas to the back of their minds. Bringing them out in front again hit them harder than they would have anticipated.

Jake and Josh looked around at everyone with expressions of curiosity and fear.

"What's going on?" Josh asked, snapping everyone out of their intense stupors.

"We… we… lost uh… a member of our team last year," Will stammered as he tightened his grip on Darla's hand. "She was… well… this is a dangerous business… and uh…"

"She was murdered," Darla finished. Nick visibly flinched at the mention of murder, and Ondrea squeezed his shoulder supportively.

"And we've had a lot of… near-death experiences between all of us," Teddy explained cautiously.

Meanwhile, as usual, Mason threw caution to the wind. "Michael helped save my life and… my legacy," he blurted out.

"Oliver saved mine," Nick whispered hoarsely. "And then Ondrea and I had to save Oliver which, surprise, killed me."

"Then Nick's dad and I brought Nick back to life," Rachel finished, shyly stepping out from her spot against the wall.

"Wow!" Josh stated, his face showing a variety of different emotions—fear, sadness, and even the pain of loss.

"And now you saved me," Jake added with a slight grin.

"We did," Nick confirmed. He stepped forward, letting go of Avery's hand and shaking Ondrea's hand off his shoulder. He wore his best smile as if attempting to smile the memories away.

"I just need to mention that the whole 'Oliver saving Nick, Nick saving Oliver, and Rachel saving Nick' thing happened in the span of like five minutes," Will explained in a mood-lightening manner.

"Yeah," Jessica added. "It was a very emotional five minutes for us!" Everyone laughed in agreement. Jake and Josh smiled, happy to see that the moment of intense sadness was over. Just in time, in fact.

Jake suddenly felt woozy. He held out his arm as if looking for something to steady himself.

"I think I need to sit down," he said, shaking a bit. He stumbled forward. Josh reached out with both hands, grasping Jake's outstretched hand and his shoulder. Teddy Teleported away and then Teleported back, appearing with a chair for Jake to sit on.

"Will, can you go get him some water?" Oliver asked, speaking as if it was a command.

"Sure!" he responded. Will looked around the room and saw a water bottle sitting on the other side of the room. He held out his hand and concentrated, manipulating the water in the bottle toward himself. The water bottle came flying toward his hand. Will caught it, opened it, and gave it to Jake.

"I'll get some crackers from our pantry upstairs!" Josh exclaimed, sprinting toward the stairs.

Jake downed the entire bottle of water in two gulps and began to feel better immediately. Then, his stomach lurched. Ondrea quickly grabbed Jake's wrist and seemed to send a calming energy through his body, but really, she was just using a bit of her Healing power to help settle his stomach to the best of her abilities.

"You drank the water too fast. When your brother comes back with the crackers, don't eat them too quickly either. If you do, you will definitely throw up," Jason sternly lectured.

"You can't forget that you were out scorching in the heat bleeding for hours on end without any food or water. Let your body adjust slowly to food and water," Oliver said.

"You're right," Jake replied quietly. "I can't forget."

"How does your stomach feel now?" Ondrea questioned, bending down to look at Jake's eyes.

"Empty, but it feels better now," Jake assured her, his voice beginning to sound thick with fatigue. Ondrea let go of his wrist and returned to Teddy's side, still looking a bit worried. Josh came back down with a sleeve of crackers, opened it and handed it to his brother. Jake began to nibble. Meanwhile, Teddy pulled Ondrea to the side.

"What's up, babe?" he wondered. "I can tell you're worried."

"I just wish I could do more," she whispered, clutching Teddy's hand. She shut her eyes tightly to keep the tears from falling down her face, but a few escaped anyway. She opened her eyes as she felt Teddy lovingly wipe the tears from her cheeks.

"I'm sure Nick feels the same way," Teddy responded. "Any Healer would, but this is something that can't be helped by anything but time. If it could be, I'm positive you would be the first to help," Teddy stated. He looked into her eyes and smiled supportively. "That's just one of the many reasons why I love you SO much."

Ondrea's eyes glimmered with tears, and she threw her arms around her boyfriend and cried. The others in the group gave the two of them some space and stepped closer to Jake.

"Thank you," she whispered. Teddy tuned out the world and focused on the intense beating of Ondrea's heart. He and Ondrea stayed locked in the hug until Ondrea's sobbing quieted and her eyes dried. By the time she pulled away, Jake had been escorted to bed by Josh, and everyone else, including Michael, went to their rooms to use their remaining time for naps.

"It's about time," Darla said quietly when Ondrea pulled away. Teddy and Ondrea turned to look at her. "I've been sitting in this chair for, like, twenty minutes just waiting for you guys to settle down a bit." Darla had her phone in her hands and was playing a game.

"I'm sorry," Ondrea said as she rubbed her eyes. Crying takes a lot out of a person. She yawned.

"Why were you waiting for us?" Teddy asked.

Darla looked up from her screen and at the wall to her left for a moment.

"I… I don't know," she mumbled. Darla immediately went back to looking at her phone. She heard Teddy and Ondrea yawn. "You cry babies should go and get some sleep."

"Yeah." Ondrea agreed, rubbing her eyes again.

"What about you?" Teddy questioned.

"I'll go to sleep in a minute. You go on," Darla demanded, eyes still on her screen.

"Alright," Teddy said, taking Ondrea's hand. They walked out of the studio door to head to their separate rooms.

As they walked, Darla painfully watched their interlocked hands. Once they were out the door, she sighed, adding that pain to the dark hole that had been growing inside her for as long as she could remember. The hole that was so empty, but full at the same time. Full of a loneliness she felt she would never shake. As she got up and trudged back to her room, one thought went through her mind, and she quietly whispered it aloud.

"How can a heart be so full of emptiness and still feel empty even though it's full?"

Once she got back to her bed, she cried for a bit and then fell asleep.

EIGHTEEN

In Which They Get Ready For the Game

Everyone had set their alarms for twenty minutes before the *Unleash Your Wild Side* game show was to begin. When the last of the team had entered the studio, Steven took them to the general backstage area and told them how to enter the stage when the cameras began rolling. Then, with ten minutes left until game time, he pointed them toward a decent sized area with mirrors and makeup.

"Just in case anyone wants to spiffy up before we start!" he announced as he went back on stage to finish setting up.

Once he was gone, Darla used her Power of Invisibility and sat in a chair in the corner, trying to gather her thoughts and practice smiling. Rachel was being dragged over to the makeup area by Ondrea, and Teddy was hovering around her so he could tell her how beautiful she looked. Avery—who was naturally beautiful and not usually one to fuss over her appearance—was just brushing her hair. Will sat down against the wall taking deep breaths and trying not to throw up from nerves. Jason was pacing back and forth, occasionally fixing his glasses and just mumbling about how excited he was.

Mason was trying to get Josh to style his short curly hair while Josh complained. Jake sat nearby in a chair, teasing Josh about his discomfort.

"Maybe you should focus on your own hair, Mason," Josh finally said.

"Why? Wait! Oh no! Does it look bad?" Mason wondered. He raced to the mirror and began running his hands through his hair in an attempt to fix his originally not-messy hair. Josh sighed, finally glad to be rid of Mason and his hair suggestions.

Oliver was off to the side doing a surprisingly amazing job of braiding his sister's hair.

"Wow, Ollie!" Nick said, smirking. "I didn't know you could braid hair like that. Can you do mine?"

Jessica giggled at the comment as Oliver finished her braid. "Thanks Nick," Oliver said sarcastically. "I bet you only WISH you could braid hair like me!"

"Oh yeah. I wish I could be like 'Oliver the Famous Hair Braider' because THAT would be just awesome!" Nick laughed as he reached out and jostled Oliver's hair. Oliver started laughing too.

"Well, when you have a sister like Jess, you must learn the art of hair braiding!" Oliver exclaimed as he slugged Nick playfully on the arm.

Michael, who had been lurking in the shadows and had nothing to do, came out of the dark and sat against the wall beside Will. They were silent for a moment before Michael asked, "You okay?"

"Why do you care?" Will grumbled, his face looking pale.

"You look like you're about to hurl everywhere," Michael stated as he copied Will's sitting position by instinctively hugging his knees to his chest.

"It's that bad, huh?" Will said quietly.

"Yeah," Michael answered.

After a minute of silence, Will said, "What about you?"

"What about me?" Michael wondered, staring straight forward at nothing.

"Are you… nervous too?" he asked, now glancing up at Michael.

"Yes," Michael replied. "Sorry, I'm not the most encouraging person to talk to right now."

"It's fine. I'm not either," Will admitted. "I feel like all I've ever done is mess things up."

"Yeah. Same," Michael stated, looking down. Then his voice faded to a whisper. "It doesn't seem like your friends think that though."

"Yeah. I guess you're right. But doesn't everyone tell you that it doesn't matter what others think of you—only how you think of yourself?" Will asked, looking toward the ceiling.

"Yes. All my therapists tell me that," Michael replied.

Will looked at him with an eyebrow raised.

"Sorry," Michael mumbled.

"It's alright, dude," Will sighed as he went back to looking at the ceiling.

"I've come to realize that what you just said is only part of it," Michael continued. "I believe there is more to life than what you think of yourself."

"What do you mean?" Will wondered, looking at Michael expectantly.

"I don't really know," he responded. "I heard my mom say that once. What do you think it means?"

Will thought for a moment.

"I think I get it," he exclaimed, grinning.

"Enlighten me please," Michael stated, turning to look at Will.

"Well, there must be a good reason why my friends trust me like they do. There must be a good reason why they keep me around. Also, there must be a good reason why they're my best friends," Will explained happily.

Michael was glad that Will now realized his place among his friends—but then realized that he himself didn't have a place among Will's friends.

"What about me?" he asked sadly. Michael's eyes went wide for a moment. "I didn't mean to say that out loud."

"Michael, you may be… uh… pretty antisocial at times, but you've got something more. I feel it. You've got something in you that's worth fighting for," Will answered.

"You'll always have a place here, Michael," Darla said, appearing beside him.

Michael jumped. "Have you been sitting there the whole time?" he questioned.

"Yep," she responded, "and I heard everything BOTH of you said."

"Oh," Will muttered.

"Will, you have always had a place here no matter what you think. You're our best friend. And Michael," she exclaimed, "you'll always have a place with us too—no matter what you think."

"Yeah. We're a team," Teddy said, walking up to them. "Oh, and sorry. I was eavesdropping."

"So was I," Ondrea added, coming up behind Teddy. "And Teddy Bear's right. So is Darla. Both of you will always have a place here. There's no need for anyone to feel like an outcast."

"We're in this for life, baby!" Mason shouted, scaring the crud out of everyone.

"True that, my brother," Jason agreed, smiling.

"Yeah, I can't wait to be fighting VORK when we're fifty years old," Avery said, looking dramatically off into the distance.

"No!" Rachel yelled. "Please, no!"

"Don't worry, Rachel. She was just kidding," Oliver sighed, rolling his eyes at Avery's comment and smiling. "Besides, we'll defeat them long before that."

"That's right," Jessica confirmed. "It's just what we do!"

"I would rather not fight villains if that's cool with you guys," Josh mentioned.

"Yeah… we'll be known as 'Friends of Superheroes' and not 'Superheroes' if that's alright with you," Jake added.

Suddenly Steven broke through the curtain and announced something that made their nerves spike.

"We'll be on in one minute!" he called. Then, he disappeared to the stage again.

"Yikes," Will mumbled nervously.

"Hey, it's alright, Will, Michael. Guys, we'll absolutely do great!" Nick exclaimed, trying to pump them up. "You know what? We need a team name. I don't just mean like for the game show. I mean more for our Superhero stuff."

"That's a great idea!" Jessica agreed excitedly. Everyone went silent for a couple seconds to think of something good.

Michael spoke up first. "How about Heroes Of Planet Earth?" he suggested. "I know it's a little cheesy and plain, but it's…"

"Dude, I LOVE IT!" Oliver yelled. Then he cringed and quieted down. "I love it!"

"Me too!" Jessica agreed. "And not just because the acronym for Heroes Of Planet Earth is HOPE."

"All in favor?" Nick asked. Everyone raised their hand.

"Awesome!" Will said. "TEAM HOPE!"

Steven poked his head through the curtain once more. "Kids! I just turned the cameras on! You'll be able to hear me talking through the curtain, so when I say your name, you know what to do. It's show time!" he whispered giddily.

Once he went back to the stage everyone smiled at each other. As Oliver heard his name called, he whispered to the others, "Heroes Of Planet Earth… it's go time!"

NINETEEN

In Which the Game Begins

HELLO my crazy adventurers, watching from the comfort of your home! We do the dangerous stuff, so you don't have to!" Steven announced in a loud voice to the cameras. "Today we have a ton of very special guests for you, including... my own sons!

"Let me introduce you to our first participant, Oliver Fletcher! Come on out, Oliver!" Steven called, gesturing dramatically to the slit in the curtains. Oliver ran out onto the TV set. He got behind one of the podiums and stood there. Oliver had no clue what to do, so he just sheepishly waved. Steven put his hand on Oliver's shoulder.

"Our next participant is the lovely Jessica Fletcher, twin sister to Oliver!" Jessica came running out looking a bit flustered and tripped on the platform. Oliver cringed and ran over to help her up. They both walked back to the podiums together.

"What an entrance!" Steven announced with a grin, so caught up in his showmanship that he hadn't realized how much the trip had embarrassed Jessica. "Now we have Rachel Fletcher, sister of Oliver and Jessica and an animal enthusiast!" Steven exclaimed.

Rachel shyly walked out the curtain with her head slightly lowered and her hands behind her back. She turned to face the camera, then immediately looked down as if she had regretted looking up. Once she arrived at the podium, she took a deep breath, put her brave face on, and smiled widely at the camera.

"Next up, we have Nick Gator, cousin of the Fletchers and a military veteran!" Steven announced. Nick had begun to walk to the podium the second his name was called but froze when Steven mentioned his military history. As far as Nick knew, since he was enlisted into the military illegally and underage, only his family and close friends knew that. Oliver and Jessica's eyes went wide. Nick quickly recovered from his shock and continued to walk to the podium next to Jessica.

"Thank you for your service, Nick," Steven announced. "Next, we have Jason Mackenzie! Get on out here, Jason!"

Jason ran out excitedly and stepped up behind the podium next to Nick.

"Hello everyone!" Jason called with an uncharacteristic wave.

"It's nice to see you here, Jason!" Steven said. "Now we have the mustard to his ketchup, the left shoe to his right, Jason's twin brother, Mason Mackenzie!"

Mason dramatically leapt through the curtain, danced his way to the podium next to Jason, and then did a flip.

"Yo, yo, yo!" he shouted excitedly. Jason couldn't help but smile and roll his eyes at his brother's theatrics.

"Wow, very impressive, Mason!" Steven bellowed. "Next up we have Avery Kendal! Let's see it, Avery!"

Avery pushed the curtain aside dramatically, cat-walked to the front of the stage, struck a pose, walked to her podium, then bowed.

"Wow! Very beautifully done, Avery!" Steven announced. "Now for her beloved sister, Ondrea Kendal!" Ondrea walked out of the curtain and beelined for the podium next to her sister. Once she arrived at the podium, she flashed a smile and a wave.

"We can't split up the happy couple!" Steven called. "Now, introducing Teddy Baird, Ondrea's charming boyfriend!" Teddy walked out looking uncharacteristically nervous and awkward. He looked at the camera and smiled charmingly, but anyone who knew him could tell his heart wasn't in it. Then he turned around and took up the podium next to Ondrea. She could tell something was up, but instead of asking, she took his hand in hers and squeezed it supportively. She meant for the gesture to be subtle, so as not to embarrass Teddy. But her goal was ruined when Steven announced, "Aw, how cute! Always there for each other! Next up we have the wonderful Darla Madison! It's your time, Darla!"

Darla confidently strode out from the curtain, struck a fierce pose, and continued her stride to the podium. She took the podium next to Teddy and, for effect only, smirked toward the cameras.

"Ah, sassy, I see!" Steven chuckled. He cleared his throat and continued, "Next up in our lineup, we have Will Brookes…" Steven paused to look at a card he'd been keeping in his pocket given to him by Will for this exact moment, studied it, then continued, "Will Brookes… ladies' man extraordinaire and… dazzler of all women!"

Will came out of the curtain with the most charming smile any of his friends had ever seen. He had his hands in his pockets and walked to the front of the stage. He then took his hands out of his pockets, stylishly pointed to the camera, and winked. His eyes went wide as he headed to the podium next to Darla, remembering that he had a girlfriend and the girl he ACTUALLY had feelings for was standing right next to him.

"Very smooth, very suave, Will!" Steven said. "Now, we have my sons, and the best pair of twins that I personally know, Jake and Josh Stanford!" Steven shouted. Jake and Josh came running out of the curtain. Josh 'accidentally' tripped Jake and continued to his podium. Once Jake got up, he raced to his podium and shoved Josh just hard enough to say, "We aren't done yet," but not hard enough to knock him over.

"I'm Josh," Josh said to the camera. "This one is Jake." Jake smiled and waved.

"Aren't they just… quirky! Don't worry, folks, we're almost done here! I know we have a lot of participants for this month's episode! Let me introduce our last participant! We have the man, the myth, the legend, Michael Atrius!" No one came out from behind the curtain. "Come on Michael!" Steven encouraged "Everyone is waiting to get a glimpse of you."

Michael hesitantly stepped out. He mumbled something to himself, straightened up, then walked calmly to his podium next to Will. Although Michael appeared to be completely calm and in control, everyone who knew him knew that inside, he was bouncing with nervous energy and exploding with anxiety. Will gave Michael a gentle pat on the back.

"Alrighty, girls and boys, ladies and gentlemen. Now that the introductions are finished, let's get right into the 'face your fears' portion of this show!" Steven announced. For some reason, he sounded nervous.

TWENTY

In Which Michael Reveals a Secret Evil

The second the cameras turned off for a two-minute intermission, Team HOPE raced toward a corner backstage. They huddled around each other and waited. Oliver realized they were waiting for him to speak.

"First, how did Steven know about Rachel's love of animals? She never mentioned that to him," he said.

"I'm not sure. As you said, I never mentioned it to him," Rachel responded. "Maybe our parents filled out some kind of questionnaire about us and gave it to Steven."

"I'm sure they did," Jake began. "I saw Steven looking at a digital form on his computer a couple hours before we left to pick you guys up. Maybe they were completed questionnaires."

Josh spoke next. "Yeah, but we can't confirm that theory," he countered. "And why did you shove me?"

"Why did YOU trip ME?" Jake sputtered.

"Guys!" Jessica called. "We don't have time for you to argue about this right now!"

"What we really need to discuss," Nick began, "is how Steven knew about my military background? My dad would NEVER put that on a questionnaire! I was enlisted illegally, I was underage, and I deserted!"

"How DID he know about that?" Avery wondered.

"How did he know Teddy and I are a couple?" Ondrea questioned, looking upset.

"I mean, you two don't exactly keep it a secret," Will mumbled.

Suddenly, Darla interjected. "What's with that entrance, Will?" she snapped.

"You know, looking back on that, I kind of regret it," Will muttered, awkwardly scratching the back of his head.

"Look, as disturbing as that was," Teddy began, "it shouldn't be our main concern. What we should be concerned about is that someone here is holding out on us. SOMEONE here knows something that we don't. Something that we probably NEED to know!"

"Nah," Mason said. "I get who you're talking about, but Michael is just a naturally anxious guy."

"I second that," Michael added calmly. But inside, he was screaming.

Jason transitioned to the topic that was on everyone's minds. He said, "Something that we really should be concerned about is this—what are we going to do during the fear simulations?"

"What are you guys so worried about?" Jake asked.

"Uh… dude, we're Superhuman," Will said.

"Let me elaborate on that," Oliver said. "We have been through many incredibly fear-raising situations—none of which have been normal. Therefore, our fears… are not normal." The reality of the risk they were about to take finally hit him.

"So, you guys could be outed on television," Josh realized.

"Thirty seconds until you're back on!" a crew member shouted. "Start heading to your places."

Before they began walking back, Nick asked, "Wait, why did Steven seem so nervous when he announced the next challenge?"

Everyone stopped and turned to look at him. "That's a good point," Jessica said nervously.

"Twenty-two seconds! Come on, kids!" the crew member yelled.

"We can't worry about that now," Ondrea sighed.

Everyone else nodded in agreement, but, in truth, they couldn't stop worrying as they took their places behind the podiums.

Steven began the countdown to go live. "Smiles everybody!" he exclaimed. "Three, two, one!"

20.2

Oliver didn't know what to expect. The cameras faced him, and his friends' nervous faces turned in his direction. As Oliver sat in the chair, ready to face his fear, a man stepped out from behind the curtains. Steven had been glancing toward the curtains as if he expected this man to appear, but gasped when he did. As curious as Oliver was as to why Steven seemed so startled by this man, his reaction wasn't the one that got Oliver's attention. When the man came out of the curtain, Oliver Sensed a strong presence, which was enough to put the man under suspicion.

What really concerned Oliver was Michael's reaction. Oliver saw Michael stiffen the second the man appeared. As Oliver further studied Michael's expression, he noticed fear and worry.

20.3

When the man stepped out from behind the curtain, the hair on the back of Michael's neck stood up. Michael quickly turned in the man's direction and, as he caught a glance of a familiar face, his eyes widened, and he faced forward once more. It was when the man began to approach Oliver that Michael really began to worry. To Michael's left, he noticed Josh's face twist into one of confusion. The strange man began hooking wires up to Oliver's head and Michael began to nervously rock back and forth on his heels. To Michael's immediate right, Will noticed the rocking and looked to Michael with his eyebrow raised.

While all the cameras were focused on Oliver as he was getting wired up, Will took this time to ask Michael a question. He nudged Michael in the arm to get his attention, but Michael didn't budge. "Michael!" Will whispered. "What's your deal?"

"I don't have a sound reading on him," Michael responded.

"What does that mean?" Will asked. "What… what are you not telling us?"

Michael hesitated. He rarely ever judged anyone based on appearance, but Michael began judging this man the second he saw him. Having walked into the man's lair and feeling the evil, Michael had proof that this wasn't the kind of guy you'd want to mess with. Michael hadn't been with his new friends for very long, and he didn't want them to think he was a bad person for breaking into the man's room. But even Michael knew that it was time to say something.

"This man…" Michael began, "he isn't good. I don't have a good reading on him."

"A little more information," Will said, now studying the man with an intense stare.

"He… he went into the purple door. I followed him. The door… it… it led to an evil lair," Michael stammered.

Will sighed and turned to stare directly at Michael. "And you thought keeping this new information to yourself was a good idea because…?" Will questioned.

"I… I don't know," Michael mumbled.

"Alright ladies and gentlemen of the home audience," Steven began in his big announcer voice, "It's time for Oliver Fletcher to FACE HIS FEAR!"

TWENTY-ONE

In Which Oliver Is On the Hot Seat

Oliver closed his eyes. When he opened them again, he was in a completely black room. Standing some distance in front of him were his mother, father, and Jessica. Oliver became nervous. In normal circumstances, he would be thrilled to see his mom, dad, and sister, but he knew he was in a fear simulation—and there they were, smiling at him. He began slowly walking toward his family… but stopped. Something felt different. Uncomfortable, but familiar. HEAT. The room began to heat up quickly. Fire sprung from the floor under his family and he began to scream.

Oliver was well aware that this was only a simulation, but it seemed so real. He was also aware that the point of this simulation is to overcome his fear, but FIRE?

"How could anyone overcome a fear of fire? And why would you want to? I mean, it's fire!" Oliver said. His voice echoed as if the room was empty. He closed his eyes as he felt the heat sear his skin. When he opened his eyes once again, the dark room had turned into an office building filled with fire.

"No! Not this!" Oliver cried. Then, he broke down and cried as the fire threatened to engulf his family. After a minute or two, he felt the fire suddenly sear his arm. He stopped crying and looked up. The fire wasn't anywhere near him.

"Wait a second," Oliver sniffed. "This isn't real…This isn't real! It's just a fear! But why should anyone get over a fear of fire?" he asked himself once more. Then, a realization hit him.

"This isn't a fear of fire," he said. "This is a fear of high-pressure situations. I hate high-pressure situations."

Oliver took a deep breath and shook out his arms.

"I can do this," he whispered. Suddenly, everything became quiet. Oliver gathered his thoughts and the first thing that came into his mind was Jess. He realized he had to do this. For his sister, his parents, his friends. He took another deep breath and, as he did, the fire roared to life again. With most of his nerves cleared, Oliver took a breath of non-toxic air and started to race into the raging blaze.

As if waking from a nightmare, Oliver thrashed for a second before realizing that he had been strapped to the chair for his safety. He noticed the sweat dripping from his face. Lastly, he remembered where he was and looked to his friends, sisters, and cousin who all appeared to be holding their breath anxiously. He looked down and blinked rapidly, his mind still waking up.

"I'm okay," Oliver said quietly to himself. "I… did it." He looked to his friends again and laughed. "I'm okay. Guys! I'm okay!"

"We know," Jessica said. "We saw the whole thing, along with the people at home. We saw it all."

"That had to have been the most intense fear session we have ever seen, folks!" Steven announced to the cameras. "Oliver, tell the world how you feel!"

Steven gently placed the microphone into Oliver's hand, and the cameraman hurried to shove the camera in Oliver's face, which provoked a glare from Steven. The cameraman backed up a couple of steps to give Oliver more room.

Oliver spoke. "I am so relieved. Relieved to be over that fear and relieved that the fear is over. I'm also really tired… and probably stinky."

"Yes, well. I think we've embarrassed you enough for today, so we're going to take a five-minute break. We'll see you, folks, when we return," Steven called and then immediately cut the cameras.

As soon as the cameras were cut, he dropped his mic on the floor and rushed to Oliver to unhook him from the wires and remove his restraints.

"Gosh, I'm really sorry about the restraints," Steven said. "You started moving and squirming, and I didn't want you to end up hurting yourself, so we strapped your wrists and ankles to the chair."

"Thank you for that, Steven, but I wish you could've warned me that it would be so intense," Oliver exclaimed.

Suddenly, Jess, Nick, and his friends came rushing over to him, pestering him, asking if he was okay. Then Will interrupted and suggested that everyone go backstage.

Once all the kids made it backstage, Will said, "Michael has a bit of explaining to do."

Michael began explaining about the man and the purple door. By the time he had finished, he had everyone on edge.

"So, you've been holding this information back from us for… how long?" Will asked with his head in his hands.

"Hey, go easy on him, Will," Teddy said, "He was probably scared to speak his mind."

"Are you always this blunt?" Michael asked, gently rocking back on forth on his heels.

"You'll never meet any group of friends more blunt than we are," Avery confirmed with a grin.

"Back to the main focus," Jason said, "Why didn't you tell us this earlier?"

"Well… I … I just…I mean I had broken the lock…and …I didn't want you to think…" Michael sighed. He continued his next statement as if thinking carefully of what he was saying. "Look, I… I've never had a group of… friends so…intrusive before and…."

"We're not intrusive!" Darla interjected.

"Let him finish, Dar," Ondrea mumbled.

Michael began again. "No… it's not that you're… intrusive. You… you just don't hold anything back."

"That's the type of people we are, Michael," Mason said with a smile the ladies would call "cute." Mason gently put his hand on Michael's shoulder.

"When Jason and I first met this crazy bunch of kids, we weren't super close as brothers. Plus, we never really thought of each other as brothers. We always thought of ourselves as 'the twins', the twins that would always stick out. Never… never family," Mason's hand dropped away from Michael's shoulder, and he stopped talking.

Jason continued. "Then we met Oliver and his crew. I was getting beat up, and I believe it was Nick who stepped in to save me. Mason was around the playground area looking for me. The bully had broken my leg, and Oliver's crew came to my rescue," he explained.

Jason smiled, and Mason ruffled his hair playfully. "Yeah, but that was back when you were a little geeky boy with zero physical control over your life," Mason laughed.

"Alright, Mason," Jason sighed, but under that sigh, appeared a small smirk. It was nice… remembering the good old days when he and Mason not only made new friends but also grew closer to each other.

"TWO MINUTES!" a crew member called.

"Guys, I know we're all laughing at better times, but we really need to talk about THIS situation some more," Nick suggested.

"I think Steven looked nervous," Jessica said. "It's almost as if he had a reason to be nervous when that guy walked out."

"You can't seriously be suggesting that our dad has something to do with this creep, right?" Jake hissed, immediately becoming defensive.

"Well, Jake," Josh began, "I'm not saying Dad is in evil cahoots with this guy, but maybe he knows what's up."

Rachel was the next to speak up. "Maybe… maybe this is your new sponsor. You know, the person who's brought in the extra money," she offered.

"Then, what's he doing hooking up the wires and stuff?" Will wondered.

"That still doesn't explain why Steven looked so nervous," Ondrea pointed out.

"Maybe he was just nervous because of the tech…?" Darla said in a tone that suggested a question.

"THIRTY SECONDS! GET TO YOUR PLACES!" a crew member yelled.

As the gang began to line back up for their entrance, Michael said, "Look, I'm sorry that I hid this from you. But here's the bottom line: we need to figure this out."

"He's right," Oliver confirmed. "Everyone be on guard."

TWENTY-TWO

In Which Jessica Faces the Flames By Herself

Hello folks and WELCOME BACK! Let's get straight into this! Next up to face her fear is Jessica Fletcher!" Steven called. All twelve kids stood at their podiums while Jessica nervously walked up to the chair. She sat down as the strange man began hooking the wires to her head. Back at the podium, Rachel subtly moved to her sister's podium and grabbed Oliver's hand for support.

Everything became dark in Jessica's head. She was immediately hit by a blinding blue sky, and she closed her eyes.

"Oh, no," she said when she opened her eyes. All around her were cloudy pieces of Superhero School. She began trying to block them out as soon as she saw them form. "The world can't know!" she thought, panic-stricken. The more Jessica blocked the image out, the more the cloudy pieces of Superhero School began to look like normal clouds.

Then, she saw her fear. Ondrea, Teddy, Avery, Will, Rachel, and Nick, and Nick's father, Damian, all surrounding Oliver's body. That's when she lost focus and Superhero School came into view all at once. The memories came flooding back to her. Jessica's heart dropped, and she fell to her knees.

It was strange. She knew the outcome of the situation. She knew her Ollie was still alive, but the emotions overpowered every logical and reasonable cell in her body. She broke down.

From outside the simulation, Oliver was shaking. Seeing his own death being broadcast to the world was… agonizing. Mason, Jason, Josh, Jake, and Michael just stared at the screen because, although no one in the audience (other than their parents) knew this really had occurred, they did. Sure, they weren't there, but still they were confident that this event had occurred.

From back in the simulation, Jessica had somewhat pulled herself together and stumbled toward her brother. She tried to touch him, hold his hand, even if the hand was dead, but her hand went right through it.

"Oh, God!" she cried, "I'm in a simulation. I've got to pull myself together." She realized that she was seeing all of this, feeling all of this, but she couldn't physically interact with any of it. Somehow that made her situation even worse and reminded her of all the times the previous year when she nearly became unhinged from events like this.

She cried out in horror and agony, tears soaking her shirt. As she felt the tears on her hand, she realized that she was the only real person in her simulated world. Jessica cried out once more and curled up into a ball, as if attempting to hide the pain and loneliness deep inside her.

After a minute, she looked up again and saw nothing. Nothing but black. No, it wasn't even black. There wasn't a color. There was no black, just darkness. But in the darkness, she saw her worst fear. The fear that used to keep her up a night and, when she did sleep, invade her dreams: No one. Not a single person in sight.

She felt her body shaking as sweat poured down her face. Suddenly, fire enveloped her. The devilish red glow outshone the orange and yellow. She saw rage, pain, and guilt, and she saw herself succumbing to the maddening internal conflicts she had been desperately trying to avoid. She felt her body heat up, and she became enraged.

"All this pain!" she screamed over the roar of the fire. "What is it all for? NOTHING! All my life, I've fallen prey to emotional torture! I always felt I was living as if something were chasing me, but I never went down that path because I have… f…friends. But in the end, I'm always so alone. Why am I so alone?" Jessica cried.

"A simulation!" she said, remembering that none of this was real. Although she had realized this vision wasn't real, the anger that burned inside remained. "LET ME OUT! LET ME OUT!" she screeched.

Outside of the simulation, trails of tears slid down Oliver's face. The moment she screamed to be let out, Steven rushed to turn off the simulation—but it wasn't working.

Michael, managing to stay surprisingly calm in the heat of the moment, noticed that the creepy man wasn't doing anything to help. He was just standing off camera… smiling.

On the simulation screen, Oliver and his friends could see Jessica throwing her hands around in the darkness as if trying to grasp onto something. Anything that was real. Oliver couldn't take it anymore and, against the rules of the show, he began to run to his sister. Suddenly, the creepy man stepped up and grabbed Oliver by his arm before he could make it to his screaming sister.

"No one can interrupt the process," he said. "The machine won't turn off until the process is complete. Until the victim has faced their fear."

Oliver tried to move forward, but the man held on tighter. Steven looked up from the machine and saw this.

"Unhand that young man, you menace!" he hissed.

The man known Steven called a "menace" glared at Steven and held on tighter. "The process isn't yet complete."

Oliver's friends and family were all in shock. Luckily, Will's instinct to cause trouble always outweighed any other emotion he had ever felt. Will ran over to the man and kicked him on the back of his leg as hard as possible, which left the menace on the floor gingerly clutching his leg. Oliver finished the distance to his sister.

Jason met Oliver there and, just as Oliver was about to pull all the wires loose, Jason stopped him. "Think about what you're doing, Oliver. What if doing this will hurt her?" Jason cautioned. "As much as I hate to say it, maybe she really does have to finish the simulation."

"She's in pain in there!" Oliver cried.

"I know, but what if just pulling the plug puts her in more pain?" Jason asked.

Despite all the emotions he was feeling, Oliver realized that he had to listen to the logical side of this. Maybe pulling the plug would be a bad idea. Instead, Oliver grabbed her hand. It felt cold, but sweaty. And just like her whole body, it was shaking.

"You can do this, Jess. You're never alone," Oliver whispered.

Back in the simulation, Jessica was still having a mental breakdown. At this point, the flames had disappeared and all she felt was cold and broken.

Then, she heard a voice. Oliver's voice. She looked around the darkness and saw nothing. "I really am going crazy," she whispered hoarsely.

"No, you're not, Jess."

"Ollie?" she croaked into the darkness. With her shaky hands, she rubbed her eyes, stood up, and looked around again. Finally, she took a deep breath. Then another and another. Her body stopped shaking and she suddenly felt something in her hand. Something warm. She looked over and saw Oliver standing right next to her holding her hand.

"This isn't right. I can feel your hand," she muttered.

"That's because I'm here with you. I took off all the restraints already, but I don't want to unhook you yet because I don't want it to hurt you. Do you think you could be calm?"

"Yeah, I think so," she whispered.

"Jess, you're not alone," Oliver said with a sad smile.

"I know. I just… felt alone," Jessica sighed.

"Yeah, we all saw that. Pretty embarrassing if you ask me," Darla said.

"Darla?" she asked.

"Yeah, you big dum-dum," Darla teased. "Are you ready to come home?"

"Oh, yeah," Jessica laughed.

"Close your eyes, sis," Oliver said.

Jessica closed her eyes and, when she opened them again, she was in Oliver's embrace surrounded by all her friends in the real world.

"You're a superstar, girl!" Teddy cheered.

"Alright folks!" Steven exclaimed to the camera, "That was insane! I think that deserves a good one-hour intermission, and we'll see you when we get back! Oh, by the way, for insurance purposes, I want to make sure you know that everything you just saw was COMPLETELY STAGED!"

With that, the cameras were turned off.

TWENTY-THREE

In Which Steven Comes Clean

After all the commotion and trauma, Team HOPE went backstage. Everyone was silent for a second…"Well, that was awful," Will remarked.

Steven entered backstage looking flustered, worried, nervous, and angry all at once. He quickly passed off his announcer microphone to one of the stage crew who accidentally dropped it. He bent down and fiddled around picking it up. The group could see that his hands were sweaty and slick. Once he had picked it up again, he hurriedly handed it to the crew member, who was ready this time. Steven whipped his head in different directions, clearly searching for something. He was making such a scene that the kids had turned and watched.

"Dude, your dad is really freaking out," Avery said.

"Yeah," Josh mumbled worriedly.

Jake peered at his dad and then at Jessica. Once again, he peered at his dad, this time with a look of disgust and confusion plastered across his face.

"I… I just…." Jake began before Steven cut him off when he finally spotted the kids.

"KIDS!" Steven called, desperation dripping from his voice. "Kids! I am so incredibly sorry!"

By this time, Steven had hustled toward them and put his hands into a begging position. "Kids, I am so, so sorry. Jessica, I… I didn't know what was happening!" Steven was practically begging for forgiveness. "Mr. Bradford said that Mr. Atrius was trustworthy and experienced! I never even thought this would happen! Kids, I'm so sorry!"

Jessica walked up directly in front of Steven. She was still a bit shaken up and a tiny bit angry, but she was also a forgiving person. She could tell that Steven was being sincere.

"Steven," she said quietly, trying to calm him down. "It's… it's alright. I know you would never do that on purpose. It was probably just a machine malfunction. I'm sure Mr. Atrius knows what happened and is fixing it now."

She gestured around her to show Steven that Mr. Atrius was not backstage and the toolbox that was on one of the shelves was now missing. "See…. I'm sure he took the tools and is fixing the simulation now. This had nothing to do with you."

Steven stared at her in shock and turned to Oliver who looked annoyed.

"Please don't sue me!" he begged.

Oliver smiled and rolled his eyes. "Alright, I won't sue you. You've convinced me. Although, I'm still pretty upset with you Steven. You seem like a good man, so I'll let you off the hook, but you need to earn my trust again. Okay?" Oliver said as he raised his eyebrow and crossed his arms.

"Yes! Of course! I understand," Steven rambled. "Yes. I understand. It won't happen again! I swear."

"Steven," Darla said loudly. Steven looked at her with fear in his eyes. "Chill, Steven."

"Yeah. We're not going to sacrifice you," Ondrea laughed.

Jake's anger had been stewing ever since Steven walked through that curtain and he couldn't take it any longer. Ondrea's lighthearted laugh set him off. Jake launched forward and pushed his dad in the chest. Steven stumbled back with a look of pure shock on his face. The entire backstage area went silent.

"How could you guys just laugh this off?" Jake shouted. He turned to Jessica. "How could you possibly forgive him so easily?"

He turned to Oliver next. "How could YOU forgive him so easily? She's your sister! Don't you have some kind of instinct to protect her?"

Oliver stepped forward and tried to put calming hands on Jake's shoulders. Jake stepped back. Oliver sighed and spoke. "I trust Jess. If she forgives him, then I'll accept that, but I told him… and you heard me… that he has to earn my trust back," Oliver tried to assure him.

Jake stomped on the floor and balled his hands into fists.

"That could have killed her, Oliver! This isn't right! NONE of this is right! Not you guys. Not what you can do! This Atrius guy isn't right. Michael certainly isn't right, and my d-… Steven… isn't right. All of this is BULL!" Jake screamed.

Everyone was shocked now. Michael was a bit offended, but mostly shocked. Josh had only seen his twin act like this one time, and that was when their mother died.

If expressions could kill, Steven's would. He looked like a wounded animal on the side of the road. Silent painful tears streamed down Jake's face as he stood there shooting daggers. Steven spoke.

"Son, I…"

"Who is he?" Jake asked in a low growl. "This Mr. Atrius. Who is he?"

"He's a new assistant," Steven responded quietly.

"Who is he, Dad? WHO?" Jake repeated, forcefully shouting the last word. "Is he the donor? The one who gave you money? Tell me, Dad. Don't lie to me. To us."

"He's just the assistant," Steven said even more quietly this time.

Jake turned away from his father, barely able to look at him. Josh put his hand on Jake's shoulder, but Jake pushed it off. Josh closed his eyes and sighed. "Dad..." he muttered. "Please stop lying."

"I'm not lying!" Steven persisted fearfully.

"Stop lying to your sons, Dad!" Josh exclaimed. "Tell us the truth! Are you in trouble? Who is this guy? And who is Mr. Bradford?"

"Mr. Bradford is just the man who suggested Mr. Atrius to me. He said that Mr. Atrius has a lot of money that he was willing to…" Steven clamped his hand over his mouth.

"So, he is the donor, then," Jake hissed, turning back around to face his father. "And you're a liar!"

Steven's face flushed in shame. "I… He… he told me not to say," Steven squeaked.

Nick interrupted, "How do you know Mr. Bradford?"

Steven's face sank deeper into shame, and he turned away.

"You don't even know the guy, do you?" Darla sneered.

Steven was quiet for a moment and then the words began pouring out in a long desperate stream.

"Yes, you're right. I don't know him. But I needed the money so badly so that this place could stay open! I was about to lose this building because I couldn't pay—but I never wanted to tell you, Jake and Josh. We live here! Not only is this the game show studio, but our kitchen and living room are one floor above us, and our beds are all around. I couldn't lose this place! I couldn't! Then I wouldn't be able to properly take care of you boys! What would your mother think if I couldn't take care of you? She would be ashamed of me!" he cried.

"In trying to keep this place, you've lost yourself, Dad!" Jake shouted, less angry and more sad. "You're terrified! It's so obvious! Something is going on here, and I know you know what it is, but you won't tell us! Why!?"

Jason, who had been silently observing and calculating, chimed in with a question that had been buzzing around in his head. "What is the name of the organization Mr. Bradford and Mr. Atrius work for? You can tell us," he assured Steven.

"It's a weird kind of name. I think they said uh… VORK… Yeah, that was it."

TWENTY-FOUR

In Which Rachel Bites Back

After Steven walked away, defeated, Will exclaimed, "Well, this is just wonderful," with great sarcasm. "The guy in charge of keeping our brains from melting is part of the organization that tried to kill us."

"Yeah…" Mason followed up. "So, what do we do now?"

"It's simple," Darla began. "Kick some VORK butt!"

"I second that!" Avery added in.

"None of this is a good idea," Jake muttered as he leaned against the wall and slid to the floor. He put his arms around his knees and sighed. "What is this all for again?"

"Honestly," Josh started, "This is pretty discouraging for us non-Supers too." He walked to his brother and sat down next to him.

"I get it, guys, I really do," Ondrea said as Josh walked closer to Jake. "But we can't give up."

"I know this all sounds pretty cheesy, but we truly CAN'T give up. We can't even THINK about that," Teddy said.

Ondrea sat down next to Jake and paused for a moment. Then she said, "One of the things my Powers allow me to do is to be nosy and pushy, but Mind Reading can be pretty helpful. Especially right now. Tell me, did you give up hope when… when your mother died?"

"No," Jake responded in a hushed whisper.

"No," Josh copied. "But Steven almost did."

"And riddle me this," Jason said. "Why didn't he give up?"

"I don't know," Jake said. "Why is this even relevant?"

Ignoring Jake's last remark, Nick answered Jason's question with full confidence. "The reason he never gave up is because YOU GUYS never gave up."

"Take this from someone who knows how much family can sometimes suck—morale is everything," Darla remarked. "When it comes to people who are close to you, everything is contagious. Pain, fear, sadness, happiness, excitement… even forgiveness."

"I never really had good friends before I met these guys," Will stated. "They have a tendency to bring people out of dark places. They did that for me, they can do that for you guys, and maybe, just maybe they can do that to the anti-social enigma known as our new friend Michael."

The corner of Michael's lips tilted up, almost forming a humored smile.

Out of the corner of his eye, Oliver saw this. He smiled amusingly and said, "Michael might be a bit of a project." Michael chuckled.

"We're pretty good at working with twins." Will added. "All you guys need to do is be there for each other AND for your dad."

"You're all you've got," Nick sighed.

Avery moved toward him and supportively squeezed Nick's hand.

The subtle motion caught Josh's attention, and he peered thoughtfully at the gesture. Slowly, he reached over a grabbed his brother's hand.

"We've got this," Josh muttered.

Jake turned his head and saw the fierce look in Josh's eyes. "Alright," he said confidently. "Let's do this."

Michael walked forward and offered his hands. Jake and Josh smiled at him curiously and took the help. "About what you said earlier," Michael said, "you two might not have Powers, but you have… hope."

"Good one, Michael," Will whispered, nudging Michael with his shoulder. Michael stayed silent.

"And hey, Michael," Jake said. "Steven said this donor assistant person is called 'Mr. Atrius.' Isn't that your last name? Is he related to you?"

Michael looked down and shook his head. "No, I never had any other 'Atrius' relatives. Now, I guess I'm glad about that."

"Anyway, what do we do about this VORK situation?" Oliver asked the group.

"We don't have much information yes, so… Let's wing it!" Mason suggested. "What do you think?"

Everyone looked around and shrugged.

"Let's do it," Jessica answered, smiling.

24.1

Rachel stepped up to the chair. After seeing what her sister had just gone through, Rachel's nerves were through the roof, and so were her friends'. She whimpered as she sat firmly in the chair. Her mind filled with the false illusion that sitting firmly on a material object would keep her grounded. As Mr. Atrius came out once more from behind the corner, Rachel's entire body stiffened. Her eyes began to water, and she looked toward her friends for emotional comfort. A tense silence filled the air. Will hated tense silences and decided to yell in order to break it.

"You got this Rachel!" he yelled, making everyone jump.

Rachel, for just one second, flashed a nervous smile his way and, seeing all pairs of eyes on her, took a deep breath.

"Time to activate the machine, ladies and gentlemen!" Steven announced, "I promise everything will be alright! No more interruptions and no more problems!"

As Rachel heard those words, she closed her eyes and prepared to be horrified. When she opened her eyes, the sight she saw caused a visceral reaction, and she howled.

"Oops," she said, moving her head and taking in her surroundings. "Oh no. I remember this… this place."

On three sides of her were blank white walls that looked as if they were made from cheap wood. There were hundreds of scratches covering them. In front of her, were thin bars, both horizontal and vertical. Like a cage. A dog cage. After Rachel began remembering what she was experiencing, she realized that she was only a quarter the size she had been when she was human. In all the shock, her five senses briefly left her.

When her brain began to wake up, she heard barking. Loud barking. Crying. Howling. Scratching. It was too much. She knew exactly where she was and when the scene had occurred. But since then, she had gained a couple of new senses. For instance, sensory anxiety. The noise was coming from all around her. Even from above, and she remembered the second floor of cages. Rachel tried to cover her ears, but realized it hurt to try to strain so hard to move her hands… no… wait… paws… toward her head.

"My elbows bend so strangely as a dog," she mumbled.

Back in the real world, everyone who knew what was happening with Rachel had broken out in a sweat.

"This must have been when Rachel was a dog, before Mom and Dad adopted her," Oliver whispered to Jessica.

"She… she looks so scared, Ollie," Jessica said.

"Maybe… maybe she was fine there as a dog, but because she has so many more memories and experiences than she did back then, she's feeling lost and overwhelmed," Oliver said as if he knew it to be fact.

Nick noiselessly slid his way to the next podium to talk to Jessica and Oliver.

"I think she has yet to realize that she's in a simulation. Or at least, that's what it seems like," Nick whispered.

A few seconds later, Avery moved to talk to the twins as Nick had done. She sighed.

"I understand what she's going through. Not to sound like I'm being inconsiderate of her feelings, but I really hope she doesn't accidentally give herself away," Avery muttered.

On the other side of the podiums, although Jake and Josh had no idea what it felt like to be in the fear machine, or what it does to the mind, they had a suspicion that something had gone very wrong.

"Josh, I don't think this is right," Jake said, glancing at Steven, then his brother, then Rachel, and back to Josh.

"Yeah, I don't either. We should go ask Dad if this is normal," Josh exclaimed.

"Sure, but does he even know?" Jake asked. "Before you say anything, Josh, I'm over being mad at him. But I'm genuinely concerned he may not know what's going on here."

"We can try to discreetly ask him," Josh offered, locking eyes with Jake. "We really need to talk to him."

Jake sighed. "I know that I specifically need to clear the air with him, Josh," Jake began in a tone that implied he knew what Josh had hinted to. "But we need talk to him about this Rachel situation. You're right about that."

"Okay, let's go now, then," Josh said as he began to sneak his way behind the other podiums toward Steven.

"Wait!" Jake said, stopping a couple steps behind him.

Josh turned around and looked at his twin with a sense of urgency. "Jake, come on," he said.

"You go," Jake said quickly. "I don't want to interact with him before I can apologize. I definitely can't do it now. We're live. Go on."

Jake turned around and went back to his podium while Josh continued on. He easily made it to Steven.

"Dad," Josh whispered. "Dad, is this level of immersion in the simulator normal?"

"I assure you the simulation is fine. The more susceptible to the fear Rachel is, the more vivid and real the simulation will feel," Steven explained. "There's no need to worry. This time, we really can pull her out if it gets too intense. But now that the machine is properly set up, she will see a pop-up asking if she wants to end the simulation or stay in."

"What if she says no? If it gets too bad and she says no, could you still pull her out?" Josh asked.

"I'm afraid not. But she seems like a strong girl and, as a game-show host, I must trust the participant." Steven responded. "Now, you aren't a game-show host, but as a friend of hers, I must ask: Do you trust the participant?"

Josh didn't hesitate to answer. "Yes. Of course I do!" he exclaimed.

Steven smiled and laid a hand on Josh's shoulder.

"Then there's your answer," he said. Steven glanced up and caught Jake's eye. He hesitated for a moment and, as Josh began to leave and go back to the podium, Steven said, "Tell Jake that I love him no matter what, and tell him that I'm sorry."

Josh smiled and nodded before continuing back to the podium. Once he got back, before Jake could say anything at all, Josh said, "Dad said that this is normal, and she will be fine. He also said that he loves you no matter what, and that he's sorry."

Jake let out a sad sigh and leaned on the podium as if he was carrying the weight of the world on his shoulders. He absentmindedly stared at Steven who was now watching the screen and said, "I love you too, Dad. Always and forever."

24.2

Rachel, back in the simulation, had been barking for about five minutes because it helped her think. She stopped when she finally remembered why she was in the kennel in the first place.

"Fear facing," she muttered. "Oh no! I've made no progress. Wait, if this is supposed to be my fear, why am I enjoying it so much?" she asked herself. "Am I overthinking this?"

She began pacing in her cage, suddenly feeling energized. Her tail began wagging in anticipation for something, but, for… what? Her nose began wiggling and she sniffed.

"Food!" she yelled happily. Since a dog's brain is much smaller than a human brain and all dogs seem to have ADHD by nature, the only thought that filled Rachel's head was food. As she heard employee footsteps coming closer, the food smell became stronger. She could no longer contain herself and, as a dog, excitedly peed.

"Oh no!" she cried. Rachel began to howl sadly and whine as she felt the pads of her paws moisten wherever she stepped. The scent of her urine was strong, and the other dogs began to bark more loudly. The employee who had come to bring the food stopped by Rachel's cage and bent down to be eye-level with her.

"Carol!" he yelled. "This one peed! I believe you're up for the duty!"

"Alright, Mr. Funnyman!" a woman hollered back. "You do your feeding. I'll clean the mess."

The male employee snickered as he continued down the row without placing food at Rachel's cage. A woman assumed to be Carol walked up and crouched down.

"Hello, little one," she said softly. "My name is Ms. Katy, but you can call me Carol. Let's get you all cleaned up."

Carol unlocked the cage door, scooped Rachel up, and began walking toward the reception office of Rachel's old kennel. She remembered that the employees had to walk through the reception office and go through another room to get to where they groomed the animals. Before Carol opened the reception office door, Rachel heard high pitch screaming, like kids playing. She yipped in fear as she remembered exactly what had happened that day—what was waiting for her in the reception room.

As the door swung open, her fears were confirmed. A small blond boy and a larger boy with brown hair were running around the room and riling up the smaller children. The receptionist was running around the room asking the children to stop and the parents to settle down their children, but to no avail.

Suddenly, the big brown-haired boy ran straight into Carol, knocking Rachel out of her grasp. Now on the floor, Rachel darted left and right trying to avoid being trampled by all the people running around. After a minute of running and panicking, Rachel found the corner and hid behind a decorative flowerpot. She could see Carol scanning the room, trying to find her. Rachel began barking, but Carol couldn't hear her over the shouting children. Suddenly, she found herself being picked up by the large brown-haired boy. He studied her closely and said three words that no dog in her position would ever want to hear.

"I hate dogs!" he sneered. The boy laughed and began poking her with his bony finger. One poke a bit too rough to the neck made her whine. She began growling and snapped at his finger. "Stop it, roadkill!" he yelled. He put Rachel down, but before she could run away, he kicked her in the stomach and sent her flying.

Rachel began crying at the top of her canine lungs, and Carol spotted her. Carol ran and scooped Rachel up once again. She looked around the room, spotted the boy who kicked Rachel, and bunched her face up into an expression that can only be described as deadly.

"Young man!" she yelled. "You DO NOT kick animals! Do you understand me!?"

The boy came over and pushed Carol, once again causing Carol to release Rachel from her grip. Rachel had had enough. She ran to the door that led to the outside world. She needed to escape. As she approached the door and looked out the clear door, she was taken aback. There was no outside world. Everything was completely blank and white.

"Oh, my geez!" she muttered. "I'm in a simulation! I almost forgot!"

Rachel's tail began to wag again as she became relieved. She thought everything she had just gone through was her real life. But she was wrong! She was in a simulation!

"None of this is real!" she said, yipping in excitement. "But I need to get out of it!"

She now remembered this day vividly. She remembered all the feelings and the horror and isolation she had experienced at this kennel. The only one she ever really liked was Carol. Rachel remembered that this was the day she had escaped from the kennel. This was the day she was found by the Fletchers, who adopted her.

Rachel thought it through and realized she had two options: Hide or fight. She chose to fight.

Rachel turned around to see that the manager of the kennel was now attempting to pull the horrible boy away from Carol. Even though it was all a simulation, a blood-boiling rage filled Rachel, and she snarled. She howled a battle cry and charged. Everyone in the room had stopped running when they heard Rachel's battle howl. Even the horrible boy with the brown hair looked over.

"Perfect!" Rachel growled. "Now you can watch as my teeth and claws tear you to shreds, you worthless heathen!"

Rachel lunged and bit into the boy's outer thigh as hard as she could, and she heard him scream in pain.

"I can't believe I was ever too frightened to take you down!" she yelled. And then, the world faded to black.

Rachel closed her eyes. When she opened them again, she was sitting in a chair being unstrapped and unwired by Steven.

"Bow wow WOW, ladies and gentlemen! That was quite a show!" Steven cheered. Rachel blinked, still recovering from the shock of it all. Steven tapped her on the shoulder. She looked up at him.

"Would you like to tell us how you feel, Rachel Fletcher?" Steven asked as he handed her the announcer mic.

Rachel's eyes wandered the room as if seeing everything in a whole new light, and she smiled euphorically.

"I… I can't remember the last time I felt so weightless. I feel so in control!" she shouted happily.

As Steven took the mic back, he smiled very genuinely, put his hand on her shoulder and said, "God bless you, sweetie."

Rachel's smile never left her face as she walked back to her podium feeling like she was floating.

"Well, folks!" Steven bellowed. "That was quite an emotional roller coaster, and what an exciting one too! It had a beautiful ending. Let's take a five-minute break and then we'll be back with the next participant."

24.3

Right after the cameras cut, the gang sprinted backstage and enveloped Rachel in the worlds' most disorganized hug.

"Wow, Rachel!" Will exclaimed. "That was super freaking awesome!"

All her friends chimed in in agreement and settled down. Everyone sat on the floor.

"In all seriousness though," Jessica began, "are you okay?"

"I'm fine," Rachel answered, unconsciously moving her hand to her stomach where the boy landed that very real-feeling kick.

Jason peered closely at her. "Are you sure?" he asked as he pointed to her stomach.

She pulled her hand away and quickly said, "What? What do you mean? I mean, yeah. I'm fine."

"Are you sure?" Mason copied. "Because it sort of looked like you were holding your stomach."

"Let's take a look at that," Ondrea said, using her Telekinesis to slightly lift Rachel's shirt so that only her bare stomach was visible.

"Oh my God," Nick exclaimed. "I did not expect to see that."

"Yeah," Darla said, "that's a bruise."

"This makes no sense!" Josh said. "I asked Steven whether the system was working correctly this time, and he promised me it was!"

"It was," said Michael, the man of few words.

"How do you know?" Teddy asked. All eyes turned toward Michael.

"During the one-hour intermission, I studied the chair for a bit. It worked the right way this time," he explained.

"Might just be a Superhero thing," Jake said distractedly.

"Are you okay, bro?" Josh asked.

"Uh, yeah, yeah, I'm good." Jake answered. "Hey, do you know if Dad's busy right now?"

"He's getting ready for the next round, but he always says that he will never not have time for his kids," Josh responded.

Jason looked at Oliver and cringed.

"What?" Josh asked.

Oliver answered, "Double negatives, Josh."

"Yeah, no one likes them," Jason finished.

"I'll be right back, guys!" Jake called.

Jake ran out from behind the curtain and found Steven talking to the cameraman about angles. Steven saw his son and turned to face him. Before Steven had a chance to say anything, Jake threw his arms around his father.

"Dad, I'm really sorry!" he exclaimed.

Steven ended the hug and sat down in a nearby chair to be eye-level with Jake.

"Son, I have never been so stupid in my entire life," Steven began. "I messed up big time, so… I'm sorry."

Jake's face twisted into a look of confusion. "What do you mean you messed up?" Jake asked. "What does that mean?"

"Not only could I have been a better father to you and your brother, but I also could have been a better influence." Steven explained. "I… I think I'm in trouble, and I wouldn't usually be telling you this since I never want to get you in trouble, but… you, your brother, and your new friends all seem to have a bold and brave presence. I need your help, but later. Right now, get behind the curtain. We're starting again in thirty seconds."

Jake began slowly walking back to the curtain, trying to process everything his father had just said. He was two-thirds of the way back to the curtain when he stopped, turned around and asked from a distance, "Dad, what exactly did you do? Give me the short version."

Steven looked at his son with a vivid expression of horror and guilt.

"I think I made a deal with the devil," Steven said.

TWENTY-FIVE

In Which Nick Earns His Stripes

And we are back once again, ladies and gentlemen!" Steven announced as all the participants lined up at their podiums. "Nicholas Gator please come forward!"

As Steven ushered a very nervous Nick into the fear chair, Steven said something to Nick with no intention of sounding creepy, but it sounded creepy, nevertheless.

"See you later, alligator!" he said with a goofy smile on his face.

As Nick sat down in the chair, he let out a nervous laugh and mumbled, "After a while, crocodile." Nick sighed and closed his eyes as Mr. Atrius began hooking the wires to his head and Steven strapped him in.

Once Mr. Atrius stepped back, Steven whispered, "Your father told me about your military background. Don't worry, I'm no snitch. Being in the military must be very fear inducing, so be brave, soldier."

That statement left Nick's brain spinning as he closed his eyes and entered the simulation. Nick knew that Steven mentioning his military background was going to make this simulation seem fearfully real. Before he opened his eyes, he thought about the panic attack he'd had in history class, and he took a deep breath.

"No way fear is going to get the best of me this time," he mumbled. Nick opened his eyes. "Whoa, what?"

What he saw before him was not related to the military at all. No. It was his old bedroom. But there were parts missing, and it looked faded and foggy in some areas.

"I've been forgetting about this place," he said to himself.

He looked directly at one of the faded missing sections and tried to remember what was there, but he couldn't pull it up because of the gaps in his memory. He sat down on his bed and bunched up the covers in his hands.

"Why am I reliving this?" he asked. "I'm not afraid of my room."

After a few minutes, Nick took off his shoes and socks. He hopped down and walked around his room, feeling his soft carpet between his toes. He never realized how much he missed this place. Nick put his socks back on, leaving his shoes by the bed, and opened the door. He barely got a chance to take in the hallway before he heard shouting.

"No way," he muttered. "That's Mom and Dad."

He ran down the stairs, throwing caution to the wind. Even if it was just a simulation, he needed to hug his mom. One thing Nick knew about his mother is that she was the reason he was sent to the military in the first place—because she could not accept that Nick had Powers. Her exact logic and reasoning were lost to Nick; all he knew was what his dad had told him. He heard his parents in the kitchen aggressively arguing. He was about to burst in to hug his mom but stopped when he heard what they were arguing about. They were arguing about him.

"I don't understand, Lisa!" Damian said. "The boy has Powers, just like me! How do you not get that?"

"I understand, but I don't care!" she yelled. "He uses his Powers for EVERYTHING! He cleans his room with them, he makes food with them, he even walks the dog with them!"

"Then all I need to do is tell him to ease up a bit, hon!" Damian exclaimed. "I'll just do that! But, you have to admit, he cleans his room, makes us dinner, and it's just very impressive how he walks the dog with Magic!"

"Who knows what his Dark Magic could be doing to our dog?" she said.

"Just because it's called 'dark' magic doesn't mean it's only used for evil!" Damian said with a hint of frustration. "That's just what our ancestors labeled it—because of the times!"

"Damian, he's joining the military! That's final!" Lisa exclaimed.

"That's also illegal, sweetie!" he responded. "He's only ten years old for God's sake!"

Nick almost jumped off the stairs when he heard that. He shook his head as he focused back on the conversation at hand.

"I don't know what else to do about this!" Lisa shouted. "He'll never stop using his Magic like this!"

"And sending him to his DEATH is going to stop him?" Damian yelled.

"Oh, please!" Nick's mother countered with a laugh. "He won't DIE! Have you seen that boy?"

"Lisa, do you not realize what this is all adding up to?" Damian exclaimed. "Here, let me add it up for you. You can't enlist him illegally. The government is by far the worst entity to find out that he has Powers. He's just a kid! He doesn't know how to fight! He's only ever used his Power for chores. He's never had to deal with people SHOOTING at him with GUNS!"

"Damian, love, he has Healing Powers! The military would love him!" Lisa said. "I've already called the General he'll be working under anyway."

Damian screamed in anger. "You did what!?" he yelled. "I can't believe you would do this! You're a psychopath!"

"Oh, shut up!" she screamed. "When the men come and pick him up tomorrow, I should tell them to take you too!"

"WHAT!?" Damian screeched. "What the hell is wrong with you, woman? This is your son! And he is also MY son!"

"What are you going to do? Use your Dark Magic on me?" Lisa snickered.

"How about a divorce?" Damian screamed. "How does that sound?"

The kitchen went silent for a moment, and Nick peeked his head out from behind the corner to see what was going on. At this point, he wasn't very focused on his original goal—which was to see his mother's face. But when he looked at her, he was shocked to see that she didn't have a face at all—because Nick couldn't remember what his mother looked like. He flinched and fell backward, making a thump. His faceless mother stomped toward him so aggressively that Nick's eyes began to water. Damian saw that Nick had been listening, and he stood in between him and Lisa. Nick was at a loss for words.

"Look what you've done!" Damian growled. "You've scared him!"

"At least now he knows!" she countered, walking closer to Damian.

Nick had never felt more helpless than he did at that moment. He did the only rational thing he could think of. He stood up and grabbed Damian's hand. Ten-year-old Nick would probably have hugged Damian's leg for comfort. But this Nick—although in desperate need of comfort—stood by his father. He still couldn't speak.

"That's my boy," Damian whispered.

As Nick's fuming and faceless mother began walking toward them, Nick exploded in anger. He screamed and punched her, knocking her out. Damian let go of Nick's hand and turned to stare at his son. Before either of them could say anything, Nick lost consciousness.

When Nick opened his eyes again, he found himself in a hospital tent. He sat up, swung his legs over the edge of the cot and stood up. He immediately collapsed. Nick looked down and saw a makeshift splint around his leg.

"Great," he muttered through his teeth. "Just what I need."

Suddenly, Nick felt a tingling sensation in his hurt leg and gasped. He knew what was happening; he was unintentionally using his Healing Power to fix his leg. Up until this point, Nick had been doing a really good job reminding himself that this was a simulation, but now… now he was confused, as well as horrified that this might be real.

"Not normal. That is definitely not normal at all," Nick said to himself. He started tearing off the splint and inhaled sharply as the wood scraped his leg leaving a small cut. "This really is just not my day."

He stood up and began to look around. There were a couple of rows of cots lined up. Some of them were back-to-back, and others were scattered in random places.

A familiar face walked into the medical tent and made a beeline for Nick. It was Spencer. When Nick got to basic training camp, he realized that he had been enrolled in 'a small and exclusive private military academy for highly gifted students', run by his mother's friend, the General. That sounded good in theory. But, in reality, he had never seen the General and had actually been tossed straight into the military's basic training as though he were fully grown, with the expectation that he would be deployed and go to combat as soon as his training was complete. So far, Spencer was the only other 'student' that Nick had met.

"Hey there, Mini-man," Spencer said. "Since you're very much up and walking, I guess your leg injury wasn't as bad as everyone thought it was."

Nick cleared his throat and turned to face him. "Uh. Yeah. No," Nick began. "It… it hurts, I guess."

Spencer gave Nick a funny look. "Still mentally recovering from that beating too, huh?" he asked, punching Nick on the shoulder.

Nick looked around and blinked a couple times.

"This is insane," he muttered. "How is this so real?"

He began walking away from Spencer as he tried to remember what the point in all of this was.

"Hey!" Spencer yelled. "I'm talking to you, Mini!"

"Right. Sorry," Nick said as Spencer appeared in his line of sight again.

Spencer knocked on Nick's head. "You in there, Mini?" he asked aggressively. "No wonder you were such an easy target. You hardly say anything at all."

"Right. What exactly happened again?" Nick asked, turning his full attention back toward Spencer. "I must have gotten hit in the head. I don't remember what happened."

Spencer scoffed. "You were in the lunch hall, and you spilled your tray all over Major Kenny," he said. "You got a pathetic little napkin and started wiping off his uniform, but he kneed you in the stomach."

"Oh," Nick said, frowning. He began to pace as he remembered. "Right… This is the day I met you, correct?"

Spencer doubled over in laughter. "Wow!" he laughed. "Very perceptive, Mini!"

Nick smiled. The nickname. Mini-man. He remembered that Spencer began calling him that after the mess with the Major. Spencer used to refer to that day as the 'Mess of the Major.' He wasn't very creative back then.

"Ay, Mini, you've gotta apologize, remember?" Spencer exclaimed, walking out of the tent. "Come on, I'll show you where he is. Then… Good luck, Mini-man."

Spencer walked out of the med tent without looking back. Nick sighed heavily and followed behind.

"I just want this to end," Nick sighed.

A couple minutes later, they arrived at a similar-looking smaller tent, and they stopped.

"Listen, Nick," Spencer said sternly. "You gotta be careful here. The last person who botched a Major apology was dismissed."

"Why do you care so much?" Nick asked.

"Because you're not that bad," Spencer said, slapping Nick on the back. "We can make a soldier out of you, Mini."

Nick was about to enter the tent. Then he suddenly remembered that when he did this the first time, he was a nervous wreck and didn't give the proper greeting. Even though what he'd do now wouldn't change anything in real life, he still wanted to do it correctly. Nick took a deep breath and felt a hand on his shoulder. He turned around and saw Spencer smiling at him.

"You've got your wits about you. You'll do fine. I'll be waiting here for you," he said. Then Spencer pushed Nick, and he stumbled into the tent.

Nick's eyes narrowed as he stared the beast in the face. Major Kenny was big, but he wasn't as muscular as Nick remembered. Then again, that could just be because Nick had grown a backbone. The Major looked up, but when he saw who entered, his eyes narrowed, matching Nick's.

Nick straightened his posture and saluted the Major as one should do. Major Kenny assessed Nick's salute and nodded.

"Rest easy," Major Kenny said as Nick put his hand down to his side and relaxed. "I assume you're here to beg for forgiveness."

"Sir, I don't think I need to beg," Nick said.

The Major leaned forward in his seat and put his elbows on the desk. He raised his eyebrow, showing that he was intrigued. "And why is that, son?"

Nick's mouth felt dry, and a bead of sweat rolled down his neck. "Uhm… I… I'm very sorry sir," Nick began.

He was about to say more when he was cut off by the Major's sigh of disappointment. "If that's all, then you may leave now."

Nick scrunched his face up, mentally kicking himself and took another deep breath.

"Sir, I'm apologizing due to an act that I performed by accident," Nick said calmly. "The fact that I am here apologizing to you, even after you kneed me in the stomach and nearly broke my leg, is quite generous, I must say."

The Major stood up and walked toward Nick, suddenly seeming larger and taller. Nick swallowed and continued despite his rising nerves. "BUT… I did walk into you and spill my tray on your uniform. I did say that I am here to apologize, so, with my pride still intact, I'd like to say that I am truly sorry. But I do not think I deserved the added violence."

Major Kenny stopped in front of Nick and looked down at him. A couple seconds of silence passed, but to Nick, it felt like an eternity. He held his breath.

"Is that all?" the Major asked.

"Yes, sir," Nick said, his voice slightly shaking.

He saluted and hurried out as quickly as possible, but the Major stopped him. "Son, wait," Major Kenny called. "I can appreciate a cadet with spunk."

"Thank you, sir . . . I think," Nick said quietly.

The Major chuckled and smiled. "I'm very observant, Nicholas. For example, I noticed an older soldier push you into my path. I still had to make an example out of you even though you did nothing wrong," he explained. "I was about to come to you to apologize, but the fact you came here surprised me…in a good way. You're an honorable man, Nicholas Gator."

"Wow…" Nick said. "Sir, I don't know what to say."

"I do, young man," he responded. "I'd like to say that you have guts, confidence, respect, honor, and will. That's exactly what we're looking for here. We'll make a soldier out of you yet."

Nick smiled as the Major held out his hand. Nick grabbed it firmly and shook it. "I'm excited, sir. Thank you, sir," Nick said happily.

Major Kenny's smile widened, and he released the handshake. "You're free to go, soldier," he exclaimed. "And no need to salute this time."

Wordlessly, Nick exited the tent to see Spencer grinning. "Good job, Mini," Spencer said. "I thought you were screwed."

"Thanks, Spence," Nick exclaimed and let out a laugh. Spencer put his arm around Nick's shoulders, and they began walking to the training grounds.

"Mini and Spence, the justice duo," Spencer announced as if he had an audience. "We're going to be good friends."

Nick felt a pressure in his head, and he closed his eyes. When he opened them, he saw Steven. He looked around and grinned. All his friends were staring at him. Steven began unstrapping him while Mr. Atrius unplugged the wires. As soon as his hands were free, Nick gave everyone a thumbs up. Everyone began clapping.

"Are you alright, Nick?" Steven asked while covering his announcer mic.

"Yeah… Yeah, I'm alright. Just a bit shocked," he replied.

Steven smiled, cleared his throat, and began speaking into the mic.

"A salute to you, Nicholas Gator!" he announced. "How do you feel? The world wants to know."

"About eighty pounds lighter," he answered. He thought about Spencer. "I miss Spencer."

Steven looked at him sympathetically and said, "I'm sorry. He seems like a good friend."

"He is," Nick said. "Thanks Steven."

"Of course. It's time for the intermission! See you in five!" Steven announced.

The cameras cut and everyone went backstage. All the kids sat in a circle in silence for a minute until Michael spoke up. "I'm sorry about your mother."

Nick had almost forgotten about that as he had been caught up in the excitement of the Major.

"Right," Nick sighed, suddenly missing Damian as well.

"Hey, Nick," Ondrea began. "If you really miss your dad and Spencer, you could call them quickly."

"You're right," Nick said as he pulled out his phone.

He clicked on his dad's contact and the phone began ringing.

"Put it on speaker!" Avery said.

Nick looked at her with a confused expression. "Okay, sure, but why?"

"We want to talk to him too," Oliver said, shrugging.

"Okay, sure." Nick said as he put the phone on speaker.

After two more rings, it went to voicemail and, instead of leaving a voicemail, Nick called again. When it went to voicemail once more, he left a message:

"Hey, Dad. It's Nick. I don't know whether you saw my fear simulation, but I just want to say that I really miss you. Call me soon. I'm a bit worried since you didn't answer. I love you." He ended the call, and the voicemail went through.

"Guys, that was weird," Nick said. "He almost always answers the first time. Since he didn't answer the first time, he'd most certainly answer the second time but... he didn't. That's a bit worrying."

"I'm... I'm sure he's fine," Jessica said. "Maybe he's just using the bathroom."

"Probably," Nick said, with a little laugh. "I've seen his eating habits, so you may be correct."

"Give Spencer a call," Darla said. "At least you'll get to talk to him."

Nick rang Spencer, but there was no answer. After trying again five times, Nick dropped his phone in his lap and put his face in his hands.

"My God. What's going on?" he asked.

At this point, his friends were beginning to worry as well.

"You have Spencer's dad's number, right?" Josh asked. "If you do, call him and see what's going on."

"Good idea, man!" Teddy said. "Do that, Nick."

Nick picked up his phone again and clicked on Vixsten's number. He picked up immediately.

"NICK!" he yelled. "Is my son with you?"

"I was just calling to ask you if he was okay!" Nick exclaimed, his eyes wide. "I tried calling him six times, but he never picked up!"

"Oh, no! I've called him like a BILLION times, and he hasn't picked up!" Vixsten shouted.

"Well, this is just awful," Mason muttered.

"My dad!" Nick said, "Has he called you?"

"No, I haven't gotten a call from him," Vixsten replied. "Why is that relevant?"

"He's not answering his phone either!" Nick exclaimed, his breathing becoming rapid. "I'm really worried about him, especially now! Call him. See if he answers!"

Vixsten immediately hung up.

"Oh, God, I hope my dad picks up," Nick exclaimed. He looked at his hand and noticed he was trembling. He held his hand in front of his face. "No. This isn't right," he mumbled.

"Nick, why are you shaking?" Will asked. "Are you having a panic attack?"

"No," Jason answered. "He's not. There's something off with him. It's been like that ever since the Heal he gave Jake. Maybe even before that."

"Oh. I hope it wasn't my fault," Jake said quickly. "I'm sorry."

"No, no, no," Nick assured him. "It definitely wasn't your fault."

"Oh, man," Oliver said to Nick. "Jason's right, bud. Your energy is all off. It's… depleting."

"Why do most of the bad things happen to me?" Nick sighed, putting his head in between his knees.

"It kind of makes sense," Rachel exclaimed. "Your main energy is Dark Magic."

"She's got a point," Teddy said. "In the past, bad things seemed to happen to you and Spencer quite often. Oliver's just got bad luck."

Suddenly, Nick's phone rang. He jumped in surprise and fumbled to get it out of his pocket. He answered.

"Boss man, is my dad okay?" Nick asked. Vixsten stayed quiet on the call for a moment. Nick didn't like that. "VK, is Damian alright?" he repeated urgently.

Vixsten's voice came through the phone softly. "I called him several times… No answer," he whispered. "Nick… something is horribly wrong."

A woman from the crew came backstage. "Thirty seconds, kids. Get ready!" she said.

"I've got to go, VK, I'm so sorry," Nick said. "I will figure this out even if it's the last thing I do. I promise!"

"Nick, for God's sake, be careful!" Vixsten said right before Nick hung up.

"Twenty seconds, kids!" The woman called out.

As Team HOPE lined up to go out again, Michael said, "I know I'm new to this, but, if there's one thing I know, it's that we can and will figure this out, Nick. We'll do it together."

Steven began counting down. "Three. Two. One. Welcome back and let's see…"

"Thanks," Nick said to Michael. He took a deep breath as everyone ran out to their podiums.

TWENTY-SIX

In Which Jason Is Forced To Leave Home

After Steven welcomed the audience back and the kids went to their podiums, it was Jason's turn to come forward. "Jason, come on down to this chair and let the fear conquering begin!" Steven yelled excitedly.

Initially, Jason had been more excited about this segment than any of his friends. He had loved this show and had watched it obsessively over the summer. But after everything he'd seen happen with his friends during filming today, he'd become less sure that this segment deserved his eager anticipation. Now that it was his turn, he felt 100 percent unsure—and 100 percent unprepared.

Jason didn't move. When Steven announced his name again, he still didn't move. In fact, he didn't show any sign that he had even heard Steven. Mason elbowed his brother in the side, and Jason jumped.

"Are you okay?" Mason whispered. He put his hand on Jason's shoulder and became aware that Jason was shaking. Mason could feel the panic rising in his brother.

"Hey, could you give us a minute?" Mason asked, turning toward Steven.

"Of course," Steven answered, forming an empathetic smile. "Five minutes."

As Mason grabbed his twin's hand and led him backstage, their friends turned to watch them go with the same question on each of their faces: "Do you need us?" Mason shook his head and continued toward the back. Once they had made it to the backstage area, Mason let go of Jason's hand and sat crisscross on the floor. Jason remained standing.

Jason became aware of the silence and looked up, realizing he was no longer on the stage. Then, he looked down to find his brother sitting in front of him.

"I did that panic thing again, didn't I?" Jason muttered.

"It's called a panic attack, and yes, you did." Mason responded. Jason put his hands behind his back and began pacing. "Let it out, Jace. You know I'm a decent listener… at least when I want to be."

Jason took a deep breath and began talking. "I feel completely out of it. As if I'm having an out-of-body experience. You know how that is, right? When you feel like you're watching yourself from someone else's perspective?"

"Okay," Mason said. "Continue."

Jason nodded. "I've never felt like this before. I feel like… like I'm not really… here."

"You feel nauseous?" Mason questioned.

"No, I feel like the only evidence I have that I'm real is that when I look down, I see myself," he exclaimed.

"You're clearly trying to say you don't want to be here. So much so, that your mind is trying to convince you that you're not really here," Mason observed.

"How in the world could you possibly have known that?" Jason asked as he stopped walking and turned to stare at Mason.

"Twin sense, duh," he said, smiling.

Jason sat down on the floor next to his brother. "In that case, what else am I feeling? You may be able to say it better than I can," he said.

Mason aggressively put his hand on Jason's head, slapping him in the process, most likely on purpose. Jason smiled and elbowed Mason in the ribs. He shushed Jason and closed his eyes. Mason began humming, and Jason rolled his eyes.

"I'm getting something," Mason said. He began rubbing his hand around the top of Jason's head, completely messing up his hair. Without stopping, Mason said, "I see now. You're feeling almost weightless. You don't want to care about anything right now, but you have to."

Jason knocked Mason's hand off his head and fixed his hair. "That's pretty accurate," he said. "How are you this accurate with my feelings?"

"Because I feel the same way, bud," Mason said. The smile left his face. He sighed, slouched over and stared at the floor.

Jason put his arm around his brother's shoulders and scooted closer to him. "Stop feeling sad," Jason demanded. "Now I feel bad for making you feel sad."

"But you're not focused on being sad anymore?" Mason asked.

"Yeah, well, now I'm focused on the fact that you're being sad," Jason answered.

Mason looked at his twin and smiled. "See, now you're focusing on something else," he remarked. "I don't actually feel sad, ya moron."

"Dude, seriously?" Jason said, pulling his arm back. "Then why did you say you did?"

"Well, now you're no longer focusing on your negative emotions, and you're spending energy focusing on something more important than sadness—me," Mason explained. "What I'm trying to say is this: whenever you're sad, scared, or angry, don't spend your energy on that thought. Spend your energy on something you find worth spending energy on. So, spend it on something you love."

Jason stared straight ahead and stayed quiet for a few seconds. "Whoa…" he mumbled. "I can't believe I'd never thought of that! It's genius!"

"That's what I'm here for," Mason said, laughing. "But Jace? This fear thing, facing your fears? It seems like it sucks, and it probably will. But I'll be here for you when you get out, as will the rest of our group. Just remember that it's all fake."

"Thanks," Jason said. They stood up and walked out together.

As soon as they came within view of the camera and went back to their podiums, Steven began clapping theatrically and turned to face the camera. "Alright, ladies and gentlemen, let's do this!" He faced Jason and smiled at him. "Are you ready?"

Jason glanced at Mason and then back toward Steven. "As ready as I'll ever be, I guess!" he exclaimed, putting on a fake smile for the camera.

26.1

The second Jason sat down in the chair, he closed his eyes and waited. About a minute later, he opened his eyes and his breath nearly left him.

Jason was laid out on a black rock that would most likely give a normal person first-degree burns. He got up and took in the smoking black mountain of rock and ash and the seemingly endless jet-black pillars.

"Oh, Lord," he muttered.

Despite the giant black volcano and the searing hot rocks, he noticed the air was as cool as a dry spring day.

"Oh, God," he said. "This is not the best time for this place to resurface." Jason didn't want this specific area to resurface because this was where he and Mason were from; this was their home planet. He knew that once he got out of this simulation, he was going to have a lot of explaining to do to his friends.

Jason began walking around to get his bearings, keeping in mind that this was a fear simulation.

"Mason's probably flipping out right now," he said to himself.

A strong gust of wind caught Jason's attention. Dust flew into his eyes, and he was surprised by the fact that he felt it. Jason knew there was no point in rubbing his eyes because the dust wouldn't come out like that. In fact, it would only get worse. He put his palms against his eyes and discreetly rinsed them out with his water vapor. Once he blinked a few times and let the dusty water drip down from his eyes, he continued forward, but in the direction the gust of wind had come from.

Jason stopped as he realized something. He was home. Although Jason was aware this is a fear simulation, he was also aware that fear was nowhere in sight. He took this opportunity to take in his home. He looked at the dust and sand beneath his feet and remembered the sand fights he and his brother used to have. They heard from their great-grandmother that people on Earth would have snowball fights. Jason thought it was barbaric at the time, but Mason really wanted to try it, so they went outside and began the fighting.

As Jason thought about this memory, he heard voices. He quickly went to hide behind a pillar of rock. He peaked out and saw five-year-old Mason and… himself. Five-year-old Jason.

From behind the pillar, Jason smiled. Seeing himself as he was before he came to Earth almost made him laugh out loud. His glasses were made out of volcano glass! And his charcoal pencil wa sticking out of his back pocket. What was mostly funny to Jason wasn't himself, but Mason. He remembered how his brother ALWAYS had dust and sand coating his hair and clothes, just as he did now. Jason would sit inside one of the wide pillars that Mason hollowed out and write on the walls with his charcoal pencil, while Mason rolled around on the floor outside.

"Mason!" Little Jason yelled. "I really don't know why you'd want to do this whole 'snowball' thing. It sounds stupid."

"YOU sound stupid!" Little Mason yelled, laughing.

Little Jason rolled his eyes and laughed with his brother. "You're so immature, brother," he said.

That just made Little Mason fall on the ground and roll around on the sand, laughing even harder.

Jason stared at Little Mason from behind the pillar and smiled sadly. Seeing the days when they were younger and much more naive made him long for that simple time. It had been a long while since Jason had that depressing thought. The one thing Jason had never even hinted to his brother was how much their old home lingered in his mind. Jason was sure his brother never thought about it at all—or at least he'd never said anything about it.

Jason snapped out of his daze when he heard someone shriek. He looked over at the Littles and saw that Little Mason had compacted sand together using his Earth element and hurled it at Little Jason. Little Mason began laughing again. When Little Jason began to cry, however, he quieted and walked toward his brother.

"Did I hurt you?" Little Mason asked as he timidly reached out to hold his hand.

Little Jason turned around and began to storm off.

"Wait!" Little Mason called, his voice shaking as if he was about to cry. "I didn't mean to hurt you!"

From behind the pillar, Jason smirked. He remembered this moment. This was what he used to refer to as his "favorite trick." As Little Mason began to follow his brother, Little Jason swiftly scooped up some sand, used his Water element to turn it into a loose ball of mud, turned around, and chucked it at Little Mason.

Little Mason stood there in shock, and his lip began to quiver. Little Jason frowned and began walking toward his brother thinking that he was about to cry. Suddenly, Little Mason chucked a sand ball toward him. He tried to duck out of the way, but it hit him right below the neck. They both stood still for a moment, staring into each other's eyes. The two boys used to have random staring contests when they were younger because their grandmother claimed it helped you develop concentration skills. At some point, they stopped using the staring contests for educational reasons and re-purposed their use just for fun, because they thought they were silly and competitive. Now, despite the previous actions of both the boys, neither was sad. They both faked it. In fact, they were smiling. Little Mason was the first to crack. He once again fell to the ground and began rolling around in the sand and dust, laughing.

"You never win these staring contests, brother," Little Jason exclaimed right before breaking down into laughter. While his twin brother was laughing, Little Mason hurled a barrage of ping pong sized sand balls at him, leaving small bruises on Little Jason's arms and legs.

"Ah, so that's how you want to play it, then?" Little Jason exclaimed. He moved his hands in a dance-like pattern and pelted Little Mason with hundreds of damp sand balls. By the time he was done, his brother was literally buried in damp, clumpy sand. All except for his head, of course. This time, Little Jason was the first one to start laughing. Little Mason smiled because, even though he had been duped, he was secretly happy to finally see his brother having actual fun—as opposed to reading and writing all the time.

Little Mason decided that his brother had had enough fun, and that it was time to bring out the big guns. "You may have mounded me, but I can break free!" he yelled as he used his Earth element once more to lift the damp sand off himself and throw it to the side.

"So, you're not going to use that sand?" Little Jason asked, still smiling.

"Never!" He responded, "You know I hate using hand-me-downs."

From behind the pillar, Jason still watched. His attention snapped elsewhere when he heard a voice coming from behind him. It was their great-grandmother.

"Kids!" she yelled. "It's time for dinner! You'd better get in here quick and clean yourselves up!"

"Okay, Grammy!" Little Jason called back as their great-grandmother went back inside.

Seeing his Grammy made Jason tear up. She was no longer with him and his brother. No one was. Their current parents weren't even their real parents.

After Jason and Mason were forced to leave their planet with nowhere to go and no one to guide them, they decided to use their extensive knowledge of the stars to find the planet they had heard so much about, Earth. Once they arrived, they walked around expecting to see only a few people. Their Grammy had told them that Earth had people just like them—which was one of the reasons they decided to go there. They were very surprised to find out there were billions of people inhabiting the planet.

They walked around asking everyone they saw question after question.

"Where can we live?"

"Where is the food?"

"Who are you?"

"Can you be our guardian?" Now that Jason really thought about it, that was probably one of the reasons they both were taken to an orphanage. A year later, they were both adopted. Later, when their new parents heard there was a school for kids like them, they were overjoyed to send Jason and Mason to Superhero School. That's how they ended up meeting their friends, and ultimately, ended up here.

As Jason thought about all of this, he realized the scene around him had shifted. The sky was now blood red, and the air felt blisteringly hot, although the heat didn't bother him at all. What bothered him was knowing what day this was; he remembered this day more vividly than any other. As the memories he had tried to block out came flooding back to him, he stepped back.

"Oh, come on, Jason," he said to himself. "How did you forget this was a fear simulation? Of course this was going to happen! It all leads up to this!" Jason mentally kicked himself for forgetting he was in a simulation. This was the day he and his brother were forced to leave their home.

26.2

As Jason was strapped into the fear simulator, Mason and his friends watched anxiously. About two minutes later, when Mason saw where the simulation had placed his brother, he nearly screamed. His suppressed emotions about their home planet came boiling up and he felt as if he was about to throw up or pass out. His emotions were so incredibly strong, and came on so suddenly, that his friends were able to sense it immediately.

They all turned their heads toward him with looks of deep concern, but Mason didn't notice and was too worried to care anyway. Mason stepped out from behind his podium and ran over to Steven.

"Steven!" he barked. "You have to take him out! NOW, NOW, NOW! You have to!"

"Hey, friend, calm down," Steven exclaimed. "You know that your brother will be okay! It's just a simulation." He attempted to put a calming hand on Mason's shoulder, but Mason slapped it away.

"Whoa, champ! You're getting a bit aggressive!" Steven whispered harshly. "Maybe you should go backstage and cool down!"

"No! I can't!" Mason cried. "Please! You have to get him out! Please!" Mason grabbed Steven's hands and clutched them tightly. "Please, you have to take him out!"

"Son, your grip is a bit tight," Steven said fearfully.

Suddenly, Jake, Josh, and Teddy were by his side. "Hey," Jake whispered, "lay off my dad, would you?"

"My brother can't be in there! No one can be there!" Mason exclaimed.

Mason's entire body was shaking, and Steven could feel it. The look on his face combined with the tone of his voice, the shaking, and the unintentional aggression, told Steven that whatever was happening on the screen was a horrible trigger. Steven understood—because this is how he'd felt when his wife had died.

"I can try to get him out," Steven said. "But I'm not sure what will happen to your brother's mind. If you're willing to risk that, then I'll do it—but I'd rather not."

"What do you mean?" Mason asked, lessening the intensity of his grip.

"Well, first of all, just like I said, I don't know what the machine would do to his mind if I unplugged it while he's still inside. Also, I don't want to get sued or arrested in case something does happen to him. It's mainly the first reason though," Steven explained.

Mason let go of Steven's hand and stumbled. "Oh boy," he mumbled. "This is not good. Not good at all."

Teddy grabbed Mason's forearm because it looked like he was about to pass out. Ondrea came over and grabbed his other arm, discreetly sending waves of calm through Mason.

"We'll take him backstage," Ondrea said firmly.

Before they led him away, Mason whispered, "Sorry about the aggression."

Jake and Josh stayed behind to check on Steven while Ondrea and Teddy led Mason backstage. As Mason walked by the rest of his friends, his vision blurred, but he blinked the dizziness away.

His friends stared at him with intense confusion and worry. Before Mason slipped behind the curtain to the backstage area, he knew he needed to say something. It wouldn't answer their questions, but it was all he could say.

Mason opened his mouth and spoke.

"I'm scared."

TWENTY-SEVEN

In Which Times Stands Still

Jason closed his eyes and sat on the ground. He could feel the sand around him getting warmer and warmer as the dust in the air began to float, coating him from head to toe.

"Dear God, this is awful," he mumbled.

He opened his eyes and realized that little Jason and Little Mason were staring at him. They looked older than the scene before, but still young.

"Hey, look at that!" Little Mason said, pointing to Jason. "It's you!"

"What?" Little Jason said as he scratched his head. "No, that must be some strange trick with the light. Because of the red sky and all."

Jason stood up, causing both Littles to scream. "Get off of this planet!" Jason yelled to them. "You're supposed to be leaving this planet!"

Little Jason screamed again and ran off in the opposite direction. Little Mason stayed behind, looking petrified.

Jason began to shake. His anxiety exploded out all at once and he broke down crying. This was a strange thing for Jason. He had never been this emotional before when it came to anxiety, fear, or sadness. Anger was a different story. Mason always said he could be a bit hotheaded.

Jason crumpled to the ground, filled with a range of emotions. Angry at himself for keeping this memory locked away for so long. Guilty for yelling at Mason every time he used to try to talk about it. Depressed at the thought of having to watch his home planet be destroyed once again. He felt someone tap on his shoulder—Little Mason.

"I'm not scared of you!" Little Mason said loudly. "You should be scared of me!"

Through his tears, he laughed at a notion that had been working its way into his brain for years.

"I am," he said. "I am scared of you."

Little Mason took a step forward and kicked Jason on the knee. Jason just laughed.

"I'm scared of you because you're free. This was my home. A little world where I could be alone with my family and my thoughts. Nothing else to worry about…"

Little Mason kicked him again. Jason knew a bruise was forming on his knee. "No one else I had to worry about!" he continued. "This place was freedom. I finally got to go back to this place and experience freedom again. But now I have to watch it be torn apart again!"

Little Mason kicked him again, this time in the stomach. "It sounds like you're more afraid of your home than you are of me!" Little Mason said.

"I am afraid!" Jason cried. "I'm afraid of this place, as well as you! I'm afraid of me!"

"You're a very dramatic person," Little Mason said, sitting down on the ground next to Jason.

Jason heard a screeching noise and looked up to see the rocket launching toward Earth.

"You're supposed to be on that!" he yelled. "Now, I've ruined everything!"

"This is a simulation, moron! I am on the rocket!" Little Mason said. "You didn't travel back in time."

Jason began to laugh.

"Why are you laughing? Are you crazy?" Little Mason asked.

"Maybe I am," Jason said. He began to take deep breaths to calm himself down. "I think I'm just having a panic attack."

"Don't panic. It's just a stupid simulation," Little Mason exclaimed.

As Jason heard the rocket's screech fade away, a thought occurred. "Wait—if you're on that rocket, then how are you still here?"

"I'm a little figment of your microscopic imagination," Little Mason said. "Let me help you feel a little less crazy though."

Suddenly, Little Mason seemed to morph into normal Mason. With his voice slightly deeper than Little Mason's, he asked, "Is this a bit better?"

Mason was no longer coated in sand or had messy hair. Now, he was just normal Mason. Normal Mason, who, just to be realistic, still had messy-looking hair. "I guess it is," Jason mumbled.

Mason pulled what looked to be Jason's phone out of his pocket and held it in the air.

"You know what's funny about our home planet?" Mason asked rhetorically. "It doesn't have good Internet, Wi-Fi, or reception."

Jason smiled. "We didn't need all that," he responded, nudging his brother with his elbow. "I'm really glad to see you. It's been lonely in this simulation."

"I'm not really here. It's just a simulation," Mason said. "Your actual brother, however, is losing his mind."

Jason's expression became one of worry, then one of confusion. "How would you know that if you're just a simulation?" he asked.

"Because, you know," Mason responded.

"What do you mean? How would I know?" Jason exclaimed, his voice full of anger.

"Because you can feel this…" Mason pointed to his own head and heart, "in here." He finished as he pointed to Jason's head and heart.

"That was really cheesy," Jason muttered as he tried to hide his smile. "You've always been a cheesy child."

"You know it too," Mason said, smiling. "You know it, and you like it, or else you wouldn't implement that trait of Mason's personality into this simulation. Remember, this is YOUR imagination."

"Yeah, yeah, I know," Jason said. "If you remind me one more time, I might have to unimagine you."

"Hey, this isn't me," Mason said, laughing. "It's you. It's you talking to you through me."

"This is paradoxically annoying and soothing at the same time," Jason said. "I assume since I'm under a lot of stress right now, my brain's defense mechanism is portraying me through you—because talking to a copy of myself would be considered unpleasant."

"You could have just said, 'Talking to myself would be weird, so I'm talking to you,'" Mason pointed out. They were both silent for a moment before Mason continued. "You don't have to be afraid of your brother— or of yourself."

Jason turned toward his brother. "So, we're back to this then," he said with a weary sigh.

"Hey, we don't have to talk about this right now," Mason said. "Just know, the longer you put it off, the longer you stay in the sim."

Jason sighed again and said, "Fine, but you know I'm not going to get all emotional… again."

Mason laughed. "Hey, I'm you and even you don't know if that's true or not!" he exclaimed. "Now, why are you so afraid?"

"It's strange because most people would love to go back to the time before they knew all the hardships, just like the Littles back there, but… I'm more afraid of when I didn't really know anything," Jason explained.

"Sure," Mason began. "But why are you so afraid of your brother?"

Jason put his head in his hands and clutched his hair tightly. "I don't know!" he yelled. "Have you ever had a moment where you just don't know?"

Mason chuckled and said, "I don't know, have you?"

Jason hugged his knees. "Oh, God," he whispered. "I'm so afraid."

Suddenly, Jason felt Mason's arm around his shoulders. "Tell me why," Mason said quietly.

"You're Mason!" Jason cried. "You're incredible and funny, but you're such an idiot! You were even MORE of an idiot when we were little like we were in this time here," Jason gestured to the setting around them. "You were a huge idiot and so was I! We didn't know anything, and we still don't know anything, but we knew even less then. I mean here. We know less here!"

When Jason didn't say anything else, Mason prompted, "And…"

"And, and…" Jason sputtered. "I guess, in my opinion, knowing nothing is scarier than knowing everything. Imagine how much less afraid we would have been when we had to leave our planet if we had known everything!"

"You can't put that on yourself," Mason whispered. "You know that your experiences make you who you are. You had experienced nothing on your planet, but now… now you're different. Now, you've seen it all. But why are you specifically afraid of your brother?"

Jason sighed and took a few controlled breaths. "It might have been an in-the-moment thing. Or…maybe it's multiple things. I'm afraid FOR my brother. I'm afraid OF him because… he always has so much fun despite it all. He's acting like he's innocent, but he's not. It's never bothered me before, but now, in this moment, it is."

Mason smiled. "Maybe you feel this way because of all the emotions you keep bottled up inside. All the emotions that you never let out. All those emotions are keeping you from letting go," he said. "You need to allow yourself to feel—feel what you need to feel."

"Yeah, I guess you're right. I guess Mason has a right to feel happy—or he at least looks like he's happy. No, what am I thinking?" Jason smiled. "Of course, he's happy! I can always sense it." Jason laughed sadly. "I guess it's… it's really the only thing keeping me going."

Mason looked at Jason and said, "If you'd let all the negative energy that has been building up inside of you go, then…"

"Then I'll be happy," Jason finished. "Then I'll finally be happy!"

"That's right," Mason confirmed. "Well, you'll at least be a big step closer to happiness. And when you are happy, embrace it!"

Jason frowned. "Well, whenever I'm truly happy, I know I'll get sad again."

"Sure, you will!" Mason exclaimed. "You can't constantly be happy forever. You'll always have those sad days. We all do. But in the moments when you are happy, embrace it. Stay in the moment. Look around you and say to yourself, 'Wow, this is incredible.'"

Jason nodded. "Yeah, that sounds right," he said. "That reminds me a bit of what Mason told me before I entered the sim. He told me to think of something that makes me happy whenever I get sad… To focus my energy on what makes me happy."

"Not so much of an idiot now, huh?" Mason exclaimed, punching Jason on the shoulder.

"I guess not," Jason said, laughing.

"I think it's time for you to be off, then," Mason said, standing up. "And, before you go, I know it's difficult for you to sense it in the sim, but your brother is very worried right now. Also, I'm sure you can already figure this out, but Mason isn't all just rainbows and unicorns. He's got some pretty deep stuff inside too."

"Yeah…" Jason mumbled. "I know. It was wrong of me to think otherwise."

"Hey," Mason said, smiling. "It's okay. You were just scared."

"Yeah, I, I was. Not anymore," Jason smiled and closed his eyes. "Thanks Mason, who isn't Mason, and is just me in the form of Mason."

When all the ambient noise faded and Jason opened his eyes, he saw Steven standing in front of him wearing a half smile. Jason blinked a couple of times. He moved his fingers and toes. When Steven unstrapped him from the chair and Jason stood up, his senses finally returned to him. Then… it hit him… hard. Jason nearly tripped when he felt a wave of Mason's grief wash over him.

"My God," he said. Without looking at his friends or focusing on anything else, Jason sprinted backstage to see Mason lying on the ground with Teddy sitting beside him. "Oh my God, Teddy, is Mason okay?" Jason asked frantically. He ran and sat by his brother's body. "Did he faint? Is he dead?"

"Whoa, whoa, whoa! Okay!" Teddy exclaimed as he slowly stood up. "He's fine now. He just fell asleep."

"Oh," Jason whispered.

Everything had finally caught up to him as he stood and staggered toward the wall. While Jason found himself in an early-life crisis, Teddy began waking up Mason. When he sat up and saw his brother, he walked forward briskly, but stopped a couple feet away from him, unsure of what to do.

"I'm still approachable, brother," Jason said. "I haven't gone rabid yet."

Despite Jason making a joke, Mason didn't smile as he usually would. He was too worried about his brother. So, instead of sitting with him or asking how he was, Mason pulled his brother into a tight hug.

Jason could feel Mason's tears. "Dude, I'm okay. It's all okay," Jason said.

The hug went on for two more minutes, before the two of them pulled away, both crying, to sit against the wall. Meanwhile Ondrea came backstage to talk to Teddy.

"Teddy Bear," she said, taking his hand. "Are you okay?"

"Of course. How could I not be when talking to you, angel?" he responded, taking her other hand.

"You're too cute for this world," she said. "Anyway, Steven called for a forty-five minute break and the others want to know if they can come backstage or if the twins need a bit more time."

Teddy looked toward the twins. "Hey guys," he called. "Care for a party?"

Jason looked up, dried his eyes on Mason's sleeve, then said, "I think so."

"Good." Ondrea said as she gestured for the others. "Because you and your bro have A LOT of explaining to do."

TWENTY-EIGHT

In Which Malice Takes Over

Once Team HOPE found a more private place to chat backstage, everyone sat in a line against the wall. Oliver was the first to speak.

"Okay, guys, this was crazy," he said. "Jason and, I assume, Mason have a lot of explaining to do, but we also need to figure out what's going on with Spencer and Damian."

"Jason and Mason first!" Ondrea exclaimed. Jason noticed a hint of anger creeping up in her tone.

"Ondrea, love," Teddy said, "what's going on?"

"That's what THEY need to tell us!" she answered. When Teddy reached to grab her hand, she pulled away and crossed her arms.

"Okay, so it's obvious that you're upset," Jason began, "but…"

"But ease up!" Mason yelled.

"GUYS!" Nick shouted. "Can everyone just shut up! We need to talk about this, so we can then talk about what the heck is going on with my best friend and my dad!"

"Don't yell at my girlfriend, Nick!" Teddy growled.

"I'm not!" Nick exclaimed, "I'm yelling at everyone! This is really stressful for me too, Teddy!"

"Guys," Jason said, "There's really no need for all this."

"That's really easy for you to say, Jason!" Ondrea yelled. "You just want to get out of talking about… about whatever that was…"

Avery interrupted her. "Look, sis, as someone who is literally a DRAGON, I can vouch for them when I say that it's really stressful to be THAT different!"

"We're all 'different' and that's great, but that's no excuse not to share whatever happened!" Rachel said, feeling bad that no one was supporting Ondrea's case, which turned out to be a mistake.

"Rach, I'm not saying that at all!" Avery said. "Also, I was talking to my sister."

"Well… I don't care!" Rachel yelled. "Yeah, I said it! I don't care! Ondrea's getting enough shade thrown at her! Last thing she needs is for her sister to be screaming at her too!"

"I'm just fine on my own, Rachel!" Ondrea snipped. "And, Avery, I know what you mean when you say 'THAT' different."

"Oh, you do?" Rachel exclaimed. "I didn't know you were so smart! What does it mean then?"

Ondrea scowled at Rachel. "It MEANS even though we're all Superpowered freaks, people who come from different planets—and those who were born dragons—are clearly even more freakish!" she yelled.

"Hey!" Rachel hissed, "I was born a Morpher! We were all born with Powers! Don't diss your sister like that!"

"Thanks, Rachel," Avery said. "And, not cool, Ondrea! Seriously, why are you being so mean?"

"Oh, shut up! I'm not being mean! Everyone else is being mean! YOU'RE being mean!" Ondrea screamed. "The only reason YOU'RE being mean to ME is because you're jealous of me!"

Avery laughed. "What? Sis, I'm not jealous of you!" Avery said. "I'm proud of you, always. You know that! I'm just really confused about why everyone is suddenly fighting!"

"Maybe you're just INCREDIBLY STUPID!" Ondrea yelled.

That comment shut Avery up. Meanwhile Nick and Teddy were still going at each other's throats.

"I already told you!" Teddy shouted, "I don't care how stressed you are! You don't get to yell at my girlfriend like that!"

"Oh, my GOD!" Nick said. "Teddy, get over yourself! Ondrea doesn't need you to stick up for her all the time! She's clearly doing a very good job of it on her own!"

"She's being ganged up on, Nick!" Teddy exclaimed, "You're her friend! You should be defending her!"

"Well, that could go both ways, Teddy!" Nick said. "You're Jason and Mason's friend! You should be defending them!"

"She's my GIRL!" Teddy said. "I'm defending her first. So, you don't yell at my girl!"

At this point, Will thought he'd intervene. While he was always a supportive person, he was typically better at starting arguments than breaking them up.

"Oh my God, guys!" Will said, "This is so stupid! Nick, you are so stupid! So are you, Teddy! Just apologize or something!"

"I'm not apologizing until Nick apologizes!" Teddy yelled. "And stay out of this, Will!"

"I'm not apologizing for making a better point than Teddy Bear over there!" Nick exclaimed.

"GUYS!" Jessica yelled. "STOP!"

When the fighting continued, Oliver felt he had lost control of his group. He immediately began losing confidence in himself—which wasn't at all like him. Jessica sensed this.

"Ollie," she said as she took her brother's hand, "let's go talk."

Oliver got up without hesitation as Jessica pulled him to a separate area of the stage.

"What's wrong?" she asked.

"All this fighting, Jess," he answered. "It's… insane."

Jessica sighed and sat down on the floor. "Yeah, this isn't how friends act… or siblings."

Oliver nodded. "Did you hear how Ondrea responded to Avery?" he said. "She called Avery incredibly stupid! She would NEVER say that!"

"I know, Ollie, but… I didn't pull you out here to talk about them," she said. "I want to talk about you. That lack of confidence you just fell into? Not liking it. It's not you."

"I know," he said. "I don't like it either and, you're right. It's not me. Besides, they're wasting a bunch of time arguing."

"Yeah, I know," Jessica agreed. "This isn't like them. Something is going on."

Suddenly the twins heard someone stomping their way.

"… really don't care, Teddy. I'm not talking to you about this anymore!" Nick called. He stopped in front of the twins and took a deep breath. "Sorry, guys."

"Um… What was that?" Oliver asked. "Why were you and Teddy arguing so aggressively?"

"He thought I yelled at JUST Ondrea to shut up, and he got mad about that," Nick explained.

"Didn't you yell at everyone to shut up?" Jessica asked.

"Yeah, that's what I told him!" Nick exclaimed, throwing his hands up in the air.

"Yeah, but you shouted that at him," Oliver reminded him.

Nick stayed silent for a couple seconds, then he sighed. "Yeah… probably wasn't my best idea," he muttered. "Why did I continue arguing? I have no clue. Suddenly, I realized I was being a moron, and I decided to escape."

Jason came speed walking from around the corner.

"Dear God, guys, it's just not slowing down!" he gasped as he plopped down against the wall. "I had to get out of there. I was beginning to get a headache."

Oliver laughed. "Yeah, me too. I'm glad Jess pulled me out of there," he said. "I was starting to zone out."

"Huh…" Nick said. "I was getting a headache too. I've still got one."

"All three of you?" Jessica asked as she sat down next to Jason. Oliver followed her example, but Nick began pacing.

"Apparently," Nick said. "You know, I've still got one. How about you guys?"

"Mine has dialed down considerably," Jason said.

"So has mine," Oliver seconded.

Nick took a deep breath and sat to face everyone. "Okay, let's list the facts here," Nick said.

"While everyone is still losing their minds?" Jessica asked.

"I have a feeling that's not going to end any time soon," Jason mumbled. He held his hand tightly around his stomach.

"What's going on with you?" Nick asked cautiously. "How do you know it's going to keep going for a while?"

"It's a gut feeling," Jason responded. "In fact, it's a bit more than that. There's a rage inside Mason that I've NEVER felt before—which is strange because this is definitely not the most rage-inducing thing we've ever partaken in."

"I felt that bubbling inside of me too," Jessica whispered, fear creeping its way into her head.

"Me too," Oliver said. "Now, it's gone, and I feel my confidence again, but it was such a strange sensation. It's like I felt so small over there, I come over here and, two seconds later, my confidence is back and my headache begins to significantly lessen."

"Same for my headache," Jason said. "And, I can't lie, I was feeling that rage too, which is probably the reason I had so much trouble sensing it in my brother at that moment. Then, I took a deep breath, realized that anger is not who I am, and, when I did, I was able to sense Mason's. It scared me, so I left and came over here. Strange thing though. Now, I can't sense Mason at all, which is… really frightening."

"Now that you say it," Jessica said, "I can't Sense anyone other than the people in this conversation. I know they're all still there because I can hear them, but I can't Sense them."

"I can't either," Nick said. He winced and put his head in his hands. "And this dang headache… it's driving me crazy."

"Still got it?" Oliver said. "Mine's gone."

"Mine is also gone." Jason seconded.

"This is… not normal. NOT at all!" Jessica whispered.

"It'll be okay, Jessi," Oliver said as he put his arm around her shoulders.

Nick shot up straight and began to pace again, but more aggressively. "No. No it won't be," he said. "There's… there's Dark Magic in the air. Not here. But there. EVERYWHERE around our friends!"

No one said anything for a minute until Jason spoke up.

"No kidding," he said, standing up. "Nick, you're right. I feel it. Oh no, Mason!"

Oliver stood up and grabbed Jason's forearm before he could go running into Dark Magic.

"Geez, Jason," Oliver said. "Think. You can't just go running back into that."

Jason sighed and turned to face his friends, all of whom had stood up. "What do we do?" he asked.

"Nick could give it a shot," Jessica suggested.

"She's right, I could," Nick agreed. "My main energy is Dark Magic, and I know the effect is has, so I can resist it better."

"As long as you're careful!" Oliver said.

"Wait!" Jason exclaimed. He turned so he was looking solely at Nick and stared at his face for a second. "How is your headache?"

"It's lessening," Nick lied.

"Okay, go for it," Jason said, jokingly pushing Nick around the corner.

Nick gave Jason a dirty look and continued walking toward his friends. They were still arguing.

"I don't know where my brother went!" Mason yelled. "He probably wants to get away from YOU!"

"You're his brother!" Darla said. "He's definitely getting away from YOU! Right, Will?"

"Yeah!" Will yelled. "Even I don't want to be around you!"

"Can everyone just shut up before I have to go and get my dad?" Jake yelled as he held Josh's arm.

Nick hadn't noticed Jake and Josh in the crowd before he left, so he went over to talk to them.

"Hey, guys," Nick said. "You okay?"

"Yeah," Josh answered. "But what's wrong with them?"

"So, you guys don't feel an uncontrollable urge to scream at people right now?" Nick asked Jake and Josh.

"Nope," Jake replied. "Seriously, what's going on with them? If this doesn't stop soon, I'm getting Steven."

Nick's knee-jerk reaction was to grab them both, so he did.

"Hey!" Josh exclaimed. "Relax."

"Sorry," Nick sighed as he released them both. "I just don't want your dad involved in this. This isn't your normal slap fight. This is Dark Magic."

"Oh," Jake muttered. He took a deep breath. "Nick, you've got this?"

"Yeah, I'll take care of it," Nick assured them. "If anyone tries to come to this part of the backstage area, can you deter them?"

"Sure," Jake said. The twins then went to stand guard.

28.1

"Oliver and Jess both left!" Mason exclaimed. "Clearly, they're tired of..."

"Everyone!" Avery yelled. "Clearly they're tired of everyone because we can't stop arguing over stupid things!"

"She's right!" Nick screamed.

Everyone stopped arguing and went quiet.

"You nuts are under the influence of Dark Magic! It's every-where!" Nick explained. "You can't see it, but it's in the air! That's why you're all at each other's throats! Can't you Sense it? Please!"

"He's right," Avery said. "I knew something was off. I… I just couldn't put my finger on it."

Everyone nodded.

Mason gasped in realization. "Whoa!" he said. "Guys, I'm so sorry! I didn't mean any of the things I said. That was so uncalled for. Not cool."

"I should be the sorriest," Ondrea mumbled sadly. "I regret everything I said. I'm really sorry for getting mad at you." Ondrea began to cry. Teddy reached his arm out to comfort her, but she politely declined. Instead, she ran over to Avery and grabbed her hands. "I'm so sorry, Avery!"

Avery smiled at her. "It's okay. You didn't mean any of it. I love you sis, no matter what you do."

"It felt so real," Teddy whispered. "When I was… Oh, man. I'm sorry, Nick! That was the worst feeling in my life!"

"It's okay, Teddy. Forgive and forget," he responded.

"Where's Jason?" Mason yelled frantically. "Is he okay?"

"I'm okay, bro!" Jason assured him, coming out from behind the corner. "The Dark Magic seemed to dissipate after all the fighting ceased."

Oliver and Jessica followed behind Jason.

"Michael, are you okay?" Jessica asked as she knelt next to him. She refrained from putting her hand on his shoulder since Michael wouldn't really be comforted by contact.

"That should never happen again," Michael whispered, rocking back and forth.

"And it won't!" Oliver exclaimed, standing in front of everyone.

Josh came out from behind the corner. "Is everything okay now?" he asked.

"Yeah. Everything's all cool again," Rachel chimed in.

Jake and Josh came to sit in the circle with the others. Jake looked at his watch. "Okay, we still have a whopping thirty minutes to discuss the whole friends-from-another-planet thing."

"Right," Jason sighed as he and the others joined the circle. "Mason and I grew up on a different planet. You guys call it Mars, but we called it Home. Very simplistic, I know, but to us, it will always be Home."

Mason grabbed Jason's hand and continued. "This is going to be really weird to hear, but our great-grandmother died when she was ten thousand years old," he said. Although the twins could see the look of shock on everyone's faces, no one interrupted. Mason continued. "She liked to take frequent trips to Earth—which she did by disguising her temperature to match the bleakness of space. That way satellites didn't pick up her heat signature."

Jason began speaking. "It was incredible, looking back at it. Anyway, years after our parents birthed us, which happened on Home, when great-grandma deemed us 'ready', she began telling us about all the wonders of Earth," he explained. "Even I have to admit, there were a lot of wonders. Mason never knew this, but I would ask her about the other stuff too, the less-than-wonderful part. She told me about wars, poverty, and all the horrors of it."

"Really?" Mason said, as he turned to look at his brother. "You thought I couldn't handle it?"

"Of course not. That wasn't it," Jason replied. "You can pretty much handle anything, Mason. Anyway, living there was pretty great. I'm sure you guys saw it on the monitor when I was in the sim."

Everyone nodded.

Jason continued. "One day, we had to leave. It was…" He began to tear up. "Oh no."

Mason put his hand on Jason's shoulder and continued for him. "Something big came and destroyed where we lived. I remember it very vividly, unfortunately. See, this wasn't a huge problem for Jason because of his Water element. But when the temperature began rising, it became so hot that the rest of the family could hardly breathe. Mom, Dad, Grandma, Grandpa, and even our Grammy died.

"The only reason Jason and I didn't burn up is because our parents had prepared for our evacuation. It was an escape pod, designed just for the two of us" Mason explained. "I remember the handle was too hot to touch, so Jason cooled it as much as he could. At that point, my brother's strength was nearly gone so I opened the door and hauled him in. Once we were in the little pod and shut the door, the temperature began to even out, and Jason began regaining his strength."

"I can take it from here, brother," Jason sighed. "He's right—I did begin to gain my strength back. There was a window on the pod door. The glass was about two feet thick; all the glass was. When I looked out the pod window, I saw someone! Yes, it was a person. Then, Mason and I felt the ground shake. But it wasn't the pod starting up—it was the volcano on our island exploding. And while I am embarrassed to admit it, I think I screamed.

I looked at the controls and realized only Mason could operate them. That appeared to be how Mom and Dad designed it. Once we got the pod off the ground, Mason and I took a second to look back at our planet and the entire thing had been mysteriously leveled. Any proof that it was ever our home had been deleted. Not destroyed but deleted. It looked just like… Mars. Home, our planet, turned into Mars. It's all that person's fault—the person I saw through the pod window."

"There's a chance it could have been… not a person, but something else," Will chimed in.

"Maybe," Jason said, "But what I saw was clearly a person-shaped figure."

"I don't mean it could've been some other machine or monster," Will explained. "I mean it could've been some kind of alien or demon shaped like a person."

"Really, Will?" Darla said. "An alien? A DEMON?"

"It could've been!" Will said.

Darla smirked and punched him in the shoulder. "Whatever…" she said.

Will smiled at her. "That seemed like submission to me."

"Shut up, idiot," she muttered, her smile growing.

Michael cleared his throat, and everyone turned to look at him. Initially, he didn't say anything, so Rachel opened her mouth to rattle off an idea. But instead, Michael did speak. "It could have been… VORK," he said quietly. "Just like VORK did the Dark Magic thing earlier."

Although the room was quiet for the next two minutes, it was the loudest silence on the planet. When Steven came out from behind the corner, everyone practically jumped out of their skin. Steven was out of breath and sweating buckets.

"Ah, kids!" he gasped. "As you can see, I've been all around backstage looking for you!" Steven laughed, then continued. "We're back on in five! If you kids could get going early, I have something important I need to talk about with Jason and Mason."

Everyone did as Steven said. The entire way to the stage, their minds were restless with the idea that VORK could have killed Jason and Mason's entire bloodline and their home planet. Meanwhile Mason and Jason stayed behind.

"What's up Steven?" Mason asked. "Is everything okay?"

"Well, that's what I wanted to ask you," Steven said, pulling at his collar. "Mason, I'm so sorry about the trauma that I caused you when I couldn't pull Jason out of the machine."

Jason looked at Mason curiously and furrowed his brow. Mason pretended not to notice and addressed Steven.

"It's okay, Steven," he said. "It wasn't you that caused the trauma; it was the scenario. You had nothing to do with it, I swear."

Steven released a sigh of relief and grabbed Mason's hands.

"Thank you, Mason," he said. Steven let go of Mason's hands and continued. "And Jason, I'm so terribly sorry for not being able to pull you out."

Jason took a step back. "What do you mean?" he asked suspiciously.

Steven's expression turned desperate. "Well… I…"

"No!" Jason said sternly. "What do you mean you couldn't pull me out?"

"Jason, chill," Mason muttered. "Steven told us he couldn't unplug the machine without possibly giving you brain damage."

"But much earlier, you said the machine was fixed and the failsafe lever worked," Jason said. "You know, the lever that can safely shut off the simulation?"

Steven's eyes darted from side to side. "Yes, I did say that, but…"

"Wait!" Mason interrupted. "You could have pulled him out?" He turned and glared at Steven.

"Kids! Kids, kids! I'm so sorry!" Steven exclaimed, looking as if he was about to cry. "Mr. Atrius wouldn't let me pull the failsafe! I tried to convince him!"

"What? What's going on, Steven?" Jason asked.

Steven just looked away. "I… I… I can't say anything," he stammered. "I'm so sorry. For the future, I doubt he'll let me pull anyone out. I'm so sorry. Oh, my. I'm so very sorry, for I have made a deal with…" Steven lowered his voice, "the Devil himself."

"What do you mean?!" Mason asked, his voice trembling. "The Devil?"

"I'm so sorry!" Steven said again. "But the show is about to start, and if I'm late, Mr. Atrius will be very suspicious! I know this is a lot to dump on you and you're only children, but please keep it cool!"

"Uh… we can keep it cool," Jason said nonchalantly.

"Oh, thank you so much! I can't tell you how much I appreciate you two right now," he whispered.

Steven scurried off to the stage and the twins followed. As soon as Steven entered the camera view, he plastered a very convincing fake smile on his face, and headed to his podium.

Mason and Jason tried to do the same. But their friends could immediately sense that something was terribly wrong. They turned to look at the twins as Mason and Jason headed to their podiums, but the twins just shook their heads. Once everyone was settled, Steven picked up his announcer mic and turned to directly face the camera.

"Sorry about that, ladies and gentlemen! Jason had quite a rumble!" he exclaimed, with exaggerated gestures. "That break was entirely necessary, but we're back here now, and the show must go on! Next up in the hot seat will be Mason! Come on down Mason and tell the world how you're feeling!"

Mason took a very shaky breath and stepped down from his podium, feeling as if he might fall over. But it didn't take him long to go from shaky and scared to steady and a bit more confident. He looked back at his friends to see Ondrea projecting Oliver's confidence and Jason's assurance into him.

Mason let out a little chuckle and continued to the chair. When Mason arrived at the chair and sat down, Steven shoved the mic in his face. As Mason got a closer look at Steven's face, he could tell that, despite the smile and charm, Steven was struggling to keep the nervous sweat back.

"Tell us how you feel, Mason!" Steven exclaimed. "Nervous, scared, excited maybe?"

"Definitely the first two," Mason confirmed.

As Mr. Atrius came walking up to strap him to the chair, Mason had to desperately hold back the urge to wiggle away. Meanwhile Jason began sweating as Mason was being strapped in.

Both the twins were thinking the exact same thing— if Mr. Atrius could control who gets pulled out, he could most likely control everything else.

Once Mason was fully strapped in, wired up, and ready to close his eyes, Steven bent down to say something.

"Good luck, Mason."

TWENTY-NINE

In Which Mason Fights For Control

Jason's body shook as Mason closed his eyes to be transported into the simulation. His mind kept racing back to when Rachel came out of the sim with a bruise on her stomach. He couldn't stop thinking that when Little Mason was kicking him, Jason felt it. Steven's words finally sank in.

When Steven hit the button to begin the simulation, Jason turned away from the monitor and sat against his podium. He didn't want to look at the screen. Of all the times he had been scared for his brother, this time was the worst. Silent tears ran down his face at the thought that Mr. Atrius could—and possibly would—do anything to Mason.

Nick looked over and noticed Jason sitting against his podium, out of view from the cameras. Nick knew he just had to say something to him, but Michael traveled from seven podiums down, put his hand on Nick's arm, and firmly shook his head no. When Nick gave him a dirty look, Michael rolled his eyes and pulled Nick backstage.

"What?" Nick growled, yanking his arm out of Michael's grasp.

"That aggression was very unnecessary," Michael stated. "Listen, I know you want to help Jason, but there is no point."

"What's that supposed to mean?" Nick wondered.

"It's very clear through all the experiences you have shared that you care deeply for him and the others, but they already know that," Michael explained. "Jason already knows very well that you will be there for him emotionally, but there is nothing you can do now."

"What are you saying, then?" Nick asked, crossing his arms. "Are you saying I shouldn't support my friend?"

"There gets to be a point where constant comfort is unnecessary, especially considering how much you have bonded with him," Michael said. "Look, what I'm trying to say is you should leave Jason alone for now."

"Alright. Sure," Nick said. "But explain why."

Michael sighed and sat down against the wall. "Judging by everything we've learned from Jason's fear simulation, it would be best to let him feel what he's feeling right now. Therefore, we need to leave him alone for now," Michael said. "He needs to feel his way. It's hard to explain, but this will help him cope better the next time he has an emotional breakdown."

Nick sat down next to Michael. "So, what you're saying is that it's always nice to let your friend know you're there for them, but sometimes they need to do things on their own?" he asked.

"Yes, exactly," Michael confirmed with a smile.

"But he hasn't rolled that way since I met him," Nick countered.

"Give it a shot," Michael suggested. "If he needs your help, I'm sure he'll let you know."

"What about reassuring glances?" Nick questioned. "Can I give him those?"

Michael stayed quiet for a few seconds, contemplating Nick's question, then nodded and said, "Yes."

Nick began walking back toward the curtain to head to his podium when Michael grabbed his arm again.

"Are you okay?" he asked.

Nick smiled. "Yeah, I'm fine," he said. "How about you?"

"I'm fine, thanks," Michael responded as he let go of Nick's arm.

The two of them went back to their separate podiums. When Nick reached his podium, he noticed Jason had recovered from his panic and was now standing at his podium wiping his eyes. Nick looked at Jason and smiled. When Jason caught Nick's eye and smiled back, Nick knew everything would be okay.

29.1

When Mason opened his eyes, he found himself lying on the floor of a red carpeted hallway. The walls were made of dark mahogany, and the ceiling he was staring at was painted maroon. He sat up and saw an arched door at the end of the short hall. It opened and he was shocked to see Jason.

"Hey," Mason said awkwardly. He hadn't figured out where he was yet, but he knew it had to be somewhere familiar or else why would Jason be there.

"It's only our second month here," Jason said. "You don't want the other kids to find you sleeping on the floor like that. Especially Dennis."

Jason held out his hand to help him up and Mason gladly accepted. Once he was standing, Mason was better able to look around. He sat down on a seat, trying to get his bearings, and noticed that Jason, still wearing the glasses he made on Home, looked a bit younger. He smiled.

"You still have your glasses from Home," Mason pointed out.

"Yes," Jason stated. "Yes, I do. I have had them since Home, so I still have them."

"Right," Mason said as he peered around the room some more. For some reason, Mason's mind felt scrambled. He knew where he was, but he didn't know how he got there or why he was there.

"Are you still waking up?" Jason asked. "Why are you acting so strangely?"

Mason completely ignored Jason as he tried to remember what was going on. He knew something wasn't right.

"Is this real?" Mason wondered aloud, momentarily forgetting that Jason was real.

"You must have been really asleep!" Jason exclaimed while laughing. "Yes, this is real, brother. No, you are not dreaming."

"No," Mason whispered. "Something is off. The contest! No! It was a game show… IS a game show."

"Stop muttering to yourself about your crazy dreams. This is why Dennis always picks on us," Jason sighed.

"Aren't you supposed to agree with me or something?" Mason asked. "You're, like, my conscience, right?"

Jason laughed, but it contained a slight feeling of unease. "I don't always have to agree with you, Mace," he said. "And, even though I am your twin, we definitely don't think the same. We are actually contradicting equals."

"That's not even a real term, Jason," Mason said distractedly looking around again. He searched for anything that could be out of the ordinary.

"Sure, it is," he countered. "Grammy always called us that."

Mason stood up and began walking toward the double doors Jason had entered through earlier.

"Right, I remember," he muttered. "We look the same but act completely different, therefore, always contradicting each other. It's still not a real term though."

"Forget it, Mace," Jason exclaimed as he too stood up and followed Mason. "Where are you going?"

"I… I need to think." Mason said as he tugged on the door handle.

"You can think here!" Jason exclaimed as he stopped at Mason's side. "Explore ideas with me! We do that all the time."

"We used to, Jason," Mason mumbled. He pulled on the door handle, but it didn't budge. He kept on pulling quite aggressively when Jason tapped him on the shoulder.

"It's a push door, moron," Jason stated. "You've been through this door thousands of times."

Mason pushed the door open and sighed wearily. Once the door was fully pushed out, a child ran right into it. The thud snapped Mason out of his daze.

"Sorry!" he exclaimed. He quickly shut the door so he could help whoever just ran smack into it, which caught Jason off guard. The door slammed right into Jason—but Mason didn't even notice.

"Hey, I'm really sorry," Mason repeated to the girl who had ran into the door. He reached out a hand to help her up, but she slapped it away.

"You do this stuff all the time, you jerk!" she screamed as she got up. "You can't just start being nice and apologizing! That won't make up for the hundreds of other times you've done stuff like that without apologizing."

"What?" Mason responded. The girl looked familiar, but he couldn't remember her name for the life of him.

"Who are you?" he asked this question very genuinely, but the girl thought otherwise.

"You know exactly who I am, you idiot!" she yelled. "I'm Fawn, Dennis' sister! You will regret this interaction! My brother WILL be hearing about this!"

She began to stomp off, but stopped, turned back around, and kicked Mason below the belt. While Mason doubled over in pain, as any guy would do, Jason grabbed Fawn's arm and stared her down. Mason glanced up at the one-sided staring contest and noticed a fire in Jason's eyes that he had rarely seen. As a startling realization popped into Mason's head, his pain vanished. Confusion, joy, and anxiety replaced it.

"Oh, my God!" Mason exclaimed. "I'm in our orphanage!"

"Yeah, idiot!" Fawn sneered while Jason was still vice-gripping her arm. "Glad you finally figured it out after two months."

"Can you just leave us alone, Fawn?" Mason asked as he stood up. "Or at least don't kick me like that again."

She just laughed. It looked like Fawn was about to try the kick again, but she yelped in pain and yanked her arm out of Jason's grasp.

"Ow!" she screamed. "You… you burned me! How did you do that?"

Jason looked at her arm, satisfied by the small red blisters forming just above her elbow.

"My body temperature runs a bit hotter than most others," he said, smirking. "Sorry about that."

While Fawn stomped off crying, Mason stood to Jason's side feeling uneasy.

"That wasn't very cool, Jace," Mason said. "I don't care how annoying she is. We shouldn't use our Powers to hurt people unless it's one-hundred percent necessary."

"She was right," Jason stated blankly.

Mason waited for further explanation, but none came. "She was right about what?" Mason asked.

Jason sighed and turned to face Mason.

"She was right that you're acting different," he answered. "She didn't say it like that, but it's true. You are acting differently. It all started since you woke up from your floor nap."

Mason's vision flashed red for just a second, and his head began to spin.

He didn't show any physical signs that anything had just happened because he didn't want Jason to ask questions. Instead, he trudged upstairs to his shared bedroom all the while wondering—if he could remember where his bedroom was located, why didn't he remember Fawn?

"What is going on with me?" he whispered.

All the other children running around the halls ignored him as they usually did. Once he arrived at his room, he pulled open the door and stood in the doorway, taking in what was once his room. It was bland like most things at the orphanage, but it had felt like home for a while.

Straight ahead there was a big window, the only window in the medium-sized room. There was only a single light bulb to illuminate the room. One of the teachers at the orphanage would always say they didn't need more than one light bulb per bedroom because natural sunlight from the single window was good for the children.

While Mason knew that to be true, he also knew it was just an excuse; budget cuts were the real reasons for just one light bulb.

The bathroom and two closets were built into the room. Across the room from the doorway, there were two bedside tables along with two small desks for homework. Next to the bedside tables there were two plain, white beds, one on the right side and one on the left.

The bed on the left was neatly made and the bed on the right wasn't. The twins shared this room and Jason, the neat freak, always made his bed and put his laundry in the bin.

Mason never saw the point in making his bed. After all, you were just going to mess it up again the next night. The only reason his side was free of dirty clothes was because Jason could never stand seeing half of the room clean and the other half dirty, so he always picked up Mason's clothes and put them in the bin for him. Some days, if Jason was feeling up to it, he would make Mason's bed for him while Mason wasn't there. But that behavior decreased the longer they stayed at the orphanage.

That was when they both had started to lose hope.

Mason walked stiffly into his old bedroom and sat on his bed. He felt it out, rubbing his hands over the rough covers. The feeling brought back memories. Some good, some bad. He glanced over at his bedside table, stood up, and reminisced over the picture of themselves that was taken when they first arrived.

Suddenly, Mason heard a click, and then the sound of a door slamming. He turned around to see Jason standing by the door, his face showing a variety of different emotions. Frustration, worry, confusion, and, most commonly of course, depression.

Jason silently walked over to Mason's bed, stood in front of him, looked Mason in the eyes, and slapped him across the face.

"Not you too," Mason whined, standing up. "Are you going to kick me next?"

Jason just sighed and shook his head. He stood there for a few seconds more, looking contemplative. Jason reached his hand toward Mason's shoulder, hesitated, then pulled away.

He shook his head again and began to pace around the middle of the room.

Mason crossed his arms, rolled his eyes, then dramatically sat on the edge of his bed while waiting for Jason to say something. After five minutes, when Jason still hadn't said anything, Mason began getting impatient. He decided a better use of his time would be thinking about things—something Jason claimed Mason often excelled at. Not this time, though. When he tried to think coherently about his current situation, his mind clouded over, and he felt a jab of splitting pain shoot through his skull.

Jason was still pacing, his head abuzz with questions about why his brother would be behaving the way he was. When he heard Mason inhale sharply, Jason's protective instincts took over, he swiftly turned toward his brother, and power walked the four-foot distance between them.

By the time Jason arrived by his side, the pain Mason felt had already begun to fade. He looked down and realized he was clutching his bed covers so tightly that his knuckles were red. Mason shook out his hands and sighed.

He felt like crying, but he mentally scolded himself for it. All the while, Jason kept on asking him if he was okay, but Mason was too lost in his crippling thoughts. Even though many horrible, awful things had happened in his life, this was only the second time he had ever felt THIS kind of despair. The despair that once buried itself deep into the hearts of both twins fell back on Mason; he could feel his brother's pain as well. This time, however, it felt ten times worse. Despite this, he knew that he had to keep going. Something was going on in his head and, while he had no clue what it was, it felt dangerous. If he couldn't think hard about his situation for a long period of time without his head hurting, he'd write it down.

"MASON!" Jason yelled. "Are you even hearing me? What the heck is going on with you?"

"Stop shouting," Mason muttered. "Hold on."

"What do you mean 'stop shouting'?" Jason growled. "You need to talk to me! I didn't want to have to say this, but I have no choice! Mason, I'm worried about you. What's going on?"

As Mason opened his desk drawer and pulled out a pencil and two sheets of paper, Jason strode over and yanked the paper out of his hands.

"Dude, what the heck!" Mason exclaimed.

"You won't tell me ANYTHING!" Jason said. "Did that get your attention?"

"Yes, it did, jerk," Mason whispered. He held out his hand and showed Jason the surprisingly large paper cut he just received.

Wordlessly, he took the papers back, sat down at his desk, and began to write down what he could remember. He had a strategy for this. He would think until his head hurt, take a fifteen second break, then think of something else. He'd do that until he had finished. Here is exactly what his paper looked like by that time:

Things I remember/didn't remember
(So technically, notes):
1. Something about game show
2. Lots of chaos all the time
3. Floor nap
4. Not remember mean Fawn
5. Dennis = big bully
6. Remember where bedroom
7. Remember happened in bedroom
8. Weird headaches
9. Flash red
10. Game show
11. Show???
12. Jace still annoying
13. I am confusion
14. Where is food?
15. Something is bad
16. Wrong
17. Remember life and other life???

Mason finished his list, but he didn't want to look over it, so he gave his list to one very annoyed Jason without any context at all. With just a single glance at Mason's list, Jason immediately had several thoughts.

"Absolutely none of the points on your list would make a single ounce of sense to anyone but you," he said. "The title is weak, but what else would I expect considering the grades you get. Your grammar is atrocious, but at least every bullet point begins with a capital letter. The multiple question marks at the end of eleven and seventeen are tacky, bothersome to look at, and unnecessary. A couple of these points reiterate the same thing and should be conjoined into one. You clearly tried hard to make sure every point was as vague as universally possible. I have no idea what you were going for with the 'where is food' point.

"Also, you can erase number thirteen since it's already obvious that you're confused and have no idea what you are doing. Number twelve is a bit rude, but I will accept it only to reciprocate it back. Finally, I can think of no situation where the bullet point 'flash red' would make sense. All in all, if this is for our schoolteacher, you would get an F and held back. And another thing, everyone would think you are four years old."

The room was quiet for a couple seconds before Mason said, "I wasn't asking for your criticism."

Once again, it went silent.

Jason sighed. He stood up and began to pace across the floor once more. "What do you want me to do, then, brother?" Jason asked without looking up.

Mason took a deep breath.

"Okay. Hypothetically, if I was stuck in a simulation, but the lines between reality and the simulation began to blur together, and I felt stuck, what would I do?" he asked.

"That's a very vague question," Jason responded. "Tell me, would you know you were in a simulation?"

"Well, I think so, yes," Mason answered. "Although… I'm not sure. Because, hypothetically, it's supposed to feel real."

"Real as in you'd be able to feel pain?" Jason wondered, still pacing.

"Yeah," he confirmed. "But, hypothetically, all the characters that I would meet would end up being conjured by my mind, and they would all spout out my deep inner thoughts. But you don't seem to be doing this. Instead, it feels like I went through a time machine."

Jason stopped to look at Mason and raised an eyebrow.

"That's strange," he said. "You talk as if you're not hypothetically speaking."

"Right… I'm pretending," Mason said hurriedly. "Totally pretending."

"Hm… Okay," Jason said. "Now I'm going to ask you a series of questions. If you truly were in a simulation where everything felt real, you would want to get out as quickly as possible to avoid brain damage. So, to save hypothetical time, I will ask you questions quickly."

"Wait!" Mason yelled. "Brain damage?"

"Yes, now tell me more about this simulation," Jason eagerly insisted, his inner nerd peeking through. "What purpose would it serve?"

"The end goal is that it would be a fear simulation," Mason said nervously, still worrying about the 'brain damage' comment. "As soon as I'd faced my fear, I'd be automatically pulled out."

"Alright. Maybe you should face your fear," Jason stated. "If you haven't found your specific fear yet, maybe it's situational. Where are you in this simulation?"

"The current setting," Mason responded.

"This place is fear-inducing in many ways," Jason exclaimed as he began to pace again. "Tell me, when you were put into this simulation, were you in control of where and when you would end up?"

"No," Mason answered quickly.

"Let's pretend you were placed into the simulation at some point in the future—after being in the orphanage—and you ended up back here once you entered," Jason suggested. "Now, I assume the people in the simulation don't know they are reliving a simulation, but you do. Unlike time travel, anything you do in the simulation would not change the past or present no matter what you did. So, you said this is a fear simulation, correct?"

"Yeah," Mason said, impressed by his brother's skill of deduction.

"There are two plausible reasons you might be stuck. Obviously, there could be hundreds more, but these are the two I can think of," Jason said. "One could be that you are afraid of not being in control, since you realize the lines between reality and simulation are blurring together. You could be having trouble distinguishing real life from the simulation and forgetting things about reality and the simulation, while also remembering specific things. The second reason could simply be that the machine is broken. Is there anything else I need to know?"

Mason thought for a minute before saying, "What if, in real life, someone was after you? Someone evil."

"This seems to be a very complex hypothetical situation," Jason said. "But, to answer your question, in that case someone could have sabotaged the machine."

"But what if someone extremely reliable checked the machine before the next person went in?" Mason asked, his nerves turning into fear.

"I'd still say something could be wrong," Jason exclaimed which made Mason's fear grow to panic. "But if a reliable source checked the machine, it's most likely the first reason I spoke of earlier."

"Okay, so what would I do in that situation?" Mason asked.

"You would have to wonder to yourself, 'If I'm afraid of losing control, then why would it be in this setting?' Then you'd have to try to overcome it," Jason explained. "Can I ask you a personal question that will most likely throw you off guard?"

"I mean, you are my brother, so go for it," Mason answered.

"Why are you discussing this with me? Why are you letting me give you all the answers instead of figuring them out for yourself?" he asked as he stopped pacing and turned to face his brother.

"You just seem like the smartest guy in the room. Plus, I know you the best," Mason said. "By the way, this situation is still hypothetical."

"Oh, for the love of God, brother, stop saying that!" Jason exclaimed. "This is too familiar to me to be fake. Tell me the truth. You know I can handle it."

"There's no point in telling you the truth if you're so against me asking you for the answers!" Mason yelled.

Jason took a step back. "Well… I believe I know the truth, and you're correct to know that this is a simulation. This is not real," he said. "I can sense your panic. I can sense the weight on your shoulders. Despite the fact that you're in the body you had when we were at the orphanage, I can tell there's more experience and age in your head."

"Geez," Mason muttered. "That's a little creepy, man."

"Get a hold of yourself!" Jason exclaimed. "If you stay here much longer, I'm worried the lines will blur too much and you'll be very stuck instead of JUST stuck."

"Then help me!" Mason shouted. When he said those words, a headache flared to life. He nearly crumpled to the floor, but Jason instantly moved to his side.

"Listen to me," Jason whispered. "I want you to get out. Real Jason wants to hear your voice again. He's worried. All your friends are worried."

"How do you know that?" Mason asked.

"I guess I am your conscience after all," he answered. "Here's an idea—why don't you just accept it?"

Mason wiped the tears that had begun forming in his eyes. He felt lost and hopeless until he looked to his brother's face and saw him smiling.

"Accept what?" Mason mumbled.

"Accept that there are going to be many situations in your life in which you may not be in total control," Jason said. "Losing control is part of living life. All that matters is that you never give up. You, Mason, are the most stubborn person in the world. If there's one trait I could define you by, it would be that you always stand strong and never give up. You always see the good in things even when times are hard. That's what makes you who you are.

"You don't have to be in control all the time because that's impossible. I know you trust your friends. Know that all your friends trust you too. While there may be situations where NO ONE has control, you have your friends. Let things play out."

"I never thought about anything like that," Mason said. "I know I try to hold back my feelings of losing control. I put on a fake smile sometimes. I've gotten good at it."

"That's not the best thing," Jason sighed wearily. "Mason, you just have to leave it to fate sometimes."

"I guess I can't always be in control," Mason admitted.

"Mace, when you said you'd never thought of anything like this, you just didn't understand that minuscule flicker of realization in the back of your mind," Jason said. "I am your thoughts. This was all you. Not me. Now you can go home and remember this. I believe that you have initiated the first step into overcoming your greatest fear."

"Wow," Mason whispered. "Thanks, me."

Jason laughed then said, "You've been in here a very long time. You should be going. Stay safe, you reckless maniac."

"I will," Mason said. He began to feel sleepy and closed his eyes.

Suddenly, he felt his body falling to the floor. Before he hit the ground, however, he opened his eyes to see Steven. He turned his head quickly and saw his friends all grinning. Jason's smile was the biggest. As soon as Steven had unstrapped him, Mason sprinted to Jason and leapt into a hug.

"Good job, brother," Jason whispered as his eyes began to water. "I was worried when I had no reason to be."

Mason burst into silent tears. He tried to speak, but he couldn't get a word out. The hug went on for a minute before Mason was finally able to speak.

"Jason," he said. "In the orphanage, I felt like I had no control over anything. I was scared and filled with hopelessness. It was an awful feeling. I had never felt so hopeless."

Jason ended the hug and took his brother's hands. "You have nothing to fear anymore, Mason."

"Except for the obvious evil organization constantly hovering above our heads," Will interrupted.

Mason and Jason laughed.

"We were having a moment, Will," Mason exclaimed.

"I'm just stating the facts," Will responded, shrugging.

"Shut it, Will," Darla stated as she came up behind him and pulled him away.

Everyone laughed as Steven made the announcement for the five-minute break.

THIRTY

In Which the Devil Makes an Introduction

Backstage, the group began to discuss the many problems at hand. "Guys, we really need to talk about Damian and Spencer now," Jessica said as soon as everyone in the group was seated.

"Took the words right out of my mouth!" Nick exclaimed, rubbing his hands together anxiously.

Jason and Mason glanced at each other, knowing that they too had something to share with the group. They just didn't know when they'd be able to bring it up.

"So, here are the facts," Oliver started. "We know Spencer is missing, but do we know why? Also, we know Nick's father, Damian, is potentially missing and we have zero information on his whereabouts."

"Right," Ondrea said. "The first thing Vixsten asked when he picked up the phone was if Spencer was with us—which must mean that Spencer was going to be coming here for some reason."

"Good observation," Jason mentioned. "Why would he be coming here?"

Josh spoke up. "Remember when he called you saying that someone was in trouble?" he asked rhetorically. "Well, he was talking about Jake."

"I see where you're going with this!" Will yelled excitedly. "Maybe Spencer wanted to help when Jake was lost, so he came here!"

"Started to come here, but didn't make it?" Avery asked.

"Guys, can we talk about this creep, Mr. Atrius?" Teddy asked. "He's very suspicious."

"We already knew that, Teddy," Nick muttered. He held his head in his hands and sighed. "Can we please talk about my dad now?"

"Are you okay, Nick?" Darla asked.

"Has your headache gone away yet?" Jason wondered. "It doesn't seem like it did."

"Is something wrong, Nick? Do you feel okay?" Jessica questioned.

Nick stood up and began to pace.

"I'm fine!" he exclaimed. "Can we please just talk about Damian?"

"Okay," Jessica said, taken aback by his harsh tone.

"We're just worried about you, Nick," Rachel said. "This has been pretty hard—on you specifically."

"Damian!" Nick yelled. "Talk about Damian!"

"Okay, okay!" Oliver said. "No more fighting, remember?"

Everyone mumbled "yes" and "sure."

Oliver smiled.

"Good," he said. "Now, everyone apologize."

"No," Nick said before anyone else could begin apologizing. "I should apologize. I haven't been myself lately."

Yeah, we've been seeing that recently," Mason said. "If you really think whatever is going on with you can wait, we should talk about Damian. But if you think something is up with you, we should take care of that."

"He's right, Nick," Michael mumbled. "I've learned the hard way that you have to take care of yourself before you take care of others."

"I'll be fine," Nick stated. "We should work on finding Damian. Now, all we know is that he didn't pick up his phone."

"That's not much to go on, idiot," Darla said.

"Darla, sweetie, not helping," Ondrea said as she put her hand on Darla's shoulder.

"We don't know much about Damian. But back to Spencer," Jake said, nervously taking the initiative. "We can now assume he was coming here to help me when I was lost in the desert, but he obviously didn't make it."

"Yes," Josh agreed. "We also know he didn't turn back around to go to his dad, or else his dad wouldn't have any reason to worry."

"Guys," Michael said. "I saw Mr. Atrius walking through that purple door. I followed him in, and it looked like a classic evil lair of a movie villain."

"We know. You already said something like that, Michael," Teddy said.

"Did I also tell you he had a bird on his shoulder?" Michael asked.

Everyone went dead quiet except for the collective sigh.

"That's a pretty important piece of information to leave out!" Oliver exclaimed.

Michael lowered his head. "I'd never seen the specific bird before then, so I didn't think it was anything to sneeze over," he said aggressively.

"You know what?" Avery said. "Thank you for telling us now, Michael. It was a big help."

"Uh, sure," he mumbled.

"So, the bird is here?" Jake asked. He began fidgeting with his shoelaces.

"Yeah, sorry," Michael responded. He stood up and began to pace. "As much as I love classic movie plots and classic villainy, it's very different when you're living what could be a movie."

"The bird that attacked my brother is in the same building as my brother," Josh stated. "Well, that's just great."

"I guess we'll have to avoid getting on Mr. Atrius' bad side," Avery exclaimed.

"Easier said than done, I think," Jason said nervously.

"Yeah, he's kind of a scary dude," Darla agreed. "And that's coming from me."

"Guys!" Nick whispered. "He's coming!"

Everyone paused and looked around on high alert. Mr. Atrius poked his head around the corner and smiled at the kids.

"Hey guys!" he said cheerfully. "Sorry about all the recent problems."

"It's… it's alright, sir," Darla said.

"Well, I'm glad all is forgiven," he said with a big smile on his face.

"Hold on!" Will exclaimed. "What's your name? You never introduced yourself."

Everyone suddenly remembered that they had only learned his name from Steven, and Mr. Atrius didn't know that Steven had told them.

"My name is John Atrius," he said. "You can call me whatever you'd like, but I'd prefer 'Mr. Atrius.'"

"Yes, of course," Teddy said. "Thanks, Mr. Atrius, for everything you've done so far."

"It was nothing, really," Mr. Atrius said. "I'm just doing my job. Oh, kids, Steven and I have talked it over. Since everything that could possibly go wrong already has gone wrong, after Avery takes her turn, we'll take a break for the rest of the day and pick everything back up tomorrow."

Everyone cheered.

"Thank God!" Will exclaimed dramatically. "We're dying here!"

Nick had finally had enough. He couldn't take the suspense, drama, and uncertainty anymore. He was just about ready to explode. Nick knew, however, that he needed to be strategic. He feigned a coughing fit. His friends looked at him with concern.

"Are you alright, Nick?" Mr. Atrius asked.

"Yeah," Nick said. "Sorry, it's just allergies—which is really funny."

"Why is it funny, Nick?" Rachel asked nervously.

"You've never mentioned an allergy before," Will said.

"I never thought it to be necessary," Nick said. "I'm allergic to birds." He turned to address Mr. Atrius directly. "You don't happen to have a bird, do you?"

"I apologize," Mr. Atrius said. "I do have a bird, but he isn't here, so I don't know why your allergies would be acting up right now."

Nick wasn't expecting that answer, but luckily, he was quick-witted.

"My allergies are really sensitive," he said. "You must have been around your bird recently."

Slowly, everyone began to catch on.

"I absolutely love animals!" Rachel exclaimed. "Maybe you could show us your bird sometime?"

"I might do that," Mr. Atrius said with a smile. "Although, I'll leave Nick out of it. If he gets too close to the bird, he might be out of commission."

Nick's eyes widened. He was alarmed by the way Mr. Atrius phrased that comment. But the next comment freaked everyone out even more.

"Apparently, if Nick gets too close to me as, he'll be out of commission as well," Mr. Atrius said with a lighthearted laugh.

As he said this, he stared directly at Nick and his smile twisted just enough for only Nick to notice. He couldn't help but let out a small gasp as he felt a jolt of pain in his head. Nick pretended to cough to cover it up.

"Well," Mr. Atrius began. "I'll be heading out now to get ready for the next simulation round. Steven and I have added twenty minutes to your break just to help everyone mentally prepare for what is to come next."

With that, John Atrius left.

THIRTY-ONE

In Which Michael Reveals His Wild Card

Well, that was really ominous," Will said as he hugged his knees close to his chest.

"Did anyone else feel his powerful magic?" Michael asked quietly.

"At this point, Michael, we all know he has powerful magic, but what do you mean by 'feel'?" Oliver questioned.

"You couldn't feel it?" Michael wondered. When everyone shook their heads, he took a deep breath. "I understand now. The reason I could feel it so strongly is because my Lightning Power is often attracted to stronger Powers, which makes it much easier for me to target my enemies. It also enables me to see other people's Magic Power. It's sort of like an aura. Not only can I see it, but I can feel it too.

"The thing is, Mr. Atrius tried to hide his Magic aura for most of the conversation. But when Nick mentioned the bird, I guess it caught him off guard, and he accidentally let go. When he did, his Magic Power felt like a punch to the gut."

"That's very interesting!" Jason exclaimed, sounding genuinely excited. Although his mood changed a second later. "I've come to a realization."

"Really?" Darla said. "Because you seem to come to a lot of realizations."

"Thank you, Darla," Jason said, choosing to act oblivious to her sarcasm. "Nick's main element is Dark Magic, but for some reason, Oliver and I can sense it too."

"He's right," Oliver said quietly. "I can for sure. Does anyone else in here think they can sense it too?"

"Honestly, I think I can," Avery said.

"Yes, you can," Michael confirmed as he nodded.

"How would you possibly know that?" Ondrea asked curiously.

Michael smiled. "I love getting into this kind of stuff with people. It's very exciting to share," he exclaimed. "Anyway, it's time for me to dive more into auras. Not only can I sense the amount of Power one holds, but I can also sense the main elements of their Power. Each element has a different color aura. Sometimes the auras combine to make some color not associated with just one element. Also, the more powerful someone is, the wider their aura extends.

"For instance, Mr. Atrius' aura is deep black with red hairs peeking through. That means his Power focuses on Dark Magic as well as a small amount of Healing which is the result of the red threads. His aura is very wide which means he is incredibly Powerful. Also, his aura smells like rotten eggs which means he has bad intentions. The way his aura flows determines the amount of control he has over his Power. By control, I mean how well he can use it. His aura flows evenly, which means he has good control. All auras flow in a wave like pattern just for reference."

"That's way too complicated," Darla stated. "How do you keep up with all these things you're talking about?"

"I've had a lot of practice," Michael answered. "Some auras can also contain colors that aren't Elements. For instance, Darla, your aura contains mostly purple with white threads which means you have something called Sneak Magic. Sneak Magic isn't an Element but a type of Magic category. Despite your aura mainly consisting of purple with white strands, you also have splashes of orange which pertains to your Fire Element. It's clear to me that, in the grand scheme of things, you use your Invisibility much more than your Fire Element. Not to mention the incredibly small amount of blue barely poking through the purple and white. Blue means you have Projectile Magic. While the word projectile refers to objects being thrown, in this sense, it means Weaponized Magic. You have a laser that can come out of the tip of your fingers. Is this correct?"

It took Darla a minute to give him a simple answer as she was still trying to process literally everything Michael had just said.

"Yes, that's true," she whispered.

"Well, that's the hint of blue in your aura," Michael explained. "I believe you rarely use that Power."

"Uh… yeah. That's right," Darla said. "I believe I've only used it once or twice within the past year and a half, so that might be it."

"How wide is her aura?" Ondrea asked.

"It's the same width as Teddy's aura. You both have the weakest auras here, which is nothing to be ashamed of, by the way. Darla's flow pattern, however, is incredibly strong. The waves are closer together and perfectly even. Meanwhile Teddy's waves are much tighter than Darla's waves. In fact, his waves are the tightest out of everyone in this room which means he has the most control over his Powers. I've never seen waves that tight before. They're practically touching each other."

"What else about me can you figure out?" Teddy asked eagerly.

"Well as I mentioned already, you have astounding control over your Powers. What I have not yet mentioned is that astounding control only pertains to your Teleportation Power, which comes off as gray. Gray is the Space Element, which means you are allowed to defy the laws of time and space—which is very cool.

"Your Earth Element, which is brown, pokes through quite a bit. That means it's Powerful, but I can tell you don't use it nearly as much as you use your Teleportation. Your Super Speed is yellow and is a category of its own. Speed Magic. As for its Power level… I had to look very hard to find the few strands of it in your aura. Basically, you have Super Speed, but you never seem to use it. In my opinion, the fact that you have Super Speed is unnecessary considering you can Teleport, but I don't decide which Powers are given to which people— so I can't really complain about it."

"That is so cool!" Teddy exclaimed. "Hey, how do I smell?"

Michael sniffed the air and his expression immediately changed to one of contemplative thought.

"Very interesting, Teddy," Michael mumbled. He looked at Teddy and began to speak clearly. "When I smell things, not only can I smell intentions, but I can also smell certain personality traits. I haven't figured out every single trait I can smell, but I've created quite a large library of smells. It's rare that a person smells of only one thing, because all people have layers. Teddy, you smell like cranberries, sugar, and roses."

"What do those mean?" he asked, looking nervous.

"Cranberries are bitter. Most likely, you have either a dark secret you don't want anyone to know about, or you have a hatred inside of you that you're trying to avoid or cover up. The reason these two possibilities involve secrets is because people who haven't tried them before would believe that cranberries are sweet because they are berries, but they're actually bitter."

Ondrea looked at Teddy curiously. He just shrugged.

"I don't doubt Michael's skills," he said. Maybe I do have something that I'm hiding. I guess it just hasn't surfaced yet. What about the other two?"

"Sugar and roses," Michael said. "Sugar is obviously sweet. Naturally, this means that you are a sweet person and have never, or rarely, had bad intentions. It could also translate to you being patient and understanding toward others. Roses means… well, it translates to romance. Clearly you care very much for Ondrea because the rose smell is very strong and doesn't blend like the cranberry and sugar smells. Not only does it mean romance, but depending on the person, it can translate to undying loyalty."

"Wow…" Teddy whispered. "That's a lot to unpack."

Ondrea wrapped her arms around his shoulders and gave him a kiss on the cheek.

"That's my Teddy Bear!" she said happily.

Will snickered. When Ondrea snapped her head in his direction, he immediately stopped. Michael sniffed the air in Will's direction and grinned. After opening up about his Power to the group, Michael was feeling giddy and bold.

"Will," Michael said. "I wouldn't be laughing if I were you. The rose smell basically overpowers all the other smells you have."

Will's face turned red, and he instinctively glanced at Darla. Darla happened to miss Will's look, but everyone else saw it.

"Will, you have a girlfriend already!" Nick exclaimed, laughing. "I know you're quite the player but show a little decency, would you."

Will's face turned a darker shade of red, and he scooted out of the circle. "You guys are really mean." He said, making a pouty face. "I know Hannah's my girlfriend—or at least a girl I liked at school. That's what Michael meant… obviously."

Everyone began laughing except for Darla, who looked very confused. "Why is everyone laughing?" she asked.

"No reason at all!" Will said quickly. His face had turned so red at this point that he wanted to curl up in the corner and hide, but he didn't.

Suddenly, Steven came bursting backstage, once again, sweating.

"Kids!" he said. "It's ten minutes until we're on! Get out there!"

Everyone began heading toward the stage all in good spirits. As Josh walked past Steven, he made sure to tell his dad what was on his and everyone else's minds.

"Hey, Dad," Josh stated plainly. "You really need to get in better shape."

Steven smiled and jokingly glared at his son.

"If I have to get in better shape, you have to stop throwing things at your brother."

"Oh!" Jake yelled. "Yeah, stop throwing things at me!"

Steven stayed where he was, while Jake and Josh continued toward the stage, arguing still.

"It was one time!" Josh exclaimed as their voices faded from the vicinity.

Steven was about to head after them when he saw that Nick was still sitting on the floor.

"Hey, Nick," Steven said. "Are you okay?"

"Yeah, I'm alright," Nick said, starting to get tired of people asking him that. "You can go ahead. I need a minute."

"Okay," Steven said. "Just make sure you get to the stage on time, please."

Once Steven had left and Nick was alone, he sighed and rubbed his eyes with his fists.

"What is wrong with me?" Nick muttered.

He felt a flash of pain rip through his skull, and he nearly screamed. About a minute later, the throbbing in his head settled, but his constant headache persisted.

"I really need to tell my friends about this soon," he said. Nick sat back against a wall and closed his eyes for a moment, trying to will his headache to go away.

31.1

Rachel stood at her podium and looked at all her friends.

"Hey guys?" she said.

"What's up?" Mason asked. "Everything okay?"

Rachel smiled and let out a small laugh.

"Everything is better than okay!" she exclaimed. "I used to fear almost everything, but because of all of you, including my three new friends, I'm only scared of some things. Even with everything going on, I'm so lucky to have you guys in my life. I know this is a really random time to say all of this, but I felt it needed to be said."

"We love you, Rachel," Jessica said.

"No matter what you're scared of, we will always appreciate you," Will added, throwing her a thumbs up.

Everyone turned their heads toward the backstage curtain as they heard Jake and Josh's arguing voices coming closer. They continued arguing even after they got on stage.

"You throw things at me all the time!" Jake said. "Don't try to tell me that was only once."

"Clearly you have brain damage!" Josh insisted. "That's not what I remember!"

"What do you mean?" Jake asked. He was clearly about to say more when Darla butted in.

"Guys!" she hissed. "Shut up! We don't want to hear about your brain damage problems. I'm getting brain damage just listening to you argue."

The twins shook hands and stopped arguing. As they headed to their podiums, however, Josh stuck his tongue out at Jake and made a spitting noise while Jake mumbled something about Josh being too immature to be his twin.

When Steven entered the stage, he announced that the cameras would start rolling in seven minutes.

"Wait, where is Nick?" Oliver asked.

Steven began fidgeting with the camera, trying to get it ready.

"Nick said he needed a minute," Steven responded. "I'm sure he'll be here soon."

Two minutes passed, and Nick still hadn't arrived at his podium. Michael urgently walked all the way down to Oliver's podium and pulled him to the front room of the backstage area.

"What's going on, Michael?" Oliver asked, more concerned than annoyed that Michael had pulled him backstage.

"After you guys came back from rescuing Jake way earlier, I instinctively read everyone's auras," Michael began. "Since it was the first time I'd read your auras, I didn't think much of it. But as time went on, I started to become unsure."

"Unsure of what?" Oliver asked. He was able to sense Michael's panic building up. "Just slow down and talk to me. What's going on?"

"As far as my aura reading goes, deep black means Dark Magic, but in the most evil form—which is why I told you Mr. Atrius' aura was deep black." Michael explained. "Nick's aura is a lesser black. Not because he's less Powerful, but because he doesn't fight for evil."

"Please don't tell me his Magic is turning deep black," Oliver said.

"No, of course not!" Michael responded. "It's sort of the opposite; Nick's aura is very gradually getting smaller."

Oliver began to panic.

"That's bad, right?" he asked, already knowing the answer.

"Yes, very bad," Michael confirmed. "He's in trouble, and he's known it since the game show started. I don't know him as well as you do—and I'm not saying I know more than you, or I'm more observant—but because of my Power, I can read people in general. I believe Nick is the kind of person who puts others before himself because he doesn't want to burden anyone."

"Yeah, that sounds about right," Oliver said with a sigh. "His behavior makes even more sense especially given the circumstances. There's so much going on with everyone else, and he's having a hard enough time keeping it together because of Spencer and Damian."

"Exactly," Michael said. "So, he's trying not to push everyone too much, and he's trying to help everyone too much. I have a difficult time caring about things in general, and even I'm a bit worried for him."

"We should go back there and check on him since he's still not back yet," Oliver said quickly. He grabbed Michael's arm and began heading backstage, but Michael didn't move.

"Come on, Michael! Let's go!" Oliver urged.

"You go on, seriously," Michael said. "I support him in every way, but I'm not good in situations like these. I'll go back to the podiums, and you go check on him. I'm sure he'll feel more comfortable if just one person is back there with him."

"Okay, fine," Oliver said. "Just don't tell anyone about this yet."

"Of course," Michael said. With that, he headed back to the podiums and Oliver raced toward the back room to find Nick.

31.2

"Nick!" Oliver called. "Dude, where are you? This thing is going to start soon!"

No response.

"Nick!" he called out again. "Nick!"

Oliver heard someone shuffling around and immediately changed course. Once he entered a different back room, he saw Nick sitting crisscross against the wall with his elbows on his knees and his head in his hands.

"My God, Nick!" Oliver exclaimed. "What's going on?" Oliver ran to him and knelt by his friend's side. "Nick. Please."

Nick lifted his head and yawned.

"I must have fallen asleep," he said.

"So, you're okay?" Oliver asked. "There's nothing wrong?"

Nick rubbed his eyes with his fists and yawned again.

"I think I'm okay," he replied. "Although, my head does hurt a little."

Oliver peered at Nick's face with curiosity and worry. He looked pale, and his eyes looked slightly glassy—which was the most worrying thing of all.

"You don't look so good, Nick," Oliver stated. "Look, I'm going to be honest with you. I'm really worried about you. So is Michael. So is everyone else."

"I'm a bit worried about me too, Ollie," Nick muttered.

Oliver paused. His sister called him Ollie, but Nick had rarely ever used his nickname. Although he loved and respected his sister, his twin sister, every time Jessica had ever used his nickname, he couldn't help but look at her as a little sister who needed protecting. With Nick sitting in front of Oliver, he suddenly saw Nick as the younger cousin he and Jessica used to play with when they were five years old.

"Nick," Oliver said softly as if he was talking to a child. "Let's get going."

Nick bowed his head again and began shaking.

"What's wrong with me?" he cried. "Will this never end?"

It was a vague question, but Oliver knew exactly what Nick was talking about. It was a question Oliver had been asking himself lately, but to hear it from someone else made his heart drop. Oliver sat down by his cousin and put his hand on Nick's back. It was all he could do.

"Nick, I don't know what to say," Oliver whispered sadly. "I've been wondering about that myself."

Nick lifted his head and, through a river of tears, smiled at Oliver.

What comes next?" he asked as he wiped his tears with his hands.

"This game show," Oliver responded sullenly. "And after that… well… we're all in this together, Nick."

"Yeah, I guess we are," he mumbled. "Hey, Oliver, my head really hurts."

Oliver sighed. "Yeah, I figured," he said. "It's bad news."

"At least the day ends after Avery's turn," Nick said. He began to stand up, but he faltered.

"Whoa," Oliver exclaimed. "Let me help you up at least." Oliver stood up, grabbed Nick's forearms and pulled him up slowly. Once he was up, Oliver released Nick. "Can you stand?"

Nick nodded and began to walk.

"Oh boy," he said as he nearly fell.

Oliver laughed. "Alright, let me help you," he said.

Oliver grabbed Nick's arm to steady him and they walked back on stage to find Steven frantically checking his watch. Team HOPE looked up as their two friends walked back on stage. Nick began to tear up again as he sensed worry emanating from all his friends. He couldn't help but reflect back on how far he and his friends had come. As Oliver led Nick back to his podium, Nick remembered the time he had encountered his cousins on the streets of New York as he rescued Rachel and the others. Someone had been trying to kidnap Rachel. He laughed to himself when he remembered that he used his vocal manipulation to pretend to be one of the kidnappers and tricked them.

Once everyone was at their podiums, Steven looked up and finally realized Nick and Oliver had come back.

"Good! Everyone's here!" he shouted excitedly. "Cutting it pretty close, boys. Anyway, I'm going to count us down and the cameras will be live when I say 'go', so be ready. Three, two, one, GO!"

The cameras were officially live.

"Alright, ladies and gentlemen. I must apologize. This show has gotten off to a rough and strange start. This month, we will be running the show just a little bit differently," Steven announced. "Due to the unforeseen complications, the last participant today will be Avery Kendal. But don't fret, folks! Tomorrow we will continue as scheduled. You know we wouldn't want to tire out the kids on the first day! Now, why don't we begin? Avery, please come on up!"

Avery walked toward the chair with a confidence only she could pull off, but Ondrea grabbed her arm before she could get to the chair. Ondrea kissed her sister on the cheek and gave her a hug.

"Go kill it, tiger," she said with a smile and a laugh.

Despite the internal fear deep within her, Avery once more walked to the chair with even more confidence. Her friends knew she was nervous but smiled. They knew that whatever fear lurked ahead for her, she would crush it mercilessly into a thousand pieces no matter how much it scared her.

Avery sat down in the chair, closed her eyes, and prepared to be put into a world of nightmares.

THIRTY-TWO

In Which There Is a Disembodied Voice

When Avery opened her eyes, she found herself in a cold dark room. She immediately recognized her surroundings and began to laugh.

"Really?" she yelled. "This place is just a dark memory! I'm not afraid anymore!"

"Really?" a voice said from behind her. "Because you seem to be shaking."

"I don't know who you are, and I don't care!" she shouted. She lowered her voice in order to sound calm. "Plus, it's really cold in here. Why else would I be shaking, idiot."

"That was a bit rude, don't you think?" the voice asked. It sounded closer to her this time.

"Oh, my apologies," she said sarcastically. "I forgot that disembodied voices have feelings too."

"Don't worry," it responded. "I'm not mad."

Avery rolled her eyes. "Oh, thank God," she said. "Hey, who are you?"

"I'm your fear," it responded.

"I'm not afraid of disembodied voices," she stated plainly.

The voice went quiet for a moment before Avery heard what sounded like an exhausted sigh.

"Yes, I know you're not afraid of disembodied voices! I… You…. You're so difficult," it said, sounding even closer this time.

"I'm bored," Avery exclaimed, annoyed. She began to kick the ground as her impatience built, but as she did, she heard a splash. "Well, that's a bit strange."

Suddenly, the voice began to laugh.

"Now comes the interesting part!" it yelled, its bold voice echoing off the walls. "You notice how your eyes haven't adjusted to the darkness yet?"

"Well of course they haven't adjusted. There's no 'yet' about it. It's common knowledge that if you're in absolute darkness, there's no light for your eyes to adjust to," Avery explained.

"Why don't I shed a bit of light for you then?" the voice responded.

Avery suddenly screamed for multiple reasons. First, because the voice rang out from inside her head. It was as if her brain were talking to her. Second, because of the light. When she saw what she was standing in, she immediately recognized where the splashing sound had come from. She screamed multiple times and looked around, desperately hoping to escape the puddles of blood on the floor.

"What the heck is wrong with you?" she screamed.

"Oh relax!" the voice exclaimed. "You're standing in a puddle of warm blood; we get it. Your screaming pains me."

Avery took a deep breath to try to calm down but had a lot of trouble ignoring the overpowering stench of iron from the blood. She took another shaky breath.

"I'm not afraid of blood," she muttered. "It just surprised me."

"I know what you're afraid of, and I know it's not blood," the voice whispered. "Look in the corner over there."

Avery sighed. "I'm in a cylindrical room, moron," she stated. "There are no corners."

The voice just laughed again.

"Then why don't you look around until you see a dead body!" it screeched.

Avery froze and shut her eyes. She wasn't necessarily deathly afraid of dead bodies—but, like anyone, she didn't really want to see one. After nothing happened for about a minute, she carefully opened her eyes and immediately regretted it.

"My God," she whispered. In front of her was, in fact, a dead body.

The creepy voice laughed and asked, "Remember when you did this?"

Avery sloshed her way through the blood while focusing on only one thing—Nick's body floating face down in front of her. She grabbed his cold arms and flipped him over.

"I… I… didn't do this," she said, unable to hide the fear from her voice. "I didn't do anything… like… this."

"You don't remember when you picked up a little passenger last year?" the voice asked. "On the evil dragon express?"

"Good one," Avery mumbled.

"That's all you have to say?" the voice hissed. "How does this make you feel?"

Avery didn't respond because she could no longer hear the voice. All she heard was loud coughing, which instantly sparked the memory of Nick and her in The Boss's dungeon after she had captured Nick. He was sick and coughing. He was dying.

"I didn't do this," she mumbled.

"Yes, you did!" the voice screamed. "You left him in here to rot! You told your friends that The Stranger killed him in front of you. You told them that you managed to escape before he could kill you too!"

"No!" she yelled. "I didn't!"

"Yes, you did!" the voice said. "The Stranger didn't kill him though! You know what happened."

"No!" Avery screamed. "I didn't do this!"

"You know you clawed at him until he was no more!" the voice screeched. "You know you did!"

Avery was having trouble breathing now. "NO!" she cried. "I DIDN'T!"

She turned around in disgust and closed her eyes. Avery took a deep breath, breathing in through her mouth and out through her nose. She continued breathing like this until she somehow felt calm even in this situation. Despite standing in a mess of blood, she smiled. When she and Ondrea were much younger, Ondrea would always tell Avery to smile the bad things away.

Now, using her Dragon Power senses, she took in EVERYTHING about the small cylindrical room. She sniffed the air and gagged as the stench of blood entered her nostrils, but she pushed through it and went deeper. She began to catch a tiny whiff of something far more disgusting than blood: it was death.

Ignoring all the sounds around her, with her eyes still closed, she turned toward Nick's body and sniffed. Surprisingly, the body wasn't the thing that smelled like death. Not even a little bit. Avery focused on the death smell and followed the scent. When her foot hit what felt like a wall, she opened her eyes and saw a wooden door. Still channeling her Dragon Power, she kicked through the wood with little effort.

The blood in the room rushed past Avery and flowed into a hallway on the other side of the door, but as it hit the floor of the hall, the blood turned into fresh water. Once she stepped through the hole in the door and looked back, Nick's body was gone. She noticed the smell of death was gone too, but that confused her.

"What are you doing, killer?" the voice asked, sounding guarded.

"I'm an artist," she proclaimed boldly. "I changed that blood into water using the power of my mind."

"That's impossible!" the voice exclaimed. "Also, why don't you seem scared anymore? Your behavior changed so drastically!"

"I'm horrified," Avery said, laughing. "But I know I could never do the things you say I did. Sure, I'm capable of killing—I'll give you that—but I'd never hurt the people I love. You can't trick me into thinking I did!"

"That's really dumb," the voice stated.

"Are you going to cry?" Avery asked in a mocking tone.

"That's a bit unnecessary," the voice mumbled. "And rude."

"Hey, dumb voice!" Avery shouted. "I bet that death smell is you, and you were using the blood to mask the scent of it. But when the blood disappeared, you realized you could no longer mask the scent, so you hid it completely."

The voice was silent for a moment before finally speaking. "How could you have possibly known that?" it asked, sounding genuinely surprised.

"It's obvious!" she yelled. "Now I know where you are too, so you can't play your mind games on me anymore. I'M NOT A KILLER!"

The voice began to laugh. Its laugh grew louder and louder until Avery thought her brain was going to explode.

"Where am I, then?" the voice asked her.

Avery smiled. "You're going to want me to say that your voice is coming from inside my head, but I won't say that because it's not true," she exclaimed. "You're above me."

"HOW DID YOU KNOW!" the voice screamed. "Stupid killer! You killer! You're a killer!"

Avery had had enough.

"Ever since last year when I hurt Nick, I've been so afraid that I would accidentally hurt someone else!" she shouted. "It was the only real fear that ever crossed my mind," Avery scoffed and let out a chuckle. "Thanks to this stupid situation that you believe frightened me, I realize that I was worrying for nothing! I know who I am! I know what I'm capable of and how to control what I can do! My heart is pure, I know that! My friends have taught me that! My friends and my sister were—and are—the best things to have ever happened to me! I will NEVER hurt them! You can't convince me otherwise!"

Avery sat down on the floor and crossed her arms. She didn't say anything. The voice didn't say anything. No one made a noise for about five minutes. Finally, the voice spoke.

"Good job, Avery," it said, now sounding like a completely different person.

"You sound like my mom, Jennifer," Avery whispered. She began to tear up, suddenly missing home. "Mom, how are my younger siblings? And you, how are you?"

The voice laughed, but, this time, it was sweet.

"We're all fine," Jennifer said. "I'm glad you finally figured out you don't have to be afraid of yourself."

"Well… thanks, mom," Avery said. "I miss you."

"I know you do," she said. "I love you."

Avery laughed and wiped her eyes, saying, "I love you too. And no, I'm not crying."

"It's time for you to go back to your friends," Jennifer said. "Say 'hi' to your sister for me—and don't do dumb stuff."

With those words, Avery's vision began to fade. When she regained sight once more, she saw Steven looking at her with worry written all over his face.

"Is something wrong?" she asked.

Steven began to unstrap her restraints as he responded, "No, not here." He shook his head. "Are you okay? We all saw the blood. That was like nothing I'd ever seen before."

Avery stood up and smiled.

"I'm fine," she answered simply. "I know who I am."

THIRTY-THREE

In Which Questions Are Asked and Answered

Steven cut the cameras and turned to face the kids. "Alrighty, children," Steven said. "As you should already know, because of all the craziness of today, the rest of you will wait to have your turns tomorrow."

"Dude, thank God," Will said with a loud sigh.

"Wait, hold on!" Oliver called. "We have some things to discuss, I'm sure."

Steven had gotten to know the kids over the short period of time they'd been together. He had been able to gather that they were a mysterious group, but also an honest one. And they were strategic—always thinking through everything they were about to say or do. They'd already even had a great impact on his sons—which was the most important thing in the world to him.

Thinking back to the fact that these kids, especially Oliver, were very careful about what they said, Steven was curious as to why Oliver had said that in front of Steven. He figured he'd speak up.

"What does this have to do with me, Oliver?" he asked, suddenly becoming nervous.

"You're going to be involved in a bit of the discussion," he answered. "Jessi, I'm sure you can take it from here."

Jessica looked at her brother and smiled.

"You got it, Ollie," she said. "Here's what needs to happen: Jake and Josh need to talk to you, Steven. I have a feeling Jason and Mason have a bit of a bone to pick with you, so they'll be joining you. The rest of you can do what you want—but, I'm going to the houses to take a long-needed nap."

"I think I'll do that too," Rachel said with a yawn.

While Jessica and Rachel went back to their separate rooms, Jason, Mason, Jake, and Josh went upstairs with Steven to talk.

"Dad, we know you're in trouble," Jake said as he and the others sat down in the living room area.

"Quick question," Josh interrupted. "Why are Jason and Mason here?"

Mason was quick to answer. With a hint of annoyance, he said, "Your dad decided that he needed Mr. Atrius' approval before being able to remove me safely from the simulation. I needed to be removed. Your dad didn't do it."

"Seriously?" Josh said, his head turning back in Steven's direction.

"I had no choice," Steven responded, practically whispering.

Jason suddenly became concerned. Every time anyone had grilled Steven about anything that was out of his control, he got flustered and began apologizing profusely. This time was different. Steven looked dejected, as if he decided to give up.

"Steven, you had better not give up!" Jason exclaimed angrily. "I know you need help, but if you give up, there's no way we can do that."

"I – I know," he said, still quiet. "I'm not giving up. I'm just tired of…tired of doing this. I'm tired of apologizing. I've exhausted myself worrying about this."

Jake's eyes began to water, and he put his arm around Steven's shoulders.

"Dad, you can do this," Jake said. "We'll do this together. My new friends have taught me that over time that you can accomplish anything if it's done together."

Steven threw his son a sad smile.

"I'm so glad you boys have found these wonderful people," he said. "I don't know why they are so different from anyone I've ever met…but I don't care because your happiness makes me happy."

"Hey, we should really start talking about this mess," Josh stated.

"He's right," Jason said. "This is a terrible situation, so we need to go over what we've learned. Mason, you first."

"So, we know that Mr. Atrius is bad news," he began. "We also know that you, Steven, are basically his puppet. We know Mr. Atrius works for VORK."

"What's VORK?" Steven interrupted. "Why is that so bad?"

Jason chuckled. "Let's just say they have a bit of history with us."

"We also know that Mr. Atrius has dark ma – madness." Jake exclaimed. "Dark madness. He's nuts."

"Idiot!" Josh mumbled under his breath.

"Anyway…" Jason said, "Steven, we're going to say a lot of things. Some of them might not make sense, but we will elaborate as much as we can. As you have probably realized, we're not your normal teens."

Steven looked up at the ceiling, sighed, then plopped to the ground, sitting with his legs crossed. He sighed again.

"Sure," he said. "Now, explain VORK."

"VORK is this horrible villainous organization that hunts kids like us. Mainly us," Mason explained. "They've been on our tails for a pretty long time."

"Shouldn't you have called the police?" Steven asked with a concerned look on his face.

Jason laughed and he couldn't help it. He wanted to stop, but he couldn't. Jason then realized just how tired he was. He was able to catch a break from laughing and sat down on the floor across from Steven with his head in his hands. Mason sat down next to him and put his hand on Jason's shoulder.

"Are you okay?" Mason asked his brother.

Jason's shoulders began to shake. Mason thought he was crying, but upon closer inspection, he noticed Jason was chuckling. Jason lifted his head and smiled with a strange glint in his eyes.

"I'm fine." Jason said. "I just think it's quite hilarious that you, Steven, would ask such a thing. 'Shouldn't you have called the police?' Absolutely not!"

As Mason caught his twin's point, he too smiled. "Honestly, Steven," Mason exclaimed, "If we could have called the police about this, we would have called a very long time ago."

"I think you guys are finally losing your minds," Josh mumbled.

"Maybe," Jason agreed. There was a long pause before he continued. "Anyway, we should finally get to talking about VORK."

As everyone began to think of a coherent way to explain this to Steven without revealing everything, Mason shouted.

"This is ridiculous!" he yelled. "Alright, Steven. Here's the deal. Listen closely. VORK is trying to kill us because we have Superpowers. And we are trying to stop VORK from killing literally everyone that is good and taking over the freaking world."

Jason looked at Mason and sighed.

"Out of all the times I've ever called you a moron, this is the most I've meant it," Jason said.

Everyone was quiet for a moment. Then Steven began to laugh.

"Why are you laughing now, Dad?" Jake asked, visibly confused.

"I already knew all of that!" Steven exclaimed.

"ARE YOU KIDDING ME?" Jason yelled. "SO, I'VE BEEN LOSING MY MIND FOR NO REASON!?"

"Steven…" Mason began, "There aren't enough words in any dictionary of any language to describe the emotions I feel."

Steven smiled nervously, closed his eyes, and rubbed the back of his head with his hand.

"Sorry about that," Steven said. "I thought Nick's father, Damian, told you that I knew. I was wondering why you guys were being so secretive."

Once again, no one spoke for a minute.

"Dad, you kind of suck," Josh said.

"Yeah… I know," Steven mumbled.

"Since my dad apparently knows the classified details, we should continue to talk about VORK," Jake said.

"Man, if only Will were here," Mason mentioned. "He's good at recognizing when we're getting off topic. It's almost annoying."

"VORK!" Jason said. "To catch you up, Steven, here's what we've learned and gathered. Mr. Atrius works for VORK. He has a giant bird that's angry all the time for some reason. Damian is assumed to be missing, and we know for a fact that Spencer—Nick's friend in case you didn't know—is missing.

"I suspect Mr. Atrius already knows we're on to him considering the obvious amounts of Dark Magic he's been throwing our way. Mr. Atrius should know that Jake suspects him. But does Mr. Atrius know we've told your sons about our Powers and our situation with VORK? We don't know."

"How would Jake suspect him—or know?" Steven asked, glancing at his son.

Jake chuckled. "About that, Dad…" He began, "When they told you way earlier that they had gone out to play hide and seek, they were actually looking for me."

"WHAT?" Steven asked, beginning to look nervous.

"Just tell him, Jake," Josh said, punching his brother on the shoulder. Jake took a deep breath.

"They were looking for me because I got flustered, ran out, got lost, and… and I got attacked by that unnecessarily large bird of Mr. Atrius'. And I couldn't… well, I couldn't… move," he said quickly.

"That damn idiot!" Steven yelled with a rage no one had ever seen from him before. He stood up abruptly and yelled in frustration. "I can't believe he would sic his stupid bird on my own son!"

"You knew he had a bird?" Josh asked, feeling a bit angry himself. "Why wouldn't you say anything before?"

"I thought he would keep his stupid bird in his stupid room!" Steven responded as he began to pace.

Josh's instincts kicked in and he stepped in between his brother and his father.

"Dad, how did you know about that bird in the first place?" he asked quietly.

Steven's eyes went wide and he immediately stopped pacing.

"He came into the job with the thing," he explained. "I told him to keep it leashed. I said it was the only way he could keep his bird and work here."

Mason jumped in. "Are you lying to us, Steven?" he questioned in a low growl.

"Of course I'm not!" Steven exclaimed. "I have no reason to lie! I swear!"

"We believe you, Dad," Jake said, stepping in front of Josh and closer to Steven."

Steven smiled with relief and gave Jake a hug.

"I'm so sorry his bird attacked you. I also apologize if I acted out just now. What you said before took me by surprise and really upset me," Steven said.

He released the embrace and hugged Josh next. "I apologize if I startled you," Steven said to Josh. "I didn't mean to make you worry."

"It's okay," Josh responded.

Mason and Jason refrained from saying anything at this moment… because they had no idea what to say. Instead, they shared a glance—a short glance that said enough. The twins officially put their guard up.

"I'm beat!" Jason exclaimed, yawning and stretching. "Before we get on our way, I do have a question for you, Steven."

Steven looked at Jason. "I'll answer it best as I can," he said as he tapped his foot.

"We did say Mr. Atrius works with VORK," Jason began. "I assume, as smart as you are, that you knew that. Why didn't you say anything?"

"I had no clue he was working for VORK!" Steven said with a look of shock on his face.

"Dad," Josh said. "Jason literally told you that in his recap earlier."

"He's right," Jake added. "But you didn't say anything."

"Kids, this is a bit much for me right now, so I'm all out of sorts," Steven said with a sigh. "That's why I probably seem a little off right now."

"Sure," Mason said slowly.

"We should all go rest," Steven said as he lumbered off to his bedroom.

When Steven had gone into his room and closed the door, Josh said, "I think we should talk."

33.1

Teddy and Ondrea watched as Jake, Josh, Mason, Jason, and Steven climbed the stairs.

"This has been quite the eventful day, Teddy Bear," Ondrea stated.

"How are you feeling after all this?" Teddy asked with a sigh.

"I'm feeling very nervous," she replied. "I'm not sure what to expect next."

"Yeah, I don't know either," he muttered. Teddy walked to the nearest chair and sat down. "It's been a long day."

Ondrea sat on the floor next to Teddy and grabbed his hand.

"How are you feeling?" she asked. "I ask because your hands are sweaty, and it's not hot in here."

"It's just nerves," Teddy replied. "You know I sweat when I'm nervous."

Ondrea smiled. "Yeah, I do," she laughed. "And it's absolutely disgusting."

Teddy let out a laugh. "Hey, your lack of frequent showers is disgusting too," he countered. "That's something you can do something about."

Ondrea let go of his hand and pretended to pout. "Whatever," she mumbled.

There was a moment of silence before Ondrea began to speak again.

"Hey, Teddy?" she said quietly. "I need to talk to you."

Teddy put on a nervous grin and said, "We are talking."

Ondrea laughed sadly. "No," she said. "I meant, like, really talk."

Teddy stood up and began to pace. He didn't like the sudden shift in her tone.

"Alright," he muttered. "What's up?"

Ondrea looked down at the floor and spoke quietly. "Well, I... we've been together for a couple years, and they've been great," she began. "But... we haven't taken any big steps."

"What do you mean by 'big steps?'" Teddy asked.

"Don't be so dense, Teddy!" she snapped. "I mean... we've held hands. We've kissed. But we haven't..."

Teddy interrupted her before she could say anything else.

"Don't even go there, babe," he stated, as he abruptly stopped pacing.

Ondrea stayed quiet for a moment, then laughed.

"By the look on your face, I can't possibly imagine what you thought I was going to say!" she exclaimed.

Teddy turned to look at her.

"Wait… what?" he said. "So, you didn't mean…"

"No, of course not, idiot!" she said, letting out another laugh.

"Then what did you mean?" he questioned as he continued his pacing.

"I meant we haven't… well, we…. we haven't actually… made out," she whispered.

Teddy stopped pacing again and opened his mouth as if he were about to say something but kept quiet. After a minute more of thought, he spoke.

"I know," he said simply. "I know we haven't made out yet which is fine, but… I wanted to be respectful since you never brought up the subject before."

Ondrea grinned. "Your undying respect is just one of the many things I love about you, Teddy Bear," she said.

Teddy felt bolder than he ever had in their relationship just then. He walked toward Ondrea, sat down on both of his knees, grabbed Ondrea's hands and asked, "What else do you love about me, my beautiful darling?"

Ondrea blushed and laughed. "You're VERY charming," she said. "You're also incredibly handsome and have a masculine smile."

"Aren't I the one who is supposed to compliment YOUR smile?" he asked, putting on a goofy grin.

"Did I mention that you're also the sweetest boy of them all?"

"No, you haven't," Teddy said with a laugh. "And I have yet to mention that you are the most radiant woman in all the world. That your glow could only match the Goddess of the Sun's golden aura."

She lifted her head from his shoulder. "Lady Caldria could be listening, idiot," she whispered playfully.

"Good!" Teddy exclaimed. He pointed his face toward the sky. "Let the lovely Sun Goddess know there is another out for her position!"

Once again, Ondrea head-butted Teddy's chest and let out a laugh. "You're crazy," she said.

"Crazy for you," he responded.

"I have the cheesiest boyfriend ever," she muttered as she lifted her head off his chest. She looked at his face and saw him smiling at her curiously.

"What?" she asked.

Teddy moved one of his hands to touch her cheek which was red from her embarrassment.

"I never realized how cute you look when you're embarrassed," he said.

That comment made Ondrea's cheeks redden even further. She took a deep breath and noted the way his eyes sparkled and leaned toward her soul. It seemed as if his eyes were caressing her heart. She focused on his thoughtful smile and noticed small, adorable dimples she had never seen before. She closed her eyes, took another deep breath, and felt time slow as she began to recall something about their past. She recalled the way his hand felt on her face the first time they had kissed years ago. It was the same as if felt today. Right now, in this very moment, her world consisted of only herself and Teddy.

Teddy felt Ondrea's cheek grow warmer and found himself staring into her eyes as if it was the only way he could live. His soul felt hot as she returned his gaze with one more loving than his. She closed her eyes and, as she did, her smile widened which made Teddy's heart melt.

This time was different than all the other times they had spent together. In fact, this time reminded him of their first, simple kiss. Her warm rosy cheeks, her serene expression, and her awe-inspiring beauty. He found himself inching closer to her to let his eyes bask even further in the sight of her gorgeous face. With her infatuating beauty seared in his mind, he closed his eyes and recreated the image perfectly. Without opening his eyes, he moved his other hand so now both were touching her face. In true love's trance, he leaned forward and kissed her.

Ondrea couldn't remember a time she had felt this happy. With their lips touching, she felt free. She felt as if anything was possible, as if the world was forever hers. She tugged on Teddy's shoulders gingerly and wrapped her arms around his neck, pulling him closer. The only people in the world were Teddy and Ondrea. They poured their emotions into each other as their souls became one and the same. The kiss lasted two minutes, and in those two minutes, the love birds communicated every word previously left unsaid. Years of sentiments they had never found the right words for had now been said in a single kiss.

The two of them hesitantly pulled away and opened their eyes, both their faces radiating newfound joy. A few seconds later, both their faces turned a bright shade of red and Ondrea let out a twinkling laugh. Teddy looked down and folded his hands in his lap. Ondrea took his hands and smiled at him. When she took his hands, he looked up and saw her glowing smile lighting up the world around him.

He began to laugh and let out all the nervous tension he had been feeling since their kiss ended. Teddy sighed and tried to speak.

"That was… that was…" He tried, but he found it difficult to get any words out. More accurately, he found it nearly impossible to describe the kiss.

Ondrea stood up and danced around the studio.

"That was incredible!" she exclaimed as she continued to dance and laugh.

"Yeah," Teddy said, still at a loss for words. "That was… incredible."

33.2

As everyone went their separate ways for the rest of the day, a thought came to Darla. There was somebody she needed to talk to. This situation was a bit different because it involved matters of the heart and she had no experience on that. She wanted to ask Ondrea and Teddy how to handle what she had been feeling, but she saw they were talking and didn't want to interrupt them. The studio had emptied and the only ones remaining were Teddy, Ondrea, and herself. She noticed Will had just left the room and was on his way to the houses. She ran after him, but stopped the second she exited the studio.

"What am I going to say?" she asked herself. "How do I… say anything to him? What would he say back? Do I tell him outright or do I ease into it?" Darla looked up from her thoughts and saw Will was about to turn the corner.

"Dang it. What do I say?" Darla sighed and stamped her foot on the ground. "Dang it! Dang it! Dang it! Get a hold of yourself, Darla. It's just stupid Will!"

She ran to catch up with Will. "I'll just do what I would usually do," she told herself. Lost in thought, she accidentally ran into Will and they both fell down. Darla scraped her knee against the gravel and winced.

"Jesus, Darla, who's chasing you?" Will questioned as he sat up and rubbed the back of his head.

Darla's face soured, and she made no attempt to move.

"Idiot," she mumbled.

"You're the one who ran into me!" Will exclaimed as he stood up. "Moron!"

"That's not how you address a woman who has fallen, Will," Darla said.

"Well, you're not a woman, but …whatever," he muttered. He reached out his hand and offered to help her up. She glared at it, hesitated, then turned her head away. Will crossed his arms and stared at her for a second.

"Oh, for goodness sakes, Darla," he said as he grabbed her arm and pulled her to a standing position. "Why are you suddenly being so difficult? First you run into me, then you stiff-arm me when I try to help you up. Come on."

Darla sighed and then sat down on the ground. Will, who had just pulled her off the ground, rolled his eyes then sat down next to her. He wanted to say something, but nothing came to mind. For some reason though, the silence didn't feel awkward to either of them.

Darla sighed again, then spoke.

"Sorry, Will," she said quietly. "I wasn't really thinking about where I was going." She looked up and positioned herself closer to him. "Did you hurt your head or something?"

Will laughed. "No, I'm good," he responded. "Just a slight concussion." Will had expected her to laugh with him, but she slouched and looked back down instead. "Hey, I'm just kidding. I'm fine, really." Another silence commenced for a short moment, then Will asked, "How does your knee feel?"

Darla looked up and straight ahead.

"It's fine," she answered. "Just a bit scraped up."

Will leaned forward and glanced at her knee. "Yeah, it'll be fine," he said to himself.

Darla turned her head toward Will and smiled. "For someone who just got mowed down by me, you seem pretty perky," she said, sitting up straight.

"Yeah. Weirdly enough, I was looking for you," Will mentioned.

Darla stood up and pushed pieces of gravel off her jeans. "Well, you found me," she exclaimed. "What do you need?"

Will stood up and faced her. "I wanted to know if…." Will hesitated. He didn't know if she was the type of person who liked walks.

"Will!" Darla yelled. "Are you having stroke or something?"

Will burst out laughing. "No! I was just wondering if you wanted to… go on a walk with… me… or something."

Darla's cheeks turned red. "Uh, yeah, sure," she said.

They turned and began walking along the gravel path.

"So," Will began. "Are you nervous for this chair thing?"

"Are you?" Darla countered.

"Well, yeah," he answered, once again rubbing the back of his head. "How could I not be? You and I both saw how everyone else's went."

"I'm sure it'll be easy," she said, waving it off. "Maybe it'll be fun."

"That sounds like something I would say," Will whispered as he looked toward his feet.

"You're dumb and immature, Will," Darla exclaimed with a smile.

Will released a small laugh.

"Exactly," he responded.

Darla was quiet for a moment before the realization finally hit her.

"Did you just call me dumb and immature, you idiot?" she exclaimed, as she slapped the side of his head.

"Remember my concussion, Darla," he said. "And no, I'm calling what you said dumb and immature."

"There's a much better way you could have put it," she muttered, crossing her arms.

"Listen, Darla…" Will paused. He stopped walking and planted his feet in the gravel. "Listen, Darla!" He said again. He looked at her with a sudden intensity in his expression. "I need you to take this seriously!"

Darla stopped walking and turned to face him.

"It was just one stupid comment, Will," she said. "You don't need to get all worked up about it. Besides, it will be easy. I'm going to nail this thing!"

"Dang it, Darla!" Will shouted. "Don't be dumb! This whole fear thing is, like, stupid dangerous. You saw what everyone else went through. It looked like Hell!"

"Will!" she shouted back. "I'm not blind! Of course, I saw it. Me and everyone else! So just shut up about it, okay!"

So many emotions began to bubble up inside Will—anger, nervousness, some excitement, but the most prominent was inevitable fear. His expression changed to show this feeling and was mixed with fiery anger. "DARN IT, WHAT IF YOU'RE NOT STRONG ENOUGH?" he screamed.

Darla's previous expression melted into rage.

"I know you didn't just call me weak," she growled.

Will covered his mouth with his hand and turned away as quickly as he could. After a minute of uncomfortable silence, he uncovered his mouth. "I didn't mean…. I… I'm…" He couldn't say what he felt he needed to say—not because he couldn't find the words, but because, if he did say them, they wouldn't be true.

Darla put her hands on her hips and glared at him.

"Go on! Say you're sorry," she said. When Will didn't say anything, she could feel her rage being replaced with sadness. Her eyes began to water.

"Go on!" she yelled. "Tell me you didn't mean it!"

Will turned to face her. "I… I can't," he whispered. "I can't because… because I meant it."

Darla's sadness deepened and she became angry once more.

"You jerk!" she screamed. "Jerk, jerk, jerk, jerk, jerk!" Darla lunged at Will and punched him in the face. Then, with one more look of disdain, she sprinted toward her housing, leaving Will with a black eye.

Will sat against the fence and looked toward the sky. After five minutes of spacing out, all the sentiments that had been shared within the past thirty minutes hit him hard. He covered his eye with his hand, then pulled it back. He looked at it expecting to see blood on his hand, but there was none. Instead, there were tears.

"I'm crying," he said to himself.

He blew it. He said something unforgivable, especially when said to a Superhero. Will called her weak and he knew it, but he didn't mean it to sound the way it had. He pulled his knees toward his chest and wrapped his arms around his knees, wanting to get as far away from the world as possible. Will began to sob.

"I'm so pathetic," he muttered. "Why did I say that?" Will looked in the direction Darla had run off, and he sighed.

"Maybe I'm the one who isn't strong enough," he said. "I wish I was."

THIRTY-FOUR

In Which There Are Bad Happenings

Jessica was in the middle of a wonderful nap when Darla threw the door open and stormed in. "Will is such a donkey butt!" Darla shouted.

Jessica woke up with a start. "Darla, what's wrong?" she asked while rubbing her eyes.

"He called me WEAK!" she screamed. "He's such a jerk!"

Jessica winced. "Alright, Darla!" she exclaimed with a sigh. "Quiet down! Don't get all worked up. You might accidentally activate your Powers."

Darla shoved her hands in the pockets of her jeans and glared at Jessica.

"I have perfect control over my Powers, thank you very much!" she growled.

"I understand, and I know you can control your Powers but… I've never seen you THIS mad before," Jessica said. She swung her legs over the side of her bed and stood up. "Just sit down and tell me what happened."

Darla sat down against the wall and began crying. Jessica's eyes widened, and she raced to Darla's side to comfort her. She knew Darla was upset, but she didn't expect her to start crying like this.

"Honey, what's wrong? Tell me everything," she said softly.

Darla looked at her and laughed. "You don't need to baby me," she said through her tears. "I'm not weak."

Jessica bit her lip and stayed quiet. Naturally, the silence somehow upset Darla even more, and she continued talking. "Jess…" she muttered. "Will called me weak, and I'm not sure why."

Jessica smiled and knew the perfect solution. "You should talk to him about it!" she exclaimed.

Darla slowly turned her head to look at Jessica and glowered. "No!" she yelled.

Jessica sighed. "Look, Darla, I'm sure he didn't mean it. Will may be an idiot sometimes, but he would never do anything to upset you," she said, laying a hand on Darla's shoulder.

Darla shook off her hand and stood up. "Why specifically me?" she asked.

Jessica smiled sadly. "You know he likes you, right?" she asked quietly. "He wouldn't intentionally do anything to ruin the current relationship between the two of you."

Darla crossed her arms and pouted.

"Whatever…" she muttered. She walked to her bed and sat down on the edge. "I… I doubt he likes me back." Darla's eyes widened and she covered her mouth with her hand.

Jessica raised her eyebrows and smirked. "Likes you back?" she asked with a chuckle. "I knew you liked him! You guys are perfect for each other after all."

Darla lay back on her bed and wiped the tears from her eyes.

"Shut up," she said. "You don't know how this feels! For some reason, this fight really hurts, Jessi."

Jessica stood up, went over to her own bed, and sat down on the edge.

"I have an idea of how it feels," she whispered. Darla looked at her with confusion in her eyes. She waited for Jessica to continue, which she did. "When Oliver and I were younger, we'd get into fights sometimes. I had just few other friends at the time, and my friends and I didn't fight very much. But when we did fight, it would be about something huge, and we would wind up not speaking for a couple of days.

"Since those fights happened rarely, when they did happen, it hurt a lot. At least, to me it did. My friends had a bunch of other friends, but they never introduced me to them, so I didn't get to know any other people. I'm sure when we got into a fight, it didn't affect them as much as it did me, since they got into fights with their other friends all the time."

"Is there a point to this story?" Darla asked.

"I'm pouring my heart out, Darla. Don't be so rude!" she exclaimed. Darla muttered "sorry," and Jessica continued.

"Anyway, sometimes random kids I had never met would start arguing with me. Sometimes they'd get physical. It was nothing too bad, but those hurt too. Mentally and physically." Jessica's eyes hardened, and she looked directly into Darla's eyes. "But whenever I got into a fight with Oliver, however, it would hurt more than any physical attack ever could. Although Oliver and I fought a lot, the aftermath would always sting, the worst pain in my life. The reason it hurt so much is because I love Oliver more than anyone else in the entire world. He means so much to me; he always has and always will.

"What I'm trying to say is this: the fights with Ollie hurt the most because I love him the most. Do you understand what I'm saying?"

Darla hesitated for a moment before saying, "So, you're trying to say that because you love Oliver so much, the pain of your frequent fights stung much more than your rare fights with your friends." Darla explained. "Am I right?"

Jessica sighed, then smiled.

"Right on the nail," she said. "Do you see how this relates to you?"

Darla sat up on her bed again, stood up, and began to pace. After a minute she said, "So, my fight with Will hurt more because I... like... him more?"

Jessica stood up, ran toward her friend, and hugged her tightly. "Now you get it, Dar!" she exclaimed happily.

Darla let the hug go on for a couple seconds longer before pulling away. "This still doesn't change that it really hurts," she mumbled. "Will's still a donkey butt."

"Sure, he is... sometimes," Jessica said with a laugh. "But he really likes you, so I know he didn't mean it the way you think he did."

Darla muttered a curse word under her breath. "Yeah, well... I'm still not going to forgive him quite yet," she said, pouting. "He needs to learn to watch his tongue."

Jessica smiled and rolled her eyes. Stubborn as always, she thought.

34.1

Since the gang had gone their separate ways, Oliver had spent those thirty minutes looking for Nick. He finally found him sitting against the back of the studio building.

"Nick!" Oliver exclaimed. "I've honestly been looking for you everywhere. You seemed so tired when I last saw you, so why aren't you resting in your room? Also, why are you away from everyone else?"

Nick looked up and gestured for Oliver to sit down next to him.

"I'm tired of worrying everyone," he said. "Last year, I seemed incredibly accident-prone and worried a lot of people. I almost died by losing my Powers, which sucked, and you all spent a long time trying to find me and rescue me. I feel like I'm just a huge burden."

Oliver laughed and put his arm around Nick's shoulders. "You're no burden, my friend!" he exclaimed. "The reason we did all those things is because we love having you around. I know we're Heroes, so it's our moral duty to risk our lives to save anyone and everyone, but you're different than anyone and everyone. You're really special to us, Nick."

"Thanks, Ollie," he whispered hoarsely. "That means a lot."

Oliver took another look at Nick's face and saw his eyes watering. Not only that, but Nick looked exhausted. "Nick, you really need to tell me what's going on," Oliver stated.

"Are you going to tell everyone else?" Nick asked.

"No, *we're* going to tell everyone else," Oliver said, tightening the grip on Nick's shoulders.

"Then… no!" Nick yelled, pulling away. "I won't tell you what's going on! I won't burden everyone with my problems!" Nick stood and began to pace.

"Nick!" Oliver yelled. "Sit down, for God's sake!"

"Oliver, I'm tired of going through the motions! I'm tired of constantly being in danger! I just want to have a normal life!" he exclaimed loudly. "I'm so done with worrying everyone, endangering everyone, having to fight for my life, and being…" Nick was cut off by a slap across his face. He stopped pacing and put his hand on his cheek, shocked by what Oliver had just done.

"You don't think I know all of this already!" Oliver whispered. "I feel the same way! WE ALL FEEL THE SAME WAY! This is our life, and it sucks more than anyone else will ever know! We have Powers—but we don't HAVE to save people if we don't want to! Well, guess what? We DO save people! We save them because we want to, not because we have to! You could have walked away from this a long time ago, but you never did."

Nick collapsed to his knees and bowed his head. Oliver knelt down in front of him and put his hand on Nick's shoulder.

"You… you slapped me," Nick mumbled.

"Yeah… sorry about that," Oliver said sheepishly. His eyes hardened again. "You were spiraling out of control, and I needed to snap you out of it. Anyway. . . you could have walked away from this life, but you never did. WE could have walked away from YOU, but we never did. You're our friend. You are NOT a burden! Do you understand me, Nicholas? You're not holding us back, you're not hurting us, and you're not as worthless as you think you are."

Nick looked up. "I never said I was worthless," he whispered.

"Then what's all this talk about being a burden?" Oliver asked. "If you think you're not worth saving, you might as well call yourself worthless. You are worth saving and we are all worried about you! Please just tell me what's wrong with you!" Oliver's eyes began to water, and he released his grip on Nick's shoulder.

After a couple of seconds, Nick suddenly pulled Oliver into a hug.

"I'm so sorry," he said. "I'm so very sorry. I don't know what came over me." Nick let go of the hug and sighed. "I do want to do this, and I understand the danger that comes with the job description. But I can't help being tired of it all. I'm also sorry I didn't take your feelings into consideration."

Oliver wiped his eyes and smiled.

"It's okay. I'm just glad we've got one issue settled. No more self-pity, okay?"

Nick nodded. "Oliver," he said, "I feel kind of sick. I feel like I did when I was in that cage last year getting my Power drained, except it feels more prolonged. And honestly a bit more painful."

Oliver peered at Nick's face again. "How long have you felt like this?" he asked.

"Since we met Mr. Atrius—which can only mean he's draining my Power, I think," he responded. Nick chuckled sadly. "Kind of ironic."

"Lift your head," Oliver said. "I just want to see how you're doing. Maybe I can use my Super Sensing Power on you."

Nick lifted his head, and Oliver saw a bit of sweat dripping down the sides of Nick face. "It's bad, isn't it?" Nick asked. "I can tell by the look on your face."

"Jesus, Nick!" Oliver exclaimed. "I know we had this discussion earlier, but we could have done something if you'd let me know sooner."

"Yeah, I know. I'm a bit stubborn," Nick said with a laugh. "You know, I probably should go and lie down."

"Yeah, maybe," Oliver agreed. "And don't worry about your dad and Spencer. Avery's on it, and I think I'm going to go and help her."

Nick nodded. He stood up, but immediately fell again. Oliver caught him before his head hit the ground.

"You want me to… uh… carry you?" Oliver asked awkwardly.

"No, it's alright," Nick answered. "Maybe just help me to my room and that'll be fine."

"Okay. By the way, Rachel said she was going to take a nap, so be a bit quiet if you can."

"Of course," Nick said.

"Alright, let's go."

34.2

As everyone headed their separate ways after the game show, Michael snuck backstage with an idea in mind.

"Time to see what this Mr. Atrius stuff is all about," he said to himself. "Back into the stereotypical villain lair I go. I just hope the villain isn't home."

Michael carefully ventured back to the purple door and took a deep breath. He noticed the door handle had been fixed since the last time he entered. He stared at it in shock as he realized what that had meant. When he first busted the lock with his electricity, there was no noticeable damage to the outside, so no one would be able to tell, but now it was fixed.

"This could only mean one thing," he said to himself. "Mr. Atrius knew someone broke in! But how is that possible?"

Michael put his ear against the door and covered his other ear with his hand to block any outside noise. He couldn't hear anything coming from inside, but that didn't mean Mr. Atrius wasn't lurking on the other side.

"Maybe this was a bad idea," he thought. "I should get backup, but... I... I can't, and I don't know why." Michael took a step back and sighed. "If I can't work out the confidence to do this with stealth, I'll just knock—because nothing can go wrong with that plan."

Michael lifted his shaky hand and prepared to knock. But before he could knock even once, a girl opened the door. She smiled wickedly and grabbed Michael's still outstretched hand.

"You must be my brother," she whispered.

The only thing Michael could register before he blacked out was a sense of unparalleled evil.

34.3

About an hour after everyone had dispersed, Oliver heard his phone ding. He pulled it out of his pocket and saw that Jason had written a group text asking everyone to meet at his place. Oliver immediately texted back, telling everyone to meet at Nick's instead. When Oliver got the okay from everyone, he began to head over there himself. Oliver was almost there when he spotted Will sitting on the ground against the fence with his head in his hands.

"Over here feeling sorry for yourself?" Oliver joked with a smile. The smile left his face when Will lifted his head and looked at Oliver.

"My God, Will, are you okay?" Oliver asked.

"I really messed up, Oliver," he whispered. "Now I think Darla hates me forever."

Oliver sat down beside Will and smiled. "Nothing you do could make her hate you forever," he said. "I'm sure you're just being dramatic."

"Do you say that to every person you try to cheer up?" Will asked.

"Nope, just you," Oliver responded with a grin. "You're the most dramatic person I know. My sister is the most dramatic person I'm related to though."

"Darla's pretty dramatic," Will mumbled, "and really strong." He absentmindedly rubbed his cheek, drawing attention to it. Oliver's eyes narrowed, and he focused on Will's face, noticing the bruise.

"Did Darla do this?" Oliver asked.

"Yeah, she did," Will answered sullenly. "I accidentally called her weak."

"Well, a couple of things," Oliver began. "I need to tell her that hitting friends is wrong no matter what. That aside, I'm surprised she didn't kill you. Also, how do you 'accidentally' call someone weak?"

"I didn't mean to!" Will exclaimed. "It was just a heat-of-the-moment sort of thing! I got all fired up about the fear simulations and I…" suddenly, both of their phones dinged.

"Will, Oliver, Michael, are you guys coming?" Jason asked.

Oliver responded saying that he was with Will and they'd be over in a minute. Oliver's phone rang because Jason decided to call.

"Hey, so Will is with you, then?" Jason asked frantically.

"Yeah, we're both here," Oliver said.

"Michael didn't say anything to you, did he?" Jason questioned, anxiety rising to the surface.

"No, he didn't say anything to me," Oliver responded. "Is something wrong?"

"We've all tried calling Michael, and no one has gotten an answer," Jason whispered. "Something is very wrong here."

THIRTY-FIVE

In Which Blackmail Is Revealed

When Oliver and Will opened the door to Nick's house, everyone began talking at once, and they were unable to make out any of it out.

"Guys!" Oliver yelled. "One at a time!"

When everyone quieted down, Jessica spoke. "I'm sure we have different things to talk about, but we should discuss the most important thing first… Michael."

"Actually," Oliver began. "Michael's disappearance is mysterious and worrisome, but Nick has something important to say first."

"Okay," Jessica said. "Nick, go on."

Nick cleared his throat nervously. "So, as you know, I've been feeling a bit… not okay," he said. "The thing is, I feel the same way I did when my Power was being drained in the cage last year."

"That's… that's not good," Teddy mumbled.

"I don't doubt how you feel, but this seems a bit different, Nick," Avery mentioned. "Am I right? I usually am."

Nick smiled. "Yeah, you're right," he admitted. "It's a bit more… painful this time."

"I guess that makes sense," Jason said. "Last year, a magic source was draining your Power and, by magic source I mean a sort of magic gauge."

"Oh, yeah!" Mason agreed. "Now it's different because a person is draining your Power. At least, I assume it's a person."

"Wait!" Josh said. "What about this cage magic draining incident?"

"Yeah, what is that?" Jake asked.

"We'll tell you later," Will said. "Right now, we need to stay on topic."

"Hold on. You're talking about Mr. Atrius, right?" Rachel asked quietly.

Oliver looked over and noticed Rachel looking very nervous. He walked over to her.

"Hey," he said soothingly. "Everything will be okay, you know that. No matter what happens, things will work out. They always do."

Rachel smiled. "Yeah, I know. It's just worrying is all," she whispered.

"I hear you, sister!" Will exclaimed dramatically.

Everyone looked up and smiled. Even Darla cracked a smile before rolling her eyes.

"Geez, Will," Ondrea said, laughing.

Will grinned. "Just trying to be a little comic relief," he said happily.

"Anyway," Nick began, "Rachel's correct about it being Mr. Atrius."

"Go figure," Jake muttered. "Wait, it could be the bird!"

"How could it possibly be the bird?" Teddy questioned with a tired sigh. "It's just a normal bird."

"It is definitely NOT just a normal bird!" Josh shouted. "It attacked my brother and stalked our bus! How likely is it that Mr. Atrius TRAINED the bird to do that? Not likely!"

"Guys!" Rachel said loudly. "There's something up with that bird. I know animals like the back of my hand, and that bird is different!"

"She's right," Jason said. "I could sense it from the very beginning. I thought maybe you guys could sense it too."

"I could," Oliver stated. "I thought the same thing. Couldn't you guys sense it?"

"I couldn't," Darla said.

Everyone shook their heads.

"You two have some kind of Super Intelligence, right?" Josh asked timidly. "Maybe that's it."

"Wait, Josh, how did you know that?" Oliver asked, very alarmed. "We told you we had Powers, but we never told you specifically what."

Josh pulled a folded piece of paper out from his pocket, unfolded it, and gave it to Oliver.

"After Mason, Jason, Jake, Steven, and I had our conversation, the four of us continued talking without Steven," Josh explained. "I went off when our conversation was over and snooped around in Dad's private office. That list is what I found."

Oliver looked at the list and gasped. He dropped it as his hand began to shake. Jessica picked it up and read it over.

"What the..." she mumbled. "How does Steven have a list with all of our Powers on it?"

"We meant to talk to you guys about that," Jake said sheepishly.

Everyone except Josh, Mason, and Jason turned to glare at Jake.

"You mean you knew about this list!" Will exclaimed.

"No!" Jake yelled in a panic. "No! That's not it!"

"Will, calm down," Jason said with a sigh. "When we talked to Steven, we learned a couple of things. One of them being that Steven had already known about our Powers from the beginning. That's most likely how the list plays into all of this."

"How could he possibly know?" Oliver asked, his voice shaking.

"Apparently Damian, Nick's father, told him," Mason answered. "I assume that's how Steven knew about Nick's military background."

Nick sat up in bed and sighed heavily.

"I don't know why my dad would have told Steven about our Powers. And why did he have to mention my military background?" Nick said. "It's not like it was a huge part of my life or anything."

Everyone turned toward Nick with confused expressions.

"Dude, are you serious?" Teddy asked.

"Yeah, I'm pretty sure your military experience was, and even still is, a pretty big part of your life," Avery added.

"Are you losing your mind or something?" Darla asked sarcastically.

Nick was quiet for a second before responding. "I'm too tired to care at this point," he said with a laugh.

"Then we'd better get on with the important stuff," Will said, once again reminding everyone to stay on topic.

"We were talking about how Steven knows about our Powers," Ondrea said.

"Sure, but in order to get the full gist, we should probably tell you what we know, infer, and suspect from our conversation with Steven," Jason stated. He pulled a piece of paper from his pocket and handed it to Mason. "Read this, would you?" he asked with a loud sigh.

"You do it," Mason countered.

"I'm feeling a bit flustered right now, and I would prefer you do it," Jason said as he sat down on the floor.

Mason sighed and unfolded the paper.

"It's a list," Mason said as he scanned the paper. "It's a list of everything we learned in our conversation with Steven. I'll just paraphrase."

"No," Jason said. "Read it exactly how I wrote it."

Mason looked at Jason and rolled his eyes.

"Okay, fine," Mason said. "Number one: Mr. Atrius dictates who gets to exit the machine early. Number two: Steven is being controlled by Mr. Atrius. Number three: Steven already knew about our Powers. Number four: Steven thought Damian had told us that Steven knew about our Powers. Number five: Mr. Atrius is onto us. Number six: Steven is clearly lying about Mr. Atrius's bird and that he didn't know Mr. Atrius worked for VORK. That's it."

"That's a lot to swallow," Rachel said quietly.

"No kidding," Oliver mumbled.

For the next couple of seconds, there ensued a deafening silence until Jason spoke.

"There are a few things I have gathered from the information we have," he began. "Related to number two on the list, I'm thinking Steven is not only being controlled by Mr. Atrius, but he's being blackmailed by Mr. Atrius—based on the way he was acting during the conversation and times before that. On the other hand, it seems that Steven ALWAYS acts flustered.

"Also, about that bird… Earlier, when Rachel said something didn't seem right about it… well… she was correct. Obviously, it's MUCH smarter than your average predatory bird," Mason explained. "I'm not sure what the bird's end goal is, but first it tried to attack me, and then it attacked Jake."

"Some birds attack in patterns," Rachel added. "The intelligent species are usually looking for a certain physical attribute like taste, smell, size, or appearance. This bird is clearly very intelligent just like Mason said, but it's also much larger than any other species of bird I've ever known. Plus, this bird doesn't appear to have any attack pattern like I mentioned. Now, some intelligent birds DON'T have an attack pattern naturally, but… there's still something off about this bird's attack sequence. I can't quite put my finger on it though."

"I was able to sense something about the bird, and I'm surprised none of you mentioned it earlier," Jessica said. "Using my Super

Sensing, I could tell that this bird has Powers, so it's obviously not a normal bird."

"What!" Rachel shouted, suddenly frustrated. "I can't believe I didn't sense that too! Animals are my thing!"

"Either the bird or Mr. Atrius must have been masking its magical presence," Oliver mentioned. "Besides that, you should know that nothing can get past Jess and I when it comes to our Super Sensing."

"Speaking of the bird," Jake said. "Mr. Atrius knows that I know how mean and evil his bird is. At least I think he does. The thing is, I'm not 100 percent sure if he knows you all have told Josh and me about your Powers."

"You could be right," Avery said as she crossed her arms. "And that could be an advantage for us."

"Unless he DOES know," Will stated.

"Even if he knows, Mr. Atrius doesn't seem to be treating us differently," Josh said. "He made the bird attack Mason, someone with Powers, and he made the bird attack Jake, someone without Powers."

Jason, still sitting on the floor, looked up at Mason and frowned. Something about his twin seemed off. He was clearly worried about something specific.

"Mason, what's on your mind?" Jason asked.

Mason walked back and sat against the wall. He then put his head in his hands and sighed.

"This is way too complicated," he whispered. "I mean, it's so obvious that Steven is being manipulated by Mr. Atrius, but Steven could also be acting of his own accord. I mean, Steven seems nice and all, but he *could* be acting."

"What do you mean?" Jason asked.

"I mean that he acts differently off camera than on camera, so he's clearly acting there. But what if everything we know about him is also an act?"

"No way!" Jake exclaimed. "We've known Dad, obviously for our whole lives, and he would never do anything malicious! Right Josh? You can back me up here."

Josh cleared his throat and looked away as he quietly said, "I'm in the same boat as Mason. I don't think I can look at Dad the same way anymore. Not until we've figured this whole thing out."

Jake stared at his brother in shock. "I can't believe you!" He roared. "This is Dad we're talking about and…"

Nick interrupted him. "Can we all just take a chill pill!" he yelled. "We shouldn't be fighting amongst ourselves! There's just no time for that!"

The room went quiet, and everyone looked down in shame.

"Sorry," Jake muttered after a minute.

"Something we're not thinking about…" Will said with a shaky voice. "Michael's last name is Atrius."

"But he told us that he didn't have any relatives with the last name of Atrius," Nick said.

"That he knew of . . ." Will added.

THIRTY-SIX

In Which a Villain is Revealed

Michael woke up to a throbbing pain in his skull. When he opened his eyes, he noticed he was tied up in a chair. Everything was blurry at first, but then he saw a girl sitting on a counter a few feet away from him. She appeared to be assembling a Star Wars® Lego® set.

Michael cleared his throat. "Is that the Cloud City set from Empire Strikes Back?" he asked.

"Why yes, yes, it is, and I've been working on it for WEEKS now!" she responded distractedly. "It's really a legendary scene!"

"Yeah, it's the one where Darth Vader says, 'I am your father,' and then slices Luke's hand off," Michael said almost smugly.

"Are you a die-hard Star Wars fan like I am?" she asked, finally looking up from her Lego set.

"I wouldn't say I'm a die-hard Star Wars fan, but I could always go for a good re-watch," he answered.

The girl stayed quiet for a second before hardening her expression.

"Hold on!" she yelled. "You're my prisoner! I shouldn't be discussing this with you!"

"What else are we going to do?" Michael asked.

She stared at him, completely bewildered.

"How are you not scared right now?" she questioned. "You should be scared!"

"I am a little scared, and I'm sure this is nothing to sneeze at," he admitted. "This is the first time I've ever been taken prisoner. So, I might as well make the best of this experience—since you're probably going to kill me anyway."

The girl's expression remained unchanged.

"WHY ARE YOU SO CALM ABOUT THIS?!" she screamed, clearly frustrated.

"There really isn't any point in panicking," he said casually. "What's your name, by the way?"

She turned away and began to mumble curse words. Then, she took a deep breath, put on her most evil grin, and turned around.

"My name is Sydney," she said with a growl.

"And you're a villain?" he asked with an amused grin.

"YES! I AM!" she exclaimed. "I'm also your sister."

"Yeah, I remember you mentioning something about that," Michael said. "You know, I thought real-life villains were supposed to be scary."

Sydney stomped her foot and glared at him menacingly. Michael couldn't help but shiver as the room seemed to suddenly drop in temperature, and her eyes began to glow a subtle red. When Sydney saw him shiver, she slowly grinned, her expression a mixture of amusement and unchecked anger. When Sydney opened her mouth to speak, he noticed that every tooth had been shaved to a dagger-like point.

"What do you think of me now, brother?" she asked in a low voice.

Michael, out of fear, was about to make a sarcastic comment, but realized his body felt paralyzed. Sydney's eyes lit up with a newfound determination, and she belted out a perfectly executed villain laugh. To Michael, however, there was something different about this evil laugh. It was much more sinister than any laugh he had ever heard in the movies or on television shows.

"This is nothing like I expected." Michael thought.

Sydney finally stopped laughing maniacally and cleared her throat. Her eyes and teeth returned to normal. Michael did not. He still shivered, even though the room appeared to return to normal temperature. He began taking deep breaths to calm his nerves, but he also gritted his teeth in anger. His body wouldn't stop shaking and his heart continued to pound.

"I bet you feel weak," Sydney whispered in her normal voice. "I bet you feel powerless."

"I still… still have my Powers," he mumbled.

"Sure, you do," Sydney exclaimed happily. "But you won't use them. You can't. Not in this situation."

Michael closed his eyes to block out the setting and focused on the metaphorical voice in the back of his head. That voice, for some reason, was his therapist telling him to have confidence in himself and believe in his resolve. This time, those words didn't help, and Michael was clueless as to why. Considering how many times he had gone to therapy, he figured the message would be seared into his subconscious by now.

"Why are you hiding from it, Michael?" asked Sydney. "You can't hide from the weakness inside of you."

Michael bit his tongue, and the pain, along with the shocking taste of blood in his mouth, snapped him out of his slump.

"I've never been weak," he growled.

Sydney laughed normally and scoffed. With a smile on her face, she said, "You can say that all you want. It doesn't matter how many times you say it because you've never believed it."

"Sure, you're right," Michael said. "But I think I'm starting to."

Sydney began to pace.

"Why? Because of those stupid friends of yours?" she exclaimed. "You just met them. You don't know anything about them. And no matter how much faith you have in them, or how much resolve you have in yourself, you'll never be able to escape from the pain that holds you back and makes you weak."

Michael's eyes widened as he began to wonder if she made a valid point.

"Maybe… maybe you're right," he began. "But I won't let that stop me from trying."

"Michael!" Sydney snapped. She turned to him with a sad smile. "You'll never outrun your pain."

"Good words of encouragement, Syd," he said under his breath.

She chuckled and softly placed her hand on his shoulder. Michael, who had been looking down the whole time, flinched and instinctively tried to scoot away before he remembered he was tied down.

"I can help get rid of that pain, Michael, sweet brother," she said as she began to stroke his shoulder.

"Jesus, woman!" he exclaimed. "Stop touching me! It's weird. Also, I'm not falling for this."

Sydney removed her hand from his shoulder and took a step back, pretending to be hurt.

"Not falling for what?" she asked.

"I'm not falling for this classic villain trope! The one where the villain gives this falsely empathetic speech about how they can make all your problems disappear—and then brainwashes you into doing whatever the villain wants," he explained.

"I'd never brainwash my own dear brother," Sydney said innocently.

Michael, for the first time, looked deep into his sister's eyes and saw something he'd only seen previously when he glanced in the mirror. He saw himself. That realization chilled him to the bone. What also chilled him was seeing genuine innocence and sympathy in her eyes when, just a minute ago, he had seen genuine burning hot rage and destructive evil.

"I'm dealing with a 'grade A' psychopath who switches from one emotion to the next in a matter of seconds," he thought. "I have to be careful. She's clearly powerful, so I don't want to set her off. She's playing the sympathy card. I need to play along. Clearly, she's intelligent and would be able to tell when I'm lying, so I'll just have to tell the truth."

Michael knew, judging by the real sympathy and sadness in her eyes, that she wouldn't be able to fathom his deceit. He played on that. He did something he swore he'd never do and let down his guard. He needed to, in order to tell the truth about his feelings. Michael sighed, preparing to vent his innermost feelings to a psychotic villain while being tied up in a chair. He looked down in shame.

"I'm not sorry for assuming the worst of you, but I am sorry I lied to you about how I've been feeling," he said tensely. He wanted to look up and judge her expression, but he kept his head bowed instead in order to appear very ashamed. After a minute of silence, he slowly looked up.

Sydney took a step back with a look of actual shock on her face. For a second, deep suspicion flickered in her eyes but then it was replaced with pure joy.

"Really?" she asked, her bubbly voice bouncing with excitement. "You really mean it? Oh, that's so great! Maybe we can be good friends! Maybe even act like real siblings!"

She skipped over to Michael and gave him a hug. He wanted to squirm out of it, but he couldn't because he was tied to a chair. His entire body tensed when she touched him. He sensed a presence darker than the void lurking deep inside of her—a presence just waiting to come out. She didn't seem to be fighting it, which let Michael know that she and whatever was inside of her respected each other, and that Sydney was in full control. She pulled away from the hug with an even bigger grin on her face, which made Michael wonder.

"Hey, do you have any friends?" he asked.

The smile left her face and turned into a frown. Then she began to sob. Michael sensed a lonely sadness within her with enough depth to drown in. She was drowning in sorrow.

Suddenly, a realization hit him like a boulder: the darkness inside her was also crying. She was shedding enough tears for both of them. They were both lonely. Suddenly her expression hardened, and her breathing settled, but tears still rushed down her cheeks like waterfalls. This was a very unsettling look.

"I have one friend," she said quietly. Her voice sounded steady and normal, but she was still crying for some reason. "I have only one, but one is all I need. I love my friend."

As soon as she said that, the tears stopped flowing, and her sluggish demeanor vanished entirely.

"My friend is happy now," she exclaimed cheerfully.

"Sorry I asked," Michael muttered, shaken to his core. He looked away from her because looking at her filled him with so much fear, he felt like his heart would stop beating.

"Well, that's just not fair!" she whined loudly. "You can't even look at me without being scared." She crossed her arms.

"Well…" Michael began meekly, trying to think of what to say without setting her off. "You just finished crying… and… and your face is a bit… red and snotty. Your eyes are puffy too."

Sydney pouted again. "What are you trying to say, brother?" she asked, a look of defiance in her eyes.

Michael looked toward the ceiling and sighed heavily. He was getting nowhere at all. He thought he'd better move this along. He then stared Sydney dead in the eyes.

"You look disgusting," he stated plainly. "I'm trying to say you look disgusting. Your nose is dripping, your face is red, and your eyes are…"

She completely cut him off and chuckled.

"And my eyes are red too?" she asked in an ominous whisper. "Because that's my preferred color. My friend likes that color too, but it's clear you don't. Will that be a problem in the future, my dear brother?"

Michael nervously cleared his throat.

"Uh… no… no, not at all," he said, his voice cracking.

"I don't believe you!" she screeched, sounding oddly bird-like. "I don't like people who can't accept me for who I am. But I REALLY don't like it when my family LIES TO ME! Liars need to be punished!"

Sydney dove at Michael with claw-like fingernails, opened her mouth to reveal razor-sharp teeth, shrieked, and then closed her jaws in Michael's shoulder. Michael screamed in pain until his throat gave out. It was only when he stopped screaming that she unclamped her jaw from his shoulder and peered at his face.

Michael bowed his head and almost passed out, but Sydney squeezed his wounded shoulder, causing him to shout out in pain. He snapped his head up to see her only an inch away from his face with a happy smile, but a look of pure rage in her eyes. She let go of his shoulder, stood back and studied him as if feeling concerned suddenly.

"I didn't want to hurt you," she said returning to her angsty self. "But that's what you get. I told you liars need to be punished."

She caressed his face gently and sighed. Michael felt too weak to pull his head away.

"This won't do," she whispered to herself. "Let me bandage that shoulder for you."

She turned around and rummaged through a drawer that seemed to hold nothing but white bandages. She jumped as she spotted what she was looking for and turned to face him. Sydney held a red bandage in her hand and began wrapping it tightly around his wound. A small cry escaped his lips.

"You'll be fine," she said nonchalantly. "How does this feel?"

When Michael didn't answer, she sighed once more. She asked again, but he still couldn't answer. He couldn't seem to get his vocal chords to work. So many things had just happened in the span of so few seconds that his mind was having difficulty processing everything.

"Maybe I pushed her a bit too hard," he thought. Michael couldn't help cracking a smile at his predicament. Sydney became impatient waiting for his answer and slapped him across the face.

"Hey, idiot!" she exclaimed. "How do you feel now? It's okay to say that you're scared for your life, because I'll understand. That's what most people say after I harm them."

"Hey…" Michael said softly. "Why is my bandage red?" He had no clue why this was the first thing to come out of his mouth. He chalked it up to the shock.

Sydney perked up, clearly glad he had asked.

"I've been saving that one especially for you," she said. "Our dad has brought in many people to make me happy, and he told me that one day, he'd bring my brother to me."

Michael's brain did a one-eighty.

"Hold on," he said loudly. "You've been saving that for me?"

"Yes, of course I have," she said as if it was obvious. "I've been patiently waiting for you to come back home, and now you have. I'm very excited."

Sydney went back to working on her Lego set as if nothing had happened, completely ignoring Michael. He was perfectly fine with that, and eventually fell asleep.

36.2

"Good morning sleepy head!" Sydney exclaimed, violently shaking him awake.

Sydney's shaking, along with an incredibly sharp pain in his injured shoulder, woke Michael up from his nightmare—only to realize he woke from one nightmare to roll right into another one. "Morning, sis," he said. "What time is it?"

"That doesn't matter!" she exclaimed with an uncharacteristically happy smile. "All that matters is all the fun we're going to have today!"

"Oh boy, can't wait," he muttered sarcastically.

Sydney's demeanor swiftly changed back to her angsty self, and she slapped him across the face. When she saw him glance at her and raise his eyebrows as if asking why she did that, Sydney just shrugged.

"I wanted to make sure you were really awake," she responded.

"Can you untie me from the chair?" Michael asked wearily. "Also untie my wrists?"

Sydney shrugged and cut him loose from the chair. Michael's wrists were still tied behind his back. She stood behind him to cut those loose too, but stopped and inhaled sharply.

"No can do on the wrists," she said.

"Well, can you at least loosen then?"

Sydney frowned at his pain and said, "No. I was just trying to teach you a lesson. I wanted the lesson to stick, which I'm sure it did. But I didn't want YOUR pain to continue. I would give you pain medicine, but I don't have any. All I have are my usual medications—anti-depressants and stuff for my anxiety."

"I'll take some anti-depressants," Michael joked, becoming used to her sadistic ways.

Sydney laughed. "If you're serious, I can give them to you. Maybe if I give you enough, they'll numb your body," she offered.

Michael smiled at her genuine sisterly concern, then rolled his eyes at her obvious lack of sanity.

"No way. I would never take your pills. That was a joke," he exclaimed. "I'd never take medicine from strangers or medicine that wasn't specifically prescribed for me. I'd never take more than the prescribed dose because any amount more could be detrimental to my health and hurt me more than help."

Sydney rolled her eyes and chuckled, saying, "You sound like one of those public service announcements." She closed her medicine cabinet, taking a couple of her pills. Once she finished chewing, she swallowed and reached to the side of the counter for water. She took a huge swig and cleared her throat.

"Also," she continued. "You're right about all those things."

"Then why did you just take those at random?" he asked. "Also… why did you… chew the medicine? You're supposed to swallow them with the drink of your choice."

"I like to lick the leftover powder off my teeth. When I do, it reminds me of powdered sugar," she said as she shrugged her shoulders.

"To each their own." Michael mumbled.

"Now it's time for the fun to begin!" Sydney exclaimed joyously.

"What fun?" Michael asked, suddenly becoming worried. Her idea of fun was most likely… questionable at best.

Sydney turned on the television set in her room, and the game show came on. Steven began speaking. Thirty seconds later, Ondrea walked toward the chair.

"So… I'm missing it then?" Michael asked with a sigh.

"Of course not!" Sydney said. As she said this, the temperature in the room dropped, her teeth became sharp, and her eyes turned a deep blood-red color. "Besides, the fun hasn't even started yet. I'm about to prepare you for when it's your turn on the chair. I'm going to make it easier for you, so you won't be nervous about your darkest fear just in case you were unsure of what exactly it would be.

"What… what does that mean?" Michael asked, voice shaking.

Sydney's voice suddenly dropped and she licked her lips, showing a snake-like tongue.

"That means… I'm going to show you fear like you've never experienced before, so when you go up to the simulation chair, you'll know exactly what you're afraid of," she whispered.

Michael froze as everything around him became silent except for the demonic sound of Sydney's voice. Michael jumped out of the chair when he heard Sydney speak right next to his ear.

"One more precaution before the fun begins," she said. She hit a button that was pinned on the wall behind Michael's chair. "The inside of this room has a magic soundproof barrier, which means no sound can get out of this room. None. No matter how… loud. We'll be needing this to… optimize… our fun."

A thin shield of magic dark magic suddenly coated the walls and door of the room, somehow making the room dim. It didn't look like much, but the Power Michael sensed from it was almost as intense as the indescribable evil Sydney began to give off in that moment. It was the kind of evil that could snuff out the sun as easily as it did him!

"I'm going to make sure to have the most fun with you, since you're family," Sydney whispered, her voice echoing in the foreboding silence. "I'm going to make sure that by the time it's your turn in the chair, I will be your deepest, your darkest, and your worst forever fear."

THIRTY-SEVEN

In Which One Door Opens

Everyone congregated at a bench near the studio the next morning.

"How is everyone?" Oliver asked with a yawn.

As a response, everyone collectively yawned with him. Oliver laughed. "I see we all had trouble sleeping!" he exclaimed.

"Nick," Teddy said. "How are you today?"

"Yeah, you think you can make it through today?" Jessica asked, putting a supportive hand on his shoulder.

Nick yawned again and rubbed his eyes.

"Maybe," he responded. "I probably shouldn't have stayed up most of the night looking for Michael though."

Everyone looked down at the ground and sighed.

"You too, huh?" Rachel said quietly.

Avery smiled sadly. "How many of us stayed up most of the night looking for Michael?" she asked as she raised her own hand.

Everyone raised a hand, except for Darla. She blinked a couple of times and then shrugged.

"What? I was tired, and I assumed you guys would take care of it—which you did," she said. "Even though no one found him, you did one of us a favor. You allowed me to sleep!"

"Not now, Dar," Will mumbled under his breath, not realizing his mistake until after he finished his statement.

"Nobody asked you, Will!" Darla growled. "So why don't you just shut up and keep your head down!"

"Holy crap, Darla!" Ondrea exclaimed. "That was beyond rude! You can't just say that to a person!"

"It's fine, Ondrea," Will said, not looking up.

Everyone gave Will and Darla looks of concern, but no one pushed the matter.

"So… no one found him, then?" Jake asked with a sad sigh.

Josh, who was standing next to Jake with his hands in his pockets, put his hands on Jake's shoulders and shook him.

"Shake the worries out, moron," he said. "That's what Dad used to say when we were younger. So, shake them out."

"Yeah, I remember I got dizzy from doing that back then too!" Jake responded with a laugh. "I've learned a few things since then, like this."

Jake brought his elbow back and jammed it into his brother's ribs. Josh fell to the ground and began to laugh. He grabbed Jake's leg and pulled it out from under him, causing Jake to crash to the ground. They both laughed and lay there for a moment. When they saw everyone else directing amused grins their way, the twins quickly stood up and dusted themselves off, acting as if nothing had happened.

"That was cute, you guys," Rachel said, her grin turning from amused to mischievous.

"That didn't happen," Jake grumbled as he cleared his throat.

Josh frowned, pretending to be sad. "Aw, come on bro," he said in a baby voice. "Is Jakey embarrassed?"

"I'll leave!" Jake exclaimed, angrily. "I'll do it!"

Josh smiled at his brother and squeezed his shoulder.

"I didn't mean it, idiot," he said.

"Yeah, I know, moron," Jake countered, chuckling.

It was silent for a minute before the twins, once again, cleared their throats.

"But seriously," Josh began. "Never speak of this."

"Okay!" Darla said, sounding exasperated. "I guess we can't tell anyone that you're acting like siblings."

"So, no one found Michael?" Will asked, getting everyone back on track. "Let's start there."

"We've started and we've finished," Ondrea mumbled with a sigh.

"What does that mean?" Oliver asked.

"I have no idea where to go from here!" she exclaimed, throwing her hands in the air. "All we know is we DON'T know where Michael is. He could be in danger!"

"He most certainly has to be in danger," Jason said. "Otherwise, I'm sure he would have appeared by now."

"You think it could have something to do with the bird?" Mason asked, anxiously tapping his foot on the ground. "Or maybe Mr. Atrius?"

"Definitely one of those two," Rachel muttered sadly.

Avery put her hand on Rachel's shoulder.

"We'll find him—or he'll find us," she said cheerfully. "One way or another, we'll get him back."

"You say that as if he's been taken!" Teddy said. He began to pace back and forth. "Do you think he's been taken?"

Ondrea grabbed Teddy's arm to calm his pacing and pulled him closer. She kissed him on the cheek and said, "Even if he has, he'll be fine. I'm sure of it, Teddy Bear."

"He most certainly has been taken," Jason stated confidently.

"Look, Jason," Oliver began. "I'm all for getting to the point quickly, but could you take it easy with the 'most certainly' stuff?"

"You're kind of harshing the vibe," Nick said with a humored grin.

"What does that even mean?" Jason asked.

Jessica sighed. "What he's saying is you're being a bit of a downer, but I disagree," she said. "You're not being a downer, you're just being you. Factual and straight to the point."

Jason frowned. "I've never thought about it like that," he whispered. "I never thought of myself as a… downer. I'm sorry."

Mason's eyes widened. "No way, bro!" he exclaimed, feeling a bit panicked. "You're no downer! This discussion is pointless, really!"

Jason threw Mason a sad smile and clasped his hands behind his back.

"Mason, you don't have to say that for me," Jason said. "If it's true, it's true."

"But it's not true!" Mason said quickly. "Right guys? It's not true."

"He's right," Jessica agreed. "I'm sorry, Jason. I never meant to make you think you're a downer."

"It's alright, guys," he said. "I get it."

Mason let out a sigh of frustration. "But we said you're not a…"

Will cut him off. "Guys! Can we seriously focus?" he shouted. "I can't believe I'M the one saying this! I never have to say that!"

"Sorry, Will," Jason said softly.

Will relaxed his tone. "It's fine. Let's just talk about Michael," he sighed.

"If you think about it, there really is nothing else to say about Michael," Josh said. "We've already confirmed he's most likely kidnapped and probably in trouble."

"Yeah, we don't really know much more about the situation," Jake added.

Everyone was quiet for a moment. Suddenly, there was a small noise, and the air began to smell weird.

"Who farted?" Avery asked, covering her nose.

"We all know it was you, Will!" Darla exclaimed, turning away from the smell.

"Sorry guys, the air was getting a little stagnant, so I decided to spice it up," he said, not being able to make the joke with a straight face. "Man, we've been so busy I haven't had the time to… expel… a fart joke in a while."

"Dang it, Will," Rachel mumbled with an amused grin.

Everyone laughed at Will's tactlessness. "That was pretty good," Darla muttered with a sigh. "Even I have to give you a point there."

"Heck yeah!" Will exclaimed. He held up his hand toward Darla for a high-five, but she rolled her eyes and turned away. "Okay, not there yet… but we're making progress!"

"Making progress on what?" Avery asked.

"Don't worry about it," Darla responded. "And from now on, you can just ignore the idiot Will."

Will, who was still holding out his hand for a high-five, frowned, high-fived himself, and put his hands to his side.

"I can give you a high-five," Nick said as he held up his hand.

Although, for Will, the moment was ruined and he didn't feel like high-fiving anyone, he knew leaving anyone offering a high-five hanging would be a cardinal sin, so he high-fived Nick anyway.

"So, what do we do now?" Oliver asked.

"About Will's terrible jokes or about Michael?" Avery questioned, genuinely unsure of which one Oliver would be referring to.

He sighed in annoyance and said, "About Michael."

Will pouted and opened his mouth to say something, but Darla glared at him, shutting him up.

"We could search the studio before the show starts," Mason offered, tapping his foot again.

"The show is starting really soon," Josh said.

"Yeah, I doubt we'd have time," Jake added. Out of nervous habit, he began to scratch his arm, but Josh slapped Jake's wrist to get him to stop.

"What if we all split up?" Jessica asked, staring off into the distance, deep in thought. "Then would we have time?"

Suddenly, Jake's phone alarm went off and everyone jumped. "I guess we had less time than we thought!" he exclaimed as he reached into his pocket to turn off the alarm. "We've got five minutes until it starts!"

"We'd better get going, then!" Ondrea yelled, startling everyone.

While everyone raced forward to get to their podiums, Will lingered behind, unaware that Darla had lingered too and was watching him, waiting for him to get to his podium.

"Idiot's going to make me late," she mumbled to herself, looking at her purple watch impatiently.

She heard Will sigh. He shoved his hands in his pockets and looked into the distance, still unaware Darla was close by, waiting for him.

"My jokes aren't that terrible," he grumbled, kicking the ground half-heartedly.

When Darla saw him walking her way, she turned and began heading to her podium, smiling the whole way there.

37.2

"Alright folks!" Steven announced in his classic game-show voice. "We're back and kicking! I hope all of you back home are feeling wonderful this morning! I know I am. Anyway, it's time for the next participant to take their chance in the chair! Ondrea, come on up… if you dare."

For today's show, the audience would see the gang smiling and ready for a face full of fear, but in actuality, their smiles were fake and their enthusiasm very much lacking because Michael's podium was empty.

Ondrea walked slowly toward the chair. She felt strange. Her movements seemed both clumsy and relaxed. But at that moment, Ondrea didn't feel clumsy or relaxed. She felt numb. All of Team HOPE felt numb. Everything was so out of sorts that the gang didn't know what to feel. They didn't know what would happen next. They didn't know what they would do next. They didn't know where Michael was, and they didn't have a clue if they should trust Steven or not.

Ondrea was seriously worried as she took a deep breath and sat down in the chair. Out of the corner of her eye, she noticed Steven looking at her with deep concern, but she pretended not to notice. She closed her eyes and sighed. Truthfully, Ondrea had no clue what her deepest darkest fear was, and she wasn't ready to figure it out. She had no choice. The time was now.

The second her mind had entered the simulation, she felt cold. The air around her felt still and smelled damp. She opened her eyes only to find herself surrounded by darkness. She stretched her arms out and swung them around in order to feel out the space, but her arms didn't hit anything.

"Anyone here?" she called cautiously. When nobody answered, she sighed loudly and sat down on the floor. She felt water seep into her pants, and realized the reason it smelled damp was because the air around her was dense with water.

"It's like a rainforest in here," she said to herself. "Where am I?"

She had been in the dark simulation for about five minutes now, but her eyes had not yet adjusted to the darkness. She began to think it could be Dark Magic, but a different idea wormed its way into her mind.

"I remember being in a situation like this," she said. "It was when my family and I were touring the Carlsbad Caverns in New Mexico. The guides turned off the lights in the caverns and everyone was plunged into darkness."

Ondrea scrunched her face up in full concentration as she tried to recall what the guides said about the underground darkness. After a minute, she gasped.

"Right!" she called. "One of the guides said that the only reason your eyes CAN adjust in darkness is because even in the dark there's always a little bit of light coming from somewhere—and that's what your eyes focus on to help you adjust."

But when you're underground—and the electric lights are turned off—there is no natural source of light.

"I forgot how surreal this feels," she whispered, her voice echoing in the cavern. "Being alone in complete darkness. Alone where everything you say or do, every breath you take echoes with no one else to hear it but yourself."

Ondrea stood up and began walking around in the darkness, feeling out her surroundings using her hands.

"This feels so familiar," she muttered. The more she thought about it, she realized the ONLY time she had ever experienced total darkness was in the caverns.

"So… am I back in the caverns, then?" she asked the darkness. "I must be. Unless this is some made-up place for my fear to be, the caverns would be the only possible option."

After ten minutes of silence, Ondrea had been able to feel the area enough to gather she was in was a large circular cavern with only a couple of branching pathways. She continued to think as she started walking down one of the branching paths.

"I'm not afraid of the dark, though," she thought aloud. "My sister is terrified of the dark, but not me. Being alone is scary, but it's not my deepest, darkest fear. Sure, I hate being lost, but I'm not necessarily afraid of it. And I'm not a fan of enclosed spaces, but I'm not afraid of them. What's going on?"

Suddenly, Ondrea heard a voice. She turned what felt like a corner and squinted in the beam of a flashlight. She saw… herself. The flashlight was held by one of the cavern guides and was aimed directly at her, but the beam continued through her as if she wasn't there.

"I'm in a memory," she said to herself. "But… I don't remember this."

Her younger self was standing next to her parents looking incredibly frantic.

"We have to find my sister!" Younger Ondrea shouted.

"Look, miss," the guide began. "Our time is up, and we have to leave the caverns. A search and rescue team is on their way down and will look very thoroughly for your sister, Avery."

"Excuse me, but my daughter is correct!" Mrs. Kendal exclaimed. "We have to find Avery!"

"Jen," Mr. Kendal whispered calmly. "I agree wholeheartedly that we need to find Avery, but how are we going to do anything about it? We have no clue where she could have ended up, and the only people who know how to navigate the caverns are those who are most familiar with it."

"Don't worry," the tour guide said. "We'll find her and bring her back to you in no time."

As Ondrea watched her younger self, her parents, and the tour guide argue more, the numbness she had been feeling was replaced with shock.

"I remember this now," she said to herself. "This is when Avery went missing. I must have blocked it out."

It seemed her family had finally settled their argument with the tour guide, so he began to escort them back to the entrance, and Ondrea followed. About two minutes later, everyone had connected with the main tour group and the tour guides began instructing everyone back to the top to exit the caverns. Ten minutes later, the light from the entrance was shining into the darkness and the tour members made their way outside along with Ondrea's family.

Ondrea was about to follow, but movement from the back of the cavern caught her eye. She turned and saw a collective group of about ten tour guides whispering near the back. She walked toward them to hear what they were talking about. But when she got closer, they stopped whispering and began heading back down the caverns—presumably to look for Avery.

"Should I follow them?" she asked herself. "Or is the answer I'm looking for outside?"

"Do you even want to follow them?" a voice questioned.

Ondrea jumped in surprise and turned around to see one of the tour guides looking at her with crossed arms and raised eyebrows.

"Yes!" Ondrea exclaimed. "Of course, I want to find her! I need to find her!"

The tour guide laughed.

"I didn't ask if you wanted to find her," he said with devious smile. "I asked if you wanted to follow them." He gestured toward the other tour guides. "Their light is disappearing. I'd hurry up with your decision. I'd like an answer to my question."

"You'll get my answer once I choose!" she growled impatiently. "Now let me think!"

The tour guide's face became expressionless as he waited, but Ondrea didn't notice the sudden change. After two minutes of fretting had passed, the light had long since disappeared down the corridor, and Ondrea began to pace. She realized her legs were shaking. She grabbed her hair in her fists, feeling like she'd yank it out if she had to grapple with this decision any longer.

"Why is this bothering me so much?" she cried out, her voice echoing throughout the main part of the cavern.

The tour guide snickered. When Ondrea glared at him with obvious annoyance, he sighed, rolled his eyes, and grabbed her arm. His forceful grip ensured that she couldn't shake free—but it didn't hurt at all, and she had no clue why. The tour guide began to pull her deeper into the caverns, away from the exit.

"Wait, I haven't made my decision yet!" she exclaimed, fear creeping into her voice. "You can't just force me into this!"

The tour guide continued to pull her as if she hadn't said anything. He didn't even hesitate at the fear in her voice. She continued to protest, but the guide continued pulling her until, twenty minutes later, they came across a giant cavern where the other tour guides had gathered.

When the guide stopped pulling her and let go of her arm, she could see a red mark where his hand had been. Distracted, she asked, "Why didn't it hurt when you were pulling me?"

He looked at her and his expressionless face slowly turned to a look of confusion and concern.

"You thought I was trying to hurt you?" he asked quietly.

"I didn't know what to think," she responded bashfully.

"Even though my grip was incredibly tight, my objective was never to hurt you," he said. "The reason it didn't hurt was because I didn't intend to hurt you—and that's that. My only objective was to get you to where you didn't want to be."

"What? That… I mean… what?" Ondrea stuttered. "That makes no sense."

The tour guide smiled with a look of amusement.

"Tell, me, Ondrea," he said. "What do you REALLY fear? Is it the loss of your sister?"

"What are you talking about?" she yelled furiously. "Of course, it is, idiot!"

The tour guide's demeanor remained the same. "Or is it finding out the truth?" he asked. "Is it learning of the tragedy and pain your sister might have experienced?" Ondrea stayed quiet, so he continued. "Could it be that what you fear most is the thought of harm coming toward others?"

"I… I don't know," she whispered, tearing up.

"You could have exited the cavern," the tour guide continued. "You could have gone toward the light that always remains. The light of the sun in the darkness. Or you could have chosen the light that had begun to fade down the corridor. The light of knowledge and truth. Your want for the truth was slowly slipping away. You were hesitating. You were scared. I had to help you choose. Your problem is that you hesitate when it comes to the difficult choice. Maybe you're afraid of choosing the harder path."

"I… I want to know," Ondrea exclaimed suddenly. "I want to know what happened to my sister, but also I don't want to know! That makes no sense. What I mean is I want to find out what happened, but I'm too afraid to move forward."

"You have courage, Ondrea," he said, putting his hand on her shoulder. "You must move forward. Think about it like this: This is a simulation. What you will see here, your sister has already experienced. It's a moment that has long passed. You might be shaken by it, but your sister isn't."

"But she never talks about it!" Ondrea said.

"There could be two reasons. Reason one is she doesn't talk about it because it makes her feel upset to recall it. Reason two is because she's already over it. You know her better than anyone. Which one do you think it is?"

"Reason two," she responded without hesitating.

The tour guide smiled. "Good," he said. "You two are peas in a pod. Both strong, courageous, and not afraid to speak up. If seeing this rattles you, at least you'll know what happened. It may bother you for some time, but most of the time, knowing the truth and facing it is better than hiding from the truth and pushing it further away."

"I guess you're right," Ondrea muttered. "I need to face it!"

"So you'll go in and find out what happened?" the tour guide asked.

"Of course, I will! I'm Avery's sister after all! I need to face the truth so I can know more about my kick-butt little sister!" she exclaimed with a laugh.

The tour guide chuckled. "Then it's time to see," he said. "The door is right there." He pointed to a wooden door located on the farthest wall in the large cavern.

"That wasn't there before," she mumbled. She turned toward the tour guide. "Was that there before?"

"It's always been there," he responded. "I'll leave you to it, then."

"Hey wait!" Ondrea called. "What's your name?"

"You can call me Pater," he responded. "When you say my name, however, you need to say it right. It's pronounced Pau-tair."

"Uh, okay," she said. "Should I…" Suddenly, Pater disappeared. "Well, that was weird."

Ondrea looked to the door and saw the other tour guides open it. When the door was fully ajar, a bright light shone from the entrance as if inviting her to step forward yet warning her to be careful.

"Here I go," she muttered with a heavy sigh. She took a second to muster up her courage and sprinted toward the door full speed. As the light grew closer, so did Ondrea's thirst for knowledge.

THIRTY-EIGHT

In Which Ondrea is Traumatized

As she emerged on the other side of the door, Ondrea was surprised to find herself in another dark cavern—despite the light she had seen coming through the door. She looked around, but once again could only see darkness. A sudden wave of sadness passed through her, urging Ondrea to use her Powers, pushing her mind in order to locate the source of the sadness. She heard a voice.

"Wake up."

"Is anyone there?" Ondrea yelled. "Wait, what am I doing? No one can hear me."

"Please, wake up!" the voice said again. "I'm scared and I don't want to be alone here!"

The voice became louder in Ondrea's mind, so she blindly began moving in the direction of the thoughts. It took her five minutes to find the voice—which continued asking someone to wake up. Finally, Ondrea entered a manufactured passageway within the cavern. She continued searching, unphased by the implications of the construction. There was no time to be scared now.

The hallway cut off in multiple directions so Ondrea went left, still following the voice. Eventually, she walked into a man-made room. Sitting in a cage at the back of the room, were her sister and another little boy. They both had strange-looking collars around their necks. A few feet from the entrance was an operating table with an older boy lying on it. He was face down, strapped to the table, seemingly unconscious, shirtless, and his back was covered in blood. Ondrea gagged. On the far side of the room, just behind the cages, was a rack filled with surgeon tools, construction tools, and the occasional weapon. Ondrea barely had to glance at them to know what every one of them was being used for—and that it was not for their intended purposes.

She walked closer to the boy on the table and looked intensely at his back. There were two slits, one below each shoulder blade. The slits were located more toward the center of his back instead of his sides, and were about three inches apart.

Ondrea gasped, covered her mouth, and turned around. She began to shake and tear up.

"I know what these slits are from," she said quietly. "This is horrible!"

It was the boy's wings. He'd had wings just like her sister, but his wings had been cut out of his back. Ondrea looked at the smaller table next to the boy and noticed a pair of wings. Ondrea felt like screaming.

"This is so sick!" she gasped as tears began pouring down her face. "This is disgusting!"

Ondrea's attention was pulled away from the scene by the screeching sound of a different boy. She looked at the cage where her sister resided and noticed the boy had woken up.

"It's okay," Avery whispered, her voice shaking. "I'm sure… I'm sure my sister will get us out of this."

Ondrea fell to her knees and looked down at the floor, feeling ashamed.

"But I didn't," she cried. "I didn't get you out of this!"

"I'm really scared," the boy said as he began to cry and scream.

"I… I am too," Avery said softly, clearly trying to be calm for the boy's sake. "Let's chat."

The boy quieted down and looked at her with confusion. "Why… why would we chat?" he asked as he wiped the tears from his eyes.

"Because, why not?" she responded, putting on a smile. "What's your name? How old are you?"

"Um… I'm Carter, and I'm eight," he said quietly. "What about you?"

"I'm Avery, and I'm…" their conversation was cut short by the loud footsteps of a large man entering the room.

"Alright! Which one of you two lucky dragons wants to go next?" he asked.

Ondrea stood up and screamed in rage. She felt so angry that she couldn't do anything about this. She wanted to kill the cruel man. She wanted to make him suffer.

"Wanda!" the man called. "Get that boy off the table! Make sure he doesn't die, and put him in the cage over there with the others!"

A skinny, nervous-looking lady with glasses came out of a far door and walked quickly toward the man.

"Of course, Mr. Mitch!" she exclaimed. Wanda carried the boy over to a metal table and began sewing his wounds shut.

Mr. Mitch walked toward the cage, opened the door, and grabbed Carter's arm. He tried to pull him out, but Avery hugged Carter close to her to keep him safe.

"Let go of him, you stupid brat!" the man growled.

Avery began to shake in fear, but she didn't release him. If anything, she held on tighter. Carter began to cry again as Mr. Mitch pulled him even more.

"Stop it!" Carter yelled desperately. "My arm's going to snap off!!"

Mr. Mitch laughed but didn't let go. "You can still live with only one arm," he said with a smile.

Suddenly, Mr. Mitch yanked on the boy's arm with so much force that Carter's shoulder popped. Avery screamed and released her hold on him. Mr. Mitch just laughed again, grabbed Carter's shirt, and hauled him on to the operating table. At this point, Carter lost consciousness.

Ondrea felt like she was about to die. Her heart pounded in her chest louder and heavier than she thought possible. Her legs felt weak, and she began having a hard time breathing.

"I can't look at this anymore!" she yelled. Her yell was drowned out by her sister's constant screaming. "Please just get me out of here," Ondrea whispered. She sat down against the wall, put her hands over her ears, and shut her eyes.

Ondrea screamed and felt her mind begin to slip into madness, but a feeling caught in her chest, and she gasped. She opened her eyes, lifted her head, and took her hands away from her ears. When she looked at her left hand, she noticed a faintly glowing hand was on top of it. It felt warm and soft. Curiously, she placed her right hand over the ethereal hand. When she did, a second glowing hand encased her own in warmth.

She moved both her hands away, feeling weirded out, but the two hands grabbed her left one and held on tightly. Despite the implications of this gesture, Ondrea didn't feel threatened or scared. The hands are the ones that felt scared. The hands squeezed her hand tightly and shook. Ondrea smiled.

"Sorry I lost my cool," Ondrea said with a shaky laugh. "There's no need to be scared."

The hands released Ondrea from their grasp. One of the hands formed a fist then stuck out their pinkie finger.

"Pinkie promise?" a faint voice whispered.

Ondrea smiled. "Pinkie promise," she said as she connected her pinkie finger to the glowing hand.

The hand disappeared and a glowing girl came out of thin air. She flew like a wisp of light and kissed Ondrea on the cheek. The little girl giggled happily and flew off smiling and waving. A few seconds later, the girl disappeared and left Ondrea sitting against the wall, speechless. She touched her cheek where the girl had kissed her and laughed.

"Such a sweetheart," she mumbled. "That kind of tickled."

Her sister's screams of sadness brought her back to the present moment.

"Please don't hurt him!" Avery screamed. She began desperately pulling at the bars. "Please, no!"

The man laughed. As he did, the sound of Carter's screams echoed off the walls. Ondrea, still disgusted, turned away, accepting that she had to listen to this. She had to get through it. Just as she felt she'd start crying again, the setting disappeared and she was in a dark circular room. It looked like a dungeon. On the opposite side of the cramped room, there was a wooden door. Ondrea walked toward the door and tried to open it, but it wouldn't budge.

"Probably wouldn't even matter because I'm not technically here," she muttered to herself.

Ondrea stopped, took a deep breath, and looked around. There really wasn't much to see except the stone walls, old door, stone floors and ceiling, the one little barred window, and her sister. Avery was sitting in the middle of the floor crying softly. Her wings were still on her back.

"I guess that horrible monster didn't take her wings after all," Ondrea said to herself.

Suddenly, the door opened, and a 3D red-eyed shadow walked in. Avery screamed and flinched back in fear.

"Look, kid," the Shadow said. "You're going to be here for a long time and, for the record, it's not my fault."

"Whatever!" Avery exclaimed. "I've given up on explanations and circumstance, but you can't make me give up on hope."

The Shadow smiled. "I wouldn't want it any other way," he said. "I'm not going to visit again… at least… not for years, but I will see you again one day. When I do, I hope I have better news for you."

"Whose side are you on, creep?" Avery asked, folding her arms over her chest.

"Not mine," he said with a sad sigh. "I'm on whatever side I'm told to be on. I can't really choose. The thing is, my boss likes you. He thinks he can use you. It's the only reason he told Mr. Mitch to let you keep your wings."

"You can tell your boss to go and suck it!" she grumbled.

"I don't think he'd respond too well to that," the Shadow said. "Tell me something. Why do you continue to fight? I wouldn't be able to fight in this situation."

Avery scoffed. "You clearly have nothing to fight for!" she yelled furiously. "I fight for my sister! One day, she'll rescue me! Who will rescue you?"

The Shadow stayed quiet for several seconds, then he spoke.

"I don't deserve to be saved," he whispered. "My kids have no clue what I do yet. My wife supports this for some reason. I had a son. He… he…"

"Don't start with the water works!" Avery interrupted harshly. "I don't want to see you cry near me! I don't want to hear it! If you think you don't deserve to be saved, then stop feeling sorry for yourself and accept it!"

The Shadow sniffed and scowled at Avery.

"Whatever, little girl!" he yelled. "See you in a million years!"

When the man left the room and locked the door, Avery burst into tears. Meanwhile Ondrea had no clue how to feel. She felt angry at The Shadow, but she also felt sympathy for him. She felt like she knew him—and she had a good idea why.

"Damian, Vixsten, my sister and I are going to have quite the chat when all of this is over," she muttered.

Along with the anger she felt, Ondrea also felt sad. Seeing her sister in this state broke her heart, and yet, Ondrea knew she would be okay.

"I'd only met up with my sister again last year," she said to herself. "And Avery never talks about her past. So… could she have been here the whole time?"

Ondrea's train of thought was interrupted by her sister screaming in sorrow.

"Sister!" Avery screamed. "I miss you so much!"

Ondrea began to tear up. Even though this was just a simulation and nothing could change, she felt compelled to place her hand on top of her sister's. Something strange happened when she did. Ondrea's hand began to glow, and her sister gasped. Avery looked at her hand, then up directly into Ondrea's eyes. She couldn't see her, but Avery somehow knew someone was there.

"I know you're watching over me, big sis," she said, wiping the tears from her face. "I know you're thinking about me right now, and it feels wonderful. I can't wait to see you again. The fact that you love me is keeping me strong. Even though you can't hear what I'm saying because you're somewhere else entirely, I want you to know that I'm going to get through this for you. You don't have to be afraid anymore."

Ondrea burst into tears and she wrapped her body around her sister's. Avery smiled and sighed. Ondrea laughed sadly.

"I'll be waiting for you, then," she whispered.

Suddenly, the world began to fade to black. Ondrea felt a wave of calming peace wash over her as she closed her eyes and welcomed the conclusion. Even though she knew her sister would be trapped in this horrible situation for a very long time, the resolve her sister showed in that moment gave Ondrea the pleasure of knowing Avery would be just fine.

When Ondrea opened her eyes again, the first thing she saw was Avery's face. She looked around and realized she was back in the studio with all her friends.

"Ondrea!" Steven yelled worriedly, while staying in game-show character. "Tell the world how you feel!"

Ondrea had been stunned into silence. When Avery squeezed her hand, however, Ondrea took a deep breath, looked at her sister, then spoke.

"That was horrible," she stated plainly. "But, I'm okay! It already happened. There's nothing I can do about it now, and everyone is okay, so I shouldn't worry about it anymore."

"That's a wonderful way of looking at it, Ondrea!" Steven exclaimed. "Thank you for sharing that breath of fresh air with us."

She looked Steven dead in the eyes and chuckled.

"I'm just happy to know the truth."

Steven smiled at her as she and Avery walked back toward the podiums. Despite Ondrea saying she was alright, her legs were shaking.

The gang went backstage as soon as Steven announced the five-minute break. Teddy was the first one to arrive and anxiously awaited his beloved's return. Everyone else walked in, but Teddy kept his eyes fixed on the entrance, waiting for Ondrea. Oliver came up behind him and put his hand on Teddy's shoulder for support, but Teddy shrugged it off distractedly. He didn't want comfort from anyone right now. All he wanted was to comfort Ondrea—and nothing else.

It felt like an eternity to Teddy, but Avery and Ondrea finally entered backstage. Ondrea was a mess, despite her calm demeanor on camera. Her legs were shaking, and she walked with her head down. Her shoulders also shook, and Teddy could hear her make small gasping sounds.

Teddy's heart shattered as he realized his love was crying. He Teleported the short distance to her, surprising Avery who jumped back, releasing Ondrea. Ondrea would have collapsed to the ground, but Teddy wrapped his arms around her tightly. Ondrea looked up and, when she saw Teddy's face, she began to sob. The others stayed far back in order to give them space. The only other person who remained by Ondrea's side was Avery. She put her hand on her older sister's shoulder. At some point, Steven popped in to tell everyone it was almost time to get back onstage but, when he saw the tears, he decided to add a couple of minutes to their break.

Five minutes had passed and Ondrea's sobs of pain and sorrow toned down to sniffles, but Teddy refused to let go of her. He held on tighter for her sake, but now, also for his sake. Teddy had begun shedding a few tears in the middle of all this too. His love was suffering, and there was nothing he could do to ease her pain besides holding her tightly. He desperately wished he could do more.

Teddy looked up at his friends behind him. Darla's eyes were red from crying, but Nick had grabbed her hand to let her know she wasn't feeling the sympathy pains alone. Will sat in the corner with his head in between his knees mainly looking tired, but Jessica was there with her hand on his back. Oliver sat on the other side of his sister with his arm wrapped around her shoulders. Jake and Josh stood awkwardly in the opposite corner, Josh with his hands in his pockets and Jake holding onto his brother's wrist.

Jason, who was never good at managing emotions, stood by the wall adjacent to the entrance with a look of embarrassment on his face. Meanwhile, his twin was next to him, trying not to laugh at his brother's discomfort since Mason was comforting Rachel as well, and he didn't want to laugh because it would be insensitive.

Teddy smiled, pulled one of his arms off Ondrea and wiped his face. Nick tossed a grin his way, made a thumbs-up, and winked in a way that made Teddy laugh. Ondrea who had begun falling asleep lifted her head off Teddy's shoulder and saw what Nick was doing. She smiled sadly and squeezed Teddy's hand to let him know he was still supposed to be comforting her. Teddy looked at the face of the woman he loved, wiped the tears from it, then planted a long kiss on her lips. When he pulled away, Ondrea was smiling and her eyes were wide. Her face was red with embarrassment.

"In front of everyone else? Really?" she whispered.

Teddy smirked. "It distracted you from being sad," Teddy said. "That's what I had intended."

He released his hold on his girlfriend and stood. Avery went behind Ondrea, glared mockingly at Teddy, and wrapped her arms around Ondrea's shoulders.

"This is MY sister!" she exclaimed. "You can't have her!"

Teddy burst out in laughter causing the rest of his friends to do the same. Ondrea sniffled and let out a laugh as well.

"Avery," she began. "Of course, I'm yours!"

Avery's eyes began to water as her face lit up.

"I know you're mine!" she cried proudly. "I've always known! I love you so much, sis! I'm so happy to have you in my life!"

"Why are you crying, then?" Ondrea asked, turning around and grabbing her sister's hand.

"I don't know!" Avery responded. "I guess I'm just so happy to be where I am right now. I wouldn't be here today if I didn't have a wonderful big sis to think of during my time in that terrible place!"

Ondrea kissed her sister on the cheek, stood up, and formed a group hug with Teddy and Avery. Within five seconds, everyone joined in—ultimately squishing the trio.

Two minutes later, everyone was sitting against the wall. They had no tears left; all that was behind them now.

Jake and Josh walked through the doorway that led to the backstage area.

"When did you guys leave?" Will asked with a yawn.

"We left after the group hug thing while everyone was settling down so no one would notice," Josh said.

"We didn't want anyone to notice just in case the extra time we asked Steven for didn't work out," Jake added. "But it did, so we have ten minutes… nope… nine minutes from this point on."

"In that case…" Ondrea began. "I have a theory. I believe it was Vixsten, Spencer's dad, who imprisoned my sister."

"Wow, we're getting right into this, I see," Will said wearily.

Nick began to protest.

"Suppose he really did have something to do with it," Nick said. "Why would he do that? He had no reason to experiment on kids, and I don't understand what his reasoning would be for kidnapping Avery and keeping her."

"That's exactly it, Nick!" Ondrea exclaimed. "You don't understand! How much do you really know about Spencer's dad?"

Nick went quiet and sighed. He sunk lower toward the floor and rubbed his eyes with his fists.

"I don't know," he muttered. "Look, I'm just really worried about them."

"Them?" Darla asked. "Who are we talking about?"

"Darla!" Jessica yelled. "Not cool! You know exactly who we're talking about. Spencer and Vixsten!"

Darla zoned out for a moment before saying, "Oh yeah. Sorry about that. There's just a lot going on. It's hard to keep track of it all."

Suddenly, Mr. Atrius poked his head backstage. Nick's eyes went wide. Without trying to hide it, he stood up and went to the farthest corner of the room.

THIRTY-NINE

In Which They Speak Of the Devil

Hey gang," Mr. Atrius said. "Have you all seen Michael?"

"What about him?" Rachel asked. "Did you do something to him?"

Mr. Atrius glared at Rachel. "No, I didn't do anything to him," he said. "Steven wanted me to ask you about him."

"Why didn't he come back here himself?" Jake asked, clenching his fists. "Did you do something to Michael?"

Mr. Atrius smiled, laughed, then sighed wearily. "Why do you kids keep asking that?" he questioned. "No, I didn't do anything to him. But I asked him if he'd seen my bird, so maybe he's looking into that right now."

"That had better be the case," Josh mumbled.

Mr. Atrius looked around the backstage area and noticed an air of hostility. He sighed, walked further in, and sat down against the far wall.

"Listen, kids," he started. "I know what all the looks are for. I know you've figured out who I am."

"How did you know?" Mason asked worriedly.

"We weren't doing a very good job of hiding it, brother," Jason whispered, putting his hand on Mason's shoulder.

"So, what are you going to do now?" Avery asked coldly.

Oliver held up a hand. "Wait. "First, what do you think we know?" he asked.

"I know you kids know I'm a bad guy who works for VORK, and I know you're confused about all of this. I am too," he responded.

"What does that mean?" Teddy asked as he grabbed Ondrea's hand.

"My bird just dragged me out to this place," Mr. Atrius said with another big sigh.

"THAT MAKES NO SENSE!" Rachel screamed. "None of this makes any sense! What's going on?"

"Down, girl!" Nick exclaimed, still sitting in the corner.

Mr. Atrius looked Nick directly in the eyes and gasped.

"I didn't know you were a Dark Magic user!" he exclaimed, sounding excited and worried at the same time. "That can't be good news for you."

"What are you talking about?" Nick asked with a yawn. "Why wouldn't it be good news?"

Mr. Atrius went quiet for a minute. Will was about to yell at him to say something, but Mr. Atrius opened his mouth and began speaking.

"What am I to you?" he asked the group.

"A villain?" Will said cautiously.

"Sure, but what's my name?" he asked. "Since you don't know my name, what would you call me in a formal environment?"

"Mr. Atrius," Oliver stated. "We'd call you Mr. Atrius."

Mr. Atrius smiled and continued.

"Good," he said. "So, you can imagine why I'm so concerned for Michael."

"I'm not following," Ondrea said quietly.

"Haven't you figured out that Michael is my son?" he asked, genuinely confused.

"We've mentioned it as a possibility before," Jason said, also looking confused. "But Michael said he didn't have any relatives named Atrius."

"So, Michael is your son, and you're concerned for him because you don't know where he is. Is that correct?" Oliver asked just to be sure.

"Yes, that's correct," Mr. Atrius confirmed. "I had no clue my son would be here. I honestly had no clue that all of our organization's targets would be gathered here either. It's why I've been so cautious and kept my guard up around you—which I'm sure is why I seemed hostile."

"Start over," Jake said, taking charge. "Why did you come here in the first place?"

"Well, my daughter is a huge fan of this show and, for some reason, after watching one of the recent episodes, she desperately wanted to come to the studio," he began. "She told me if I didn't get her down here before the next episode, she'd murder our neighbor."

"Dude, what the hell!" Will exclaimed. "You're daughter's a psychopath."

Mr. Atrius sighed and rubbed his head anxiously.

"Yes, she is," he said. "Then again, like father, like daughter."

"You don't seem that bad," Rachel said quietly.

"I taught her the family business, so I'm the one who taught her how to kill," he muttered with a sigh. "I've been going cold turkey, but I can't seem to get my daughter to do the same."

"Nothing surprises me anymore!" Josh exclaimed, folding his arms across his chest. "I'm used to this now!"

"Please continue your story," Jason stated.

"Right. I researched this show online and found out multiple things. First, the show has had a lot of money troubles, and—being part of a wide-ranging evil organization—I'm loaded. After

I finished researching, I contacted Steven and told him I'd be happy to fund the show as long as I could be on set and bring my bird," he explained. He was about to continue, but Jessica interrupted him.

"What does your daughter have to do with your bird?" she asked.

Rachel shifted and began to tap her foot nervously. "Please don't tell me that bird is your daughter," she whispered fearfully.

"That bird is my daughter," he confirmed. "She's a shape-shifter, or a Morpher. Whatever you want to call it. Anyway, the second thing I found out was the Mackenzie twins—Jason and Mason—would be the main participants on the next episode and, I must admit, I got excited. My daughter opened the possibility to eliminate two of our targets at once. When I called Steven to tell him that I would bankroll him, I required him to tell the participants the donor was anonymous—if it ever came up in conversation."

"So, you do want to kill us!" Darla exclaimed!

"I'll get to that in a minute," Mr. Atrius mentioned casually. "Anyway, my daughter and I got to the studio, but I didn't want to hint to Steven that I was a super villain, and my bird was actually my daughter who happened to be a villainous murderer."

"Obviously," Will muttered rolling his eyes.

Mr. Atrius continued. "Steven told me a boy named Michael Atrius would be featured as well, which caught me extremely off guard. The reason is that my wife left me when my daughter was just a small girl—but she took my younger son, Michael, with her because she didn't want him to be tainted by the family business.

"At the time, I couldn't have cared less. But, things change with time and, now, I'm overjoyed to hear about Michael and see him. I stayed away, however because I didn't want to confuse him and I didn't want my daughter to do anything rash. She has a morbid and extremely messed up way of expressing love."

"Skip ahead," Avery said. "Why haven't you made any attempt to attack us?"

"I've been too busy worrying about Michael and my daughter, Sydney," he said. "I figured I'd strike during the Environmental Dome portion of the show—when Sydney and Michael won't be in the same building. The risk of him being injured would greatly decrease if that were the case."

"Way to keep your plans a secret…" Will said with a sarcastic grin on his face.

Teddy glanced over at Will's face and scowled. "You're actually enjoying this, aren't you, Will?" he asked incredulously.

Will looked away and crossed his arms.

"No," he answered with a pout on his face. "I'm not."

"Whatever you say," Teddy muttered, rolling his eyes.

"What I want to know is why you're draining Nick's power!" Oliver exclaimed as he glanced at his friend to see him nodding off.

Mr. Atrius promptly stood and walked over to Nick. Everyone in the room immediately tensed up, and Nick stood as he tried to run to the other corner. Nick had only made it halfway to the other corner when he stumbled. Mr. Atrius caught him by the arm before he could fall.

"If I'd wanted to hurt you, I would have already done it," Mr. Atrius said as he led Nick to the center of the room and seated him in front of his friends.

"What's going on?" Rachel asked. "What are you going to do?"

Mr. Atrius sat down in front of Nick, put his hand on Nick's shoulder, then stared into his eyes. The room went dead silent. After a minute, Mr. Atrius said,

"Remember when you I told you that being a Dark Magic user wasn't good news for you? It's because my daughter feeds off it."

"She really is a little gremlin, isn't she?" Will said with a smile.

"Look who's talking," Darla muttered.

"Will, you think she's a creature that was imagined in the twentieth century to explain malfunctions in military aircrafts, commercial planes, and other machinery or their operators?” Nick asked curiously.

“What are you even talking about?” Will asked, looking incredibly confused.

“That’s what gremlins are,” Nick stated, turning to face Will.

“I think Will’s talking about the make-believe kind,” Jessica said patiently. “The kind that come from fairy tales. Mischievous, annoying little creatures known to be evil, creatures who enjoy other people’s misfortune.”

“That would make a lot of sense, actually,” Jason said, nodding his head. “For some reason, I was thinking the same thing as Nick.”

“Nick’s a military junkie, so I’d… kind of expect that sort of thinking from him, but not you, Jason,” Teddy exclaimed.

“My daughter is now more of a demon than a gremlin, but when she way younger… oh boy,” Mr. Atrius said with a sigh. “Anyway, my daughter is the one draining your Magic Energy, not me.”

“Is there any way to stop it?” Avery asked, twiddling her thumbs anxiously.

“I would ask her to stop, but she’d probably say ‘no’ and throw a fit,” Mr. Atrius responded, looking oddly disturbed. “I hate having to clean up after her fits. Imagine deep cleaning a gore pit the size of the Grand Canyon.”

“Are you scared of Sydney?” Ondrea asked. “Because it seems like a good idea to be scared.”

Mr. Atrius laughed. “No, I’m not afraid of my own daughter!” he exclaimed with a smile. “She’s actually more afraid of me. But I don’t use scare tactics on her because of our contract.”

“Your contract?” Mason asked, having a difficult time following the conversation.

“Yes,” Mr. Atrius stated, suddenly looking serious. “Where I was born, contracts are a very big deal, and breaking them would mean forfeiting your life—and spending eternity in Hell.”

"As intriguing as this conversation is ultimately becoming…" Oliver began, tugging on his shirt anxiously, "Is there any way to stop her from draining Nick's Magic Energy that won't resort in a… fit?"

"Nick, if you can get on my daughter's good side and appeal to her interests, she may willingly stop," Mr. Atrius suggested.

"I'll think about it, but I have to ask, what are her interests?" Nick wondered.

"She likes cold treats like ice-cream and milkshakes. She also loves Star Wars movies and building Lego sets. Another thing she loves—and I assume this is NOT a mutual interest—Is torturing people. It helps her wind down," he explained. "Also, she's inspired by nature. Most of her torture techniques come from years of watching Animal Planet. Obviously, her favorite color is red. She's a very talented cook…"

"So…" Josh interrupted quickly. "Some of that information is helpful."

"I've decided I don't want to get to know your daughter to appeal to her interests," Nick said, looking frightened. "In fact, I think I'd rather die than get to know her."

"Her mother felt the same…" Mr. Atrius muttered as he gazed into the distance wistfully.

"Dude, this couldn't get more awkward," Jake said, scratching his head. "So, interacting with Sydney is out of the question. Maybe give us more plausible, safe, and less complicated options."

Mr. Atrius thought for a minute, then said, "I can't think of anything, but it's imperative, NO MATTER WHAT, that she does not find out I've spoken to you about any of this!" he exclaimed strictly. "She can't find out you know she's a bird. She can't find out you know anything! If you see her in her mock human form, be wary and act as you would toward a stranger you've never met. If you see her in her bird form, act the same way you have been previously."

"What would happen if she found out?" Rachel asked, hands shaking.

Mr. Atrius put on a grave expression and sighed. "All of you would die here," he said.

The room fell completely silent for a long time. The silence was interrupted by Will's laughter.

"She can try!" Will said, chuckling. "She can try to kill us, but she won't!"

Mr. Atrius's expression turned dark with annoyance.

"You arrogant idiot!" he yelled. He raised his hand and performed a slapping motion in the air. Will yelped in pain as a black air current slammed into his face. Will recovered quickly and began to Freeze Mr. Atrius, to turn him into an ice sculpture. Mr. Atrius's darkened expression softened and turned to one of impatience. He sighed heavily and without saying anything, shattered Will's ice just by touching it.

Nick sighed wearily and put his face in his hands.

"Will!" he yelled. "Mr. Atrius is not an immediate threat, and I'm honestly shocked you guys haven't noticed how powerful he is before all of this."

"That's the thing, Nick," Mr. Atrius said. "My power and my daughter's power is different than anything else in the universe. Only people with vast amounts of Dark Magic can sense my aura. It's a defense mechanism—not that I can't handle myself, of course."

"Hey, guys!" Jake exclaimed loudly, "It's been way more than nine minutes!"

"Is Steven still looking for your bird?" Josh asked.

"Do you guys want to go and look for him?" Oliver questioned. "Is that a good idea, Mr. Atrius?"

"They can go if they want, but they should take…" Mr. Atrius paused and swept the room with his eyes "…Will. Take Will with you."

"Safe-mission-gone-wrong time, baby!" Will cheered excitedly.

"Will Brookes!" Mr. Atrius yelled. "It would be in the best interest of us all that you keep my client's children safe! I'm worried that my daughter is up to her old antics. Be wary and watchful."

"Uhhhh… right," Will said.

"If we end up dying, it's not our fault," Josh said as he rolled his eyes.

"You can blame Mr. 'safe-mission-gone-wrong,'" Jake mumbled as the twins followed Will.

"Now!" Mr. Atrius yelled. "Back to business. Will Brookes, I'd advise you not to be so cocky. I was able to wipe out your ice with the touch of my fingertip. Although my daughter only has a little over half of my power, unlike myself, she has no restraint. And, half of my power is still an extreme amount. Attempt to attack me again and I will not hesitate to put you down like a dog with just a flick of my finger."

"Fine." Will mumbled as he pretended not to be petrified with fear. "You don't have to be so intense about it."

Mr. Atrius put on a friendly smile. "Sorry, just trying to get my point across," he exclaimed. "The reason experienced Dark Magic users are the only ones who can sense my family's power is because it's derived from the source of all evil on Earth. To put it simply, the name I was given when I was born is not the name I have now. The name I was given, Lucifer, isn't inconspicuous at all."

"Wait!" Oliver said, his voice shaking. "Are you trying to tell me that you're the… the…. devil?"

"Exactly," Mr. Atrius responded with a wide smile.

FORTY

In Which Teddy Comforts
the One Who Matters Most

After a couple minutes of silence, Darla sighed. "We're Superheroes, we've met an angel, and now we meet the devil himself!" she exclaimed with another deep sigh.

"I apologize," Mr. Atrius said with a look of regret in his eyes.

"You apologize for what exactly?" Avery asked. "Because besides wanting to kill us all, you've done nothing wrong… I think."

"I apologize for revealing my strength to you," Mr. Atrius said sadly. "I made your lives much more complicated by doing so."

"Our lives were already complicated," Oliver stated. "As Darla said, we've met an angel."

"Even though I never intended to reveal my strength, I knew I had to make a tactical decision," Mr. Atrius began. "I didn't want to reveal my true nature because I'm now at a disadvantage for when I need to destroy you. Nick told you of my immeasurable strength and, if I tried to deny it, you would have even more of a reason to be suspicious. That would not be ideal since my current objective involves asking for your help."

"You want us to help you find Michael?" Jason asked. "Because, if so, we were already trying to do that."

"Yeah, no luck," Mason mentioned sadly. "Whether or not he's the son of a bad dude, he's still our friend and a part of our team, so we really need to find him."

"What are you going to do when it comes time to eliminate us?" Nick asked. "Are you going to kill your son, too?"

Mr. Atrius smiled. "You are my targets," he said simply. "My son isn't a target of our organization."

"That settles that," Teddy said with a weary sigh. "We're doomed."

Mr. Atrius's smile widened.

"I'm glad you've come to terms with that!" he exclaimed happily. "It will make my job easier. I'd still like you to put up a fight, though. If not, destroying you will not be fun."

"We are going to put up a fight!" Ondrea exclaimed, squeezing Teddy's hand. "And we will win! Teddy was just kidding! We won't let you have your way, Lucifer!"

"Then I look forward to this," he responded confidently. "Right now, however, we are allies in the quest to find my son."

Will came sulking in the backstage area with a dejected expression.

"We found Steven," he muttered.

"That's good," Rachel said excitedly.

"Yeah, it is, obviously," Will stated. "But there was no action!"

Oliver glanced at Mr. Atrius then looked at Will. "There will be plenty of action later, Will," Oliver said nervously. "You don't have to worry about being bored for long."

"Why not? What did I miss?" he asked, glancing at everyone's expressions curiously.

"Mr. Atrius is literally the devil, Lucifer," Darla explained. "He wants to kill us. But right now, he's our ally since he wants our help to find Michael."

Will began jumping up and down in excitement. "Cool!" he yelled. "Mr. Atrius is the devil! That's so cool!"

Mr. Atrius began to laugh, clearly amused.

"I'm glad he can see the positive," he said with a friendly smile.

"Will, you moron! Don't forget that he wants to kill us!" Darla yelled angrily. "You're such a meathead."

Will frowned. "Sorry," he muttered. His excited demeanor changed, and he sulked toward the wall.

"We've got to fix this eventually," Jessica whispered to Darla.

Darla just scoffed and looked away. "Whatever," she stated with her arms crossed.

"Where are Jake and Josh?" Mr. Atrius asked, glaring at Will. "Did something happen to them?"

"Cool your jets, Satan!" Will exclaimed. "They're helping Steven set up since he's behind schedule now."

"It's Lucifer, not Satan," Mr. Atrius muttered, looking surprisingly offended just as Jake and Josh entered backstage.

"Dad's ready. We're going live in one minute," Josh said.

"Hey, give us the quickest recap on what you found out," Jake said.

"Mr. Atrius is the devil himself," Avery said simply. "Oh, and he plans to murder us all. That's pretty much it."

Jake and Josh just looked at each other, then back at everyone else.

"Why are we not surprised anymore?" Jake said with a grin.

"You two are taking this well," Mr. Atrius chuckled.

Steven poked his head backstage. "Get to places, kids!" he exclaimed, looking flustered. "Fifteen seconds!"

With that, Mr. Atrius rushed outside to his position and the kids lined up, preparing to go to their podiums.

40.1

"Ladies and gentlemen!" Steven bellowed with extra enthusiasm. "I apologize for the long break. Our schedule has gotten a little wonky. This day has been quite the doozy."

From their podiums, Jason asked, "Steven, don't the fear portions last a week total?"

"Yes, but because of recent complications, we've been trying to squeeze them all into a couple of days. That's why we could afford to take yesterday off," Steven answered, smiling.

While Steven addressed the cameras again, Jessica leaned toward Oliver.

"That just raises a couple of questions for me," she whispered.

"Yeah," he agreed. "Like why do the fear simulations usually take a week?"

"Actually…" Jessica began. "I was thinking more along the lines of, if this segment is supposed to take a week, why are we almost done after… what… two… three days?"

Oliver nodded. Suddenly Rachel leaned toward Jessica and whispered, "I've never seen this show before, so I'm not sure how this whole thing plays out. But with traditional game shows, the episodes are filmed with a live audience in advance, but are released once every week."

"That's right," Oliver confirmed. "The way Jason made this game show sound, however, was that there was only one episode every week or month. I can't remember which one."

Jason popped up behind them. "I don't remember doing that," he said suddenly, surprising Rachel and the twins.

"But you did," Nick argued, butting in.

"I still don't remember that, but I'll let you in on the real layout of this show," Jason offered. "The term 'game show' is used very loosely in this scenario. You could call the first segment a game show. That's the part we've been doing so far. But the next segment is the Environmental Dome. That part isn't even technically a game show because it doesn't involve games. I'll refer to this whole show as UYWS which is an acronym for the show's actual name, *Unleash Your Wild Side*."

Jason then explained that UYWS takes place over the course of a month. The fear segment is broadcast on live television for the first week. Once those episodes have aired, they're available on UYWS's official website to watch again.

Once all the participants have finished the fear segment, they spend two weeks in the Environmental Dome. A hardcore and creepy UYWS fan could go to the official website and watch the full 336 hours live from the Dome. But normal people just watch the daily thirty-minute episodes that are available on the UYWS website. The last episode of the UYWS's show is live on television since it's the conclusion."

"Huh?" Oliver muttered while he, Jessica, Rachel, and Nick processed this.

"So…" Rachel began. "How's all of our show stuff going to air, or go up, or be where people can watch it?"

"I'm not sure, but I could make calculations." Jason said with a smile. "Oliver could help out."

"Sure, I'd be happy to later… when this all somehow becomes relevant again, but… for now we should probably pay attention," Oliver said hesitantly. "Teddy went into the simulation like three minutes ago."

"Oh right." Jason stated. He walked back to his podium and immediately spaced out.

"Good talk," Nick muttered as he and the others brought their attention back to Teddy.

"So far, everything in his simulation is looking normal. Which makes me even more nervous," Jessica said, shuddering.

40.2

When Teddy entered the simulation, he found himself in a long, dimly lit hallway. Along the wall were lines of lockers. The lockers—and every square inch of the walls—were coated in dust. Teddy walked cautiously toward the lockers and wiped off just enough dust to see that the lockers were red.

He turned his head, and when he looked in the direction he had first appeared, he saw his back had been facing a blank wall. The wall looked out of place. It looked as if someone had put it there using scraps of wood. But it also looked new, as if someone had recently built it.

"This is too weird," Teddy said as he looked the looked down the hallway and couldn't see an end. "In a way, this is actually pretty cool. I love horror games, and this seems like the start of one. The first thing you do in a horror game is take a deep breath and get your bearings. Then, you look around for anything weird."

With that, Teddy leaned against the wall, relaxed his muscles, and took a deep breath. After a few moments, he took in his surroundings.

"Weird wall..." he muttered as he began listing things he thought were strange. "Dusty hall, never-ending walkway, and dimly lit atmosphere even though there aren't any light bulbs."

Teddy took another deep breath, tensed his body, and began venturing down the foreboding hallway. After about fifteen minutes of walking, Teddy noted that every two minutes the hallway seemed to loop back around. He walked for fifteen more minutes, taking great care to notice details and look at his watch.

"Okay," Teddy sighed. "When no progress is being made and everything looks the same, just keep walking and something is bound to happen."

He continued walking. Twenty minutes later, he froze. Teddy began to hear crying. That's when he felt an air of familiarity about this hallway. He gasped as he realized he had been walking down the main hall of Superhero School this whole time. He refocused, but couldn't tell where the crying was coming from, so he did what instinct called for and calmly kept walking.

The further he walked, the louder the crying became. Teddy looked at his watch and calculated that at his current pace, he should come across the person crying in a minute or so. Teddy took another deep breath and, in order to be on the safe side, slowed his pace by half.

"That should add another minute," he whispered to himself. Just as he had calculated, he spotted the source of the crying two minutes later.

There was a shadowy figure curled up on the dirty floor sobbing excessively. The dim light was making it difficult for Teddy to see, but he could tell by looking that the silhouette was a female about his age. He walked forward a few feet and shouted. The girl was Ondrea! He threw caution out the window and ran toward her, but he hit a glass wall. He tried to Teleport to the other side, but he found he couldn't use his Power.

"Ondrea!" he shouted as he began to bang on the glass. "Ondrea, my love, it will be okay! Please don't cry!"

Despite the sound of his fists echoing off the glass and his shouting ringing in his ears, she didn't look up or reveal any sign she had heard or noticed him.

"Please!" he yelled again. "Ondrea, I'm right here! Please don't cry!"

Once again, she didn't notice him at all. As her cries turned into choking sobs, he felt his heart shatter. He covered his ears, but her cries seemed to fill his head even more.

"No!" he growled. "I won't accept this!"

Teddy removed his hands from his ears, stuck his elbow out, and charged the glass as hard as he could. The glass splintered into hundreds of pieces, and blood from the cut on Teddy's elbow dripped onto the floor. He gritted his teeth and pushed through the pain toward Ondrea. His steps slowed significantly as some kind of wind began pushing him away from her.

"I'm almost there Ondrea!" Teddy yelled over the howling wind. "Please stay strong!"

Ondrea looked up and appeared to finally see Teddy. She smiled and held out her hand for him. As he reached out to take it, the image of Ondrea scattered into the wind like a sandstorm. He could hear her shout his name as she disappeared into the wind.

"No!" Teddy screamed as he fell to his knees. "I almost had you, baby."

Suddenly, the scene around him began to shift and he found himself kneeling in front of Ondrea. She looked a bit older, but still as beautiful as ever. She was staring at him expectantly, and he immediately realized why. In his hand was a beautiful diamond ring. The sun hit it perfectly, and it sparkled as brightly as her eyes.

Teddy, although confused, held out the ring in proposal. Her eyes lit up as she waited for him to pop the question. Teddy opened his mouth to speak, but nothing came out. He brought his hand to his throat and didn't feel anything wrong with it. When Ondrea noticed he wasn't saying anything, she frowned. Teddy saw her frown deepening the more he tried to talk.

"What am I even trying to do here?" he asked himself with a sigh. His eyes widened as he realized he had just spoken. Teddy looked toward Ondrea again and tried to continue to proposal, but nothing came out of his mouth. He stood and reached for her hand to show her he still cared, but she purposely moved her hand away before he could grab it. Ondrea scowled at Teddy and began to walk away. He tried to call out for her, but, once again, nothing came out of his mouth. Teddy pocketed the ring and chased after her, but the faster he ran, the farther behind he fell.

"Ondrea!" Teddy cried. He gasped at the realization he could finally speak to her, and he called out again, "Ondrea, please come back!"

She looked back at him with a look of sadness and disdain. Teddy sighed and fell to his knees in surrender.

"I'm beginning to see a pattern here," he said to himself. He glanced up and saw that Ondrea had completely disappeared. He sighed once more and twiddled his thumbs.

"So," he began wearily. "This is a fear simulation, so I should determine what to do given the information I have. I'm not afraid of Ondrea obviously. In both scenes I've been so close but haven't been able to communicate with her. She'd notice me at the last second but, by then, it's been too late."

Teddy stood up and put his hands in his pockets. He looked at the ground and began to walk forward.

"I have always been terribly afraid of losing her, so not being able to communicate with her is pretty terrifying too. I had no clue it was my deepest fear though," Teddy stated. "It would make sense. She means more to me than anything in the whole world." Teddy smiled to himself, took a deep breath, stopped walking, and looked toward the sky. "Even if I can't communicate with you, my love, I will never stop loving you, and I will never leave you behind," he said to the sky. "I won't let you leave me behind either."

Teddy stood still for a minute longer so his message would really sink in, and then he continued walking with a bit more pep in his step. "Maybe I just need to be patient and stop hounding her," Teddy mumbled. "This is confusing because we've rarely had miscommunications in the past, so why would this be brought up?"

Teddy stopped walking and sat down on a grassy lawn. He laid down, watched the clouds roll by, and shuddered.

"I guess I really am afraid of not being able to communicate with my girl," he said with a sigh. He sat up quickly. "I will be patient. Next time I see her, I will be patient. I'll survey the situation and try not to jump to conclusions."

Suddenly, the scenery began to change around him, and he found himself sitting on the pew of a church. His friends were all around him as were their parents. Everyone was crying and clinging on to each other. Ondrea however, was sitting near the front of the church with her mom. Teddy had no clue what was happening, but Darla was crying on his shoulder, covering his sleeve in tears and snot. He gently pushed her off his arm and ruffled her hair with a smile.

"It'll be okay," he told her, still oblivious to the situation. "As long as we're together, we can overcome anything."

Darla looked at him and wiped the tears from her eyes and the snot from her nose. "And please don't snot on my shirt," he added with an amused grin.

Darla's tearful frown changed to a hesitant smile and she wrapped her arms around Teddy's stomach and buried her head in his chest. Teddy rubbed her head as he looked around at the rest of his friends, wondering what could have them so upset.

"I'm going to go and talk to Ondrea," Teddy said, gently pushing her off him once more. He stood up and quietly walked to the front of the church. He looked straight ahead and paused in his tracks. Teddy's eyes began to water and he took a step back, riddled with confusion, disbelief, and sorrow.

He saw a casket. It was beautifully decorated with flowers and dragons. On the table in front of the casket, was a picture of Avery and her sketch book.

"No way," he whispered. He began to wobble and almost fell back. Teddy gripped one of the pews to steady himself. That's when his mom and dad came over to him and wrapped him in a big hug.

"I know it's hard, Teddy, but you need to accept it," his mother said as she rubbed his back.

"It's terrible, son, but you can't act like it's the first time you've seen it every time you think about her death," his father exclaimed sternly, but quietly.

"What… what happened?" Teddy asked, his voice trembling. "How did this happen?"

"You were there, son," his father said as he released Teddy from his hug.

"Honey, he's traumatized," his mom said. "Maybe he doesn't remember."

"Just tell me," Teddy demanded furiously.

"VORK shot her out of the sky," Spencer answered, coming up behind him and putting his arm around Teddy's shoulders.

Teddy began to seethe with rage, but hearing Ondrea's wail of pain and sorrow immediately brought him back to his senses. He looked at her sadly.

"You should go talk to her," Spencer said with a frown. "She could really use you right now."

"Will she listen?" Teddy asked distractedly.

"That all depends on you," Spencer answered as he walked away.

Teddy took a deep breath and slowly made his way to the front. He cautiously sat next to Ondrea on the pew and reached out to take her hand. He was able to grab it and hold it tightly, but she didn't look at him or seem to notice him. He scooted closer and put his other arm around her shoulders but, once again, she showed no sign of noticing. This time, Teddy didn't say anything. He just sat by her side and held her close to him. He didn't know if she could feel him or if she even knew he was there, but he didn't budge.

"I could stay here forever, my love," he muttered quietly. "As long as it meant being next to you."

Ondrea's pained frown twitched, but she continued to cry and didn't seem to notice Teddy. He gently took her face in his hands and kissed her on the forehead. Then, wordlessly, he grabbed her hand again and continued to sit in silence. About five minutes later, she let out another sob and buried her head in Teddy's shoulder. He jumped a bit, surprised she had noticed him, but smiled and gently stroked the back of her head.

"I love you, baby," he said as his eyes began to water. "We'll get through this together, just like we always do."

Ondrea looked up at him. "I love you too, Teddy Bear," she whispered, her voice hoarse.

Teddy began to cry and pulled Ondrea as close as he could. After a couple of minutes, both had settled down again.

"Do you want to… go up there?" she asked him quietly.

Teddy nodded. Ondrea took his hand and led him toward Avery's picture. He picked up her sketch book and flipped through it. When he came upon the old drawing of Mason and Jason, he smiled and thought about how far everyone had come. He let out a sad laugh and continued flipping through her sketch book.

"If she were here now, she would be very upset at you for looking through her book without permission," Ondrea said with a comforting smile.

"I bet," Teddy responded, matching her smile. Teddy was going to say more, but his voice caught in his throat. The last drawing in the book was of everyone in Team Hope. There were others too. Mrs. Thomas, Mrs. Macintosh, Damian, Vixsten, Steven, Jake, Josh, Solis, Lady Caldria, and even Francis.

"I'm such a mess," Teddy grumbled as tears began flowing once again.

Ondrea tapped on his nose then kissed him on the cheek.

"You're my mess," she said with a laugh. "You're our mess, Teddy Bear." Ondrea gestured to his friends and all the parents sitting in the pews.

Teddy smiled, pulled Ondrea in close, closed his eyes, and gave her the longest kiss he could have ever imagined. When he opened his eyes again, he was back in the studio. Teddy looked at his friends standing behind their podiums and laughed.

"Why are you guys crying?" he asked with a humored grin.

"That was the sweetest thing ever!" Jessica cried happily.

Oliver rolled his eyes and hugged his shaking sister. He nodded his head toward Ondrea whose makeup was running down her face. Her eyes were red and puffy, and she couldn't stop crying. As soon as Mr. Atrius unhooked the wires and let him out of the restraints, Teddy ran to his beautiful girlfriend and wiped the tears off her face.

"Babe, you're on live TV," he said.

Ondrea laughed happily and smiled.

"Are you saying I look ugly?" she asked.

"No! Never," Teddy answered immediately. "You always look so beautiful—all the time every day." He playfully kissed her neck, which made her crack up.

"I'm ticklish!" she exclaimed, squirming.

"I know that," he responded mischievously.

"Teddy," Darla said, having recovered from crying. "As you said before, you're on live TV, dingus."

He pretended to pout as everyone rearranged themselves at their podiums.

"Alright, boys and girls at home!" Steven announced, his voice cracking. "As usual, a five-minute break is in order, and I'm delivering! See you loyal viewers after the break!" When Steven cut the cameras, he turned around and wiped his eyes.

"Why don't you go to the bathroom to clean up or something?" Josh said as he pushed Steven in the direction of the bathrooms.

"Yeah, Dad," Jake agreed. "You're sort of a crippling mess right now."

"But I'm your mess, right?" Steven asked quietly.

Everyone began to laugh, and Jason stepped out.

"Steven, you're our mess," he said as Team Hope began to make their way backstage. Steven smiled and hugged his boys, then made his way to the bathroom to clean himself up. Jake and Josh rolled their eyes as they met up with their friends backstage.

FORTY-ONE

In Which a Flower Blossoms

After everyone had made it backstage, no one spoke as Teddy went to sit in a far corner.

"Teddy Bear," Ondrea said quietly as she knelt in front of him and lifted his head so he was looking at her eyes.

"You don't have to worry about any of that. Our communication skills are top notch."

Teddy smiled and grabbed her hand. "I know," he responded sadly.

"Uh… what's bothering you, then?" Nick asked as he hesitantly sat down next to Teddy.

Everyone was looking at Teddy. The group had a variety of expressions, but most looked concerned. Teddy laughed sadly, glanced at Avery, then looked down at his lap.

"Not being able to communicate with you, Ondrea, was terrifying, but…" Teddy glanced at Avery again and then continued. "But the last scene was… way too… um… surreal."

Everyone turned their heads to stare at Avery, which made her shake her head aggressively.

"No way!" she exclaimed. "Don't you all dare look at me like that! I'm still alive, and that stupid scene was all fake."

"Let's all just take a deep breath," Jessica said calmly. "Everyone is okay."

"Teddy," Jason said softly. "Just say what you're thinking—because I guarantee most of us are thinking the same thing you are."

Teddy sighed wearily and let go of Ondrea's hand. Despite feeling exhausted, he also needed to move around. Teddy stood up and began to pace around.

"What if it was some kind of premonition?" he asked, his voice shaking. "What if VORK really is going to be the death of Avery?"

Will's eyes went wide. "Whoa…" he gasped. "I wasn't thinking that at all, but you have a good point."

"Idiot," Darla mumbled as she clasped her hands behind her back.

"Look…" Avery began as she too started to pace. "Having Dragon Abilities means I'm partly a creature of ancient eras, so I have the ability of Foresight or the ability to see glimpses of the future."

"We know that," Oliver said. "Just like last year when you drew Mason and Jason in your sketch book before we'd even met them."

Mason and Jason exchanged concerned glances.

"Exactly," she continued. "I haven't seen anything in a while, but that's because my Power, or Foresight, activates when it predicts important scenes that could kick-start sequences of life changing events—like when the Twins of Legend, aka Mason and Jason, came into our lives. That's when VORK really began coming after us and set us on the path that ended in the school's destruction."

"Why didn't you predict the destruction of the school?" Rachel questioned.

Avery looked at the floor and frowned. After a couple of seconds, she said "Well… I kind of sort of… did."

"Okay…" Mason said through clenched teeth. "Completely putting aside the fact that you predicted our school's destruction and didn't tell any of us, how did you see that? I thought you said you could only see thing that begin a chain of important events."

"While the school's destruction did technically start a new chain of life-changing events, I can also see the outcome of the chain," Avery explained. "I have to admit, I saw a glimpse of us walking into the game-show studio for the first time, but we were all looking around in awe and smiling, so I didn't think it worth mentioning. Anyway, back to the whole point of me explaining my Foresight, I haven't seen a vision of me dying—or of anyone dying."

"That's great and all," Oliver said. He stood up slowly and glared at Avery with intense fury. "Why didn't you tell me about the school's destruction the very SECOND you saw it?" he asked with a growl.

Avery looked at him with shock and curiosity. "All premonitions are final," she whispered. "Trust me, I would know. I saw the… cave scene and… it happened."

Despite her sad tone, Oliver's glare remained unchanged.

"Did you try to change it?" he asked. "Did you try to change your fate?"

"I saw it, Oliver!" she exclaimed, looking him directly in the eyes. "It happened. You can't change the future!"

Oliver punched the wall. "You CAN change the future!" he yelled. "People aren't even supposed to KNOW the future—but you do! You can see it! You can see it, and yet you do nothing to try and change it when all you can see is destruction!"

"It's not that simple!" she yelled back.

"You're right!" Oliver said. "It's not that simple! It's. Not. Simple. NOTHING in life is simple, Avery! We work hard ALL THE TIME! So, what would it really do to us to work a bit harder to save our school… our home?!"

"I… I don't know," Avery muttered as she began to see that this was a losing argument.

"We could have saved our school!" Oliver exclaimed. "We could have TRIED. We could have done what you never did—and TRIED to change fate!"

"I'm sorry," Avery whispered as she looked toward the floor.

"I don't even BELIEVE in fate!" Oliver continued as if he hadn't heard her. "Fate is nothing but a concept! There is no fate, only the future. The future is UNDECIDED! Even if you see the future, it can ALWAYS change! Nothing is set in stone."

Everyone had backed away from Oliver to give him and his sudden outburst some space. Jessica, however, remained by his side. She gently grabbed his hand to calm him, but he yanked his hand out of her grasp and punched the wall again.

"Nothing is set in stone," he repeated as he stomped out the backstage door. "I'll be in the restroom."

Just then, Steven poked his head backstage. "I don't know what that was about," he said quickly, gesturing to where Oliver had just stormed out, "But we're on in thirty seconds!"

Silently, everyone lined up to go to their podiums.

41.1

"Welcome back ladies and gentlemen, boys and girls!" Steven shouted with an exaggerated smile. "Up next in the hot seat is none other than Darla Madison! What does our simulation have in store for you?"

Darla nervously stepped down from her podium and walked slowly toward the chair. She began to mumble anxiously.

"I don't want this," she whispered. "I don't want people to see this. I'm not supposed to be scared."

Darla paused and did everything she could to hold back her tears.

"I don't want them to see my fear," she continued. "I can't do this."

Darla put her hands over her face. Suddenly, she felt someone's hand on her shoulder. She turned around to see Ondrea looking at her with a sad smile.

"Baby girl, you can do this," Ondrea said sweetly.

Darla's eyes began to water and, for some reason, she found herself looking at Will.

"I don't want him to see it," she muttered to Ondrea. "I can't do this."

Will looked at her curiously and began to head her way, but Darla turned back toward the chair aggressively and sat down.

"I'm not weak!" she shouted at Will.

He flinched back and looked down at the floor.

"I know," he said, his voice barely audible. "I never thought you were."

Darla's eyes went wide, and she scoffed.

"You're really serious, aren't you?" she said with a small grin.

Will smiled at her sadly, nodded, then looked back toward the floor.

"Let's do this!" Darla exclaimed as her expression flipped to one of determination.

Ondrea chuckled and made her way back to her podium.

Mr. Atrius hooked up the wires and buckled in the restraints. Darla closed her eyes and took a deep breath. When she opened them again, she found herself in her home surrounded by her sisters. Each of them was looking at her with a different expression on their face as if they were trying to peer into her soul. Darla shuddered.

"Go away!" she exclaimed. "You guys are annoying."

Absolutely nothing happened. Darla froze in horror as she realized everything around her seemed to be held in place. The only things moving in the scene were her sisters' eyes.

"Alright you guys," Darla sighed. "This is creepy. Just go away."

Angie, the oldest sister, stepped forward and began to play with Darla's hair. Darla tried to swat her hand away, but found she couldn't move at all.

"Okay, this ISN'T funny!" Darla shouted. The one thing she always hated was when her sisters played with her as if she were a little doll they could dress up or makeover. When she was younger, her older siblings would always pick out her Halloween costume for her, and they'd usually choose something cutesy like a bunny or a dog. She never wanted to wear it, but her sisters always pressured her into it. They would tell her they wouldn't take her trick-or-treating unless she put on the costume and acted cute.

Darla had always been a candy connoisseur, so she'd begrudgingly say yes. As of two years ago, Darla got a part-time job and began buying her own costumes. Her sisters would say she was too old to be trick-or-treating anyway. Then they'd walk away with a look of disgust on their faces. Two years ago, Darla thought she'd left all that behind, so, naturally, as her sister stood twirling her hair, Darla began to shake with rage. She tried to move even though she was frozen in place.

"Dar-Dar," Angie said as she studied Darla closely. "We should do something with your hair. It looks so bland and upsetting."

"Gee, thanks," Darla muttered.

The third oldest, Caroline, stepped forward and began testing different hairstyles on her. "I think a top bun would be super cute." She said with excitement.

"There's that word again!" Darla shouted. "Cute! I can't stand that stupid word!"

"Oh hush!" Angie hissed as she yanked on Darla's hair. "Maybe a new look would change that attitude."

The second youngest sister, Zina, stepped forward with her hands clasped shyly behind her back.

"Guys, let's just leave her alone," she said quietly. "She clearly doesn't want to be messed with right now."

Darla grinned. "You've always got my back, Zina," she said as she reached out her hand and ruffled Zina's hair. Even though Zina was a bit older than Darla, she was still the shortest sister in the family.

When Darla realized she could move her hand, she stepped toward her sister and gave her a hug. Zina sighed happily and returned it.

"I miss you, big sis," Zina said quietly. "The girls are so mean. When are you coming home?"

"After this ridiculous game show ends," Darla responded with a smile. "Then I'll come home, and we can get ice cream or something."

"Make sure to bring back a boyfriend," Carrie, the fourth oldest sister said as she scrolled through her messages on her phone.

"And make sure he has hot friends," Angie added.

All her sisters nodded.

"I… I'd also like a hot boyfriend," Zina said awkwardly looking at her sisters.

"For sure, girly!" Caroline cheered. "You can share mine if you want."

Zina's eyes widened and she looked at Caroline with curiosity and shock.

"That's a bit… not okay, sis!" Zina exclaimed.

"What the crap is wrong with you, Caroline?" Darla yelled. "You're all such a pain in the… God! I wish you'd just all… die, die, die!"

"That's totally not okay to say, Dar-Dar!" Carrie said as she dramatically threw her phone across the room in over-exaggerated shock.

Zina stepped back and looked at Darla with fear in her eyes. Darla took a step toward her and tried to explain, but Carrie stepped in front of her.

"Get away from Zina, you freakish monster!" she shouted.

Darla brought up her fist ready to clock Carrie in the head, but Angie came up behind her and pushed her away. Darla tumbled to the ground with angry tears in her eyes.

"You guys suck!" she screamed. "All of you suck! I wish you were never born! I wish I was never born into such a horrible family!"

Her sisters began to laugh at her, including Zina. Darla shoved her head into the carpet, so she wouldn't have to look at her sisters, and cried. Everything around her suddenly went quiet and she found herself alone in a room. The floors were gray cement and the walls were made up of gray painted brick. There were a couple of windows, but they were small and too high up to be much use. Sunlight shone through the windows.

Darla stood up and walked around slowly, wiping the tears from her face.

"Nothing here," she muttered hoarsely. Darla stopped in her tracks and sighed wearily. She laughed sadly and felt her eyes begin to water once more. "No one here," she whispered. "I'm all alone."

Darla crumpled to the floor and curled up with her arms around her knees.

"I've seen this before," she said to no one. "I just sit here and wait for the scene to change. I've figured out your tricks."

Twenty minutes of waiting went by, and nothing happened. Darla growled in frustration. "So now that I've figured out your tricks, you're done?" she asked no one. "Well, I know what you're trying to do! You're trying to trick me into thinking I'm alone! I'm not scared of being alone. I have my friends, and I don't need my annoying sisters in order to feel like I belong to a loving family."

The stillness of the air around her became eerie. "What are you waiting for? Throw something at me!" she yelled. "I have friends and family! I don't need anyone or anything else!"

Darla thought she heard a girl laughing in mockery as the scene around her faded again. She blinked and noted she was now sitting on a vibrant mosaic floor. Darla looked around and took in the smoky glass walls around her. There was plenty of sunlight shining through the glass walls, but she couldn't see through them.

"You can't make me feel lonely in a place like this!" she exclaimed with an amused laugh. "It's beautiful!"

Darla walked around, dragging her hand across the cold glass. Butterflies appeared out of nowhere, which made her stop dead in her tracks. Sure, the butterflies were gorgeous, but the fact that they appeared out of thin air made Darla realize something.

"I understand," she mumbled. Darla scoffed and raised her voice. "You're showing me all these beautiful things. You could have fooled me if it weren't for the magical butterflies—normal butterflies don't just appear. Don't think I didn't notice the door at the end of the room."

Darla laughed impatiently. "I'm not afraid of ANYTHING!" she screamed, suddenly losing her cool. "So stop showing me all these pretty things that will NEVER, EVER matter to me and kick me out of this stupid simulation!"

Tears began to well up in Darla's eyes.

"Wow," she whispered, sitting crisscross on the floor. She smiled and continued, "Wow… look at me. I'm so pathetic."

Darla sniffed and wiped her eyes with her fists, but she couldn't stop the waterworks.

"I'm in such a magical place, and this is really what bothers me," she exclaimed, sitting up straight. "I don't really know what I'm afraid of."

She glanced toward the clear glass ceiling and saw more butterflies appear above her. Darla jumped up and stomped her foot angrily.

"Stop it with all your stupid tricks! They don't bother me!" she screamed. "I'm not afraid of ANYTHING! You can't beat me! I'm not afraid of being alone!"

Darla began to full-on cry as she watched the butterflies sparkle in the sunlight coming in from all sides.

"I want out!" she exclaimed. "Get me out!"

41.2

Will watched despairingly as the monitor showed Darla screaming in a glass room.

"This is awful," he muttered, forcing himself to watch. "I have to watch."

"I know you guys are in some kind of fight, but that's just cruel to say," Josh said, leaning from his podium.

"That's not what I meant," Will said, his voice barely audible. "I have to watch because I can't be a good friend if I don't know what she's going through."

"That's one way to look at it," Jake said, coming up behind Josh. "It's still pretty messed up."

Will glared at Jake and turned back toward the monitor. Jake sighed anxiously as Will began to tear up.

"This is what I mean," Jake said as he gestured to Will's tears.

He looked back at Jake and wiped his eyes.

"What do you mean?" Will asked, his voice shaking.

Josh sighed. "He means this," Josh began with a grin, "You've seen enough. You've already seen what she's going through, so there's no reason to torture yourself by watching it more. Just go to the back or something."

Will's eyes widened and he glared at Josh with intense anger.

"I would never do that," he growled. "I'd never leave her to suffer like this. I can't turn a blind eye!"

"Alright! Cool it!" Teddy hissed, coming up behind Will and grasping his arm firmly. Will tried to pull his arm away, but Teddy's grip held as he continued to talk. "He was just suggesting that you go and take a break, but there are MUCH nicer ways to decline the offer." There was an unusually venomous intensity behind Teddy's words. "If you two are really going to keep acting like this, then why care at all?"

No one said anything. All that could be heard now was the background noise of Darla's simulation. The others had turned toward Teddy with guarded looks. No one dared to approach him, as they had just been introduced to a side of him they'd never seen.

"I know the signs better than you know your own mind!" he exclaimed with a furious passion. "You both feel the same way, and if neither of you are willing to admit it to each other or even MAKE UP from this ridiculously stupid quarrel, then you don't deserve to worry the way you are right now!"

"What... what do you mean?" Will asked quietly.

Teddy's grip tightened. "I don't know what happened between you and Darla, but I know what you both WANT! I know how you feel about her, Will. She feels the same way! Can't you see this is what her fear is about?"

Jason came up behind Teddy and tapped him on the shoulder. "Why don't you cut to the chase," he offered. "Will isn't very perceptive."

Teddy laughed and tightened his grip on Will's arm to the point of bone-crushing pain.

"I know this hurts, Will," he growled. "This is just to get my point across, so listen closely." Teddy leaned forward and whispered harshly in Will's ear. "She's not afraid of being alone. That's true. She's afraid of ENDING UP alone. She. Loves. You. You need to let her know how you feel. You had no clue how she felt, so this simulated fear isn't a factor of your ignorance. But if you keep your feelings a secret after this, you will be a contributor. If you don't have the guts to tell her how you feel, you don't deserve to feel sorry for her."

Even though Teddy stopped talking, Will could still feel his hot angry breath against his ear. "She's... she's mad at me," he whispered fearfully.

"She's stubborn, and you're clueless," Teddy said, pulling away from Will's ear, but keeping his firm grip. "That's a bad combination. Not only are you clueless, but, when it comes to feelings, you're also a coward. The reason you rush into everything all the time is that you're afraid to spend even a second thinking about it— which is a horrible way to go about things! Therefore, you are absurdly useless when it comes to girls. I'll spell it out for you. You need to be the bigger person and apologize, even though you probably didn't do anything wrong. Pull back your pride and make up with her, moron. Then, you can tell her how you feel."

"Teddy…" Will whispered. "That was… intense."

Teddy let go of Will's arm and smiled. He gave Will a hearty slap on the back. "I just know how it feels to be in love, Will," he said with a wink.

Will gently rubbed his bruised arm and flinched. He turned around and glared at Teddy. Teddy scratched the back of his head and laughed. "Yeah, I apologize about that," he said, sounding genuinely sorry.

"Moron," Ondrea muttered with a grin. She walked past Teddy and grabbed the bruise on Will's arm.

"Ondrea, what the heck!" Will exclaimed.

"Relax, Will," she said quietly.

Will felt a sudden warmth in his arm and realized Ondrea was discretely using her Powers, Healing him.

"Thanks," he muttered sheepishly.

41.3

Back in the simulation, Darla had been screaming for someone to get her out for about ten minutes. Suddenly, Darla felt deflated and sank to the ground.

"This is pointless," she said with a hoarse voice. "Of course, Mr. Atrius isn't going to let Steven take me out of the simulation. He loves fear. After all, he is the de…"

Darla immediately covered her mouth as she remembered this was being broadcast over live TV.

"He is the decider," she finished as she took a deep breath. "Since I'm not out of the simulation yet, it clearly has more in store for me, so I'll just tough it out."

Darla knew what was about to happen next, so she walked toward the door.

"I'm ready," she said with a sigh. "I don't know what you've got for me, but I think I'm ready."

Darla heard a clicking sound which indicated the door had been unlocked. She grabbed the handle, took another deep breath, and threw open the door.

She had expected to see something horrific on the other side, but she saw a park filled with gorgeous multi-colored flowers and people who were laughing and holding hands. The air was thick with the smell of flowers, and the sun shone down on them, highlighting their beauty. Despite the bright shining sun, the air felt cool. She saw more butterflies, but was more at ease since these did not appear out of nowhere. Every person seemed to be in groups of two or four and were holding hands, smiling, and laughing like couples.

"Like… couples," Darla muttered. "Oh, gee, thanks, you stupid simulation."

Darla began to walk down the glimmering path with her hands in her pockets and her head down. Even though her head was down, she could sense the couples turning to stare at her. Despite their judgmental stares, Darla smiled ever so slightly.

"This isn't too bad," she said as she looked straight ahead. "At least I'm not in a life-or-death situation. I honestly don't think this could get any worse."

Darla stopped in her tracks and covered her mouth again.

"Oh no!" she exclaimed. "Why did I say that? Nothing good ever comes from saying that."

She sensed a familiar presence to her right. Even though it was familiar, it made her feel uneasy—and that uneasiness made Darla upset. She closed her eyes, turned to face the presence, stomped her foot on the ground to release her pent-up anger, and opened her eyes. She immediately swung away from the presence and threw her hands in the air dramatically.

"Of course it got worse!" she exclaimed with an annoyed laugh. "This couldn't get any wo… Nope, not going to say that."

She sensed the presence walking toward her and sighed.

"Didn't even have to say it," she grumbled. "It got worse anyway."

"Hey, Darla," the presence said shyly.

"What are you doing in my simulation, Will?" Darla asked with a snippy tone. "I'm not afraid of you!"

"Please don't start with that again," he begged quietly. "I hated seeing you do it the first time, so I don't really want to see it again."

"Wait…" Darla exclaimed loudly. "Are you the Will from the real world or a simulated Will?"

Will smiled coldly.

"Which one do you think I am?" he asked with a smirk. "Or rather, which one do you want me to be?"

"Don't play games with me, idiot!" she yelled. "I'm not in the mood!"

Darla turned around and began walking away, but Will suddenly appeared in front of her. Darla jumped in surprise and fell back on her bottom.

"You can't run from me, Dar," he said, still donning a cold smile. "I don't want to stalk you or anything, but I do want you to hear me. So, no running."

"I'm not running, stupid!" she said. "You're being creepy and annoying so I'm 'excusing myself from the situation,' as my counselor always says."

Will sighed and the cold smile disappeared.

"Okay," he said as he slumped over. "The simulation realizes trickery that won't work on you, so I'm going to switch it up."

"Aha!" Darla shouted as she stood up. "You ARE simulated!"

Will laughed. "Yep, sure am," he confessed. "Listen, this may not be real, but I'm pretty sure feelings are."

"I have a question for you," Darla said, crossing her arms. "This is all in my head, so shouldn't you be acting how I picture you in my head?"

"I am," he said simply. "I'm not super good with feelings or anything, but I'm pretty sure the ONE fight you had with me doesn't dictate how you feel about me since we met. At least I hope it doesn't. That would suck because it would mean you're shallower than I thought."

Darla scoffed.

"Seriously, dummy, you think I'm SHALLOW?" she exclaimed furiously. "You're such a moron! I can't believe you would say that! What have I ever done to make you think I'm shallow?"

Will shrugged his shoulders.

"I'm not sure," he said simply. "I never really know what you're thinking. Be real with me. Do you even know what you're thinking? Especially recently."

Darla let out a sad laugh and sat down on a nearby bench.

"No," she said. "It's all so confusing. I mean, I'm so confused that, for some reason, I'm having a heart-to-heart with YOU of all people."

"Technically, you're having a heart-to-heart with yourself," Will said with a goofy smile. "I'm going to tell you things you already know, but these are things you've seem to have forgotten. That's why I'm going to tell you."

"I know, moron," she said as Will sat down on the bench next to her. "Get on with it."

Will hesitantly put his arm around her shoulders which took Darla by surprise, but she didn't move away.

"Darla, you're an incredible person," he began, looking directly into her eyes. "You have your flaws, and you're not as perfect as you want everyone to think you are. You're not fearless. It's okay to be confused or scared. You know that. That's why you have friends like us to move you along. You're not an idiot. You're incredibly insecure—which is something you always keep on your mind.

"Despite all the fear in your heart and insecurity in your head, your courage is unmatchable, and your willpower is unrivaled. You have this thought in your mind that you can do anything, but you can't. You know that phrase 'nothing is impossible'? Even for Superpowered weirdos like us, that's not true. There are a lot of things we can't do. But something you can do is to use your incredible courage, heart, and mind to face your fears head on."

"Thanks for all that," Darla said as she crossed her arms. "But you're not going to convince me to apologize."

Will growled in frustration, put his hands firmly on Darla's shoulders, then shook her.

"GET OVER YOUR STUBBORNNESS!" he shouted. "It's not charming! Please just work this out!"

Darla put her hands on her hips and pouted.

"Rude! Rude! Rude!" she shouted as she kicked Will in the shin.

"You don't want to end up alone, do you, Darla?" Will asked with a glare. "Keep this up and the people who love you now will begin to fade until no one in the universe will be left in your life to love you."

As Will said this, he began to fade away. A couple of seconds later, Darla was left frustrated, confused, and speechless. She noticed the couples were now going out of their way to avoid her as if she had the plague. Without a word, she ran toward a couple and tried to talk to them, but they beelined away.

"Why won't anybody talk to me?" she whispered, her voice shaking.

Darla began frantically rushing the couples in hopes that one would stop and talk to her, but they continued to avoid her.

"Why won't anybody talk to me!" she shouted, bursting out in tears. "Will! You're such a jerk! Why can't you just stop?!"

Suddenly, Darla began to feel lightweight and tired. She closed her eyes and sighed with relief as she sensed everything was about to get easier.

"Darla!" a voice yelled. "Darla, wake up!"

She felt someone shaking her and holding her hand. Darla slowly opened her eyes and saw her friends.

"I'm not in the simulation…" she said quietly.

"I took the liberty of taking you out," Mr. Atrius stated as he began to take her out of the restraints on the chair. "It was all too clear you weren't making a single ounce of progress, and to allow you to continue would have just been torture."

Darla shook her head and blinked rapidly. Once she had adjusted to being out of the simulation, she looked around again. Will was in front of her with his hand on her shoulder looking deeply concerned. Darla's eyes filled with fury, and she kicked him in the stomach, sending him stumbling across the room.

"Darla!" Nick exclaimed with a look of shock. "We all saw what happened and what the simulation said to you, but that wasn't actually Will!"

Mr. Atrius sighed and put his face in his hands while Steven cut the cameras.

"Will!" Steven called in a panic. "Are you alright? Do you need medical attention?"

Will didn't say anything. He stood up, shuffled to the nearest wall, then leaned against it with his hand on his stomach. Still looking at the floor, he began to laugh despite the pain it caused him.

"Will?" Avery asked hesitantly. "Are… are you okay?"

"Why wouldn't I be?" he said as he looked up with a pained smile. "The woman I admire is no longer suffering."

Darla slowly stood from the chair and began to walk toward Will at a snail's pace.

"I'm… I'm sorry, Will," she blurted. "I think I just panicked."

"No, that wasn't panic," he countered. "That was just you being you."

Darla stopped and frowned deeply.

"Me being me," she said quietly.

Darla's eyes widened as she looked down at herself, but mainly at her foot. She couldn't believe she had just done that. Sure, she'd done things like that to her friends in the past, but this time felt different. Much different.

"Why aren't you yelling at me, Will?" she asked as her eyes began to water. "Why aren't you mumbling sarcastically or cracking some funny, but dumb, joke?"

Will put all his weight against the wall and slid down to a sitting position. He grimaced in pain and let out a small laugh.

"There's no point anymore," he said, looking Darla in the eyes. "I don't think you'll ever learn."

"Learn what?" Darla asked as she resumed her walk toward Will. "What are you talking about?"

Will smiled supportively as Nick began to discretely use his Healing Powers to help Will with his injury.

"What that simulation said to you… about how there would be no one left to love you… it was wrong." He stated. "Everything you heard in there came from your own mind, and none of it came from reality."

At this point Darla was standing in front of Will.

"Darla," he continued. "Truth be told, I know who you are on the inside. Even on your worst days, I will never… never stop… loving you."

Darla's eyes widened in shock. She fell to her knees and began to cry.

"I'm sorry!" she exclaimed tearfully. "I was being so blind and stupid! I should have been stronger!"

Will tried to stand and support her, but Nick put his hand on Will's leg and shook his head.

"Almost done," Nick muttered. "Stay still."

Ondrea jogged toward Darla to provide emotional support, but Teddy grabbed her arm to stop her.

"Darla!" Will exclaimed sharply. "I want to get one thing straight! I have never thought of you as weak. You're the strongest and most powerful person I know, and when I see you doubt yourself, It hurts me."

Darla looked up and wiped her eyes. The firm, confident look in Will's eyes startled her.

"You're… you're really serious," she stated. "You really mean it."

"Of course I mean it, moron!" he responded. "Even though you can be a big pain sometimes, so can I! I accept you, Darla. We all accept you. You don't need to be afraid of ending up alone anymore."

Will glanced at Nick as if waiting for confirmation. Nick nodded, indicating he had finished the Healing. Will slowly stood up and made his way to Darla. He took both her hands in his and smiled at her.

"I won't let you feel alone anymore," he whispered. "You mean a lot to me, Darla. I don't want to lose you to pain, insecurity and sadness."

Darla hesitated, then wrapped her arms around Will in a tight hug.

"Thank you," she said tearfully. "Thank you so much."

Will put his arms around Darla to return the hug and sighed.

"You're quite a handful!" he exclaimed.

Darla pulled away and smiled.

"You're no better yourself, idiot," she mumbled. "Always getting yourself into trouble."

"Look who's talking," he responded with a laugh.

The members of Team HOPE exchanged glances, and each person let out a sigh of relief.

"You two really know how to carve us down to our last nerve," Jason said as he scratched the back of his head awkwardly.

"Way too much drama," Jake said. "There's no catching a break when it comes to you guys."

Everyone nodded.

"Speaking of drama…" Jessica began with a hint of concern in her tone. "Has Oliver come back yet?"

FORTY-TWO

In Which the Devil's Purpose Is Revealed

Everyone but Steven had gathered backstage.

"So," Mr. Atrius began with his arms crossed and an eyebrow raised. "Does anyone want to tell me where Mr. Oliver Fletcher ran off to?"

"If you couldn't tell," Mason began pointedly, "We have no clue."

"He got pretty upset earlier and ran out," Rachel stated. "I hadn't noticed he was still gone."

"We can add him to the list of missing campers," Teddy muttered sarcastically.

"No way!" Jessica said. "I'll give him a call. He has to come back eventually."

"Put him on speaker!" Nick shouted. "Please!"

Jessica, who had her phone in her hand, turned to look at Nick.

"Honestly, I kind of want to talk to him on my own," she said quietly. "I'm sorry, Nick. I know you're really worried too, but…"

"It's alright," he said wearily, cutting her off. "I'll just take a nap or something."

Jessica nodded firmly and marched further backstage out of earshot. Mr. Atrius suddenly disappeared then reappeared in front of Nick. Nick jumped up in surprise.

"How are you feeling, Nick?" Mr. Atrius asked, peering deeply through Nick's eyes.

"Why do I feel like you're trying to pierce my soul?" Nick wondered hesitantly. "You're a bit close."

"You should have let Ondrea take care of Will," he responded. "Using your Power has slightly sped up the draining process."

"Awesome," Nick sighed sarcastically. "Just what I need. More problems."

Mr. Atrius sighed and sat down on the floor with a thump.

"Why are you so calm about this?" Mr. Atrius questioned, yawning. "I know you realize that having too much of your Power drained is fatal."

"Naturally," Nick answered with a grin. "But I have a bunch of wonderful friends who are going to help me though. Plus, it doesn't matter what you have or don't have—as long as you have the mental courage to stand up for what you believe in."

"You kids are so optimistic," Mr. Atrius said. "I would usually find that annoying, but… it suits you guys well."

"Mr. … um… Lucifer, I need to pick your brain," Jason stated abruptly.

"You should be searching for Oliver and my son," Mr. Atrius said with a stern look in his eyes.

"Oh, sorry," Jason began sarcastically. "I'll put my people right on it."

"I'd be willing to go find them," Will offered. "I'm really bored."

Darla rolled her eyes and smiled.

"I'll go with you!" she exclaimed.

"I'm done with you two," Mr. Atrius said. "The only way you would be useful is to do what you just offered."

"Now I'm not so sure I want to go," Will mumbled with his arms crossed.

Darla snickered, stood up, grabbed Will's forearm, and pulled him off the ground.

"I'm going!" she said with a laugh. "So… you are too!"

"I feel like you're trying to rip me apart or something," Will said. "First the front kick, then the arm tearing."

"Speaking of…" Nick butted in. "Are you feeling well enough to go wandering the halls?"

"Duh, you used your Powers to Heal me," Will answered, rolling his eyes.

Nick opened his mouth to speak, but he was cut off abruptly when Darla sprinted out of the room, Will in hand.

"Let's go!" she yelled.

"Anyway…" Jason said. "Time for you to answer my questions."

"Alright, fine," Mr. Atrius pouted with crossed arms.

"Grow up!" Avery exclaimed, giving Mr. Atrius a hard stare. He glared at Avery.

"My first question…" Jason began. "When we all came back-stage minute ago, you seemed very adamant about finding Oliver. Why?"

Mr. Atrius smiled and released a quiet laugh.

"You're the smartest one here, Jason. So, naturally, I'd like to know your take on the matter," he said. "Why do you think I care so much when it comes to the location of you children?"

"It makes sense for you to be worried about Michael and Sydney since they're your children," Jason began, thinking out loud. "Jake and Josh too since they aren't a part of your current hit list. It also makes sense for you to be concerned about Steven since, from a business standpoint, he's technically your boss. You're a villain, and we're your targets, so it would be easier for you if one of us was to go missing—but you've made it clear that's not the way you want to end things. So, there's no way you'd be behind any prolonged disappearance of any of us."

"Jason?" Mason said, tapping him on the shoulder and breaking Jason's train of thought. "You might be getting a bit off-topic here. Maybe if we do our brainstorming technique, it might help keep you on track."

Jason smirked.

"Are you sure you can keep up with me?" he asked.

"I know how you operate, Jason," Mason answered. "I know I can keep up."

"Let's do this." Jason said.

Mason took a deep breath, then began to speak.

"He's the ruler of Hell!" Mason exclaimed. "Let's start off with that."

"He's been displaying a strange form of paternal instincts for us and not just his own children," Jason said with his eyes closed. "Something one wouldn't expect for him to show to his targets. Mason."

"Something else we know about him is that he can control who gets to come out of the simulation early," Mason mentioned. "I thought that became relevant when he pulled Darla out."

"Yes," Jason began. "Darla was the only one he pulled out. He most likely pulled her out because her stubbornness was creating a severe lack of progress. Mason."

"I know we're not necessarily regular humans and we have Superpowers, but the simulations seem way too intense," Mason stated. "Much more intense than they should be even for our crazy standards."

"Yes, yes, you're right," Jason exclaimed, opening his eyes. "We can connect the dots a bit better, brother! He's Lucifer. He can control who gets to leave the simulation!"

"I understand!" Mason gasped. "He's literally controlling the simulations. It makes sense! He's Lucifer! We don't know exactly what kind of powers he has, but since he judges people by searching their souls before he sends them to Hell, he can see our souls too!"

"He can see our fears, our worries, our hardships, the whole nine yards!" Jason whispered in awe. "He made our simulations more powerful!"

"Boys." Mr. Atrius interrupted, looking thoroughly amused. "What about my paternal instincts?"

Jason looked at Mason with wide eyes.

"He interrupted our flow, brother!" Jason exclaimed. "What do we do?"

"Are you open to outside suggestions?" Rachel asked.

The boys nodded.

"As you said, he judges people," Rachel began. "Mr. Atrius is a psychotic murderer, so we won't ever really know what he's thinking, but I can come pretty close. In a way, I think he's trying to clear our consciousnesses before he offs us so we can move on with little to no regret in our lives. I think that's where the paternal instinct comes in. He wants to kill us, but, in a weird way, he wants to protect us too."

Mr. Atrius began to laugh hysterically. Everyone turned and looked at him in confusion.

"Ding, ding, ding!" Mr. Atrius said as his laughter settled. He wiped his eyes and gave one final chuckle.

"She hit the nail on the head!" he exclaimed. "I don't WANT to kill you all, but I MUST. That's just how it goes! It's my job."

"Which job?" Teddy asked, raising an eyebrow. "Your VORK job? Or your…main duties?"

"My VORK job and my main duties often conflict with my morals. This is for my VORK job. VORK is an evil organization. They require me to kill you and make you suffer. I will make you suffer, but I also want you to be at some kind of peace when you die," Mr. Atrius said with a strange smile. "Besides, the more painfully you die, the more of a hero's death it will be!" He began to laugh again.

"God, you're creepy!" Ondrea said, squirming uncomfortably. Teddy scooted closer to his love and held her hand.

"He IS the ruler of Hell," Teddy said with a sigh.

"Why, thank you, Teddy," Mr. Atrius said with a smile. "Where are the Fletchers? Also where is the silly boy and the aggressive girl?"

"Jess is calling Oliver," Josh answered as he prepared to give his twin a wet willy.

"Now that I think about it," Jake began, "it's been a bit of time since we've seen Will, Darla, and Jess."

"I just realized something," Avery exclaimed. "Our sense of time is really messed up. For some reason, on this game show, five minutes can feel like ten, and ten minutes can feel like five. It's really weird."

"Yeah, that's really bizarre," Ondrea agreed as she pulled up the clock on her phone.

Nick leaned over and glanced at Ondrea's phone screen.

"We get five-minute breaks, but I'm pretty sure it's been around seven minutes, maybe ten," he said.

"It's been exactly eight minutes and now fifty-seven seconds," Jason stated, chewing on his fingernails out of boredom.

"I didn't know you could do that!" Mason exclaimed, slapping Jason on the back.

"Boys, would you stop!" Avery yelled toward Jake and Josh.

"He stuck his saliva-covered finger in my ear!" Jake growled.

"That may be so, but that doesn't warrant you trying to shove Josh's finger up his own nose," Avery said with a dragon-like growl in her tone.

Jake and Josh immediately stopped goofing around and sat completely still.

"I think we're getting a bit off topic," Mr. Atrius said, no longer looking amused. "We need the kids here. Right. Now."

"Guys!" Jessica and Oliver said, as they launched themselves into the room.

"Will… and Darla passed by that purple door… during their search and felt a… strange Dark Magic… presence!" Oliver gasped, completely out of breath.

Everyone's eyes widened. But Rachel, who had been growing ever more wary of Mr. Atrius, glanced at him to see how he would react to the news. His facial expression didn't change, but she noticed his eyes flash red. This also caught the attention of Ondrea and Oliver, who turned to look in his direction.

"Where are Darla and Will?" Teddy asked quickly. "Are they in trouble?"

"They should be here any minute now," Jessica replied. "They texted us the information and then said they'd be backstage soon."

"What is it about this situation that angers you the most, Lucifer?" Ondrea questioned suddenly.

Mr. Atrius laughed quietly and sighed.

"My daughter is most likely up to her shenanigans again," he responded with another sigh.

"Shenanigans?" Mason muttered. "What exactly do you mean by shenanigans?"

"GUYS!" Will shouted as he and Darla burst through the backstage door. "Bad news! Horrible news!"

"This is really bad news," Darla stated, walking in behind Will.

"What do you mean?" Mr. Atrius asked, looked amused.

"YOU!" Darla shouted at him.

She stuck her arms out in front of her and used her Fire Power to shoot white flames directly at him.

"You are such a jerk!" she screamed. "I don't know what you're hiding behind that purple door, but I bet it's some kind of horrible weapon!"

Mr. Atrius held up his hand as her Fire came blazing toward him. When the Fire contacted his hand, he performed a flicking motion and sent the fire right back at her. The motion surprised Darla and she didn't have time to react. She closed her eyes and braced for impact, knowing the fire wouldn't burn her, but it would send her flying backwards. She opened her eyes when she heard Fire boiling away water and saw the air fill with steam. When it cleared, she noticed all her friends were in a fighting stance around her and Will stood in front of her panting.

"Darla, those were some intense flames," he said, looking back at her and smiling.

He stumbled backward and sat against the wall. Darla stood still in shock.

"Hold on, what just happened?" she asked, her voice noticeably shaking.

"You became illogically upset and shot fire at me," Mr. Atrius said in a casual tone. "Then I flicked it back at you. Your new boyfriend jumped in front of you and formed a surprisingly strong water barrier around you and all of your friends."

Darla glanced at the others, then sat against the wall next to Will.

"He used his Water Power," she said to herself. Then she asked Will if he got burned.

"I'm alright," he responded, still out of breath. "But that was some flame."

"Also," Darla continued, staring directly at Mr. Atrius, "he is not my boyfriend."

"I'm not?" Will asked, looking disheartened.

Darla laughed and rolled her eyes.

"Not yet, loser," she said, punching him on the shoulder. "If we get out of this show alive… I'll… think about it."

Will chuckled. He suddenly went limp and slumped against Darla's shoulder.

"I'm a little worn," he said as he began to fade off into sleep.

Darla smiled and let him lean on her shoulder. Her eyes widened as she remembered they had something important to tell everyone.

"Will and I saw burn marks on the purple door's handle. I bet you anything Michael burned the lock with his Electrical Power and went inside."

"I guess my son and daughter must be playing together then. Getting acquainted and all that," Mr. Atrius said with a genuine smile on his face.

"What is that supposed to mean?" Nick asked as he bent down in front of Will to Energize him.

"Nick," Mr. Atrius said sternly. "Let Ms. Kendal, Ondrea, help him."

"Right," Nick mumbled with a sigh. "Too weak."

Ondrea came up behind Nick and put her hand on his shoulder. With that, Nick moved aside and let Ondrea get to work.

"So, about Michael and Sydney 'playing' together…?" Nick continued.

"I'm curious to know what that insinuates," Jason said, with his arms crossed.

"Well, my daughter isn't very good at playing nice, so I assume it's some friendly torture," Mr. Atrius responded while casually fidgeting his fingers.

"TORTURE! Oh yeah, that sounds like a bunch of fun," Will exclaimed.

"Glad to see you're alive, Will," Mr. Atrius stated, looking genuinely happy for some reason. "It wouldn't be fun to kill you while you're not at your best."

"That's so messed up," Mason muttered.

"Wait a second!" Jason said sharply. "Torture is torture no matter which way you look at it! Are you really okay with your daughter torturing your son?"

"She's not going to kill him," Mr. Atrius replied with a shrug. "The most he'll have is mental trauma."

"Holy crap!" Darla yelled. "You're TERRIBLE!"

"I was born this way," he said simply.

Suddenly, Avery began to laugh.

"You are so funny, Lucifer," she said, unable to control herself. "I'm so perplexed by your behavior. I've never met anyone as vile and disgusting as you."

Mr. Atrius looked at Avery, feeling genuinely unsettled by her comment.

"In fact," she continued, "I've never met anyone who has the guts to sit by while your psychotic daughter tortures your already-depressed son. You should be ashamed of yourself. Just because you're the devil doesn't mean you need to be such a devilish parent. I hope you die soon!"

"You interest me, Avery Kendal." Mr. Atrius said in a hushed tone. "I think I'll kill you last."

"Intense threats aside," Oliver said as he stepped in between Mr. Atrius and the rest of his friends and faced his adversary, "you're going to tell your daughter to let our friend go!"

"I don't think so," Mr. Atrius said as he disappeared and reappeared in front of Oliver.

He put one finger against Oliver's lips to shut him up. Oliver went stiff with fear and his friends tensed.

"If I can end your pathetic life by flicking my finger, what do you think I can do when I'm in physical contact with you like I am now?" he whispered, his eyes turning red.

"What the…" Will began as ice began to form at his fingertips.

"Play nice, children. You too, Atrius," Steven demanded as he poked his head backstage. "Sorry about the delay, but we ran into some problems. We're about to go live in one minute!"

When Steven went back to the front, Mr. Atrius stepped away from Oliver and glared at the kids.

"You're very lucky my employer stepped in," Mr. Atrius said in a low growl. "I can't get on his bad side. At least not yet. He could find out my intentions."

Mr. Atrius smiled and stared right at Jake and Josh.

"Then again, he's just a powerless human," Mr. Atrius continued. "I could do anything to him."

Josh's eyes widened in shock and Jake's eyes filled with rage. Jake began to march forward but Jason stuck out his arm to stop him.

"He could rip you apart with ease," Jason cautioned, clearly frustrated as well. "If the Superheroes in this group are not up to par with his skills, then you two are definitely no match for him. I know you're both very upset right now, but we won't let anything happen to your father."

Mr. Atrius smirked.

"Big words Jason Mackenzie," he said.

"Kids!" Steven called, "Get in line! Atrius, get out here now!"

Mr. Atrius rolled his eyes, pouted, and made his way out. Wordlessly, team HOPE lined up.

FORTY-THREE

In Which There Are Zombies

I apologize for the delay, ladies and gentlemen!" Steven exclaimed with his chest puffed out to look more confident than he felt. "You know, this has been one crazy show, but at least the fun never stops! Next up, we have Josh Stanford, one of my rambunctious teenagers!"

Josh visibly flinched and ducked behind his podium. Jake looked at him and grinned humorously.

"Get on out there, rambunctious teenager," Jake whispered, grabbing his brother's arm and pulling him up against his will.

When Josh begrudgingly stood up, he slapped Jake on the back of the head, took a deep breath, and began walking toward the chair. Suddenly, Josh felt someone grab his arm in a vice grip, and he quickly stopped. He looked back to see Jake's worried expression. Josh noticed his brother was shaking. Josh rolled his eyes and stepped toward Jake.

"I'll be fine," Josh said confidently.

His grip didn't loosen, but Josh saw Jake's eyes wander to Mr. Atrius standing behind directly behind him with a smirk on his face.

"Come on Josh. Don't be scared," Mr. Atrius said, grabbing Josh's other arm. "It's time to face your fear."

Mr. Atrius glared at Jake, then made a squeezing motion with his unoccupied hand, transferring pain into Jake's wrist. Jake quietly gasped in pain and pulled his arm back. He looked down and noticed his wrist had turned bright red.

"As long as everything goes alright, you won't have to worry about your brother," Mr. Atrius said to Jake.

Jake's eyes began to water as Mr. Atrius pulled Josh into the chair. During this entire interaction, the tension in the rest of team HOPE grew immensely.

"Are you okay?" Will asked, softly touching Jake's wrist.

"I… I'm okay," Jake responded as he cleared his throat and wiped his eyes with his fists.

"Your wrist?" Will whispered.

"It's alright," he responded quietly.

"Alright, boys and girls, women and men," Steven began. "Let's get this show on the road!"

Even Steven's confident demeanor had shifted. Once Josh was strapped into the chair, Oliver noticed Steven gently ruffle his son's hair then squeeze his shoulder to reassure him. Josh closed his eyes.

When he opened his eyes, Josh found himself sitting against a tree and surrounded by his friends.

"Uh, hey… guys," he said awkwardly. "What's up?"

Nick glared at Josh and scoffed.

"You know what you did!" Nick exclaimed. "You really messed up this time."

"Wait… what did I do?" Josh asked nervously. "I just got here."

"What the heck are you talking about?" Oliver said in a haunted whisper. "You had one job."

"To protect your twin brother," Jason said, staring sadly at the ground.

"You let Lucifer drag him into the underworld," Mason growled. "Twins are supposed to look after each other."

"Hold on!" Josh yelled as he jumped up. "I did what?"

"He trusted you, Josh!" Avery screamed, tears running down her face. "We all trusted you!"

"But… but… I'm not like you guys!" he responded as he began to pace back and forth. "I don't have Powers!"

"You're just as strong without Powers, you stupid idiot!" Darla shouted.

"But, I've been doing everything I can!" Josh said, burying his face in his hands. "We found him in the desert!"

"But YOU didn't do anything!" Rachel exclaimed, finally losing her patience. "WE did everything!"

"All you did was panic," Ondrea stated. "You're useless."

"Way to let everyone down," Teddy mumbled.

"Hey… that's a bit harsh," Josh whispered, backing up against the tree. "I'm feeling a bit cornered here. Could you guys maybe backup?"

"You really put us in a bind," Jason shouted. "You put us in a bind, and now you want space?"

"You can have it," Oliver said with a low growl. "We don't need you anymore."

"All that time and effort you put into helping us was wasted," Jessica said. "You can just wander off into the desert."

"We're a team!" Josh yelled, his voice shaking. "We're supposed to stick together!"

"And how did that work out for your twin brother?" Will asked as he walked aggressively toward Josh.

Josh began to run as fast as he could in the opposite direction. As he ran, all he could see around him was sand. No matter how long he kept going, he never seemed to run out of breath. Soon, the scenery around him began to turn gray and ash-like. The air became hot, and he found it hard to breathe, but he kept on running. Within a matter of minutes, the scene had completely shifted. Now everything around him was gray and desolate. The heat intensified, and he began to see horrifying creatures. Some were hovering in the air, and others were skulking on the ground.

Josh saw a river that seemed to run black with ash and dust. He stopped running and slowly approached it. The closer he got, the more pain he began to feel. Screams rose from the black river and he could see charred hands barely reaching through the surface. One of the hands grabbed his wrist and began to pull him under.

"Welcome to Hell," said a deep voice that echoed in his head.

The last thing Josh saw before he went under was Mr. Atrius's face, but it was distorted and ugly. Josh tried to swim toward the surface, but more hands clasped onto his legs and arms. One hand grabbed his hair and pulled him even deeper. Not only was he beginning to lose his breath, but he felt like the river was sucking all the light out of his soul.

An image of his friends flashed through his head. They were standing around him in a huddle and reaching for him. He took their hands and was about to smile when an image of Jake flashed through his head. Jake's arms and legs were tied up and silent tears ran down his cheeks. He looked too weak to do anything, but Josh saw Jake muttering his twin's name. Josh suddenly let go of his friend's hands and closed his eyes.

"Time to accept this darkness," Josh thought, his face full of determination. "I know my friends care about me. They would never say those things to me. This is all in my head. I need to accept this darkness in order to overcome it."

Finally, Josh felt his oxygen run out and he instinctively gasped for air, but all he got was a mouthful of dark sludge and pain. Despite the horrible agony coursing through his body and his lack of oxygen, he began to swim upwards as hard as he could. The hands that were holding him down tightened their grip, but Josh kicked and punched as he slowly broke free from them. Finally, he broke the surface and clawed his way out of the river.

"Holy crap," he whispered just before coughing up what felt like gallons of dark sludge.

After ten minutes, Josh lay down on the ground and closed his eyes, temporarily forgetting why he clawed his way out of the depths in the first place.

"I have to rescue my brother," he said suddenly, panting.

He stood up and yelped in pain.

"Guess I'm going to have a couple of physical scars… as well as mental ones," he mumbled with a sigh. "Time to go."

He pushed through the unimaginable pain and began to sprint ahead. This time, he seemed to be running out of energy quickly, but he pushed through.

"I may not have Superpowers," he began. "But I have friends. I have myself. I can do this. I need to accept my situation."

Suddenly, Jake appeared before him along with a grinning Mr. Atrius.

"Welcome to Hell," Mr. Atrius said.

Mr. Atrius looked completely different this time. Instead of his dark brown hair, it was blood red. So were his eyes. The tips of his fingers were charred and on fire. A pair of veiny black wings protruded from his head where his ears should have been, and his body was white as snow. What made Mr. Atrius look the most hideous were the black and silver veins protruding from his neck and face. He wore a tattered robe that looked as if it was modeled off a human skeletal system, and his grin literally stretched from ear to ear.

"You look much better this way, Atrius," Josh exclaimed with a growl. "You look more like your heart."

"I don't care what you have to say to me. And call me Lucifer when we're in this realm."

"Alright, Lucifer," Josh said in a mocking tone. "Let my brother go right now or I'll show you REAL Hell."

"You're a powerless nobody," Lucifer said with a smirk.

"I may be powerless, but I am somebody," Josh responded, returning the smirk. "I have friends—and an awesome, but mostly annoying, twin brother."

"How sweet," Lucifer said. "Now, it's time for you to die."

"I don't think so!" Josh yelled as he charged toward his brother.

Then, something strange happened. When Josh grabbed the ropes to untie Jake, they disintegrated in hands. Josh didn't have time to ponder that because he knew every millisecond counted. He threw Jake over his shoulder and raced away from Lucifer.

Josh expected Lucifer to chase after him, but when he looked back, he saw Mr. Atrius looking normal and smiling. It wasn't a creepy smile this time. It seemed to be a smile that radiated satisfaction. Josh turned around to continue his trek but was surprised to see all his friends standing right in front of him.

"You got him," Oliver said with a smile. "To be honest, we're all really sorry about what we said."

"We didn't really mean it," Rachel said nervously. "I guess we all lost our cool."

Josh laughed.

"It doesn't matter whether you meant it or not," he said, still chuckling. "I don't need to listen to the judgmental things people say to me."

Will laughed and punched Josh in the shoulder.

"You know, I think I figured it out," Will said. "You know this is all in your perspective. There's no way in… well, Hell… that we would do this to you in real life."

"We'd give you a hand," Jessica said.

"Since we're saying this in your simulation, that just means you knew it all along!" Ondrea exclaimed as she giggled.

"Geez," Josh muttered. "I kind of forgot this was a simulation."

Suddenly, he felt Jake kick him in the ribs.

"Let go of me!" Jake said as he continuously kicked his twin in the ribs. "I'm not some kind of rag doll!"

Josh aggressively set his brother down on the floor.

"Last time I save your sorry butt," Josh said with his arms crossed. "And try not to break my ribcage."

"No promises," Jake muttered, standing and brushing off his pants.

"I think it's go time." Darla said, crossing her arms as if bored.

"I've had enough of this," Josh mumbled as he stared at his twin brother.

Just as he said this, Josh felt himself fall asleep. When he opened his eyes, he found he was in the simulation chair. Josh blinked a couple of times then turned to look at his friends. When his eyes met Jake's, Jake gave his brother a huge smile.

"Wow, folks!" Steven exclaimed excitedly. "Now that was one 'hell' of a simulation, wouldn't you say? Now, ladies and gentlemen, it's time for that classic five-minute break. This time, it will ONLY be five minutes."

Wordlessly, after Mr. Atrius had unhooked the wires and undid the restraints, the kids returned backstage. Mr. Atrius began to follow them when Steven called him over.

"What can I do for you, boss?" Mr. Atrius asked.

"Why were you in my son's fear simulation?" Steven questioned as he fearlessly glared at Mr. Atrius. "What are you doing to my kids?"

"I'm not harming them," he responded simply. "I don't know why your kids are so afraid of me."

"I don't believe you!" Steven whispered harshly. "My kids mean the world to me. They ARE my world. If you do anything to hurt them, you'll instantly regret it."

Mr. Atrius began to laugh.

"I wouldn't make threats like that to me, boss," he said with a grin.

"I'm beginning to suspect there is much more to you that I don't know," Steven stated. "Given my experience with the… unknown… I'm going to assume you're not a good person."

"That would be wise," Mr. Atrius said, still grinning. "Considering that you're still my employer, I won't do anything to further upset your family dynamic."

"That's not good enough!" Steven said in a low growl. "I understand those kids can hold their own with you, but I don't want to hear anymore threats, arguments, explosions, or screams from backstage ever again."

"I'm not sure what to say to that," Mr. Atrius responded, his grin fading. "What if the children instigate it?"

"For God's sake, be the bigger person, Atrius!" Steven exclaimed, throwing his hands in the air. "I'm sensing you're not the most trustworthy person, but at least be an adult!"

Mr. Atrius laughed once more. "Yes sir," he responded. "I think I'll go and keep the children company now."

Steven was about to say more, but Mr. Atrius turned away and walked backstage.

43.1

"That really blew," Josh said as everyone sat against the wall backstage.

"You're okay though, right?" Oliver asked.

"Yeah. I'm fine," Josh responded, twiddling his thumbs.

Everyone went silent for a minute.

"You know we'd never do something like that," Jessica said softly, interrupting the silence. "We wouldn't say things like that to you."

"I gathered that," Josh said wearily.

"Thanks for saving me," Jake said, as he walked over and sat by his twin.

"I had to in order to get that fear simulation over with—but you're welcome," Josh said.

Jake stood up and kicked his brother's shin.

"Wow, thanks for that," Jake exclaimed. "I'm sorry I burdened you and got in the way."

"Okay, I didn't mean it like that!" Josh yelled in alarm.

"Children!" Mr. Atrius said, sounding unusually cheery.

He entered backstage with a big smile on his face.

"I have to be nice to you since I just got chewed out by my boss," he exclaimed.

His smile vanished for a second and he said, "What a pain." Then he smiled again.

"Gee, thanks," Teddy said.

"Yeah, we really appreciate it," Will stated, rolling his eyes. "What are you going to do, then, nice guy?"

"I haven't really thought that far," Mr. Atrius said. "Why don't I start with this?"

He sat down in front of the kids and cleared his throat. "It would be charitable for me to say this, I think. Not only is Michael in my daughter's custody, but... and this is the nice part... Nicholas, your friend Spencer is in MY custody."

Everyone went completely silent.

"How is that for nice?" Mr. Atrius asked in a mock happy tone. "Now you don't have to worry about your friend's whereabouts."

"You piece of..." Will started to shout in fury.

"Will, don't finish that statement!" Avery exclaimed. "You'd better leave Spencer alone, by the way, Lucifer!"

"He has nothing to do with this!" Jessica yelled.

"You'd better not hurt him!" Teddy shouted. "You're going to pay for this!"

Nick laughed. "I kind of figured that out by this point," he said directly to Mr. Atrius. "I love Spence like a brother, and at least I know you haven't killed him yet."

"Hold on, Nick," Rachel said with surprise. "That's a bit of a mellow reaction considering what he just said."

Everyone, including Mr. Atrius, looked at Nick curiously. When he saw this, Nick spoke.

"Sorry, I'm just too tired to care right now," Nick muttered.

Mr. Atrius stood up and walked toward Nick with a creepy grin on his face.

"I see now," Mr. Atrius said. "You're not doing so well, are you?"

Ondrea quickly got up and went straight to Nick's side.

"Don't you dare do anything to him!" She growled intensely. "Try anything, and I'll use my Super Strength to crush your bones."

"Poor, poor Nick," Mr. Atrius said, laughing. "Seems like my daughter's doing quite a number on you."

"Hey, back up, Lucifer!" Nick exclaimed as he sat up straight. "I'm still plenty strong and I've got my friends… no, my FAMILY to back me up."

"It seems like you children have forgotten your place," he responded.

"Why don't you put us back in our place, then," Jake said, stepping directly in Mr. Atrius's path.

"Gladly," Mr. Atrius stated.

He turned toward Oliver, but, before he could do anything, Josh stepped in his path. As Mr. Atrius turned to aim his wrath at a Superhero, Jake stepped in his path again.

"You can't do anything while we're in your way," Jake said with a glare.

The rest of the gang looked at Jake and Josh in shock. But despite the incredible courage and bravery the boys were showing, their legs were shaking.

"True," Mr. Atrius said causally. "But… I could just kill your father, and then I could kill you two."

"Fat freaking chance!" Mason exclaimed as the ground began to tremor.

"You don't want to cause an earthquake, Mason," Jason muttered. "Just calm down or you'll kill us all."

"Yes, listen to the smart twin," Mr. Atrius said with a laugh.

"Mason is smart!" Jason yelled, coming to his brother's defense. "You're the idiot here!"

"Idiot!" Darla said, snickering.

"Forget what the boss said!" Mr. Atrius screeched. "You kids are going to witness a TV announcer's death on live TV!"

"ATRIUS!" Steven screamed from the stage. "Shut it! I said no yelling! You too, kids!"

Mr. Atrius narrowed his eyes and sighed.

"Stupid boss," he muttered, pouting like a child.

Steven suddenly popped his head backstage. "I heard that," he said pointedly. "Also, start the line up, kids! We're going live in thirty seconds!"

43.2

"Alrighty, folks!" Steven exclaimed, making dramatic sweeps with his body for extra effects. "Next up in the chair, we have Jake Stanford!"

"Getting right into this, I see," Jason muttered wearily. "This is becoming a pain."

"We just found out Spencer was taken by Lucifer and Michael still has yet to appear," Nick sighed, leaning against the back wall behind the podiums.

"Yeah, this is no good," Rachel whispered. "Plus, your dad's still missing, Nick."

"I know," Nick stated quietly. "This is a nightmare."

"Guys," Will said from a few podiums down. "Isn't Michael supposed to go in the simulation after Jake?"

"He is," Ondrea confirmed.

The kids were interrupted by Steven.

"Jake, I know this is a bit frightening, but you need to come to the chair now," he said. "It's your turn."

"Wait, you haven't gone to the chair yet?" Avery asked. "We've been talking for like two minutes."

"For good reason," Jake muttered.

He gestured to Mr. Atrius who was looking at Jake with a creepy hunger in his expression. Steven looked over at Mr. Atrius and sighed.

"Mr. Atrius!" Steven exclaimed with a mock smile. "Could you please refrain from smiling? It will scare away our younger viewers."

Mr. Atrius's face immediately went blank.

"That works too," Steven announced, continuing to project a fake smile to the camera. "Now, come on up, Jake."

With a small nudge from Josh, Jake hastily walked to the chair, suddenly in a hurry to get it over with. He sat down, and Mr. Atrius began to strap him in and place the wires on his head. Jake's throat felt dry, and he let out a nervous cough. Steven put his hand on his son's hair and kept it there for a few seconds. Jake kept his face forward, but his eyes lingered on Steven's expression. Steven looked horrified and there was nothing Jake could do about it. He knew that. Jake took a deep breath and closed his eyes. When he opened them again, he stood in front of a grocery store with his brother standing next to him.

"Well, this is a really strange place to be afraid of," Jake muttered, taking a better look around.

"Not that strange of a place, idiot," Josh said harshly. "This was your idea."

"This place looks like it could be a zombie apocalypse movie set," Jake said, unintentionally ignoring his twin. "It's looks pretty cool, don't you think?"

"Idiot!" Josh exclaimed.

He grabbed Jake's arm and began pulling him away. Jake absentmindedly let Josh pull him along as he continued to observe the scene around him. The reason his brother was trying to pull him away soon became obvious. Horrifying humanoid creatures emerged from the entrance of the parking lot in front of the store. They had chunks of flesh and skin dangling off their gray bodies. Some of them had no face at all, while others had bones and muscles showing.

"Oh God, those are zombies!" Jake yelled as his body stilled.

"Yeah, already knew that!" Josh shouted. "Move your feet! We have to go!"

The zombies that did have faces had no eyes, just empty eye sockets constantly dripping with a never-ending supply of blood and flesh.

"These zombies are fast," Jake muttered. "This… this can't be real."

"It is real, you absolute idiot!" Josh screamed. "So, stop being such a coward and move your feet!"

"Right," he said. "We've got to move!"

With that, Jake and Josh began to run as fast and far away as they could, but the zombies continued to chase after them, leaving bloody footprints in their wake. After five minutes of nonstop running, Jake and Josh found themselves surrounded.

"This isn't good," Josh mumbled under his breath. "We have no way out of this situation."

Suddenly, a zombie lunged at Josh. It grabbed him by his arm and bit down. Josh screamed and his blood began to run to the floor.

"Dang it, Josh!" Jake yelled, his voice quivering with fear.

Jake grabbed his brother by his uninjured arm and barreled through a section of the horde of zombies. Even though he was already out of breath, Jake continued to run, dragging his injured brother behind him.

"Jake!" Josh said after a while. "Stop. Seriously, just stop."

Jake slowed to a stop behind what looked like a gas station.

"Josh…," he began. But his words caught in his throat as he examined the bite wound on his brother's arm. As he stared at it, everything he had seen about zombie bites from movies came flooding to his brain. He glanced at Josh's face and saw Josh looking at him with sad eyes. Josh knew what his twin was about to ask him.

"Just… just ask it," Josh muttered.

Jake's eyes began to water. His brother's tone of voice said all he needed to know. Jake didn't want to ask. He didn't even want to know. Either way, he knew Josh would turn. Jake took a shaky breath and asked his brother the question.

"Josh…" he whispered, his voice cracking. "Are… are you going to… to turn? You know… into a… zombie?"

Josh started to sigh, but that sigh turned into a coughing fit. He grimaced in pain and grabbed his wounded arm. Jake wiped his eyes, took off his jacket, and tied it around Josh's arm. Josh let out a weak laugh.

"It doesn't matter whether I bleed out or not," he said quietly. "You and I both know how this is going to end."

Jake looked at Josh's face and saw beads of sweat forming. His body and face became pale, and Josh began to shiver. Jake grabbed his twin's hand and hugged it to his chest. The hand felt cold.

"Holy crap, I can't believe this is happening!" Jake exclaimed as tears began running down his face. "There has to be some kind of cure!"

Josh tensed as he broke into another coughing fit. His face contorted in pain and blood dripped out of his mouth. Jake wanted to scream, but he suddenly couldn't find the will to do that. He couldn't find the will to do anything except hold his brother's freezing hand close to his chest and cry.

"Hey, moron," Josh croaked. "I know what you're thinking, but not every ailment has a cure."

Jake squeezed Josh's hand tighter and moved closer to his side. His body shook with unchecked rage and fear.

"But this isn't like diabetes or cancer or anything like that!" Josh yelled. "This is a zombie bite! Every zombie movie has a cure, right? This one should too."

Josh struggled to sit up, grunting in pain the entire time. He was about to say something to comfort his brother, but he broke into another coughing fit. He tasted blood. Jake squeezed his hand even harder and began to sob.

"There has to be a cure!" Jake yelled. "Please Josh, you can't leave me!"

Out of nowhere, the boys began to hear zombie moans. They were quiet, but clearly getting louder… and closer.

"Josh, let's go!" Jake said as he wiped his tears away.

Jake tried to pull Josh off the floor and up onto his feet, but Josh yelped in pain. Jake kept pulling, ignoring Josh's cries, too hell-bent on trying to get his brother to move.

"Jake, for the love of God, stop!" Josh cried. "I can't move! The zombies are getting closer! You need to go!"

Jake's body went from tense and ready to slouched and drained. He fell to his knees beside his brother and wrapped him in a tight hug. Josh could feel his brother's tears soaking his shirt sleeve. Jake was no longer sobbing. He was no longer shaking. It felt as if Jake had completely given up.

"Hey," Josh began, his voice cracking. "Don't make this difficult. All you need to do is walk away."

"I… I can't," Jake croaked weakly. "I can't lose you. I don't care if you're turning. I don't want you to go like this."

The zombie's moans were now noticeably closer. Josh pushed his brother off him.

"You need to go," Josh said. "But if you really don't want this to happen, you could always… kill me now. So I don't turn."

Jake began to laugh hysterically.

"You idiot!" he screamed. "I can't do that! I won't do that! YOU CAN'T DIE! I NEED YOU!"

Josh's body went limp. When Jake took another hard look at his twin, he noticed Josh was now slick with sweat and his skin had begun to turn a light green.

"Hey," Josh said, his voice barely audible. "You should…"

Suddenly, Josh's body began to twitch and he screeched in agony. Blood poured from his mouth and his veins began to pop. Jake could see blood vessels explode and rot forming around his body. Jake jumped away in horror and tears burst from his eyes as he realized he had just lost his brother. Josh's body went limp for a moment. A second later, he opened his now gray eyes and stood. He looked at Jake with very little recognition.

"Jake," he growled with a creepy smile. "They're here. You'd better go."

Jake looked around and saw the zombies converge on him. When he looked back at Josh, he saw his brother walking toward him with an unreadable expression. As zombies from all sides lunged at Jake, Josh threw himself on top of his twin. Jake thought he was about to get eaten by his own brother, but he quickly realized Josh was letting himself get torn apart by the other zombies in order to save Jake.

"Push through," Josh grumbled as he felt himself begin to lose control. "Get away. Push through."

"I… I love you, Josh. Thank you so much," Jake cried at he pushed Josh's half-devoured body off him.

Jake put his head down and sprinted through the zombies. He stopped after a couple of seconds and looked back. Josh had begun ripping apart all the zombies that dared to go after Jake and very soon, Josh was the only one left. Jake smiled, thinking he could still save his brother.

"Thanks for saving me!" Jake called, silent tears dripping down his face.

Josh gave Jake one last heartfelt smile. He then let out a guttural screech and began walking menacingly toward his twin. Jake could tell Josh was trying to keep from a full sprint—still fighting with the last of his human strength not to hurt Jake.

"Dang it," Jake muttered, his voice cracking. "I know you're in pain, Josh!"

Josh let out a growl that sounded like a warning.

"Josh, you don't have to fight it anymore!" Jake said, quickly backing away from his brother. "Just let the zombie take over! I'm going now! You will always be the best zombie in the entire world!"

Josh let out another guttural scream and began to speed up.

"I love you so much, Josh!" Jake yelled as he turned around and began sprinting away as fast as he could. "I will always!"

Jake didn't realize he was sobbing until he had run for thirty minutes. He stopped in a parking lot and screamed at the top of his lungs. All his pain, grief, anger, and sadness exploded from his body in one breath. With that, he sat against the tire of a car and began to fall asleep.

43.3

When Jake opened his eyes, he found himself staring at Josh's face. Jake let out a scream. His scream was interrupted when Josh slapped him across the face.

"Take a deep breath, idiot," Josh said. "Welcome back to reality."

Jake looked around to gather his bearings and realized he was indeed back in the game-show studio.

"Oh, God," Jake whispered hoarsely. "That was… awful."

Jake began to cry, as Mr. Atrius unstrapped him from the chair and took the wires off. As soon as Mr. Atrius had finished, Josh wrapped his arms around Jake.

"Stop crying already," Josh whispered, his own voice shaking. "You're on live TV. This is just embarrassing."

When Josh pulled away, Jake noticed he was tearing up. He didn't have time to think much about that because he found himself caught up in a very uncomfortable group hug by all his friends.

"Jeez, guys," Jake mumbled. "Get off me."

"We're just happy you're still sane," Oliver exclaimed as everyone began moving back to their podiums.

"If that had happened to Mason, I'd probably lose my mind," Jason said, rubbing the back of his head.

"If that had happened to any of us, we'd lose our minds," Nick said with a laugh.

"That was intense!" Steven shouted into his mic, making everyone jump. "I am excited to announce that, after the five-minute break, our last participant of the day will be making his fearful debut! See you then, ladies and gents!"

With that, Steven cut the cameras.

FORTY-FOUR

In Which Michael Makes His Formal Debut

Instead of staying out front to prepare, Steven went backstage with the kids and Mr. Atrius.

"Children!" he exclaimed as he began to anxiously pace. "Where is Michael?"

The kids looked at Mr. Atrius and narrowed their eyes. Steven put his face in his hands and sighed.

"Atrius, where is your son?" he asked wearily.

"He's been in my evil lair hanging out with my bird-daughter," Mr. Atrius responded nonchalantly.

Steven sighed again.

"I don't pay myself enough for this," he muttered, waving his hand and dismissing Mr. Atrius. "You have four minutes. Fix this."

With that, Steven headed to the stage muttering to himself and shaking his head. Mr. Atrius smiled and took his phone out of his pocket.

"Who are you calling, jerk?" Darla questioned with a snarl.

He just looked at Darla and smiled. Wordlessly, he clicked on a contact and put the phone to his ear. About three seconds later, there was a click on the other end of the phone.

"Oh, sweetie," Mr. Atrius sang out cheerfully. "My sweet little fallen angel. I'm going to need your brother back in about three minutes tops."

Without waiting for an answer from Sydney, Mr. Atrius hung up and silently put his phone away.

"This fear simulation should be very interesting," he whispered.

Section 44.1

Sydney sat in her father's lair and stared at the unconscious Michael sitting beside her. She began to play with his hair.

"Oh, brother," she whispered sweetly. "You're going to need to wake up soon. It's almost your moment."

She gave him a once over and rolled her eyes.

"I can't believe I almost forgot!" she said as she headed to her personal bag and pulled out makeup. "You're covered in bruises and scrapes! Can't have THOSE making an appearance on camera."

Sydney rummaged through her makeup and came up with a concealer that matched Michael's darkish tan skin color. After she had applied concealer to all his bruises and scrapes, she began to work on his wrists. Before she got started, however, she looked at them thoughtfully.

"Probably shouldn't put makeup on this," she said to herself. "The wounds are still open. That reminds me… I need to change his bandages. Don't want his major wounds to get infected. That wouldn't be fun."

"Piece of garbage," Michael murmured as he began to regain consciousness.

"Michael!" she exclaimed, tearing up. "We were just having fun! I was just playing with you! There's no need to be so rude just because my idea of fun is a little different than yours."

"Oh, dear God," he said under his breath.

"We might have time to play a little bit more before you have to go on," she said, twirling her hair on her finger. "Your friend

Jake just got out of his simulation. Steven is about to call the five-minute break."

Michael's eyes widened and he stayed completely quiet. No movement. No breathing. No sound. Nothing. He stilled completely.

"God, no," he whispered painfully.

"Fine." Sydney crossed her arms and pouted. "Brother, I can't wait to see what you fear the most."

"Probably you," he muttered with a sigh.

"Ooooh! That would be fun!" she cheered, clapping her hands with genuine excitement. "Oh! It seems the five-minute break has begun. Get excited."

Section 44.2

"Boys and girls! Ladies and gentlemen! People of all ages! Welcome back!" Steven announced to the cameras. "Get excited, folks! Our last participant of the day is on his way! According to my assistant, he should be here any second!"

Team HOPE waited anxiously at their podiums.

"I suspect this is not going to be pleasant," Jason mumbled, clenching his fists.

Everyone else nodded in silent agreement. Suddenly, a loud bird call echoed through the studio. Everyone turned their heads toward the side stage hallway to see Michael slowly walking out.

"Holy crap," Will gasped as he caught sight of Michael's appearance. "This is… awful."

Tears came to everyone's eyes as they watched Michael slowly drag himself toward the chair. Rachel growled in undying fury at the sight of Sydney perched on Michael's shoulder. Rachel clenched her fists as she noticed Sydney digging her claws into Michael's shoulder. It wasn't visible to most, but Rachel knew exactly where and how to look.

"This sucks," Nick said, suddenly feeling most of his strength leave him.

Nick leaned to the side, nearly losing balance. He would have fallen, but he felt Rachel grab his hand and Jason grabbed his opposite arm.

"Are you going to be okay?" Jason asked.

"You should probably go backstage," Rachel suggested, looking at Nick with deep concern.

"No way," he whispered. "I need to see this through. That bird will not get the best of me."

"Uh… Alright, folks," Steven exclaimed hesitantly. "It's… It's time for Michael Atrius to show us his deepest fear."

Michael turned his head to look at Sydney then immediately looked away. She turned her head to look at Michael, cawed, then detached her claws from his shoulder, and flew off toward the podiums. As she left Michael's shoulder, he flinched in pain and squeezed the shallow claw wounds. When Sydney landed on Nick's podium, he fell to his knees. Rachel hissed violently and accidentally let a snake tongue slip out. When Sydney saw this, she flew away and landed on Mr. Atrius' shoulder.

"Stupid bird!" Darla whispered venomously.

Michael carefully sat down in the chair and began to shake in fear. As Mr. Atrius began strapping the wires to Michael's body, he seemed subtly careful to avoid Michael's bandaged wounds. Mr. Atrius strapped his ankles to the chair like he did for everyone, but Michael noticed he loosened the straps that went over the wrists before he strapped on the restraints. Michael, even in his frantic state, assumed Mr. Atrius did all of this to avoid making his wounds worse.

"Thanks," he mumbled unconsciously.

Mr. Atrius gave Michael a gentle pat on the head before walking away and starting up the simulation. Michael closed his eyes. When he opened them, he found himself lying on the floor of a concrete room. He would have looked around, but there wasn't much to see at all. The walls were made of gray concrete and appeared to be covered in dirt and mold. They also appeared to be covered in dry blood; but it was dark, so he could barely tell. He looked up and noticed the ceiling was the same as the floor and walls. Concrete. Dirty. Moldy. Probably bloody. It smelled damp and earthy as if he was buried in wet dirt.

"I have a feeling this is going to be some metaphor about the hypothetical cage or prison I'm locked in," Michael muttered with a sigh.

Suddenly, a girl's laughter erupted from the walls, although there was no girl in sight.

"YES! YES! YES!" she said excitedly, her voice echoing inside Michael's head.

He held his hands over his ears in pain as the word 'yes' reverberated in his skull. Finally, the girl let out a small childish giggle, then went completely silent. Michael slowly removed his hands from his ears.

"Dear God," he mumbled, shaking his head. "I think I expected this."

Michael began to laugh sadly.

"I knew Sydney would be in here somewhere," he said. "Who else could that have been?"

Michael stood up and walked around the border of the room, brushing his fingers across the wall as he went. Despite how gently he was touching the wall, he could still feel the hard crusty dirt scratching his fingers.

"What am I doing here?" he asked aloud. "When is something going to happen?"

After two more minutes, he laughed as he realized why nothing was happening.

"I see," Michael said with a sigh. "I'm in this empty, quiet, dark room because I'm supposed to be thinking about life or something like that."

Michael was very well versed on classic movie tropes and potential villainous schemes. He knew, at this point, where this simulation was going ... or so he thought.

"I'm guessing I'm going to be sitting in complete silence for most of my simulation before something 'unexpected' happens," he observed with a weary sigh. "Just get this over with."

Michael lay down on the floor with his arms spread out and waited. He told himself he wasn't going to fall for this fear trap, but, as time went on, he became impatient and angry. Michael's emotions began to well up inside of him, and before long, he noticed warm tears flowing from his eyes and soaking the floor.

"Holy crap," he muttered. "This is what I get for doing absolutely nothing with my life, I guess."

He wiped his eyes and the sides of his face with his sleeve, then sat up.

"This is so boring," he yelled, his voice echoing off the walls. "I expected something to happen by now!"

The room answered him with complete silence. But then water suddenly began to drip from the ceiling, and it continued dripping steadily. Michael knew that at that rate, the room couldn't possibly flood, so he wasn't worried and just ignored it. After ten minutes of listening to the drip, he became anxious and rocked back and forth. He held his head in his hands and took deep breaths.

"Just get this over with," he whispered to himself.

The dripping water became louder, and Michael growled in frustration. He stood up and punched the wall repeatedly until his fists bled.

"What do you want from me?" he screamed, his voice cracking in annoyance.

"Tee-hee," a girl's voice said, once again echoing through Michael's mind.

"Sydney, you're the worst sister EVER!" Michael exclaimed in a low growl.

"How did you know it was me, little bro?" she said in an eerie tone.

"When you speak, you literally sound exactly like her," Michael said with a sigh. "It's obvious. I'm not stupid, you know."

"Why are you so angry?" she asked in a haunting voice. "Is it the water? Is it me? Or is it… you? Are you angry because you know how worthless and alone you are?"

"Well, that was blunt," he responded, crossing his arms and shivering. "You need to work on that."

"Oh, brother," she sang quietly. "Don't you wish to be included? Why are you so angry? Why? Tell me why!"

Michael stamped his foot and punched the wall again.

"Because you won't shut the hell up!" he yelled furiously. "You won't leave me alone! I never had a sister, and I don't want one!"

"You're very rude," she stated simply. "YOU should work on THAT."

"Shut UP!" Michael begged as his voice cracked. "You're driving me crazier than I already am!"

"You're crazy, Michael!" she screeched with a laugh. "You're INSANE! You know you'll never be anything else!"

Michael fell against the wall and curled up in fetal position. He began to aggressively rock back and forth. He opened his mouth to speak, but nothing came out. Sydney stayed quiet for minutes on purpose to let Michael process what she had just said. Then, she spoke.

"Embrace your insanity," she whispered. "You were born this way. It's why you have always thought and observed things differently than others. It's why you're so lonely. It's your destiny."

"Oh, God," Michael croaked. "Why are you doing this to me?"

Sydney released a high-pitched laugh loud enough to crumble a building. Michael's head snapped up and his eyes went wide.

"SHUT UP!" he screamed, tears flowing from his eyes. "I've never wanted to kill someone more than I do right now!"

She continued to laugh until Michael snapped. His body heated up and he screamed in pain. Sydney joyfully harmonized with his scream and laughed louder. He felt his entire body burst into flames. His eyes turned red and the temperature in the room skyrocketed.

"Let it out, brother!" Sydney exclaimed, still laughing hysterically. "LET IT OUT!"

Michael screamed in rage, and the flames around his body exploded, taking up the space of the whole room. He looked to his side and saw his demon sister staring at him with her glowing red eyes. She had her wings out, and her teeth were sharp and shiny as if they had been polished. She touched his shoulder lightly and his body went numb with arctic temperatures. His flames dissipated and he closed his eyes, expecting to open them to see the studio and his friends, but instead, he saw Sydney hovering directly over his face grinning.

"You thought you could escape?" she asked in a high-pitched whisper. "That's rich."

Michael's eyes widened.

"I'm… I'm trapped," he said, his voice echoing in the silence.

Sydney smiled sweetly at him, and the numbness disappeared. Michael shakily sat up and observed the room through blurry eyes. He noticed the walls had been completely charred. Despite that, he flinched as he heard the water dripping. He gripped his pants in frustration and gasped in pain. He was in agony from punching the wall, and he stared at his raw bloody fists.

"You think you know it all," Sydney screeched in his ear. "You thought you had it all planned out."

Sydney cleared her throat and replicated Michael's posture. She began to mock him.

"Oh, what am I doing here?" she said in a deep voice. "I'm in this empty, quiet, dark room because I'm supposed to be thinking about life or something like that."

Michael scoffed and put on a slight smile.

"Well done," he said. "You just made yourself sound like more of an idiot than you were before."

"I wouldn't do that if I were you—which I'm glad I'm not since your life sucks," she exclaimed. "Remember, you're stuck with me."

Section 44.3

From outside the simulation, Steven was begging Mr. Atrius to let Michael out. Mr. Atrius gave his bird daughter an exasperated look.

"Why did you have to scare him this badly?" he asked her. "You were supposed to PLAY with him."

Sydney nuzzled her beak against his face and cawed.

"You can be such a pest sometimes, my sweet birdie," he said with a smile. "But … I'm going to have to do some reassuring, so Michael doesn't go down the same path as your mother."

"Such a tragedy," she whispered into his ear. "You loved her so much."

Mr. Atrius widened his eyes and brushed Sydney off his shoulder.

"Too bad she lost her mind because of us," Sydney whispered. "Now she's gone."

For the first time in years, Mr. Atrius felt tears well up in his eyes. Tears of anguish and… fear.

"It was only you. She left because of YOU," he said, his voice shaking. "You made her leave. You're the reason. The cause of all my loneliness and sorrow."

"Yet, you love me all the same," she mumbled.

He could hear the smile in her tone.

"Of course, I do," he responded. "You're … you're all I have left."

"Now you have Michael," she said in a casual manner. "Unless he breaks like she did."

"Be quiet, child!" he hissed.

She rolled her eyes and perched on the armrest of the chair Michael was currently seated in. After a moment more of watching Michael on the monitor, Mr. Atrius closed his eyes and gritted his teeth.

"Steven!" he said loudly. "Let him out."

Steven hastily nodded and flipped the kill switch on the simulation. Michael opened his eyes and began to scream wildly. His eyes turned red for a split second before he heard Mr. Atrius clap in front of his face.

"Snap out of it!" he yelled. "Behave yourself!"

Mr. Atrius sighed as tears fell from his eyes. Michael looked at him with a curious expression and opened his mouth to speak. Before he could get a word out, Mr. Atrius wiped his eyes and glared at his son as if saying "not a word."

"Go back to your podium now, Michael," he stated, pointing aggressively to the empty podium.

"Can't," Michael muttered. "Still strapped in. Still got these wires all over me."

Mr. Atrius rubbed his eyes in exhaustion.

"Right," he said.

He began to unstrap Michael. When he finished, Mr. Atrius grabbed his son's arm and stopped him from getting up.

"I'm sorry, Michael," he whispered.

Michael shrugged his father's arm off and went back to his podium.

"Well, folks!" Steven exclaimed, his voice cracking. "I can't believe the fear portion of this show is over so quickly!"

Steven cracked a sarcastic smile.

"See you tomorrow, my friends!" he continued. "For the Environmental Dome!"

FORTY-FIVE

In Which Power Has Been Stored

After Steven turned off the cameras for the final time that day, the kids stood still. There were so many emotions to process and so many things to say, yet no one could think of any way to say them.

Michael didn't wait for words. The second the cameras were off, he rushed backstage and began breaking things. Steven flinched.

"We'll… we'll take care of this," Oliver muttered, as he turned to look at the backstage entrance. "Yeah… this is a job for us."

He cleared his throat nervously and sped backstage. The rest of the gang followed.

"Michael!" Will yelled. "Chill out!"

"It's not that easy!" Michael screamed in response. "It's not easy!"

"You have to try and settle down!" Jessica begged, eyes watering. "Please. I couldn't POSSIBLY know what you're feeling right now, but this is destructive!"

"That's all I can do!" He exclaimed as he briefly turned to glare at Jessica. "All I can do is be destructive, and nothing ever changes that!"

"You're not destructive," Ondrea said. "You're perfect the way you are. I know that it may be difficult to accept who you are compared to who you THINK you are, but you have to try."

"I've been trying!" he cried in response. "Now I know I'm the brother of a demon! How could I possibly accept that?"

"You're the brother of a HALF-demon, Michael," Mr. Atrius mumbled from the corner of the room. "You're the son of the ruler of the underworld."

Michael ceased his rampage and backed into the opposite corner.

"This… this is… it's… it's real?" Michael stuttered. "This is all real?"

"Yes," Mr. Atrius stated with a sigh.

"I knew I was weird, but I never thought I'd be this weird!" Michael yelled, laughing hysterically. "Son of the devil! Brother of a freaking psychopath!"

"Oh, boy," Darla muttered with a sigh. "Here comes the crazy."

"Michael, settle down at once!" Mr. Atrius exclaimed. "You mustn't create such a racket, or you'll wake up your sister! She just went to the lair to rest."

Michael immediately silenced.

"I hate her," he said quietly. "I hate her so much."

"I do as well," Mr. Atrius responded quietly almost as if he didn't want to admit it.

"Hold up," Mason said, looking very confused and angry at the same time. "You always talked her up when you were threatening us!"

"What changed?" Jason added, putting a calming hand on his twin's shoulder.

Mr. Atrius let out a short chuckle.

"I will tell you only since I'm just going to kill you anyway," he began. "Nothing has changed. Sydney was born evil. My wife never knew who I truly was. The reason I wanted to marry a human woman and have a child with her was so I could have a child to be proud of as opposed to a Hell child."

"What's a Hell child?" Rachel asked anxiously.

"A Hell child is a child created from the hatred of the underworld," he answered. "As long as I am the ruler of the underworld, one of my jobs is to use the negative energy to create more children. It's more of a political end goal, so I won't go into that any further."

"You said you wanted to marry a human woman," Teddy began. "Does that mean you didn't love her? That you only married her so she could have your child?"

"I loved her, yes," he answered. "In fact, I still love her. But she's gone, and there is no point in wasting my love on a woman who will never come back."

"Geez!" Jake exclaimed. "What happened to her?"

"Nothing extreme, I assure you," Mr. Atrius said with a small grin. "She left my daughter and me. It was my fault, really. I should have known that having a half-demon child would cause problems. Sydney was born with evil in her heart, and she only ever wanted to use her powers to hurt people."

"You're a horrible dad," Michael mumbled. "You could have stopped her."

Mr. Atrius sat down and sighed heavily.

"I could have," he admitted. "I should have. I was a coward. As soon as she showed signs of malice, I began to keep Sydney away from her mother because I didn't want to frighten the woman I loved. I took on the weight of my child because I didn't want to burden my wife. I taught Sydney how to limit and control her powers the only way I knew how, which was through the ways I taught myself. Since I was born evil, and no one ever nurtured me, the ways I taught myself weren't the most wholesome and… I turned her into even more of a monster."

"Serves you right," Nick muttered.

"I'm not asking for pity or sympathy, Nicholas!" Mr. Atrius snapped. "I'm simply telling my story. Anyway… one day my wife discovered how truly horrible Sydney was. I decided to tell her what was going on, but it's a hard situation to explain, and an even harder one to accept. She wrote me off as insane and as a poor excuse of a father. That's how she left."

"That's understandable," Michael said. "I'll bet she hated you after that."

"Yes, she does," he replied with a sad smile. "I know I'll never get her back, but it's still a bit of a sore subject for me. After all that drama happened, I just took Sydney down to the underworld to live. I realized a bit too late that the underworld has a different effect on humans who are still alive. Since Syd is half human, she began to go even more insane. By the time I realized what was happening, it was too late to raise her in the human world. If I tried to live a life with her in the human world, she would wreak havoc."

"So where do I come into play?" Michael asked.

"I'm glad you finally calmed down, son," Mr. Atrius said with a smile.

"Yeah, yeah," he said, waving the comment off. "I asked 'where do I come into play?'"

"Well…" Mr. Atrius began. "Your mother was pregnant when she left. I assume she had you and decided to keep you. Since she told me I was insane when I told her Sydney was half demon, I'm assuming she thought it wasn't true. If she thought Sydney being half demon wasn't true, then she wouldn't even dream of you being half demon."

"Why wasn't Michael born evil?" Avery asked.

"I'm not sure." Mr. Atrius responded. "I wish I knew the answer to that."

"Me too," Michael mumbled. "Me too."

Section 45.1

That night, no one spoke, no one planned, no one discussed.

The next morning, the kids anxiously sat backstage, waiting for instructions about the Environmental Dome.

"If Mr. Atrius is to strike, it would be today," Jason stated as he attempted to look cool, calm, and collected.

"I agree," Oliver said with a sigh.

"We're totally dead!" Will shouted with frustration. "You've seen what he can do with just one finger's worth of power! We're toast!"

"Hey, no way!" Jessica exclaimed. "We CAN do this! We must do this, so we will do it and we will win! Right, Ollie?"

Oliver stayed quiet and his expression turned grim. Suddenly, the rest of Team HOPE and the Stanford twins didn't feel so confident.

"Oliver?" Teddy asked.

"Will's … Well, he's … he's right," Oliver stammered, his voice cracking with fear.

Everyone remained completely silent, baffled by Oliver's lack of confidence and hope.

"You can't mean that!" Darla yelled furiously. "Look what you did, Will!"

"Hey, I'm sorry!" Will said. "I didn't really mean it when I said we were going to die!"

"Oliver, you're supposed to be optimistic and ready for anything!" Avery exclaimed, losing her cool. "You're supposed to act like a leader."

"I don't think I can be ready for this," Oliver said in a terrified whisper. "All I can say is… there's no way we'll… ALL make it out of this… alive."

"Ollie," Nick muttered, suddenly feeling more drained than ever. "You can't say stuff like that. I'm serious."

Nick stood and began to walk toward his cousin to give him a supportive pat on the back, but he coughed and stumbled forward.

Nick fell to his hands and knees and closed his eyes, trying not to throw up. After a minute, he looked up and noticed Oliver, Jessica, and Rachel kneeling by his side. The others were a bit farther back, but still surrounding Nick with concerned looks. Nick coughed again and let out a weak chuckle.

"Might just be me that dies today," he said, smiling sadly.

"And you told me not to say that kind of stuff," Oliver said with a sigh.

Nick coughed once more and felt his arms giving out. He almost collapsed to the ground, but felt his family grab him to keep him up.

"This sucks," Nick mumbled.

Ondrea came forward, grabbed Nick's arm and helped him to a sitting position against the wall. She put her hand on his shoulder and began to pour Healing Power into his body.

"Since this is because of his energy loss, I don't know how much your Healing Power is going to do," Jason said sadly.

"He's not going to die," Michael stated, coming up beside Nick. "I can sense his energy. At this point in his life, his energy storage has been so abused, he almost seems to be immune to death by draining."

"Jake, Josh, are you guys alright?" Mason questioned, looking back at them, where they were simply sitting in the corner.

"This isn't really our area of expertise," Josh said, gesturing to the situation at hand.

"We figured we'd let the experts deal with this." Jake added. "Nick will be okay though, right?"

"I'll be fine," Nick said. "I do feel a bit better thanks to Ondrea's Healing, but I'm not too sure how long I can keep this going."

"It doesn't matter!" Jessica shouted, making everyone jump. "Once we defeat Lucifer and his crazy daughter, EVERYTHING will be fine!"

Oliver sighed and buried his face in hands. He still felt completely unsure they would even be able to do any damage to the two of them, much less defeat them.

"I just don't know about this," Oliver said as his built-up inner anxiety began to surface. "We've never faced anyone so powerful. I know I should be supportive and optimistic, but… I don't want to be dishonest about our chances here."

Ondrea suddenly gasped and glared at Michael with so much intensity, Michael visibly flinched. Teddy immediately put his hand on his girlfriend's arm.

"Are you okay, my love?" he asked, feeling half nervous from her glare and half concerned about her own health.

"Michael!" she began roughly. "As a bit of a Mind Reader myself, I'll ask this: do you have something you want to share with the group?"

"Hang on, Ondrea," Jessica said as she walked to face her. "What's going on?"

"I'm sure whatever it is, it doesn't mean you need to be so harsh," Rachel muttered quietly.

Now, all eyes were on Michael. He sat down crisscross and looked over to the side.

"It's not what you think, Ondrea," he stated in an anxious whisper.

"Then explain, TRAITOR!" she exclaimed as her eyes began to water. "Why would you do this to our team? To him?"

"Okay, what is going on?" Nick asked abruptly. "Who is 'him'?"

"Michael is not a traitor!" Jason shouted, immediately silencing anyone about to speak.

"I agree," Darla said. "He's too shy, emotionally unstable, and socially awkward to be a traitor."

"Ondrea, what's wrong?" Oliver questioned with a weary sigh. "Just tell us."

"Michael has been stealing Nick's power this whole freaking time!" she yelled furiously. "You monster!"

Michael's eyes began to water, and he felt a knot form in his chest. He scooted away from Ondrea's accusatory eyes until his back hit the wall. His throat stung. He opened his mouth to say something, but he felt a wave of guilt wash over him and found he couldn't get words out. Everyone was silent. Jake and Josh looked at each other, feeling exasperated. Jake stepped into the light.

"I'm not your childhood best friend or anything, but, from all the time my brother and I have spent with you guys, I know you would never be friends with someone who has even a remote chance of being a traitor," Jake said, crossing his arms.

"We're kind of tired of this stupid mess," Josh stated as he stepped forward next to Jake. "This is honestly ridiculous."

"Back off, you two!" Ondrea exclaimed. "You have no idea what's really going on! I used my Mind Reading Powers and ..."

She found herself cut off by the sound of Nick laughing.

"You read his mind, then," he said with a humored smile. "In that case, you must know EVERYTHING about him."

"What are you saying?" Will asked, thinking Nick had finally lost his sanity.

"Ondrea," Nick began as his grin faded and a tired smile replaced it. "You read his mind for ONE second. You can't just assume you know everything about a person just by reading ONE of his thoughts."

"But he's been taking your energy," she said.

Ondrea still felt upset, but Nick's words finally began to sink in.

"Listen," Nick continued. "I know my Power is being taken. I know it's not Michael. Even if it was, I wouldn't worry."

Everyone went silent again for a couple of minutes before Michael finally spoke.

"Nick," Michael said quietly. "I have been taking your Power, but ... but not with malicious intent and not to hurt you."

"I thought so," Ondrea said. Instead of sounding smug, she sounded tired and confused.

"I've been … collecting it," Michael elaborated. "It's hard to explain but I'll try my best. When I walked down to get in the fear simulation, despite having been tortured and traumatized, my Powers were aware. They are always aware. They help me focus. I noticed, when I walked by you, that your Power was significantly worse off than it had been before. And that's when I finally realized Sydney's power had increased ten-fold since I last saw you. I was able to connect the dots quickly. So, before I was put in the simulation, I cut Sydney's supply by half and began collecting the other half of your power."

"Why didn't you just cut her off completely?" Nick asked, now sitting by Michael's side for emotional support.

"If I had done that, she would have noticed," Michael answered. "I'm going to explain to you how I managed to get away with this without Sydney noticing, so bear with me here."

"I'm walking to the chair. I have already noticed Nick's Power shortage, acknowledged my sister's Power enhancements and have connected the dots. Now, I'm sitting in the chair. I then began using MY power to connect to both Sydney's and my father's Powers. Now, I can't give people Power like my father can, but in my years of being alone and bored, I've had plenty of time to experiment with my own Powers. So, and this is tricky, I began to phantom enhance Sydney's Power by taking from my backup reserve—which gives her the illusion that her Power is as strong as ever. At the same time, I was also draining half of Nick's energy from her. Since my backup reserve had been used up in planting the illusion of Power on Sydney, that gave me room to store Nick's energy, and only his energy. After I overloaded my backup reserve to Sydney, I was able to store some of Nick's Power with me."

"This is just confusing," Avery muttered.

"Yes, it is," Michael agreed. "Here is what has happened so far in my explanation. I have drained my backup Power reserve and gave it to my sister to make her feel more Powerful than she actually is at this time. I took half of Nick's energy from her and put his energy in my backup reserve in order to keep it from becoming MY power. Keeping it from becoming a part of my main Power reserve is essential because I can't GIVE people MY Power."

"Very, very clever!" Jason exclaimed clapping with excitement. "What you can do with your Power seems endless!"

"Thank you," Michael said humbly. "Now, I will continue. After restoring half of Nick's Power which Sydney had drained by placing in my backup reserve, I strategically left Sydney with only fifty percent of Nick's energy that she had originally. Then, as the wires were being strapped to me, I cut Sydney off. That means I stopped her from draining any more of your power, Nick. After that, I halved Nick's power in my power reserve. I transferred that one half to Nick in that very moment since he looked like his power wasn't going to last through the day and he clearly needed a boost.

"Now that Sydney was completely cut off, all I had to do was worry about the potential of her sensing Nick's Power becoming stronger. With the other half of his power in my backup reserve, I began pulling Power out of Nick at the same rate Sydney had been and building up his Power in my backup reserve. All through the simulation, the aftermath, the night, and this morning, I have been draining Nick's Power from him at the same rate Sydney was."

"Why?" Will asked, scratching his head.

"As I said, I am doing this so Sydney doesn't realize I have cut her off and that Nick is no longer getting weaker," Michael responded. "Nick, the only difference between what Sydney was doing and what I am doing is that I'm not 'stealing' your Power. I'm borrowing it. When the time comes, all you need to do is touch me in order to get ALL your power back which, for anyone who forgot, I am keeping in my backup reserve."

"I thought you said you couldn't give your Power to anyone," Teddy said, clearly confused.

Michael sighed and slumped further against the wall.

"I get it," Oliver said. "Michael CAN'T give HIS power to anyone, but, since he's been keeping Nick's power in his BACKUP reserve, it isn't mingling with Michael's own Power. Therefore, Michael wouldn't be giving HIS Power away. It would be Nick's own Power. Michael is storing Nick's Power for sake keeping. He's making sure it's there for Nick when he needs it, and that Sydney can't use it for evil."

Everyone nodded like they understood. Nick, however, nodded very slowly as if he was thinking about something profound.

"The terms 'Power' and 'Energy' can be as confusing in the Superpower world as they are in normal terms," Nick began. "In both theoretical worlds, power and energy are the same things… technically. For a normal person when talking about energy, that could mean electrical energy and many other types of energy, but, also, PHYSICAL energy. It's very rare for a non-Superhero to refer to what is in their body as 'Power' but energy…"

"Nick!" Rachel interrupted, defaulting to her anxious state. "What are you going on about? Have you finally lost your mind?"

"I'm pretty sure he's just trying to get his thoughts out before he sorts through them and tries to make sense of them. Authors to that too," Mason stated with a smile. "Plus, I'm pretty sure I know what he's getting at. One of his Powers is Power Steal. He's done it to Oliver before. For anyone who forgot, Power Steal allows Nick to 'steal' another person's Power for however long he needs it."

"We didn't forget, Mason." Darla mumbled, rolling her eyes.

Jake and Josh abruptly sat down next to everyone.

"It's been hard to follow this, but I think we're doing okay," Josh said.

"So," Jake started. "I understand so far that Nick's philosophical rant about power and energy as well as this Power Steal thing has something to do with … If I remember correctly, I think we're trying to find out a way Nick could get his … 'energy' back from Michael."

"Yes!" Michael exclaimed, sitting up quickly. "Now, please just be quiet so Nick can work this out for himself. With the way this conversation has been dragging on, I just need Nick to figure this out."

"Got it!" Nick yelled, startling everyone. "Since, in this context, 'power' is referring to the skills we have, 'energy' is referring to the duration in which we can use our skills. Also, naturally, energy is quite literally our power's source. I can use my Energy Transference and my Power Steal at the same time in order to 'steal' my energy from Michael's backup reserve."

"Finally!" Michael yelled.

"In that case," Oliver began with a grin. "I think Michael just helped us turn the tide on the upcoming battle."

"Not only will we have a fully charged Nick, but we'll also get to see what ELSE Michael can do with his powers," Ondrea said happily. "Oh, and sorry about the incredibly terrible way I accused you earlier. I didn't even think about the fact that I was making you upset. I was too self-focused in how I was feeling. Again, I'm sorry."

Michael grinned.

"It's okay." He replied. "I'm glad to have gotten all that out in the air anyways."

"Now all you have to do is pull us through this family feud of yours," Jake mentioned, coming up behind Michael with a nervous expression.

"Right" Michael muttered. "No pressure."

FORTY-SIX

In Which Death Seems Imminent

After the previous conversation, everyone felt justifiably emotionally drained, so they went back to their rooms to take naps for a couple of hours until Steven's voice woke them all up at the same time.

"Hello, children!" Steven shouted. "I'm sorry if I surprised you. I am coming to you from a mini speaker. All the rooms have mini speakers, installed for situations such as this."

"Why don't people tell us these things?" Will groaned as he sat up in bed.

Teddy hopped down from his bed.

"Whatever this is, it's probably going to be chaotic," he said, rubbing the sleep from his eyes.

"Anyway, kids," Steven continued. "It's time for everyone to gather in the studio. There will be a bus waiting outside to take us to the Environmental Dome for the next part of your gaming experience! Naturally, your driver will be yours truly.

"Rules of the Dome: Anything you take with you from your rooms will be placed in a locker before you enter. As you should already know, this is about surviving—starting with nothing. Nothing."

"Awesome," Will mumbled, slowly getting out of bed.

Teddy and Will got dressed and ready, but Will seemed to be fumbling with his shoes quite a bit.

"You okay, Will?" Teddy asked as he waited by the door for Will to finish putting on his shoes.

Will looked up and laughed.

"Yeah, I'm fine. Seriously, I'm fine," he said with a smile.

"Right," Teddy said with a sigh. "Are you sure?"

Will nodded and finally finished tying his shoes.

"Okay," Teddy said. "Let's go then."

He opened the door and began to walk through, but Teddy felt Will grab his wrist, pulling him to a quick stop. Teddy slowly turned around to see Will with his head down looking directly at his feet.

"Will?" he asked. "Everything… okay?" Will didn't say anything, and Teddy noticed Will's grip tightening almost painfully around Teddy's wrist.

"Will…?" Teddy said curiously.

He felt Will begin to shake slightly and saw tears running down his face.

"Teddy," Will whispered, still looking down. "I don't want to go. I… I don't want to be killed by Lucifer and Sydney. I… Teddy, I don't want to… die."

Teddy was speechless, so Will continued.

"I'm so afraid," he said as his voice cracked. "Why is everyone else so cool with the fact that we may die today?"

Will's grip tightened more, now becoming slightly painful.

"Will…" Teddy said, his voice sounding loud in the silence. "We're not…"

Will cut him off. Still looking at the floor, through his tears, he smiled.

"Don't say that it won't happen, Teddy," he croaked.

His grip tightened further and Teddy could feel Will's nails digging into his wrist. Teddy opened his mouth to ask him to let go but Will began yelling before he could get a word out.

"Teddy, we're not supposed to have to worry about this!" he screamed as he snapped his head up to look at Teddy.

He could see fury in his eyes along with sadness and desperation. Will's hand slowly frosted over as his own pain began to consume him.

"I've barely been living as it is! I can't DIE like this, Teddy!" Will exclaimed. "I've just found it! I just found a reason for me to keep going and now we're going to die!"

Will collapsed to his knees causing him to release his grip on Teddy. Despite the beads of blood left on Teddy's wrist from Will's fingernails, Teddy dropped beside him and did something very out of character. He put his hands on Will's shoulders and pulled him into a hug. Will tried to pull away but, after a couple of seconds, he stopped struggling and sunk down, surrendering himself to Teddy's comfort.

"Teddy," Will muttered tearfully. "My reason… my… She's… She's going to die today too."

"No," Teddy said softly. "Darla isn't going to die today."

Teddy pulled back, put his hands on Will's shoulders once more, and looked at him square in the eyes.

"I know you can't fathom the possibility of us living through this, but we will," he stated firmly. "If it comes down to it, I'll make sure everyone lives. No. Matter. What."

Will stayed quiet and looked at his hand. The frost that had formed began melting away and he finally noticed the fresh blood underneath his fingernails. His eyes filled with tears again.

"I'm so… I'm so sorry, Teddy," he mumbled. "I didn't mean to… I just… I just lost control."

"It's okay," Teddy said with a reassuring smile. "Everything will work out."

Teddy took his hands off Will's shoulders and stood. He offered a hand to help his friend, but Will just looked away and continued to cry. Teddy sighed sadly. Suddenly, he felt his phone buzz. Oliver was calling so he answered.

"Hey," Oliver began. "Everyone's waiting on Will and you. What's going on? You're on speaker, by the way"

"Will is having the worst mental breakdown of Superhero-kind," Teddy responded. "He's freaking terrified. He's in quite a bit of emotional pain."

Teddy glanced at Will who was now hunched over with his head against the floor and his hands grasping clumps of his hair. Teddy cringed and walked to the other side of the room.

"Hey, guys," Teddy started. "I don't know if Will can do this. He made a point earlier, and I think it's a pretty good one. He said he doesn't want to die. I tried to tell him that he's not going to, but he's completely set on believing that he and everyone else are going to croak today."

"Tell him to get off his sorry butt and get to the bus!" Darla exclaimed through the phone.

"It's not like that," Ondrea told her. "Teddy's right. This one's bad. I can feel Will's pain from the other side of the phone."

Suddenly, Will stood, walked a couple feet to the door, opened it, stepped outside, and threw up in the bush.

"Holy crap," Teddy mumbled. "He just threw up."

"You think you can handle this, Ted?" Mason asked.

"I can try," he responded hesitantly. "I'm not too good at comforting people, and I hate to say this, but I think Will is a bit of a hard sell when it comes to optimism."

"You can do it, Teddy!" Jessica said, and then immediately hung up.

Teddy put his phone by his side and sighed.

"Thanks, guys," he muttered.

He looked at the corner and saw Will sitting on the floor now half asleep. Teddy quietly went and sat by Will.

"Hey," Will whispered. "I just want to go back to sleep."

"Darla wants me to tell you that you need to man up." Teddy said with a hesitant humored grin.

Will slowly looked at Teddy and smiled sadly.

"That's my girl," he said. "I wish she'd have something nice to say though."

Teddy snickered. "Don't we all," he replied. "You know she's only saying this stuff because she cares."

"Yeah, I know," Will responded. "I… I've decided that I think I'm ready to die."

Teddy's eyes widened and he stayed quiet for a moment.

"Will…don't," he finally said. "Why would you say that?"

"That's not what I meant, Teddy," Will answered sternly. "I meant that I realize I'm satisfied with the way my life has gone and, if I were to die today, I think I'd have very few regrets."

"You're not going to die today," Teddy stated without much emotion.

Will looked at Teddy and wiped the last tears from his cheeks.

"You're not a prophet, Teddy," he said. "You can't see the future. You don't know whether that's true. Either way, thank you."

Teddy sighed with defeat. "Okay, you win, Mr. Downer," he said with a smile. "Sure, I can't promise you no one is going to die, but I can guarantee everyone is going to try as hard as they can to keep that from happening."

"I guess that's all anyone could ever hope for," Will said.

"Yeah…" Teddy muttered. "Hey, your emotional state did a full one-eighty. What happened?"

Will shrugged. "I guess I must have thrown up all my fear," he responded casually.

Teddy cringed at the memory.

"…Yeah… you did throw up a lot," he shuddered.

After a few moments of silence, Will jumped up, grabbed his phone, then held out a hand for Teddy.

"Shall we go?" he questioned.

Teddy stood up on his own. "We shall," He responded, now standing. "But after you wash your hands."

Chapter 46.1

About time!" Darla exclaimed as she and the others saw Will and Teddy walking toward the bus.

"Will just had a hard time," Ondrea whispered from the seat behind her. "Try not to make fun of him."

Darla smiled sadly and turned around.

"Yeah, I know," she said. "I really have to learn to be less mean."

"It takes time," Nick said from the seat in front of her. "Besides, you're not actually mean. You're just incredibly impulsive."

"Yeah, thanks," she responded, rolling her eyes.

"So sorry we're late, everyone!" Teddy called as he walked into the bus with Will in tow.

"Understandable," Michael muttered with a humored smile.

"Thanks for that, Michael," Will stated as he sat down in the empty row in front of him.

"Sorry," Will said, still not being able to hold back a smile.

Next to Michael, Avery mimed a vomiting motion.

"Please have a laugh at my expense," Will said, throwing his arms in the air.

"Guys, it's not that funny!" Darla yelled as she stood.

Everyone turned to stare at her. As soon as everyone was looking, she cracked a smile and mimicked Will throwing up. From his seat, Will sighed, grinned slightly, then turned to look out the window. Darla walked over to Will and stumbled into his lap, pretending to faint.

"Alright, enough already," he said with a smile. "It's fine coming from you, I guess, but if you had been anyone else your nose would be punched in right now."

"Okay, tough man," she said as she once again mimed him throwing up.

Will turned to look out the window. Darla smirked, got off his lap, and sat down in the seat next to him. When he didn't say anything for a couple of seconds, she realized she might have made fun of him a bit too much. Darla gently grabbed his hand and gave a short squeeze. He was shaking.

"Hey!" she said as she hooked her arm underneath his and put her head on his shoulder. "I'm… sorry."

Will turned to face her.

"It's alright," he said with a chuckle. "I like it when you make fun of me. It's your weird and twisted way of saying you care."

"Thanks," she whispered with a small, uncharacteristic giggle.

"You totally just giggled," he said, smirking.

"I did not!" she exclaimed, sitting up straight.

"It's okay," Will said. "I won't tell anyone."

Chapter 46.2

Thirty minutes into the drive, Avery tapped Michael on the shoulder.

"Hey, are you okay?" she asked.

"Why wouldn't I be?" he countered, turning to look at her.

"Well, let's see… your dad's the devil, your sister's evil, you have this completely unique experience no one else can relate to, and we're all about to fight your evil family and potentially die," Avery replied. "That's all."

"Yeah, I'm fine," Michael responded after a couple seconds of silence.

"You can't be!" she exclaimed, clearly frustrated. "Your entire family is evil and wants to kill your friends! You were tortured by your sister! How are you so fine with this?"

Michael shrugged.

"I've been a weirdo for a very long time. I guess I expect nothing less than this strange new lifestyle," he explained calmly.

Avery growled in frustration. "This isn't a LIFESTYLE, Michael. This is a NIGHTMARE. I'm not usually one to ponder over the past and what can't be changed, but how have you already come to terms with this?" she asked.

"I don't usually feel things," he stated.

"You're impossible," Avery mumbled with a sigh.

The two sat in silence for a couple of minutes until Michael spoke.

"I will admit…" Michael began. "This whole experience is a bit… jarring. I've never really had friends before, but now I do."

Avery smiled.

"Yeah, but that's a good thing, right?" she prompted.

"Yes, but… I've never really had anyone to care about before now," Michael admitted. "Maybe that's why my evil family possibly killing my new friends doesn't affect me that much. Not yet, anyways."

"I don't know what to say to that," Avery whispered, anxiously swinging her legs back and forth.

Michael looked at her again.

"I'll figure this out," he assured her. "You don't have to worry about this."

"Michael, that's what friends do. They worry about THEIR friends," Avery said with a sigh. "We care about you a lot. It's sort of like what you said just now. I know having friends is new to you, but we're your friends. You'll learn to worry about us eventually."

"Sounds exhausting," he mumbled with a smile.

"Definitely," she confirmed, laughing.

Chapter 46.3

Forty-five minutes into the drive, Mason turned to the seat behind him to talk to Nick.

"Hey, how's the energy level doing?" he asked.

"Still pretty bad, but I think Michael said he'd give my energy back to me in bulk when the time came to fight," Nick responded.

"So, when Michael cut Sydney off from your energy supply, you didn't begin to feel any better?" Jason asked, turning around.

"I felt better, but now it's all kind of blurring together," Nick mentioned, scratching the back of his head.

"What does that mean?" Rachel asked quietly from beside him.

"Things don't feel different anymore. I don't feel like anything is changing. Like, I feel drained, but I don't feel it getting better or worse," he answered.

"I get it," Mason said with a sigh.

"Same," Jason seconded with the same kind of tired sigh.

"The orphanage felt like a never ending hell," Mason mumbled with a small laugh.

"I guess that explains why it was your literal hell," Rachel said with a sad smile.

"It's okay," Mason said with a huge grin. "I'm over it."

"No, you're not, brother," Jason said as he crossed his arms and raised his eyebrows.

"I mean, I'll never really get over the things that make me afraid," Mason responded with a shoulder shrug. "All I know now is that it's about being brave even when we are afraid."

"Well said," Nick muttered. "Is anyone else really tired?"

Nick's eyes closed, and he immediately fell asleep against the window. Jason opened his mouth to say something, but Rachel beat him to it.

"Guys, it's okay," she said. "He's been doing this on and off this whole time."

"Poor dude," Mason said quietly.

Jake and Josh stared out the window, attempting to process everything they'd been through. Although the Stanford twins were acutely aware of their bizarre situation, they were also aware that this doesn't happen to normal teens.

"Are we… not normal anymore?" Jake asked his brother quietly so no one else could hear.

Josh stayed quiet for a moment, then spoke.

"I… don't think so," he said also quietly. "I think we're all in now."

"In?" Jake wondered, returning to his normal speaking volume. "What do you mean by 'in'?"

"You know… we're in the whole Superhero club thing." Josh clarified.

"That's a creative way of putting it," Teddy said from the bus seat next to them.

"Oh, hey," Josh mumbled, his quiet tone indicating embarrassment. "Sorry."

Ondrea snickered. "It's alright!" she said, still grinning. "I like it! We're Team HOPE!"

Teddy smiled, squeezed Ondrea's hand, and rolled his eyes. "I love it when you laugh," he said, kissing her on the cheek.

Jake and Josh widened their eyes and turned away.

"Guys, it's called affection!" Teddy exclaimed with a laugh.

The twins didn't say anything. Ondrea put her hand lightly on Teddy's shoulder and gave him a concerned look.

"Hey, guys," she began softly. "What's going on? I know this whole Superhero thing is overwhelming, but you seem to be doing fine."

"We're… we're okay," Jake answered. "I think I'm still in the whoa-this-is-like-a-fever-dream stage."

"I'm alright," Josh said. "I've pretty much accepted this, but it's still kind of weird."

"And cool, right?" Teddy asked, a hint of excitement in his voice.

"Glad you're still excited about the fact that you have Powers even though you've had them your whole life." Jake said with a small grin.

"Are you kidding me?" Teddy exclaimed. "Of course I'm still excited! If I wasn't who I am today, I wouldn't have met the best group of friends in the entire world. I wouldn't have been able to experience everything I have. Chaotic as my life has been up to this point, I wouldn't take anything about it back."

"That's pretty cool," Josh let Teddy's works sink in. After a minute, he said, "But I think 'chaotic' is a bit of an understatement."

Teddy smiled.

"Yes, you're right," he admitted. "But, I still wouldn't take any of it back. I have super great friends, a beautifully awesome and wonderfully lovely girlfriend, and I couldn't be happier. It's always better to live in the moment than to think of things in the past that can't be changed—or things you're worried about for your future when you don't even know what's going to happen."

"That's really nice, Teddy Bear," Ondrea said as she hooked her arm under his.

Suddenly, a voice from the front halted their conversation.

"We're here!" Steven exclaimed happily. "Alrighty, children, unload and be merry!"

FORTY-SEVEN

In Which There Are Unwanted Participants

As the kids filed off the bus, they immediately noticed a gigantic dome the size of Mt. Rushmore. Jason stopped in his tracks and stared in awe.

"Oh wow. This is amazing," he muttered.

"Too bad we're going to get ambushed by the Devil and his psychotic daughter," Will said while staring at the dome.

"Thanks," Jason said with a sad sigh.

"Alright, kids!" Steven began. "Follow me into the first building. This way!"

Steven started walking to a building that was attached to the dome by a long hallway. When he and the kids entered, they immediately noticed lockers lining the walls of this small room. Off to the side were two bathrooms and on the other side of that was a room labeled "medical."

"So… has anyone had to use the medical room before?" Will asked nervously.

"Not yet," Steven assured him, completely unaware that the phrase 'not yet' was foreboding and very worrisome to Will.

"Oh great," Will muttered, clenching his fists.

His stomach began to turn at the prospect of potential death in their near future, and he gritted his teeth. Suddenly, he felt Darla squeeze his hand.

"Don't focus on that pain right now. Just focus on the fact we've all got your back, and you've got ours," she whispered reassuringly.

"Here's the drill, children," Steven began. "Put your things in these lockers, go use the bathroom, and sit down on the benches when you're all ready to go."

As everyone went about the instructions, Steven hurried outside. The Stanford twins saw this and shared concerned looks. When they finished putting up their things and Josh finished using the bathroom, Steven still wasn't back inside.

"Should we go out and talk to him?" Jake asked quietly.

"I think so," Josh answered, also quietly.

The twins walked outside and saw Steven briefing all the crew members.

"… and whatever you do, don't get eaten by the alligators," he finished.

The twins looked at each other and raised their eyebrows. As soon as the crew walked off to perform their duties, the twins swallowed all their new questions about the alligators to see if their dad was alright.

"Dad…" Josh said, tapping Steven on the shoulder.

Steven jumped in surprise then turned around.

"Hello, boys!" he said, putting on a fake smile. "I was just briefing the crew about the instructions and the alligator security team."

Once again swallowing their many questions about the alligator security team and more, Jake asked the one question they were most concerned about.

"Dad, are you okay? I know things have been pretty confusing and difficult, but you seem to be handling everything alright. On the other hand, we know that looks can be deceiving."

"Well… I'm a bit worried," Steven whispered, looking around anxiously. "I haven't seen Mr. Atrius or that creepy bird of his. I don't know how they could be missing since he's the one who drove the bus with the crew on it."

"That's not good," Josh mumbled. "I'll go tell the others."

"No!" Steven exclaimed. "Please don't! I don't want to worry them!"

"Dad!" Jake yelled. "You're insane for saying that! Of course, we're going to tell them!"

"Did you forget the connotations of what this might mean?" Josh asked as he face-palmed.

"I understand Mr. Atrius is evil and the ruler of Hell, but why are you kids constantly so worried?" Steven questioned with a blank expression.

"My God!" Jake said as he threw his arms in the air. "I couldn't possibly participate in this conversation any longer. Please take over, Josh. I'm going to tell the others what's is going on."

With that, Jake sulked back through the door leaving Josh and Steven alone.

"Dad, I won't sugar coat this any longer," Josh began with a heavy sigh. "Father… Mr. Atrius is very obviously trying to kill us. He openly stated so several times. There is a very high chance we will be fighting him during the Environmental Dome segment of the show, and an even higher chance we're all going to die.

"He doesn't want to kill you or any of the crew, just us and our friends. He didn't originally want to kill us twins since we don't have Powers. But now, I'm pretty sure he wouldn't hesitate to kill us. Also, he doesn't want to kill his son, Michael, who is half demon. But, with this turn of events, he might end up fighting his own son. That bird is a human girl. She's Mr. Atrius's daughter and Michael's sister. She is part demon and completely insane."

Steven stayed quite for a long time, so Josh continued.

"That's the complete story for now. You're all caught up. Please don't do anything or try to get involved. While you process this, I'm going inside."

"Hang on…" Steven mumbled. "I… I need to end this."

"Wait!" Josh exclaimed angrily. "Didn't you hear what I just said!"

Steven picked up his radio.

"All crew, pack it up," Steven spoke. "We're canceling the Dome. That's final. No questions asked. Anyone who opposes my decision will be let go."

With that, Steven walked off sadly. Josh stood there for a moment then shook his head in frustration. He didn't have time to worry about his dad. He needed to warn the others.

"Guys!" he yelled as he burst in the front door. "Steven just canceled the Dome!"

Everyone stayed quiet for a very long time before a sigh came from Jason's lips.

"I was… really hoping to see how this all works," he said quietly. Jason put his hands in his pockets and gently sat down on the bench.

"Sydney's angry," Michael whispered, his eyes widening.

"How can you tell?" Teddy wondered.

Nick fell against the lockers with a bang. "She's so angry," he muttered, holding his head in his hands.

"Nick! No!" Oliver yelled.

Oliver, Jessica, and Rachel all rushed to Nick's side.

"Sorry," Nick said after a minute. "She just upped the power intake."

Suddenly, Nick felt his Power come back just a little. He looked over at Michael, who had his eyes closed in concentration. Michael had just given Nick more of his Power.

"Thanks, Michael," he said, struggling to stand. "Thanks for the Power."

"Yeah," Michael mumbled. "Sure."

Michael leaned against the lockers and sunk to the floor.

"This sucks," he said. "I can really feel her anger. It's terrifying. It's like a magnetic pull, though."

Michael stood up and promptly punched the locker as hard as he could, leaving a decent-sized hole in the metal and his fist all cut up.

Teddy, who had been standing right next to him, gasped, and pulled back.

"Geez, man," he exclaimed. "Honestly, there are better ways to vent your anger."

While everyone else stood in shock, Nick sighed, walked over to Michael, and cupped Michael's bleeding fist in both hands.

"Moron," Nick muttered. "Don't let her anger become your anger. Keep it together, Michael. We need you for this."

Michael closed his eyes and took some deep breaths as he felt Nick spread this Healing Powers throughout Michael's injured hand. When he opened his eyes, Nick was cleaning the blood off his and Michael's hands with a towel from the medical room. Michael clenched and unclenched his fist.

"Thanks for the Heal, Nick," he said with a deep troubled sigh. "But you shouldn't be using your Powers right now."

"Well, no one else looked like they were going to do it," he replied looking directly at Ondrea.

"I was shocked!" Ondrea said, blushing. "I… I would have done it."

Nick looked toward the entrance of the Environmental Dome.

"That's not fair," Nick said quickly. "No way! No way they would… Sydney! Sydney and Mr. Atrius are in the dome!"

He made a beeline for the entrance and would have made it into the Dome if Teddy hadn't Teleported over to stop him.

"What's got you in such a hurry?" Teddy asked as he grabbed Nick's arm.

Teddy looked into Nick's eyes when Nick remained non-responsive.

"Nick!" Teddy said aggressively. "What's going on?"

Ondrea gasped and put her hands over her mouth in shock.

"I swear," Will began pensively. "If someone doesn't tell me what's going on, I'll pee on you."

Everyone turned to look at Will; he didn't even crack a smile.

"Oh, God, he's serious," Avery muttered, eyes widening.

"What's going on?" Rachel wondered. "Seriously Nick, Ondrea…one of you say something."

"It's Spencer and my Dad," Nick said quietly. "They're in there. They are trapped in there… with Sydney and Mr. Atrius."

"We have to get them out!" Jessica yelled frantically. "Teddy, why did you stop him?"

She began running toward the entrance, but Jason and Oliver grabbed her arms.

"Teddy stopped him because we need to formulate a plan," Jason said quickly.

"We can't just rush in there, sis. You know that," Oliver added.

"I'll go in and scout," Rachel exclaimed. "I can turn into a mosquito. It's nice and small, so even if they detect my presence, they won't be able to spot me."

"That's a good idea, but what if something goes wrong?" Mason asked.

"Someone should go in with you, Rachel. Maybe it should be Teddy, since he could Teleport away at a moment's notice," Darla said.

"I'm in!" Teddy shouted.

"Hey, Oliver," Jessica began. "Can you let go of my arm? And Jason too, please."

"Right, sorry," Jason muttered.

"Here I go!" Rachel yelled as she ran ahead of Teddy and threw the door open.

"What the...?? Hey!" Teddy said with frustration.
He Teleported after her.

FORTY-EIGHT

In Which Michael Is Attacked By a Plant

After going through half of the long hallway, Rachel stopped at a door that looked like the entrance to an air lock. That gave Teddy time to Teleport to her before she turned into a mosquito. Teddy Teleported behind her and startled her when he spoke.

"The fact that there is a smoking hole where the lock should be on this door is both problematic and telling," he said.

Rachel jumped. "You should really be careful, Teddy!" she hissed.

She pushed the door open. Rachel immediately noticed the other airlock door that marked the entrance to the dome had been opened.

"That doesn't bode well for us," Jason said as he studied the door.

"Where did you come from?" Teddy asked.

"I smelled smoke as soon as you guys opened the door," Jason explained as he tapped his nose. "Heightened senses, remember."

"What do you mean when you say that the door being opened doesn't bode well for us?" Rachel asked.

"I'm not sure how good they are at planning ahead, but, judging by this airlock, oxygen is supplied through a vent in the Dome," he began. "That being said, a ton of bad things could be in store for us. They could run smoke through the vent and suffocate us. That's just one example."

"They could also suck all the oxygen out of the dome and lock us in," Mason interjected. "Or run poisonous gas through it."

"Yes, good job, brother," Jason said, deep in thought. "They could also mess with the temperature settings in the Dome and bake us to death—or they could freeze us."

Teddy and Rachel just stared at the twins in horror as they continued to be deep in thought and name off the many ways being in the Dome could kill them all.

"They could also flood the whole thing with the weather setting," Mason added. "Isn't the dome case supposed to be unbreakable?"

"Yes, and impenetrable, Mason," Jason mentioned. "Nothing can break it or get through it. Given the settings of the Dome, heat and cold wouldn't be able to break the Dome since those settings are in place specifically for this structure."

"I assume many people have tried to escape the Environmental Dome by pounding on the walls because this is a very pressure-inducing challenge, so the Dome must be unbreakable. Then again, the Dome has never been tested by someone with Super Strength," Mason went on.

"GUYS!" Teddy yelled. "Stop it, please! This is not helping my nerves."

"Sorry, Teddy," the twins said at the same time, sharing the same expression and the same posture. Mason immediately perked up.

"So, are you guys ready to go?" he asked.

Rachel and Teddy sighed.

"Less ready," Rachel answered quietly. "But still ready, I guess."

"If anything goes wrong, I can get us both out of there," Teddy assured Rachel.

"By the way," Mason began. "We all agreed after you left that Avery, Ondrea, and Michael would stand near the entrance in case something goes wrong."

"Yes, that's a good idea," Jason exclaimed. "Michael can Sense if something goes wrong, Avery can 'Dragon-Out,' and Ondrea can use her Healing Powers. Perfect!"

"In you go!" Mason said, pushing Teddy and Rachel closer to the door.

Teddy nervously unlocked the mechanism and pushed the door open. When the two of them entered the Dome and shut the door, they stared in awe. It looked like they were in a jungle with enormously tall trees. Some of them were covered in vines. Others were bare but had large, wide trunks. All of them were perfectly green and beautiful. The natural smell of rain filled the Dome and it began to sprinkle lightly.

"How is this even happening?" Teddy asked quietly. "The rain seems like it's coming from all over but… but there are no holes in the roof for water to come from."

"We can ask Jason later," Rachel whispered. "Let's just get this over with. Then the difficult part will begin."

"Yeah… I guess," Teddy mumbled, still looking up.

Rachel used her Morphing Powers to turn into a mosquito, and she began to fly up. Teddy quietly made his way through the foliage, heading to where he imagined the center would be. Every leaf and branch smelled as if it were taken from the jungle itself. But despite all the beauty around him, he remained tense and wary. He flinched at every animal call and gritted his teeth every time a low-lying plant brushed against his pants, soaking them in dew.

Teddy had walked for about twenty minutes, and realized he was completely unsure of his location in reference to the center of the Dome.

"This thing is huge," he muttered.

He jumped at the sound of his own voice. Even though he spoke very quietly, he felt as if he had shouted. Teddy stopped and took a few breaths before he heard an unfamiliar noise. A rustling in the trees and then a voice.

"Dad, what are we going to do with the two we captured earlier?"

It was Sydney.

"Well, they are also our targets so we will kill them, darling," Mr. Atrius stated patiently.

Teddy carefully took a steady step forward, focusing on the ground below him as not to step on a stick or make any noise.

"Then why don't we just do it now?" she exclaimed, pouting as if she were a ten-year-old child—and not a teenage demon.

"We want their friends to see them first," he answered with a weary sigh. "Can you stop acting like a child?"

"At least Nick isn't as difficult to handle as your daughter," a familiar voice said loudly.

"Damian!" Teddy whispered, eyes going wide. It was Nick's father.

Suddenly he tripped and began to fall forward, but someone caught his arm before he fell and made a loud noise. He did manage to brush leaves on his way down, but the noise was slight. He turned around and saw Rachel holding his arm.

"What was that!" Mr. Atrius called.

"Teleport away!" Rachel said very quietly.

Doubting Rachel would say that without a plan in mind, he used his Powers to Teleport away, staying inside the Dome, no questions asked. Meanwhile, Rachel turned into a bird she had seen frequently in the Dome and fluttered around in the bushes Teddy had brushed against. A second later, she came face to face with the ruler of the underworld.

"It was just a dumb bird," he said loudly. "I hate this place."

When Mr. Atrius turned away, Rachel flew high into the clearing to scout the enemy. But nothing could have prepared her for what she saw next.

Section 48.1

Teddy had Teleported away per Rachel's instructions, but he didn't know where he'd landed. All he knew was that he was still in the Dome against the side. A couple seconds later, he let out the breath he hadn't realized he'd been holding, and he sank down against the wall of the dome.

"Holy geez…" Teddy whispered as he began to catch his breath. "This is bad. I have to tell the others."

After another minute passed, Teddy stood up. Then he Sight Teleported by looking as far as his eyes could see, Teleporting to that spot, and then doing the process again and again. By that procedure, it didn't take long for him to have gone all the way around the Environmental Dome and arrive back at the metal door.

Before exiting the Dome, he squatted down and took some deep breaths. But he snapped to attention as soon as he heard a rustling sound up ahead. As soon as he set his eyes on the display in front of him, he sighed, rolled his eyes, and smiled. He saw Avery opening the door and Michael attempting to get through the door, despite some jungle leaves wrapping around his face and tangling him.

"I hate the jungle," Michael said with a muffled sigh. "Really, I just hate anyplace with too much foliage."

"Honestly, man," Avery began as she struggled to push past Michael who continued to tangle with the leaves. "Get a hold of yourself."

"These cursed leaves!" Michael yelled as he finally began untangling himself.

"Michael, are you okay?" Ondrea asked, coming up behind him to help.

"He's fine," Avery said with a mischievous grin.

She put her hand over Ondrea's to stop her from helping him.

"He walked into a demise of his own doing. To escape the leaves, he must walk the path of virtue and escape by himself. Only then can he be redeemed by the jungle gods," Avery explained calmly.

Ondrea sighed heavily.

"Be sensible, you two," she said sternly. "And Michael, stop messing around!"

Michael had freed himself and was spitting bits of leaves out of his mouth.

"I didn't ASK the leaves to ensnare me," he mumbled. "Plus, I said it was minor trouble."

Through all this, they still hadn't noticed Teddy standing a few feet away from them, watching the entire scene unfold.

"Hey, guys," Teddy said, stepping into their view. "I wish I'd recorded that."

"Teddy Bear!" Ondrea squealed as she hugged him aggressively. "Oh, I've been so worried about you and Rachel!"

"Don't worry, I'm fine!" he said quickly. "And so is Rachel. I just almost got caught, and Rachel saved my skin. She's okay though."

"That's good," Avery said as she flicked a piece of leaf from Michael's hair.

"I need to talk to the others as well!" Teddy exclaimed as he rushed toward the door.

"Hey!" Michael said, stepping in his path. "Watch out for the plant on your way in."

"Right," he responded as he quickly reached up and removed another piece of leaf from Michael's hair

Then Avery stepped in his way.

"Hang on," she said, stiff-arming him. "What's wrong? Don't go in there with that kind of pace and tone. The others will freak out before the punchline even happens."

"You're right," he said with a very heavy sigh. "This is… well… it's really super bad."

"I'm not going to read your mind, Teddy," Ondrea said calmly. "But we need to know what's going on."

"I don't want to have to tell it more than once. Please can I just tell you with the others?" He asked, taking calming breaths.

With that, they began to head back through the small hallway toward the entrance of the main room. Michael had decided to fill the leaves with five hundred volts of electricity before going in, which made Avery turn around and douse the very small fire Michael had started. A minute later, they met up with the others.

"Hey!" Oliver said with a small smile. "How did it go?"

His smile vanished when he saw the solemn look on Teddy's face and saw that Rachel wasn't with them. He ran up and grabbed Teddy's shoulders.

"Teddy, where is Rachel?" Oliver asked, clearly trying not to panic.

"Hang on," Ondrea said quickly, putting an assertive hand on Oliver's shoulder and guiding him away from Teddy.

"Don't worry, Oliver," Teddy said. "I know she's okay. I'm not exactly sure what she's up to right now, but I trust that she's perfectly alright. I nearly got caught, and she saved me by distracting Mr. Atrius. I'm sure she's doing some scouting."

At the mention of Mr. Atrius, Michael gritted his teeth.

"So, he is there," Jessica said with an angry growl. "If he hurts my sister, he's a dead man."

"Please try to keep it together," Jason said as he walked forward and put one hand on Jessica's shoulder and the other on Michael's.

"Sydney is there too…" Teddy said quietly. "Someone else is there too. Knowing how awful they are, I suspect there are two people there."

"What are you talking about?" Nick asked.

"I'm so sorry, Nick," Teddy muttered, his voice shaking.

"What's going on?" Will asked, tapping his foot anxiously.

"Shut up, Will," Darla hissed. "He can't explain with you talking."

"Teddy…" Mason said apprehensively.

"It's Damian," Teddy finally said. "Nick… you were right. Your father has been captured. It's natural to assume… Spencer is in the same position. I'm so sorry."

Nick punched a hole through the wall.

"No need to be sorry," he whispered. "We'll get them out of this. Then I'm never letting Spence out of my sight again… or my stupid dad."

"I won't let this stand!" Michael yelled, clenching his fists so hard that his demon claws came out and dug into his skin. "I'm confronting him! I'm doing it RIGHT NOW."

Without another word, Michael sprinted down the hall as sparks of Lightning were left in his trail.

"Um. Should someone go after him?" Jake questioned.

"Oh, I kind of forgot you guys were here," Darla said, being completely serious.

"I'll go after him," Jessica said as she immediately left with her Super Speed.

"Teleportation, here I go," Teddy said with a sigh.

"Speeding off," said Ondrea, whose Powers also included Super Speed.

"Oh yeah, the rest of us will just walk," Will shouted, throwing his hands in the air.

FORTY-NINE

In Which Sydney Reveals Her True Desires

It was the last straw for Michael—hearing that his own father had kidnapped Nick's father. He cracked. Michael's claws came out and dug into his skin. Suddenly, Michael took off down the hall, his Lightning Power giving him a speed boost. As soon as he blew the door off the entrance to the Dome, red and black wings unfolded from his back as his eyes glowed red and he took off into the sky straight toward his evil family. In less than a second, he was hovering above the clearing where his father and sister resided. He looked down and saw two people strapped to large poles. Mr. Atrius looked up and saw his son.

"Ooooh, hello, son!" Mr. Atrius called.

Sydney screamed, and her entire body caught fire.

"Why do you always ruin everything?!" she shrieked. "You're literally the brother I never wanted!"

She gathered up a fireball in her hand and hurled it at Michael. He felt like a different person entirely than the person he used to be—the guy with no confidence, no self-esteem. He held out his hand and caught the fireball with ease. With a wide grin and a great laugh, he began to juggle it almost effortlessly.

"I remember you saying something completely different when you were TORTURING me!" he yelled.

The fireball dissipated in his hand.

"You really shouldn't use fire in a jungle, sis," he said calmly.

"You're so annoying!" she yelled, stamping her feet and throwing a tantrum.

Suddenly, Jessica and Ondrea appeared in a flash of speed near the edge of the clearing and gasped at Michael. Teddy teleported right beside them.

"Dude!" Teddy yelled. "You're on fire. That's kind of a hazard here."

"Oops," Michael calmly responded, putting out his own flames. "Thanks, Teddy!"

"You seem to be feeling better!" Ondrea called.

"I'm proud of you, Michael!" Jessica added.

"Thanks, guys!" Michael responded. "I'm kind of in the middle of something."

All this time, Mr. Atrius had been sitting to the side watching his kids.

"Guys!" Spencer called. "Oh my God, you're here!"

"Shut up!" Sydney screamed. "I'm fighting with my brother!"

Sydney formed a massive fireball and threw it in the air spreading fire everywhere. The trees were immediately engulfed in flames.

Michael didn't know what to do. He looked around to make sure his friends were okay. Jessica's Force Field had blocked the fire, but just barely. He quickly turned to check on the hostages and his eyes went wide. The adult he assumed was Damian had been knocked unconscious. Suddenly, a tidal wave washed over the entire dome. Once all the fires were out, and everyone was soaking wet, the rest of Team HOPE came out to the clearing.

"Fire hazard!" Jason yelled. "You're lucky I'm here."

"Dad!" Nick yelled, pain ringing in his voice. "Spence!"

Michael took advantage of the distraction and dove for Damian to get him away from the chaos, but Mr. Atrius shot one of Michael's wings with a bolt of black lightning, causing Michael to scream and fall to the ground.

"No!" Nick yelled furiously.

Using his Super Strength, Nick launched himself off the ground and landed hard right next to Michael. He heard his ankle break as he landed, but he wasn't focused on that right then.

"Michael! Are you okay?" Nick asked frantically.

"Nick, you idiot!" Michael exclaimed. "I'm fine. It's just one wing. But YOU hurt yourself!"

Suddenly, Nick felt all his energy return and his ankle immediately healed.

"I gave you the rest of your power I had stored." Michael explained quickly. "That should bring all your Powers back to full strength including your Healing. Now, I need to take out Sydney so she can't suck up your Power anymore… or your friends' Power." Michael gestured to Spencer.

"Or your dad's Power," he continued. "It seems Dark Magic is my sister's forte. Now, stay here."

During this conversation, Jason had decided to challenge Sydney to an intellectual debate… for some reason.

"What are you doing?" Michael asked. "This is annoying and ridiculous."

"Stalling…duh," Jason said, rolling his eyes.

"Sydney, why did you agree to that in the first place?" Michael inquired.

"So someone could appreciate my smartness!" she exclaimed.

"But you're not smart," Michael stated simply. "Not at all. You're just really mean."

"Alright, that's enough, children!" Mr. Atrius said calmly. "All the guests have arrived. It's time for the party to start. I think I'll start with the main threats."

"No way!" Ondrea yelled, reading his mind.

As Mr. Atrius held up his finger to attack, Ondrea used her Power of Molecular Kinesis to gently but very quickly move Jason and Will out of the way.

"Clever girl," Mr. Atrius said with a laugh. "But you can't protect your water types for long."

Mason ran toward Will and Jason, ready to defend them. Mr. Atrius flicked his finger toward Mason to launch him backward, but Mason saw this coming. He used his Earth Element to make a pillar of earth rise from beneath him. Mr. Atrius' flick missed Mason, but it hit the bottom of Mason's earth tower, breaking it and causing Mason to fall from the air. Mason used his Wind Power to catch himself. He flew in front of Jason and Will to protect them.

"Ah, I see," Mr. Atrius said, looking genuinely intrigued. "So, you have Earth Magic and Wind Magic. The one who looks just like you has Water Magic and, I'll assume, Fire Magic. You ARE the Twins of Legend. How fun."

Mr. Atrius turned around very suddenly and quickly.

"Oh, no, no, no," he said, waving his finger in the air. "Nick, stay away from your father and friend. We wouldn't want any problems, would we?"

Jessica used her Super Speed Power to race toward Nick and put her Force Field up around him just in time to block a barrage of black lightning. Oliver watched all this happen in slow motion and, knowing her shield wouldn't block the lightning, he used his Power of Flight to knock his sister and cousin out of the way before the lightning impacted. Oliver immediately felt a burning sensation unlike anything he had ever felt before, and he screamed in agony. To stop Mr. Atrius from delivering a killing blow, Michael managed to use one wing to swoop down and move Oliver out of the way.

"Oh my!" Mr. Atrius shouted suddenly. "The elusive one. The shy one. I didn't even notice she wasn't here! Where is dear Rachel?"

Rachel had been hiding in the shadows, waiting for a good time to strike. The time was now, she decided. Rachel used her Morphing Power to become a gnat, and she flew over to the pole where Spencer was tied. She discreetly Morphed into a woodpecker, and she stood on Spencer's shoulder to let him know she was there. Then, she got to work pecking at his ropes from behind the pole and out of sight.

Rachel noticed her beak burn every time she hit the ropes. That's when she realized that the ropes were preventing Spencer and Damian from using their Powers. Despite the pain, Rachel kept at it.

Meanwhile, with the comment Mr. Atrius had made, everyone was understandably on edge.

Michael, however, began sensing her power signature. But he couldn't do anything about it because he was on the opposite side of the Environmental Dome taking care of Oliver. He needed to do something fast, or Oliver was going to die.

Luckily, Michael knew what to do.

"I'm sorry, Oliver, but this is the only way to save you," he whispered. Michael wasn't completely sure he could pull it off, and he knew it would be very awkward if it didn't work. But he had to try . . .

Michael brought out his fangs and bit Oliver's neck. As blood flowed from Oliver's wound, Michael spat out the blood and put his hand over Oliver's neck. Michael took a deep breath and began transferring most of his own Power into Oliver. After a few minutes, Michael felt like he was going to pass out, so he stopped the power transference. He could already see Oliver's skin glowing.

"Hopefully that's a good sign," Michael muttered to himself.

Michael put Oliver on the ground and lay beside him.

"Hey," he whispered to Oliver, not knowing whether his friend could hear him or not. "I'm sorry for turning you into a half demon. It was the only way to save you."

As Michael began to fade, he saw the wound on Oliver's neck heal instantly, and he knew the transformation had worked. Michael smiled before he passed out… possibly for forever.

Section 49.1

"Wait, hold on, where are Oliver and Michael?" Jessica asked as she caught her breath.

"I don't care about them anymore," Mr. Atrius snapped impatiently. "Where is little, shy Rachel?"

Jessica and Nick ran across the clearing to join the rest of their friends. But before they arrived, they stopped dead in their tracks, expecting Mr. Atrius or Sydney to throw an attack at the group.

When Mr. Atrius felt the battlefield still, he sighed.

"Yes, yes, go on," he said, waving them along. "I don't want to deal with you anymore. I'm no longer in the mood."

"I'm going to go look for my bro," Sydney said as she stood up and took flight.

But she stopped immediately, screaming in rage, "Oh my, no way! Daddy! Spencer is free!"

Spencer rubbed his wrists from the rope burn and tried to use his Magic, but to no avail. The rope's effects hadn't worn off yet. His eyes went wide as he saw Sydney aim a fireball at him—with no time for him to run. Suddenly, a woodpecker with a slightly smoking beak flew in front of him and transformed into a blazing phoenix, absorbing the fire from the attack.

"Ah…" Mr. Atrius said with a grin. "There she is. Hey, congratulations, dear Rachel. You pulled a fast one on the king of the underworld. Spencer, go on and join your friends."

Mr. Atrius used his powers and waved in the direction of Team HOPE. He sent Spencer flying at nearly impossible speeds, and Mr. Atrius knew there was no way for Spencer to land safely.

Once again, his friends came to the rescue. Nick managed to use his Energy and Super Strength Power to time Spencer's arrival perfectly and keep himself from being carried away by Spencer momentum. They landed, but with a jerky movement. Spencer shook himself off, then immediately turned to Nick to thank him—but Nick was sitting on the ground holding his shoulder in pain.

"Nick, did you seriously dislocate your shoulder doing that?" Spencer asked with concern. "You should… stop hurting yourself."

"You're right," Nick muttered through gritted teeth. "I should have dislocated YOUR shoulder instead, since you decided to leave early and not tell me at school."

"Hey!" Spencer exclaimed as he bent down to help Nick. "I thought we were past that. Also… let me help you… pop that back into place."

Nick didn't say a single thing as Spencer pushed Nick's shoulder aggressively back into its socket. He let out a yelp when it finally popped back in.

"You'll be fine, Nick," Spencer said with a grin.

He stood up and offered a hand to help Nick up. His friend took it.

"Thanks, Spence," he said. "I missed you… a lot. I'm glad you're okay."

As they quickly returned to the group, Sydney came flying into the clearing dangling Michael beneath her. She was clearly about to say something, but Darla beat her to it.

"What did you do to him?" Darla yelled, balling up her fists.

Sydney looked at her with almost no regard.

"I didn't do this. I found him like this," she answered in a prickly tone. "Daddy, I found Michael lying by the by the edge of the Dome's wall."

"Outside or inside, darling?" Mr. Atrius asked as he distractedly chewed on his claws.

"Inside, obviously," she responded, rolling her eyes. "Anyway, here he is."

Sydney, still being high up in the sky, dropped him. Will raced out and used his Ice Powers to create an ice slide. Michael's body hit it at the perfect angle so that he slid down, unharmed.

"Oh, someone let their watery guard down," Mr. Atrius said with a very evil glimmer in his eyes. "I have a fun idea. I can't believe I haven't thought of this yet."

As he finished his statement, he began gathering electricity from the air into his palm and laughed with glee. A few seconds later, he released it and the entire dome filled with enormously dangerous waves of electricity. Mason, who anticipated this coming by just a few seconds in advance, raised a large metal pole from the earth and began to siphon the lightning through it, directing it away from everyone.

"Now, we can't have that!" Mr. Atrius screamed as he continued to laugh. He shot a black fire ball at the pole, causing it to explode.

Mason was caught in the explosion and was hurled straight toward the roof of the dome—bound to be crushed by the pressure. Suddenly, Oliver Flew into view and caught Mason just before he collided with the roof. Just as quickly as he used his Power of Flight to catch Mason, he was setting him on the ground. Ondrea, Nick, and Jason rushed toward him.

"Oh no! Mason!" Jason yelled frantically. "Mason, bro, you have to wake up!"

"Most of his bones are broken from the explosion," Ondrea whispered, tearing up.

"Yeah…" Nick said quietly. "His ribs… they're pretty bad."

"Nothing you two can't heal?" Oliver asked as he gripped their shoulders. "Get to it."

"Hang on, Oliver," Nick said. "This might be…."

"You have to do this!" Oliver yelled frantically. "There is no way anyone else is dying today! GET. TO. IT."

"Dying…" Jason muttered, confused. "Anyone else… what are you talking about?"

"Just use your Powers and Heal him," Oliver said quietly, almost looking defeated.

"Oh my!" Mr. Atrius said, sounding genuinely surprised and even a little sad. "I see."

"See what?" Jake asked. "Seriously, what is going on? This entire thing has been a blur to Josh and me."

"Well," Mr. Atrius began. "I critically wounded your friend Oliver a bit of time ago. My son took him somewhere so Oliver could heal. But … the problem is that the wound I dealt to Oliver was fatal. He was already dying before my son swooped down and saved him. Your friend is alive which means… my… son is not."

Everyone went completely quiet and stared at Oliver for confirmation. That's when Oliver's face turned hard as steel, and he said nothing.

"That can't be!" Rachel yelled. "Explain! Now!"

"I'll explain…" Oliver said loudly, his voice cracking. "I woke up with bite scars on my neck. I didn't have those before… I guess Michael did that. When I woke up, I noticed blood all over Michael's hand and some on his mouth."

"So…. he sucked your blood?" Will asked quietly.

"No. He bit me as a demon, then… I think he transferred… most, if not all, of his energy to me which healed me completely."

"But killed Michael," Jason said, wiping tears from his eyes.

"Oliver Fletcher!" Mr. Atrius began. "You killed my son?"

"NO!" Oliver yelled, beginning to break down. "I didn't do a thing to him! He SACRIFICED himself for me. I did NOT ask him to do that! He did it because he was a really good person—and a better half demon than you'll ever be as a full one!"

"That doesn't make any sense!" Sydney exclaimed loudly. "Brother killer!"

"I didn't do anything to him!" Oliver exclaimed as his eyes began to turn red. "YOU killed him! He was killed by you two! His own father and his own sister! His own family."

"This is stupid," Rachel said quietly. "Death is so stupid."

"Want to know what's really stupid?" Damian asked. "That no one has rescued me yet."

"Dad, you were unconscious, and someone just died." Nick exclaimed. "So, chill for a bit."

"It's okay," Rachel said. "I can meow."

"Oh, yes," Damian said. "You certainly can."

"Guys, we still need to beat the snot out of Mr. Atrius and Sydney," Ondrea said with a sigh. "Let's just do this."

"That's what I was thinking too," Damian growled. "I'm tired of playing with you, Devil. Time to get serious."

Damian ripped off his restraints and jumped down from the pole.

"Dad…" Nick said with a shaky voice. "Please calm down."

"This man and his dead-weight daughter killed one of your friends!" He as a exclaimed angrily as a dark cloud enveloped him. "It's time to end this charade."

"Honestly," Will began. "I'm SO down to end this."

Since Nick and Ondrea were still busy Healing Mason, Will used his Ice Powers to surround them in a thick sheet of ice protection.

"Will!" Darla shouted. "Don't stretch yourself too thin."

Will smiled and nodded. He used his Powers to encase Mr. Atrius and Sydney in a thick block of ice. Meanwhile, Rachel and Oliver began to work on Michael. Mr. Atrius was frozen in a smile. He understood that Will's Ice tactic was pointless and a last-ditch effort.

"Silly boy!" he screeched. "Have a taste of your own medicine!"

As Mr. Atrius shouted, the ice cracked at the sound of his voice then exploded around him, forcing chunks of ice everywhere. Will nearly threw up as he felt a chunk of ice impact his stomach, but he managed to stand his ground. Darla quickly came up beside him and wordlessly held his hand as she glared daggers at

Mr. Atrius. She clenched her other fist in rage because she knew her Fire Power wouldn't do anything to them. All she could do was stand by Will's side and feel useless.

"Who else wants to take a shot at me?" Mr. Atrius yelled. "Or my daughter, obviously."

"Daddy!" she exclaimed. "What the heck?!"

"I'll give it a go!" Ondrea shouted.

She broke through Will's ice shield. Ondrea then used her Super Speed to climb the Dome walls and build up even more speed. For just a second, Sydney and Mr. Atrius seemed to be caught off guard. As Ondrea used her Super Strength to attempt to deliver a crippling blow to Mr. Atrius, he caught her fist and, using the momentum Ondrea had gathered, attempted to push her back. To his surprise, he found he legitimately had to try hard to do so. Even then, she persisted.

While Mr. Atrius was finally distracted, Jessica used her Wind Ability to send a jet stream toward him, but Sydney intercepted it and hit it back with a fireball.

Jason stepped in front of Sydney and easily blocked the intense wind by using his Water Power to set up a solid sheet of water. He snickered and formed a rain cloud above Sydney's head. It began to pour rain on her as if she was standing under a waterfall. True to Jason's nature, he made the cloud follow her around wherever she tried to go.

Jessica used her Wind Power to shoot a jet stream at Mr. Atrius once more. But he somehow saw this coming and moved to the side; he avoided the full force of Ondrea's punch and caused the jet stream to hit her instead. Ondrea yelped in surprise as she was carried by the wind, but Teddy Teleported through the air and grabbed her, then immediately Teleported away.

"The girl almost got me," Mr. Atrius said with a laugh.

He looked over and saw Sydney struggling with the rain cloud.

"Sweetie, stop playing," he mumbled.

As he said this, the rain cloud disappeared and dark cables shot out of the ground, wrapping around Jason's arms and legs, pinning him in place. Jason struggled. Despite his Power of Super Intelligence, he didn't know what Mr. Atrius had ensnared him with. He began to panic and tried using his Powers, but found he couldn't.

"Feeling powerless, Jason?" Mr. Atrius asked with a grin.

From behind Will's Ice shield, Mason finally sat up, startling Nick. He immediately used the force of his Wind Power to speed toward his brother. As soon as he touched the cables, they shocked him and sent him flying back. Luckily, Damian caught Mason, preventing further damage.

"Brother, please stop being reckless!" Jason yelled, his eyes now wide with panic and fear.

"He's okay," Damian called out, to try to calm Jason's nerves even slightly.

Suddenly, Nick and Spencer were at Jason's side, and they began tugging on the cables. Despite the electricity flowing through their bodies, they continued; it seemed to have less of an effect on them. Even in Jason's panicked state, he recognized this was because they had Dark Magic.

"Please be careful," Jason whispered to them.

"We're all good!" Rachel yelled, coming out from behind a big tree. "Everyone, look out! Michael is alive, and he is furious!"

Suddenly, Michael came flying out of the trees and pinned Mr. Atrius to the ground.

"I should claw your throat out for what you're doing to my friends," he growled. "Actually, I think I'll go ahead and get that out of the way."

Sydney flew in and grabbed Michael by his hair. She threw him against the wall of the Dome, but instead of slamming into it, he used his feet to push off the wall, cracking it. Michael used the momentum to rocket toward his sister.

From the ground, his friends saw no more than a blur. He grabbed Sydney and pushed her to the other side of the Dome, knocking the wind out of her. Now they were separated from everyone.

"You're quite the half-demon, brother," she gasped, catching her breath.

He didn't say anything in response. He just locked his red eyes on his target and prepared to launch at her.

"You're letting the demon control you," she said in awe. "My inner demon has never done that before. That's so cool!"

"I am in control," he said. "Me—Michael. I am in control. You're the one who has had the demon controlling you this whole time. Or I should say the Devil."

"So dramatic," she said with a high-pitched laugh.

"You may be older than me, but you're such a child." he exclaimed. "I'm done playing games with you, Syd!"

As Michael said this, his entire body lit on fire. Horns appeared on his head and his teeth turned to daggers.

"Sydney, our dad may be the ruler of the underworld, the king… but I can be more of a devil than he has ever been!" Michael yelled as he dove for her neck.

She barely managed to fly out of the way and began to cry.

"But I love playing games with you, brother," she exclaimed through her tears. "If you would come back home with us, it would be so great! The only reason dad and I are doing this is because we know that if we kill all your friends, you won't have any more attachments. Then you'll come home with us."

"Stop lying!" Michael yelled, grabbing her leg and dangling her upside down. "Stop crying! We know the truth: VORK wants to assassinate our team."

"I don't know who VORK is, but that's not true!" Sydney exclaimed. "We just want you back."

"So, you think killing all my friends will persuade me?" Michael asked. "That's ridiculous!"

Michael dropped his sister on the ground and bared his claws. Suddenly, Sydney began to laugh.

"How about this?" she began with an evil grin. "How about we hold prisoner the only people on your little team who don't have the ability to fight back?"

Michael's eyes widened and the flames around his body dimmed. He flew away from his sister as fast as he could to get back to his friends. What he saw next horrified him.

FIFTY

In Which a Strange, Buff Man Appears

Steven walked in the desert for a little while as the gravity of the situation finally settled in on him.

"While I'm out here sulking, the rest of the crew is just waiting on the bus… oh, and the kids are in horrible danger, and I can't do anything about it!" he exclaimed.

After a few more minutes of walking, Steven froze and then grinned.

"But I do know someone who can!"

Section 50.1

"Hello, son! So glad you're alive!" Mr. Atrius cheered, seeming genuine. "So, I have some of your little friends here and your other little friends over there."

Michael looked down in horror as he saw Jake and Josh unconscious beside his father. The rest of his friends were tied up in dark cables.

"Sydney told me something ridiculous!" Michael yelled. "If what she said is true, then you're in big trouble."

My silly daughter says a lot of things," Mr. Atrius said as he waved off Michael's statement. "What was it she told you?"

"That you want to take me to your home!" he said. "She told me that you're going to kill all my friends so I have nothing left. She told me that VORK didn't target us this time. That you were doing this for your own selfish reasons—to get me down to the underworld."

"That's true," he confirmed. "This has nothing to do with VORK. Why do you think I'm holding your powerless weak friends here with me? Jake and Josh."

"They were NEVER meant to get hurt or involved in this!" Michael screamed.

"They'll be fine!" he exclaimed cheerfully. "Your other friends… well, that's something else. I'm draining them. I'm taking all their Energy."

Michael stilled. A few seconds later, he softly floated to the ground.

"You've lost, son," Mr. Atrius yelled as he gestured to the scene around him. "Give up and come home!"

"Michael!" Oliver called fearfully. "You can't go! You're our friend! Team HOPE, remember?"

"How about this?" Mr. Atrius whispered loudly.

He sped toward the unconscious twins, held his claw to Jake's chest and menacingly ripped the shape of an "X" onto his T-shirt.

"If you don't go back home, this is where my claw will go!" he finished, with a sharp-toothed smile.

Michael's eyes widened and, to his surprise, he felt tears dripping down his face.

"You can't do that," Michael said, as his tears put his flames completely out. "Please… dad… you can't do this."

"Then go with me," Mr. Atrius said simply. "We'll have so much fun in MY realm."

"Michael!" Josh said quietly, slowly waking up. "Don't go. You have a lot to do here. You have friends now. You said you haven't really had any before. You do now. There's so much for you to do."

"Your brother is on death row," Michael muttered, in shock. "You can't be serious, Josh."

"I don't know what else to do," Josh said, now fully sitting up.

"I think I shouldn't have shooed dad away," Jake croaked softy, as he woke up with a claw a centimeter away from his chest.

"Everything will be okay," Michael said as he choked down his tears. "You'll get to see your dad again."

"What does that mean?" Sydney asked, coming up behind Michael.

"I'll go," Michael mumbled, letting his tears fall.

"Michael!" Will screamed. "You're not going anywhere!"

All his friends began to protest at once. Michael sat down and really began to cry.

"I have to!" he exclaimed. "What else can I do? Oh wow, this sucks!"

"Michael, there has to be something you can do!" Josh yelled furiously as he clasped his brother's hand. "You can refuse to go!"

"I HAVE TO!" Michael repeated. "I have to go!"

Mr. Atrius wordlessly held out his hand toward his son. Michael stood up, feeling numb. He walked toward his father, as tears of defeat continued to roll down his face. Sydney came up beside him and put her arm around his shoulders.

"It'll be fun," she whispered with a sincere smile on her face.

Michael looked at her and saw a hint of sadness in her eyes. He noticed her look at his friends and the sadness deepened.

"We'll have fun," she said. "I won't be alone anymore. Neither will you."

Michael froze.

"I feel alone right now," he said loudly. "Knowing I'm leaving behind the only people who ever cared about me."

Mr. Atrius opened his mouth to say something, but Michael continued.

"You never cared. Not once. If you cared, you never would have done this to me! You wouldn't have raised Sydney the way you did. If you really cared, you would have raised Sydney to have friends that she could count on. You never did that."

"Son…" Mr. Atrius said, "I had no choice."

"You're wrong. There's always a choice! Sydney has feelings too. She is alone! You RAISED her that way!" Michael explained.

"She was an oddball!" Mr. Atrius exclaimed. "Nobody liked her."

Sydney's eyes widened.

"You knew no one would like me!" she yelled, feeling betrayed by her own father. "You married my mother, saw how normal people acted, and you raised me to be like this. I didn't even know I wanted friends until I FINALLY met my brother!"

"I raised you the way you should have been raised!" He shouted. "You have a title because of me! You have power!"

Sydney fell to her knees as her fists caught on fire. She felt her entire body begin to burn as tears slipped down her cheeks.

"I don't know what to do," she whispered.

Suddenly, she felt a cold hand on her shoulder, a supportive hand.

"Maybe you don't have to have a title," Will said quietly as he began to quell her flames with his Water Powers.

"Friends can be pretty awesome," Mason said as he knelt beside her—and gave her his classic million-dollar smile.

"He's right. You don't have to have to have a title to be powerful… especially when you already have Superpowers," Ondrea said with a little laugh.

Sydney's body no longer burned, but her tears began to flow like a waterfall.

"I don't want to hurt my father!" she cried. "I'm so sorry! I can't have friends… GET AWAY FROM ME!"

"NO, Sydney!" Michael shouted. "Don't be such a stubborn idiot!"

As she opened her wings and took off into the air, Michael flew above her and tackled her to the ground. She landed with a hard thud and hit her head, knocking herself unconscious. Michael stood up, put his hands on his hips, and looked down awkwardly.

"Well," he began, "that's one way to sedate her."

Mr. Atrius was fuming. "You stupid kids!" he screeched as his body lit up like a barrel of fireworks. "You've confused my daughter! And now my own son has injured her!"

"You are such a hypocrite!" Darla shouted angrily from the side.

"Darla, shut up," Avery muttered, genuine fear filling her voice.

"Power is flowing through him like crazy!" Damian warned. "This is about to be a boss fight."

"Yeah, very funny, Damian," Spencer said blandly. "Good one."

"You're finished," Sydney warned, slowly waking up. "He has this whole blast-radius thing where he blows up literally everything around him.

"Well, that's just not fair," Teddy remarked.

"I'm ready," Avery growled menacingly.

Her wings powerfully extended from her back—setting off a wind current so powerful, it blew most of the surrounding trees out of the ground.

"Everyone get over to Michael and the others!" Oliver shouted. "Put your shields together!"

"It's too late!" Rachel exclaimed as she pointed out the white light surrounding Mr. Atrius.

Suddenly, it seemed as if time slowed. The kids looked up as they heard a loud bang.

"Stupid glass!" a flying man yelled loudly in genuine confusion and frustration. No one recognized him, or knew where he had come from, but the bang appeared to have come from him trying to enter the dome.

Suddenly the man flew up, up, up, out of sight of everyone in the dome, to almost five-thousand feet in the air, moving at what seemed like light speed. A few seconds later, he was diving straight toward the glass.

"This is going to end in a splat," Jake stated grimly as he and Josh joined the rest of the group.

But to everyone's surprise, the man burst through the unbreakable glass, shattering the entire Dome all the way down. Avery quickly spread her wings over the heads of her friends to protect them from the glass. Her wings were badly cut, but she knew she had more important things to worry about.

"Friend or foe?!" Michael shouted at the man as he began his descent to the kids.

"Obviously, I'm your friend!" the man said with a hearty laugh. "But you can call me Super Dad!"

"What? No," Will immediately said as he raised his eyebrows.

"You remind me of my dad," Josh said skeptically.

"Oh, my goodness, you two!" Super Dad yelled. "Your father was a college buddy of mine. He sent for me."

"How dare you make a mockery of me!" Mr. Atrius exclaimed, looking angry but mostly baffled.

"Who's your friend?" Super Dad questioned, pointing his thumb in Mr. Atrius' direction.

"Wait, hold on!" Jake said, as he held up his hand. "My dad sent for you?"

"Yes. Your father told me you kids needed help," he responded, putting his hands on his hips and pushing out his chest in a Superhero pose.

Standing before Team Hope and friends was a man who called himself Super Dad. He wore an embarrassingly tight red suit, defining his exaggerated muscles. Behind him flowed a blue cape. He seemed supremely self-assured and clearly had a large ego—and rightfully so.

"I'm definitely having a nightmare right now," Jessica said quietly as she pinched herself.

"Don't forget about my crazy dad," Sydney mentioned, pointing to Mr. Atrius who was now completely on fire.

"The enemy!" Super Dad exclaimed, eyes blazing with determination.

With unexpected Speed and Strength, the incredibly strange Superhero launched himself toward Mr. Atrius.

"DEMON!" he roared. "I'm going to send you back to the underworld one way or another! Children are precious!"

In the middle of Super Dad's sentence, he used his Super Strength to send Mr. Atrius flying toward the ground. Upon impact, Mr. Atrius caused a massive crater. Cape flapping in the wind, Super Dad plunged down to deliver the final blow to Mr. Atrius, who was lying in the middle of the crater. But just before Super Dad reached him, the Devil opened his all-black eyes and showed his sharp-toothed smile. He stuck out his claws, attempting to stab Super Dad through the chest.

"Reckless fool!" Jason shouted at Super Dad.

Mr. Atrius thrust his hand in front of him, sending an incredibly powerful jet of wind toward Super Dad, forcing him backward. The wind knocked Jason back, too, slamming him into a tree. Jason let out a loud curse.

"Jesus, bro!" Mason said, sounding very impressed but mostly worried. "Are you hurt?"

"No. I'm alright," Jason exclaimed. "I'm not sure if the wind damaged Super Dad or not. We have to get to him before Mr. Atrius finds him."

"Right, we've got you covered!" Nick shouted. "Teddy, you need to go check on Super Dad!"

"NO, YOU DON'T!" Mr. Atrius screeched, as he dove at Teddy with his jaw unhinged—making his mouth look bigger than his face and his pointed teeth look one hundred times more horrifying than usual.

"No way!" Mason exclaimed.

Mason knocked Mr. Atrius off course by using his Earth Powers to shoot a column of titanium straight at him. Teddy then Teleported to Super Dad.

"Avery!" Will called. "Get me up!"

"On it!" Avery swooped down using her Dragon Abilities, grabbed Will by the waist, and flew him high into the air. Although Mr. Atrius assumed Will would use his Ice Powers, Will instead used his Super Stretch to wrap his arms around Mr. Atrius' entire body, rendering him immobile.

"Bad idea, idiot!" Sydney shouted to Will. "Here comes the bite."

Just as she was saying that, Mr. Atrius smiled his sharp-toothed grin and chomped on Will's arm. He shouted in pain and tried to pull away, but Mr. Atrius grabbed Will's arm and bit deeper.

"You're insane!" Will shouted.

Darla, who was invisible right below Mr. Atrius, saw him unleash his claws out of Will's sight. But instead of claws, they looked an awful lot like knives. Darla squeaked in fear as she realized how skinny Will's arms were, stretched so thin. Darla's body was shaking so badly she doubted her spur-of-the-moment plan would work.

But suddenly, Darla felt waves of calm running through her whole body, and she realized Ondrea was using her Mind Reading and Healing Powers to soothe her. Darla took a deep breath, gathering all the passion, anger, determination, and love for Will that was in her body and pushing it toward her hands. She aimed her Finger Laser Power to send a blinding laser of heat out two of her fingers directly toward Mr. Atrius' eyes. They hit their mark.

"Ahhhh, NO!" As he screamed, he pulled his head back, taking his teeth out of Will's arm.

"Who did that?" Mr. Atrius yelled. Then he looked directly below him and smiled. "Oh, an almost-invisible little bug…" he waited a second more and scratched the back of his head. "…who is fireproof. But that won't stop me."

"DARLA, NO!" Will cried.

Will used his Ice Powers to gently freeze Avery's feet, causing her to let go of him. As Will began plummeting toward the ground, he created an ice slide directly in Darla's direction. But it was too late; an evil cloud had enveloped her. Will hardened his face and began to enter the cloud, but Spencer knocked him out of the way with a blast of condensed Magic.

"Will, you'll turn!" Spencer screamed. "Think rationally!"

Will sat on the ground a couple feet away from the edge of the dark cloud, feeling helpless.

"What do you mean?" he asked quietly.

Nick, Spencer, and Damian were immediately at Will's side. Damian put his arms under Will's armpits and began dragging him much further away from the cloud. Will grimaced and finally began feeling the wound on his arm.

"That's right!" Mr. Atrius cackled. "Your precious girl is doomed!"

"No, no, no, no," Will mumbled, still in a bit of shock.

"Will, you need to pull yourself together," Spencer whispered directly in his ear.

Nick put his hand over Will's open wound and began to Heal it with his Powers. When Nick's hand made contact with his arm, Will shouted, and pain radiated throughout his entire body.

"Stop!" Michael and Jason yelled at the same time.

They both looked at each other for a second, and then sprinted in Will's direction. Then Jason pivoted and ran toward the cloud of Dark Magic instead. Rachel was about to call for Jason to stop, but Mason put his hand on her shoulder.

"He's not stupid," Mason said gently. "He knows what he's doing."

"Michael, what's wrong?" Nick asked, looking frightened.

"My father infected this bite," he said grimly. "Will's going to turn."

"Okay, I'm tired of this!" Josh said as he and Jake sprinted toward the group. "What's going on?"

"What do you mean by 'turn?'" Jake asked.

Damian cursed and began to squeeze Will's arm as hard as he could. Will screamed in pain as dark blood began to flow out of the wound.

Damian then answered Jake's question with a whisper. "He'll. Turn. Evil."

FIFTY-ONE

In Which There Are Two Caged Lovers

As Teddy Teleported next to Super Dad, he noticed his eyes were closed.

"Oh no. Are you okay?" Teddy asked, kneeling down beside him.

Super Dad opened his eyes and smiled, his bright white teeth shining at Teddy. Teddy rolled his eyes.

"Oh yes, I'm fine," Super Dad said as he sat up and opened his eyes.

Teddy grimaced. "Oh, man," Teddy said, quickly standing up. "Your eyes are so red. Is that some kind of medical condition or…"

"Your friend's Wind Power dried out my eyes. I had to lie here for a while with my eyes closed so I could 'un-dry' them," Super Dad said as he stood up.

"What is wrong with you?" Teddy muttered under his breath.

"I just told you: nothing," Super Dad said as if he was scolding a child. "I'm just fine. No injuries here."

"That is not what I meant," Teddy responded. "You do realize we're in actual danger here, right?"

"Of course!" Super Dad exclaimed. "I am fully aware of the situation." He puffed up his chest, struck a pose and stuck his thumb up for confirmation.

"Let's just go," Teddy said with a sigh as he grabbed Super Dad's arm and Teleported them both into chaos.

"Oh my goodness, what is happening?!" Super Dad exclaimed loudly.

His ears perked up at the sound of Will screaming.

"A CHILD IN PAIN!" Super Dad exclaimed as his eyes turned a bright white, and the air began to smell of… lavender.

Suddenly Will's screaming stopped, and the vortex of darkness dissipated. Everyone looked up at Super Dad in shock.

Then Mr. Atrius laughed.

"Your friends are still infected!" he screeched. "They'll turn evil, but there's a catch."

"Of course there's a freaking catch!" Avery exclaimed, throwing her hands up in the air.

"Yes, there is always a catch," Sydney said as she appeared behind Avery.

"They'll fight each other," Michael said through gritted teeth. "Isn't that right, sis?"

"How did you know that, son?" Mr. Atrius asked. "I don't think there's any way you could have known that."

"Why are you bringing me into this?!" Sydney yelled, clearly upset by Michael's question.

Michael flew at his sister, tackled her to the ground, and just barely lifted her shirt to reveal a bite mark on her lower back.

"Very astute of you, Michael," Mr. Atrius said happily. "Yes, I bit my own daughter to assure her loyalty to me. Anyway, the two brats will fight each other. Isn't it funny? I mean, I'm sure they love each other…"

"That's cruel!" Ondrea screamed as she began to tear up.

Teddy rushed to Ondrea's side and wrapped his arm around her.

"It will be okay!" he whispered. "I'm sure Will and Darla's love will prevail."

"UGH!" Mason said as he rolled his eyes and pretended to gag. "You guys are gross."

"Oh, please!" Mr. Atrius said with another laugh. "Of course I made my infection love proof! I've read too many gross stories about love to not do so."

"But have you made your infection DAD PROOF?!" Super Dad yelled as he once again struck a pose and then flew at Mr. Atrius, his blue cape flapping valiantly in the air. Super Dad grabbed him by the throat.

"You will undo the infections you have placed upon these children at once!" he exclaimed. "As a fellow dad— although a really bad one—you should understand the importance of pre-serving children!"

"Are you kidding me?" Mr. Atrius said as he casually removed Super Dad's hand from his throat. "I bit my own daughter to assure her loyalty, kidnapped my son's friends, tried to kill them, and then tried to kill my own son. Do you think I really care about preserving children?"

"He has a point," Nick said, looking at Super Dad.

Super Dad made eye contact with the other kids and saw them shrug their shoulders in agreement.

"Even the people I've tried to kill agree with me," Mr. Atrius said. "Anyway, enough delaying. Let the fighting commence."

He snapped his fingers. Will, who had been in a trance since Super Dad infused the area with lavender essence, popped up and dove at Darla, who woke up just in time to avoid a deadly ice spear to the chest.

"Will, stop this!" Oliver shouted as he flew toward Will to grab him.

"No interfering!" Mr. Atrius said harshly.

As Mr. Atrius attempted to stop Oliver with a wide burst of blood-red energy, Super Dad blocked it by seemingly absorbing it into his chest. He wordlessly turned to look at the kids and winked.

As Oliver wrapped his arms around Will to keep him from attacking Darla, he noticed her running at him at top speed. She had a sword of Fire Power in her hands and came in to slice off his head. Oliver tried to push her back with a strong gust of Wind Power, but she wasn't even phased. Suddenly, a large column of rock appeared in front of her thanks to Mason's Earth Power. Instead of running into the rock, Darla stopped with the reflexes of a cheetah and turned toward Mason with a sharp-toothed scowl and eyes as black as a void.

She slashed the wall of rock like it was butter, grabbed Oliver, and threw him off Will. Avery managed to catch Oliver in her wings.

Will turned around and dodged Darla's attack at the last second. He quickly froze her feet in place and punched her in the gut. Seeming to be unphased, Darla's feet began to glow orange. She immediately melted the ice and kicked Will in the stomach, sending him flying and catching his shirt on fire.

Jason flew up and caught Will, simultaneously putting out his shirt with his Water Power. He tried to hold on to Will but Will twisted his arms around, grabbed Jason's shoulders, and launched him into the ground. Mason grew a patch of grass and managed to catch his brother before he slammed down on the rock.

As Will's arms turned into icicles ready to impale Darla, her body became red hot, and she continued her charge. Instead of being impaled when she hit the ice, she melted right through it, throwing Will off guard. For just a millisecond, his eyes widened as recognition set in. He suddenly found himself being pummeled into the ground by a flaming Darla.

"A momentary lapse in judgment," he said to himself as his eyes once again rolled to black.

He felt bones in his back break, but that didn't stop him from trying to kill Darla. Will grabbed her by her hair and stretched high in the sky. He waved her around like a doll then dropped her, sending her plummeting to her death.

"Oh my God!" Teddy yelled. He Teleported midair, grabbed Darla's arm, then Teleported them both back to the ground. "This is ridiculous! Darla! Will! You have to stop! You LOVE each other."

Mr. Atrius let out a laugh just as Darla quietly said, "Love makes you weak, Teddy."

Teddy's eyes went wide as Darla sprinted away to fight Will again. Ondrea appeared beside him and pulled him into a hug.

"You better not listen to that, Teddy Bear!" she exclaimed. "She's evil, remember!"

"As cheesy as this sounds, we need to help her remember that love is quite possibly the best thing that can happen to anyone," Jason exclaimed, glancing at Jessica.

"CHILDREN, YOU MUST STOP!" Super Dad screamed, his voice booming in the air.

At light speed, he flew in between Darla and Will and grabbed them by the hair. He held them at arm's length as Darla and Will began to struggle for release.

"Or… Super Dad could just do that," Jake said from his hiding place behind a tree.

"You kids should be ashamed of yourselves!" Super Dad exclaimed, looking at Will and Darla with the most disappointed look ever to exist. "This Power is called Super Disappointment because I'm super disappointed in you two."

"This is weird," Josh said, staring at Super Dad.

"Yeah, this is by far the weirdest thing we have experienced," Rachel agreed. "I don't think anything could top it."

Super Dad stomped his foot on the ground, and a titanium cage grew in that exact spot. He quickly tossed Darla and Will inside the cage. As soon as they were in, the door disappeared.

"What can't this man do?" Jessica asked.

"Now," Super Dad began with his arms crossed. "I'd like to interview this boy to make sure he's best for my Darla, but now doesn't seem to be a good time."

"My God," Teddy said with a weary sigh.

Will and Darla tried to attack each other, but they found themselves bound to opposite sides of the cage by an invisible chain, unable to reach each other.

As the two began to charge up their Powers, Nick came forward, reached through the bars, and touched the two of them, stealing all their Powers away.

"I have no idea why I didn't just do that before," he said as he backed away from the cage.

Darla and Will sank to the floor and stared at each other with a sort of longing.

"They just seem empty," Jason said, coming next to the bars. "It's sad."

"Damian?" Nick asked quietly. "Can we get them back?"

"Absolutely, but we have a problem," he said with a weary sigh. "Mr. Atrius seems to have left."

"You've got to be kidding me!" Sydney yelled. "That's just like him!"

"Totally forgot you were here," Jason said.

Sydney ignored him.

"Let's fix your friends or whatever," she continued.

"This is getting really exhausting," Jessica said as she sat on the ground. "This is dumb,"

"Kiss and make up, you two," Super Dad commanded, striking a pose with his hands on his hips.

Darla and Will looked at Super Dad slowly and blinked for the first time.

"I think their infections are wearing off," Spencer said.

"Dad must have gone back to the underworld… And left me here," Sydney said somewhat sadly.

"That doesn't matter," Jake said, still a little bit afraid of her but also feeling bad for her. "You could become a friend now… I think."

Sydney smirked in his direction and stepped toward him quickly, brandishing her claws. Michael immediately went on high alert and released his own claws. Jake curled away in fear. Suddenly, Sydney began to laugh.

"Calm down, Jake," she said. "I'm not going to eat you."

"Very funny," he murmured.

FIFTY-TWO

In Which Will Gets Punched for a Good Cause

Darla felt her heart racing as the redness began to fade from her eyes. Her heart felt as heavy as stone, and she let out a small cry as she realized how sore her body was.

"Darla!" someone shouted, sounding a bit muffled.

For some reason, Will was the first person who came to her mind, but she knew the voice wasn't his.

"Where is Will?" she mumbled, her blurry vision finally beginning to clear up.

"He's sitting right across from you," Oliver said.

Her vision cleared completely, and she stared in horror as Will sat smiling at her, looking creepy with blood red eyes and razor sharp teeth.

"What's… what's wrong with him?" she asked, her voice shaking.

"I'm pretty sure since he was bitten, the evil effects are still in play for him," Damian said with a weary sigh.

"Maybe I can just…" Nick trailed off.

He reached his hand inside the cage and attempted to touch Will so he could heal the infected wound one more time, but Will immediately snapped his teeth in Nick's direction, and Nick felt someone pull him back. He turned around to see Mason shaking his head.

"Not yet," Mason said firmly.

Darla was still staring at Will in horror when she felt a hand on her shoulder, and she jumped.

"It's just me coming in with a Heal," Ondrea said as she reassuringly squeezed Darla's shoulder.

Darla felt a calming warmth flow through her body as her pain began to fade, but she thought the emotional pain of seeing Will in his condition would never fade. She reached out her hand to touch his ankle, but the chain holding her back stopped her. She frowned and pulled against it.

"Sorry about that, Darla," Super Dad apologized. "It was just for safety."

He snapped his fingers and Darla's chain vanished. She once again reached for Will's ankle just to tap him, but he snapped his teeth at her and his eyes glowed. Darla's eyes began to water, but she held strong.

"I'm not going to let this stupid evil continue its stupid hold on you, you stupid idiot," she said to Will as she crossed her arms.

Section 52. 1

Will found he couldn't control his actions, and he felt himself snap at someone. His vision was blurry and red. He could barely see in front of his face. He became conscious of the fact his heart was filled with a fiery anger and a deep hatred. Will noticed a figure in front of him and his eyes flared. He didn't recognize her, but he felt the urge to kill her. He couldn't hear very well, but he knew she said something, and that made him even more upset. He screamed as blind rage filled his heart and he struggled against his chains, reaching his claws toward her and kicking the air.

The girl jumped back and he saw a tear roll down her face. Suddenly, among all the hate and anger, he felt a small hint of sadness. He began to taste salty tears of his own and a small hint of recognition appeared in his expression. He saw the girl smile, but Will just repeated his previous sentiment as his eyes glazed over again.

"A momentary lapse in judgment," he exclaimed with a smirk. "I could easily break out of these chains."

"Not without your Powers," a boy with blond hair said.

"Nick, I'll kill you!" Will yelled.

Once again, a hint of recognition flashed in his mind as he said the word 'Nick,' and he tilted his head in confusion as he stared at the boy known as Nick.

"Nick…" Will growled as images of Nick flashed through his mind.

With Will's vision completely cleared, he once again looked at the girl in front of him and his eyes widened.

"Darla…" he muttered, shaking his head as if to clear it.

Now he heard her voice loud and clear.

"I love you," she said strongly. "You know I do. I know you do, knuckle head. So, snap out of it!"

Will growled like a wolf, but he felt the claws on his fingers retract. Nick touched Darla and returned her Powers. Will suddenly felt paralyzed due to confusion and a pain in his chest. Darla came up and punched him in the face.

"What's wrong with you, Darla!" he exclaimed. "I can't see why I love you, but… I do."

"I guess I just needed to knock some sense into you," she said with a smirk. "Not that you ever had sense anyway."

He found the red fading from his vision as he looked around him, remembering everything he had done. Super Dad saw this and removed Will's chain. Suddenly, Will lunged at Darla. But instead of attacking her, he embraced her and began to cry.

"I'm so sorry," he whispered. "I never ever want to hurt you. I totally deserved that punch."

Darla remained quiet for a few minutes and stroked the back of his head.

"You're too dumb to hurt me," she whispered in his ear. "I totally kicked your butt."

Will pulled away and smiled at her.

"I bet you did," he said.

All of a sudden, Will fell back and gasped. He clutched his arm where he had been bitten and yelled.

"Super Dad!" Rachel exclaimed as her voice cracked with worry. "Get rid of your cage! He needs Healing!"

Without a word, Super Dad stomped on the ground and the cage lowered into the earth. Nick, Damian, Ondrea, and Spencer rushed to Will's side.

"Just stay still!" Spencer exclaimed. "I think now that your infection has worn off I can remove the remaining darkness."

"That would be nice," Will responded, feeling nauseous. "Man, am I on cloud nine or what?"

Damian pinned Will's legs to the ground, Nick held his arms in place, and Ondrea grabbed his head. This all took Will by surprise but he didn't have much time to be surprised as he suddenly felt a blinding fiery pain in his arm. He screamed, feeling his body convulse as Spencer squeezed the flesh around Will's wound. Will felt the remaining hatred disappear. In fact, he felt like everything disappeared; he blacked out.

Once Spencer finished, he pulled his hand away and clenched it into a fist. When he opened it, there was a massive ball of Dark Magic swirling around just above his palm.

"Was he supposed to pass out?" Avery asked, sneaking up behind them.

"Well, I'm not sure," Damian responded. "But at least all the darkness is out."

"What do we do with the darkness?" Jessica asked, peering at it curiously.

"Well, we can't waste it!" Sydney exclaimed, looking genuinely appalled by the question.

She took it from Spencer and aggressively split it in half. Randomly, she tossed one of the halves in her mouth and swallowed. Then she let out a burp and a satisfied sigh.

"What in the ever-living heck…" Teddy said.

"Michael, you should try it," Sydney suggested. "It tastes really good! It's different for each person!"

"That would make some sense," Mason started. "I hope I get this right since Jason's usually the one in the know. Darkness equals temptation, so eating darkness, if you can handle it, would probably taste good. I say that because if you're tempted to eat it, it would probably taste like your favorite food."

Jason chuckled.

"Bingo, bro," he said.

Michael shrugged and popped the darkness in his mouth.

"Hm…" he began with a satisfied look. "Tastes like sugar."

"Told you!" Sydney yelled with a smug look.

"Guys," Oliver said with a hesitant look on his face. "What do we do with the super elephant in the room?"

He pointed directly at Super Dad.

"I can take care of myself!" Super Dad exclaimed. "We should probably get you kids back to the studio."

"Right," Josh said. "Is my dad there?"

"Yes, he's there," Super Dad confirmed with a reassuring smile. "I think it's also time for you kids to go home. You've been through quite a lot."

"What are we going to do about the fact that Mr. Atrius is literally gone?" Jake asked. "Will he come back?"

"You don't need to worry!" Super Dad said. "I will always be there to help children in distress!" He struck his most dramatic

pose yet and held it for literally a minute in complete and awkward silence.

"Well, let's go take a one-hundred-year nap!" Will yelled,
sitting up very suddenly.

Darla jumped back.

"Watch it, moron," she sneered. "You could have given me a
concussion."

"Maybe you shouldn't hover over me," Will said with a pout.

"I'll fight you again," Darla jeered as she playfully messed up
his hair.

"Okay, kids!" Super Dad yelled as he suddenly pulled up in a
flying car. "Let's head out!"

"That is so incredibly extra," Avery mentioned. "You can fly
by yourself—but you have to have a flying car."

"I usually use this bad boy to pick up chicks," he answered
with a wink and a smile.

"Gross," Jason mumbled as Super Dad landed the car safely
on the ground. "How old are you anyway?"

"Older than I look," he said with another wink.

"I highly doubt that," Darla said as she climbed into the limo-
like flying car. "My parents say that baloney all the time."

Once almost everyone had gotten into the car, Nick stopped
both Spencer and Damian.

"Hey, are you guys okay?" Nick asked quietly. "You've been
through a lot."

Damian smiled lovingly at his son. He pulled Nick into a hug
as his eyes began to water.

"I'm alright," Damian responded. "Mr. Atrius said he was going
to kill you. I hate to say it but... with his power... I thought he
would."

Nick pulled away.

"I get it," he said with a sad smile. "I'm just glad you're okay."

Nick turned to Spencer.

"Your dad is going to have an aneurysm if you don't call him and tell him you're okay!" Nick exclaimed with a humored grin.

Spencer's eyes widened as he searched for his phone. When he couldn't find it, he looked at Nick frantically.

"The Devil took my phone too," Damian said. "Use Nick's."

"Come on, my children!" Super Dad called from the front seat of his car. "We're on a tight schedule. Steven called everyone's parents and told them what happened. They are all very anxious to see you."

As Damian, Nick, and Spencer loaded into the car, Rachel leaned on Jessica's shoulder.

"I miss our parents," she muttered.

"You've been very strong," Jessica assured her, giving her sister a light kiss on the forehead.

Super Dad began to lift the car off the ground.

"I think you have all been very brave," Damian said with a smile. "Even you, Sydney."

"What are we going to do with her?" Michael asked. "My mom will not want her running around our house—especially considering where she was raised."

"I can hear you," Sydney sneered, flicking him in the ear. "I'll be a golden child. Besides, you're a demon too, Michael."

"She doesn't know about any of this…" he responded hesitantly. "Especially the whole 'Superpower' thing."

"No wonder your mother seemed so confused when Steven called her," Super Dad mumbled.

"Oh, hell," Michael whispered, twiddling his thumbs anxiously.

The ride back to the studio was relatively silent. Most of the kids were asleep—but not all.

"Michael, do you think your dad will stay in the underworld?" Jake asked quietly.

"I hope so. For your sake and your family's sake," Michael replied. "He knows all of us, but you guys would be in the most danger."

"Not as long as Steven has me on super speed dial," Super Dad cut in with a wink.

Michael smirked.

"Okay, so maybe you're even more safe than the rest of us," he said.

FIFTY-THREE

In Which the Next Adventure Begins

Once the car arrived at the studio, Super Dad began to wake everyone up.

"Get out of my car!" he called. "I have a single mom with twelve kids who are waiting on me!"

With that, everyone woke up quickly.

"Are you dating her?" Avery asked with a yawn.

"No! I help her with the children!" he exclaimed, appalled. "I only date single woman without children."

"Okay, everything about that sounded wrong," Mason grimaced as he and the others began unloading from the car.

"I don't understand what your brand is," Teddy stated, referring to Super Dad, but talking to only himself.

Jake and Josh were the first ones through the studio door. They began to call out for Steven who immediately sprinted from behind the backstage curtains and wrapped his kids in a tight hug.

"I'm so happy you two are safe!" Steven cried, becoming emotional. "I was so worried about everyone, but… my kids…"

"Dad, I'm sorry I was so mean to you outside the Environmental Dome," Jake whispered, becoming choked up.

Josh pulled away from Steven and looked at the floor. Steven just smiled and ruffled his hair.

"I'm so glad you're back safe," he repeated to his sons. "I'm glad Super... uh... Dad pulled through."

Super Dad just stood in the doorway frozen in his Superhero pose. The door was open, so the setting sun behind him cast a very convenient glow around him, accentuating his cheesy pose.

"How did you deal with him as your college roommate?" Teddy questioned with an eyebrow raised.

"I have no idea," Steven answered with a relaxed sigh. "And before you ask, no, he did not make me call him Super Dad in college... he made me call him Super Daderson."

"Oh... my... God," Sydney said, rubbing her temples. "I cannot handle this guy anymore."

"Super Dad?" Will began. "Were you dropped on your head when you were younger?"

Super Dad laughed and stepped fully into the building, closing the door behind him.

"No, but I did learn to kick criminals in the head," he said with an almost smug-looking smile.

Darla looked at Will and giggled.

"Clearly they kicked back," she whispered, slugging Will in the shoulder.

Super Dad's smile fell a little.

"Sorry, Super Dad!" Ondrea began. "They didn't mean it. You're just very... eccentric."

"It's okay!" he said very quickly. "My ego is so inflated all the time, I could fill the entire World Trade Center."

"Impressive," Jason said genuinely.

"Well," Super Dad shouted as he dramatically pushed the studio door open to leave, accidentally launching it off its hinges. "I've got some children to look after. More specifically twelve children. They are very ungrateful, but that's okay because I love to care for children."

"A lot of things just happened at once…" Steven exclaimed.

With that, Super Dad left. After a minute of baffled and confused silence, Steven clapped his hands loudly, scaring everyone.

"Alright, everyone!" he shouted, returning to his announcer voice. "I think it's time we get you back to your parents! Go back to your rooms, pack up your bags, then we'll head to the bus!"

After a couple of seconds, the kids turned around and went to get their things while Jake, Josh, Spencer, and Damian stayed in the main building.

"This has been rough," Spencer exclaimed with a wide yawn.

"How was being kidnapped?" Josh asked. "It's never happened to me, so I'm curious about the experience."

"Well," Damian started. "It's annoying to say the least. Very tiring. Also, a bit dangerous."

Josh nodded his head, deep in thought.

"You wouldn't want to get kidnapped," Spencer added. "It's not worth the experience."

"We'll keep that in mind," Jake muttered, rolling his eyes.

"It's been strange meeting people like you," Josh said. "No offense, but I don't want to do it again."

"I've had too much adventure," Jake agreed. "I think I'm ready to retire."

"Hey, Steven!" Spencer called. "What are you going to do now that your Environmental Dome is shattered into a zillion trillion billion million pieces?"

"Cry and hope my insurance covers the damages," Steven answered after some thought.

"Yeah, that's fair," Spencer mumbled.

"As an adult, I'll be real with you," Damian said. "The insurance will not cover the damage. However, Super Dad will help you. I have a feeling he is loaded with money."

All the kids came back into the studio. Everyone loaded onto the bus, even Jake and Josh.

"Why are you coming with us?" Oliver asked as everyone settled on the bus.

"We just want to spend a little more time with you before goodbye," Josh answered.

"I don't think we'll be talking much," Oliver said with an extra big yawn.

"That's okay," Jake said. "It's better when you're not running your super obnoxious mouth."

"Yeah, so demanding," Darla said as she turned around from the row in front of them.

"Alright, whatever guys," Oliver responded, waving them all off.

Some hours later, everyone was back home and unpacking.

Nick, however, went back with his father to New York for the time being. Everyone agreed they'd give school a bit of a break, then very begrudgingly take an accelerated summer school program to try and catch up on what they'd missed.

Unfortunately for Sydney, she was sent to charm school for a long time due to her being "a destructive force of nature." Aside from being grounded for, as his mother put, "the rest of eternity," Michael just enjoyed being back home. Spencer went back to studying VORK with his dad.

Meanwhile, Jason, Mason, Oliver, and Michael all met up in the Fletcher family basement to work on something new.

"Oliver, why did you want us here?" Mason asked. "It's been three weeks since we got back from that whole near-death experience."

"Yeah, I know. I just couldn't wait anymore," he answered. "My dad wants me to help him with a new project. He wanted it to be like a father and son thing, but I told him there's no way we would ever finish this, just the two of us. It took a full week but I managed to convince him to let me get help. He requested you guys specifically. And Damian, Nick, and Spencer. They're busy right now."

"Okay!" Jason said quickly. "What is this thing?"

"Why would he need all of us specifically for this project?" Michael wondered hesitantly.

"Apparently, you're all super smart so he wanted me to get you guys in on this," Oliver responded.

"Oh my God!" Jason shouted as he began to pace around the room. "Apparently? Apparently? There is nothing 'apparently' smart about me! I am smart! Very smart! I'm literally the smartest…"

"I will slap you, bro," Mason stated bluntly, putting his hand on Jason's shoulder to stop him from pacing. "Cool your jets, Einstein."

"Anyway…" Oliver started. "My dad also thinks you guys would be the most interested in this kind of thing— given each of your pasts."

"I'm ready to know what this idea is," Michael said, tapping his foot.

"Okay, guys. You're going to love this," Oliver said with nervous excitement. "We are going to build a multi-dimensional portal machine. That's what my dad calls it."

Everyone went silent for a couple of seconds.

"So… we're going to get to travel to other dimensions?" Mason asked, jumping up and down in excitement.

Before Oliver could answer, Jason jumped in.

"No way! Too dangerous!" Jason shouted. "As cool and awesome as it would be, it's too dangerous!"

"I'm fine with this," Michael said. "Earth is boring, and I've heard the weather at Home is a pretty consistent 150 degrees Fahrenheit, so I'm good with pretty much anything else."

"Horrible things could happen!" Jason shouted.

Oliver put his hand on Jason's shoulder and clamped down firmly. He looked at Jason and smiled, a hint of mischief in the reflection of his eyes.

"That's why we need you to work out all the kinks," Oliver began. "Without you here to be overly cautious and extremely paranoid, we would probably blow up the planet the first time we try to activate the finished product."

"There is a large probability of doing that without your help," Michael mentioned, the same mischievous glint in his eyes.

While Oliver and Michael looked at him mischievously, Jason turned around to see Mason with a look of pure innocence and excitement in his eyes. Jason laughed.

"Please!" Mason begged, grasping Jason's hands in his. "This will be so much fun, and it will be so safe!"

Jason laughed again and shook Mason's hands off.

"Fine," he said with a smile. "I'll do it."

Suddenly Mr. Fletcher came speeding down the stairs and threw his arms around the kids.

"Oh, I'm so excited!" he shouted happily. "With a great group like this, what could possibly go wrong?"

Special Thanks

I'd like to thank my wonderful editor, Janis Dworkis, who has guided me through this process and made it both easier and fun. She is definitely the best of them. I love her so much and I'm so grateful to her. I would also like to thank my wonderfully beautiful family for everything they've done to support me throughout my whole life. Without them, I would be lost and broken. I would also like to thank my silly, fun-loving pets who have always been by me, teaching me patience, tolerance, and a different kind of love. My adorable fur babies—Sandy, Lily, Ruthie, and Snowball—are almost everything to me and I would give up the world for them. And, finally, a very special thanks to my friends who have both driven me insane and kept me sane. They also taught me a different type of love. My friends helped lift me out of my depression and gave me a new purpose in life. I appreciate everyone in this section so much. They all honestly deserve more than this acknowledgment.